V. CARSON TAYLOR

Guided by Voices

First edition

ISBN (paperback): 979-8-9925601-1-4
ISBN (hardcover): 9798314513620

Agent: Kelley Dorning

This book was professionally typeset on Reedsy.
Find out more at reedsy.com

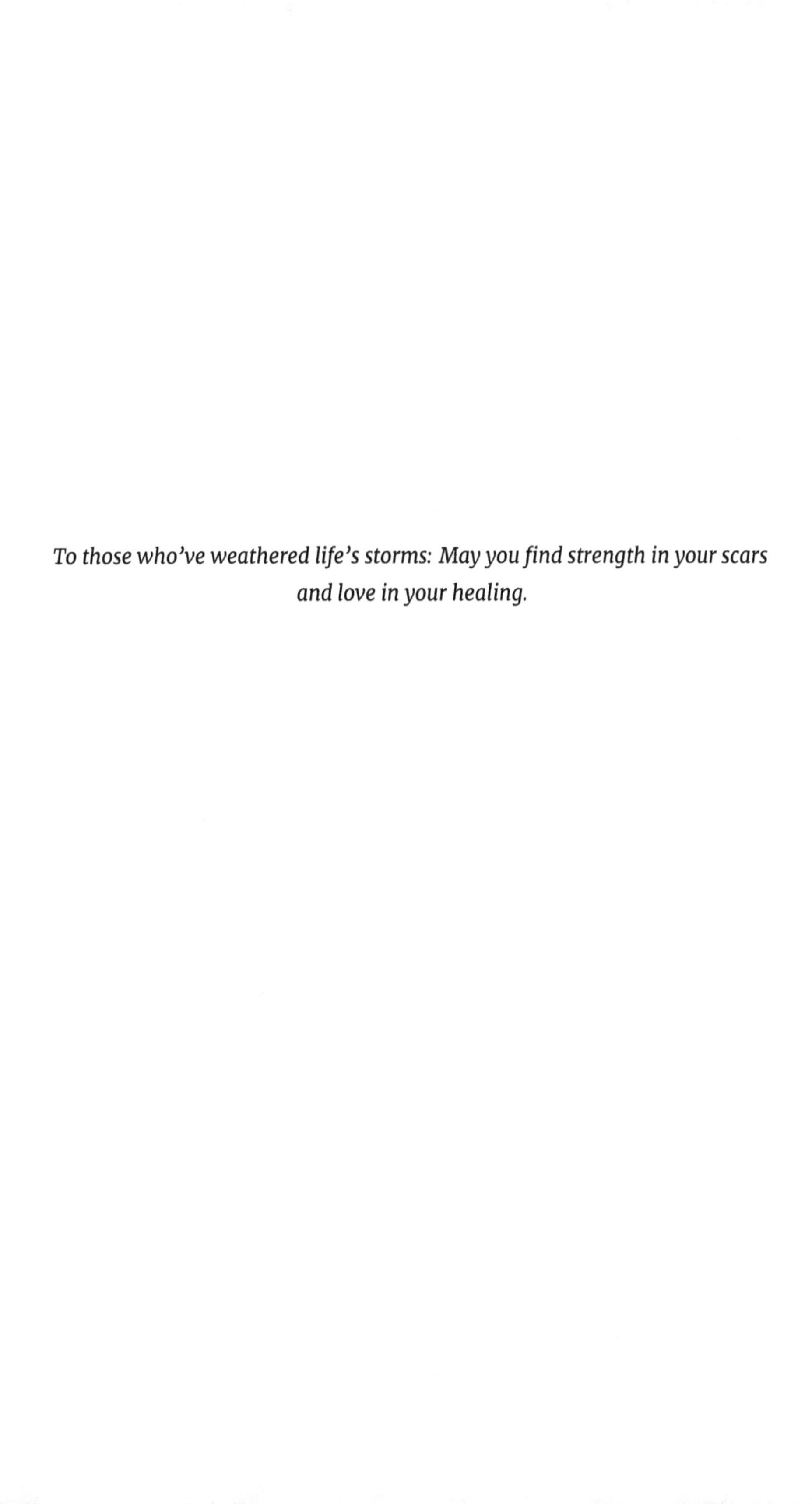

To those who've weathered life's storms: May you find strength in your scars and love in your healing.

"Only those who will risk going too far can possibly find out how far one can go."

T.S. Eliot

Preface

As you journey through these pages, know that while some locations may have evolved, the spirit of San Francisco endures, eternally vibrant and calling me back to its bright lights.

In the midst of the uncertain, and often frightening times brought on by the COVID pandemic, I found myself finally putting pen to paper for a story that had lived in my mind, rent-free for many years. As I changed and matured over time, so too, did this narrative evolving alongside me in the rapidly changing world around us.

The seed of this story was planted during the early days of the internet's rising popularity, when chat rooms and the allure of anonymous interaction first captured our collective imagination. Yet as the digital landscape transformed - bringing with it new forms of social media and communication - the story took on a fresh direction, adapting to reflect our ever-changing reality.

My excitement grew as I crafted this psychological thriller, focusing on strong female characters who could stand toe-to-toe with any challenge. Among them, Loghan became particularly dear to me. Watching her character develop and grow was a deeply personal journey and when it was time to let her go, I found it harder than anticipated. But as they say, all good things must come to an end.

This book represents not just a story, but a years-long journey of personal and creative growth. It's a testament to the power of dedication, time sacrificed and the support and love of others. It's a celebration of the human spirit's ability to create and connect, even in the most trying of times.

I'm incredibly proud of the journey and the story that unfolded along the way. It has been an unforgettable adventure and my greatest hope is that you, dear reader, will find just as much joy, excitement and meaning within these pages as I did while bringing them to life.

Welcome to my world. I hope you enjoy the ride.

Acknowledgments

This book is dedicated to my wife, Kelley and my mom, Donna.

Kelley, thank you for supporting my need to spend weekends researching and writing. You listened patiently when I hit roadblocks, talked through scenarios, calmed my mind and always encouraged me. You are my number one fan and I love doing life with you. I am incredibly lucky to have you in my corner.

Mom, thank you for always believing in me and my writing. You introduced me to a site where new authors could share their work and receive feedback and that was the final kick-start I needed to finally complete this book. Your consistent guidance, support, feedback and chapter reads mean the world to me.

A special mention for my Uncle Jerry - you were a kindred spirit, fellow writer and constant encourager. Your belief in me shaped my journey and I miss you dearly. Your inspiration lives on in every word I write. I hope to make you proud.

I would like to acknowledge the following:

The city of Sacramento, where I call home and lived for much of my life. To your warm weather, distinct mix of urban energy and suburban calm, you have provided an ideal backdrop to express my creativity, build a life and raise my son.

To the enchanting city of San Francisco, whose warm embrace and captivating spirit have been the heartbeat for this story. You captured my heart many years ago, and your endless inspiration continues to fuel my imagination. Though penned during the challenging times of COVID, your essence remained undimmed, even as I watched some beloved locations change, or quietly bid us farewell.

While countless places have their mark on these pages, special recognition goes to:

Sacramento Delta King

Old Sacramento

Myka Estates

Gwinllan Estate Winery

Mark Hopkins Hotel and Top of the Mark

Sir Francis Drake Hotel

Fog Harbor Fish House

Embarcadero Farmers Market

Sutro Baths Ruins

Bourbon and Branch

Our beloved Cliff House, which closed its doors as this tale unfolded.

Guided by Voices

Chapter 1

The computer screen cast a dim glow, its pale light flickering against the darkened walls. The fan turned in slow, measured rotations, stirring the air hinted with lavender and cold coffee poured earlier in the day. Shadows pooled in the corners, stretching and shifting with each subtle movement, as if the room itself breathed. Outside, the muffled sounds barely reached through the rain-streaked window, leaving only the hush of white noise and the quiet tapping of fingertips on the keyboard.

It was late and the large flat was eerily quiet. She was familiar working late into the night while the rest of the world slumbered. It was here that her mind was free of the distractions of the office and the chaos of life. The break-neck pace of deadlines, meetings and yet another article to research or pitch was all too familiar to Loghan Riley. In the tranquility of her home, she could retreat to a secluded space, tapping away at the computer keys without the distraction of the incessant noise of the office.

Tonight was no different from most nights - Loghan couldn't sleep. The 9:00 A.M. deadline loomed over her like a dark storm cloud, heavy and unrelenting. She had assured her editor she would finish her article and it would be in his inbox by morning, but at the rate she was moving, that was a damn lie. Loghan was still trying to piece her article together and now it was 2:00 A.M. The nagging sense of incompleteness; some key point to wrap up her writing to make it flow, gnawed at her, keeping exhaustion at bay.

"Damn," Loghan murmured out loud. She had been staring at her screen for the last ten minutes and could not get her thoughts and fingers to cooperate.

She sighed, leaning back in her chair. The words weren't coming, at least not the right ones, and she knew forcing them would only make it worse. *I need a break.*

Loghan rolled her head, feeling the tension crackle through her neck, then let her eyes drift shut, hoping a moment of quiet would untangle the knots in her mind. A familiar rustling broke the silence - soft paws shifting against paper, a slow, deliberate stretch. She opened her eyes to find her over-sized tabby sprawled across her desk, his golden-green eyes half-lidded with feline superiority. With a lazy roll, he exposed his belly, a silent but unmistakable demand.

Loghan smirked, unable to resist, "You're so predictable, Harry," she murmured, her fingers finding the soft fur of his chest, just as he liked. A deep, rumbling purr vibrated against her touch.

Satisfied, he stretched once more before rolling onto his side, fixing her with a look that suggested she was only mildly worthy of his attention. Then, changing his mind, he flicked his tail dismissively and turned his gaze to the darkened window.

Loghan exhaled a quiet laugh, "Thanks for the support, buddy."

She minimized her article and moved over to check her email. Nothing but junk mail. The ridiculous promises spam offered. Too much debt? We have a simple answer. Weight loss? Take this pill; drink this shake; you will see results in a week. Loghan swiftly deleted all the junk email that made its way to her inbox. There was an email from her mom, sharing a healthy recipe and touching bases. Loghan perused it briefly, making sure all was fine. Both she and Dad were doing well, blah, blah, blah. Loghan had no disrespect for her parents, it was just late and she could read the email in the morning when her mind was where it needed to be. Right now, she was looking for distraction. She could always count on the endless areas of the internet to let her mind wander.

"I'll get back to my article in a minute," she said aloud. Harry flicked his ears, stretching again, only to settle down closer to the warmth of the laptop. "Let's see if anything is exciting out there tonight, huh Harry?"

She smiled at the computer and stretched her long legs under the desk.

Her fingers swept over the keys with graceful agility. What was going on in the world today? What currents books were on the New York Times bestseller list, items of interest to her and every bit of information a person may or may not need.

Web pages, latest news, Threads, Instagram, Snapchat, Tik Tok, hell, even Facebook, she enjoyed it all. Everything was at your fingertips. It was a perfect escape to the night, if only for a few brief minutes. A rush of bright colors escaped the screen across the dimly lit room. Information illuminated brightly across Loghan's face in her dimly lit office.

Let's see who's out there tonight, Loghan thought.

Time ceased to exist in the endless maze of late-night digital wanderings.

Hmm, I think I'll see what's going on with my Poetry and Writers page tonight.

Loghan deftly guided the mouse to the page and typed in the site's name and clicked. What were the recent posts? Was there anything good she could invest a few minutes in discussing? She wanted a distraction, a deep exchange to get lost in a thoughtful post. Loghan loved this page because many people claimed to be well-read, published and prolific writers. It was the internet. There was the ability to be someone you claimed, whether truthful or not. She loved the anonymity this page allowed, allowing her to write from her heart without revealing her true identity, embracing the freedom to embody her thoughts and desires.

The page was filled with like-minded writers and poets. People sharing their works and seeking honest feedback. Some were good writers, others, not so much. The writers, good or... challenged, wanted to share their craft. She moved the cursor to the Welcome page to read more information and refresh herself with the admin rules.

As she scrolled through, a message from an unfamiliar sender caught her eye. She hesitated a moment before clicking on it. The sender's name: David Rothchild. There was no personal photo next to the name. Loghan clicked on his page and there was nothing but a few images of landscapes, nothing to see who David was or how she may be connected to him.

"Hello, Loghan." The typed words ran across the screen. She leaned back in her chair and waited to see if they would continue to type; nothing.

Hesitantly, Loghan responded. *"Hi. Do I know you?"* She typed and waited.

She peered at the screen and furrowed her brow. *Oh well, it must have been a mistake.* The lack of response was her excuse to get back to work. She started to move the mouse to exit the message when she saw:

"Hello Loghan, here I am."

Again, Loghan typed back. *"Hi... I'm sorry...do I know you?"*

"Well, I feel as though I know you. We're on the same writing page and have both commented on others' writings before." Came the reply. They continued; *"I do see your writing is every bit as beautiful as your profile picture."*

Loghan exhaled sharply, rolling her eyes before realizing - was she blushing? Loghan angled her head to the side. *Wait a minute...on my writing page. Does he know me?? I don't recall his name. Surely, he's not flirting with me?*

Curious, she clicked back to his profile, scanning through his posts, searching for something - anything that may jog her memory.

Nothing...she clicked "About Me" and didn't find anything that would help her determine the mystery man. Very basic information: Male, birthday was Dec 5th with no year indicated. Sparse details that would pinpoint anything that Loghan could put the pieces together. Was this intentional to be so vague?

She knew she shouldn't go one moment further without knowing more information about this person, but she couldn't help herself. She was cautiously interested by the stranger's direct compliment and anonymity. She couldn't remember the last time she felt like someone was 'interested' in her. Flirting? Maybe in grade school, "I know someone who likes you...!" No, this was different. There was no face to the name, adding to her intrigue.

"I would suspect you're even more beautiful in person than the photos do you justice." His written words jarred her out of thought.

Oh my gosh...! I don't know him and he doesn't know **ME!**

Loghan's fingers hovered over the keyboard, a faint frown creasing her brow. The message on her screen puzzled her. She had a nagging feeling this exchange should end right away, but something made her respond, even if begrudgingly.

I must have communicated with him on the writing forum, she thought, but I talk to many people there. I don't remember him specifically.

Loghan moved over to the page and looked for her last comments on a recent short story she posted. She didn't locate anything and wanted to return to the welcomed interruption from work.

Well, I've been told I am beautiful, as uncomfortable as that makes me...so, there...now what? Who are you, David Rothchild?

She poised her fingertips above the keyboard and continued: "*I assume we've talked on the writing page from your comment. Why do you ask if I'm beautiful? Does that matter?*" Her interest was somewhat piqued. Why in the hell she asked this question was beyond her. She waited for his response as the dots in the chat indicated he was typing.

"*I do think it matters to most of us, don't you? I know we hear beauty is, in fact, skin deep, but I also know we are creatures that expect desire and passion. Those feelings can only come to us if we find beauty.*"

Loghan shook her head, eyes flickering over the words on the screen with pure incredulity.

Who spoke like this anymore? It was as if she had stumbled into a lost era where language was more eloquent and unexpected. She hesitated, her gaze catching on her own reflection in the window. Auburn waves cascaded past her shoulders, catching the light, her skin luminous, her features a contradiction of strength and softness. More than once, she had been told she was beautiful, but that wasn't what held her attention now. Taking a steadying breath, she let her fingers fly over the keyboard, drawn into the mystery of this exchange. As she typed, she leaned in closer to the screen, almost as if she could pierce the digital veil and see the person on the other side.

She sat rod straight in her chair and looked about the room, trying to shake off the feeling she was doing something she shouldn't. Loghan quietly considered. Why in the hell was she drawn to this conversation? Why hadn't she pressed him to find out who he was? Or better still, why was she still engaging? She had to admit to herself, the anonymity of the interaction both thrilled and unnerved her.

She returned to the writing page and looked for other names, anything that might tell her who he was. Loghan rarely chatted online with anyone she didn't know, with the exception to work. Never had she intentionally engaged in a conversation with a stranger without knowing them to some extent and they were on a page they had in common.

Yet, here she was - spending time searching a strangers page, seeking more conversation with him.

That's what I'm doing. Encouraging more conversation.

She glanced over at Harry as if to receive his permission to continue. The orange Tabby curled up and perfectly unaware, his tail flitting and flicking. She poised her fingers again and typed, aiming to change the subject.

"Tell me, where are you right now?" She winced at her lame question.

"I'm at a beautiful woman's home, of course."

Loghan smirked. Who is this guy?! She shook her head and pointedly tapped the keys.

"Well, I should think you need to get back to her and not spend time discussing great poets with me."

"I don't believe we've done any such thing. I was, however, hoping to hear more about you. I imagine you must be quite lovely. You seem to be even a tad... contentious, might I say?"

Loghan's response came quickly. *"Please, you must be joking. Do you think I'm here to "cyber" or webcam, or whatever it is you're looking for tonight??"*

Loghan felt a slight smirk escape her lips. She knew she should get back to work. Responsibilities were awaiting, but she was having a bit of fun here for some reason. She was entertained by this exchange this evening and it was a welcome respite from her feelings of late.

"Well, I do love a woman to be forward, Loghan. If you wanted to turn on your webcam, I would enjoy that very much, but it's not my style. I'm far more interested in the... 'written word'." His pause was intentional and palatable. He continued. *"I find it's gone by the wayside a bit since the onset of computers. Tell me, darling, is your mind as equally beautiful, as your photo? I so appreciate engaging with beautiful and intelligent women. Your page doesn't allow me to see but one picture of you and I must admit, I would very much like to see you*

and hear more about you."

Loghan was drawn to the computer by his words, strong arms, reaching through the screen, pulling her closer. There was something intoxicating about the way he strung words and sentences together - clever, poetic, laced with just enough mystery to keep her wanting more.

Summoning her courage, she sat up straighter, her fingertips hovering over the keyboard. She refused to be another puzzle piece for him to study, another name on his list of 'conquests.' If he wanted a response, she'd give him one, on her terms.

"*I find it refreshing that you love words; I do as well. However, from our small exchange, you still seem to have a bit of a one-track mind. Wanting to know what I look like and if I'm intelligent - if I'm beautiful. I told you already - yes, I'm attractive and I don't like strangers stalking me on my page. Where did we have any interaction on the writing page?*

Loghan closed her eyes for a moment, willing the strange feelings to subside. Why in the hell was she taking the time to talk to this apparent "stalker?"

"*No matter, Loghan. I didn't "stalk" you as you say. Might I remind you; we are on the same writing page? I merely said hello and hoped to have an exchange of conversational topics. Perhaps, you're just shy, or worse, rude and unable to entertain the idea of a conversation with a "stranger." I really would love to chat with you again; however, the hour is late and I must go.*"

Loghan grimaced at the screen, "No, not yet." she whispered, wishing he would stay; she wanted to chat more. He can't just dismiss her before she could ask him questions. Why did he reach out to her? What did he want? Did he really want to talk about writing, or was he just another creeper?

"*I'm not rude! Well, wait...what if I'm not finished talking to you?*" He said he liked forward women, right? She typed the words as quickly as she could. Damn it, this "David Rothchild" wasn't leaving already, was he? "*Let's talk about those great American writers or poets...whatever you choose.*" Loghan realized that she was pleading with her words.

He responded, "*Not now, my dear. I really must go. I have something of great importance I must tend to. I'm confident we'll chat again soon. Goodnight, beautiful Loghan."*

Loghan watched the screen for a moment, wondering why she hoped he would change his mind. Was she really that desperate to avoid her work that was quietly waiting?

The cursor blinked dully. Loghan leaned back in her chair and let out a long sigh. "Damn."

Harry jumped up at her voice, looking slightly agitated and flitted his tail once or twice. Loghan closed her laptop with a quiet click. Perhaps this was the beginning of something exciting - or dangerous. Either way, she was ready for the challenge and hoped he would reach out again.

"I'll finish my article before heading into the office. Come on, Harry." Loghan stood and stretched, turning away from the den and padded down her dark hallway to bed.

* * *

He smiled at the computer screen, shut down his laptop and removed his VPN token.

So many possibilities, he thought. This lovely specimen seemed to be interesting enough. He did insist a woman be able to entertain him in conversation. It meant so very much to him.

He stretched his long and lean arms above his head, allowing a yawn to escape his lips. Rising from the chair, he walked into the large bathroom and flicked on the light. His reflection was youthful, strong and vibrant. He ran his hands through his thick, wavy dark hair and studied himself in the mirror.

He had always liked his appearance.

Standing tall with effortless grace, he exuded quiet confidence. His lean, athletic build spoke of discipline and strength, without excess. Broad shoulders tapered into a toned frame. His face, a striking balance of sharp angles and smooth lines - high cheekbones and strong jaw and a straight nose that lends him an air of quiet intensity. But it's his eyes that unsettle - piercing blue, so striking they seem almost unnatural, their depth both hypnotic and unnerving.

His lips curled slightly at the corners as he admired his reflection.

Indeed, not bad at all. I need to work a little more on my arms, he mused, slightly flexing the back of his arm and studying the symmetry of his triceps.

Quietly, he finished dressing. Everything seemed to be in order. He glanced over the room and reached for a towel and neatly wiped off the counter. He turned and left the bathroom, placing the towel in a leather duffel bag.

His gaze moved toward the bed in the middle of the room.

She lay on the bed. Her long, sinewy body cradled in the luxurious white sheets. Her long, chestnut hair, cascading out on the pillow. She was a vision and he admired her beauty before him.

"You were just wonderful tonight, darling. Simply wonderful."

She appeared to be quietly asleep. Her eyes closed; face tilted toward the door. He touched her gently on her arm, caressing her soft skin with his fingertips. Turning, he strode back over to the desk, placing the bag inside his briefcase and picked up his overcoat and laptop bag.

His piercing eyes surveyed the room once more as his eyes rested on the painting above the desk. Some knock off artist, no doubt. It was a lovely painting, though. There were touches of art throughout the home. Decorated subtlety for one such charismatic woman, he thought. He would have thought her to be more the modern art type when it came to her choice of art and arrangements. He quickly dismissed the thought that he was incorrect in his assessment of her in any way.

This is a lovely space, indeed. He mused once more at the decor and noted how tidy she kept her home. "Very inviting," he murmured.

Positioning himself in the full-length mirror for a final time, he straightened his tie and pulled on his overcoat. Nice, he thought. He looked very sharp. He always made damn sure of that.

"Well, goodnight to you, my dear. I had a lovely time." He reached the doorway to her bedroom and glanced at her once more.

This time, he noticed her lips were faintly blue. It was a shame their beauty never lasted long after he killed them. Smirking, he dismissed the thought as quickly as it entered his mind and closed the door behind him.

Chapter 2

Loghan darted in and out of traffic. The freeway was no place to be at 8:00 A.M. on a weekday. She was running late and behind schedule, two things that were not her norm when moving through her life. She rushed out of the apartment this morning, coffee and bagel in hand.

Dependable as they came, Loghan's weekday routine included a light breakfast at her favorite coffee shop, after her morning run. Not one to waste time, she checked her email and meeting schedules on her iPad while she ate, to determine what the day had in store for her. She had two cups of coffee, avocado wheat toast and a small glass of orange juice. She tipped the same amount every day, as Marie, her waitress, would say. She arrived at work at precisely 7:00 A.M., neatly groomed and ready for the day.

Loghan tamed her wild mane of auburn hair with a simple, yet creative twist - effortlessly gathering it up, leaving just a few strands of hair to frame her face. She always played down her striking good looks, preferring an understated elegance: a soft touch of lipstick, just enough to highlight her full lips and the barest hint of makeup to enhance her naturally glowing complexion. Despite this modesty, Loghan had a presence that couldn't be denied. Wherever she went, she was the first to capture attention, her magnetic beauty impossible to ignore, though she never seemed to believe, or fully accept the admiration that followed her like a quiet shadow.

Today, Loghan was not on her usual, "A Game." It started when she tried to catch a little sleep before jumping up at 5:00 A.M. to finish her article. She didn't wake to her alarm going off and its melodic sounds did nothing but lull her into a deeper sleep.

She finally woke to the vibration of Harry purring and butting his head against her and she flew out of bed and followed up with an obscenity under her breath.

Her start of the day was so fractured; she wondered what the rest of her day would present.

Loghan embraced familiarity. Her morning routine worked for her and the unwanted disruption of waking late made her slightly annoyed. Even with the rocky start to her day, Loghan completed her article and was pleased with the finished product.

In Loghan's close circle, it was no secret that she was known for being slightly strict about her daily life structure. Her family and friends gently teased her about her "imaginary" timeline in her mind, but everyone turned to Loghan when it came to coordinating events or getting everyone together. She recently started to mix up her strict scheduling, trying to prove to her friends and coworkers she could be flexible. Or maybe, she was trying to prove it to herself.

It was pointless to try and change a trait that was intrinsic to Loghan. She would often say to others when teased; so, she loved structure in her life and was comfortable in knowing what came next - what was wrong with that? She was always on time and came prepared. People depended on her, right? Hadn't she done well for herself? Why, then, did she feel like she still had something to prove to someone?

Jesus, I need to lighten up a bit, she mused quietly.

Driving through traffic, Loghan considered her reasons for needing structure.

As a child, she was hesitant to jump into whatever new game her playmates were invested in learning until she was comfortable with the surroundings and rules. When she reached her teens, she was cautious but wildly curious about people or new situations.

Now, as a young woman, Loghan seemed to take fewer risks in her life. Loghan wasn't this way when she first started out on her own. She applied to several top colleges that included applications to NYU, Columbia and the Seven Sisters. She toured a couple of campuses, but none struck her as she had hoped. Never expecting to get into any of the Ivy League campuses, she was thrilled when Columbia accepted. She knew the moment she set foot on campus - this was the right college and decision. Loghan couldn't wait to begin her new life. A life to build, new experiences and, far away from her loving, yet overly protective eyes of her parents.

Loghan had always been driven, a quiet determination burning within her from the moment she stepped onto her college campus. With a major in journalism and a minor in business management, she juggled the pressures of academia with shifts at the trendy coffee shop just off campus. The smell of freshly ground coffee beans became a familiar backdrop to late-night study sessions and conversations with friends about the future. While many of her classmates relied on cushy college funds or parents footing the bill, Loghan took a different path. She hustled-applying for grants, snagging scholarships when she could and balancing work with school. Every cup of coffee she served felt like another step toward self-sufficiency. By the time she graduated, she wasn't just walking away with a diploma; she had earned every bit of her success with grit and resilience.

Loghan had always been full of dreams, brimming with ambition, but something seemed to hold her back when it came to being adventurous and taking risks. She couldn't quite put her finger on it for the longest time, but she eventually began to suspect it had something to do with the way she was raised - good ole' Irish Catholic. Her family was the picture perfect, devout and loving family. Always together - and Sunday mornings were sacred, not just because of church but because of the unbreakable ritual of family unity. Her parents insisted all the children attend mass, rain or shine and while Loghan appreciated the sense of togetherness as a young girl, that feeling began to wane as she grew older.

As she edged toward her teenage years, Loghan craved something different - independence, space, freedom. She didn't want to be dragged along to every event like a reluctant extra in her family's production of The Sound of Music. The Von Trapp family might have been cute on screen, but the constant togetherness at home was suffocating.

It wasn't that she didn't love her family; in fact, her family was a beautiful kind of chaos - a house full of four siblings, two dogs, three cats, a mom, a dad and, of course, the ever watchful presence of the Father, Son and Holy Ghost. The divine trio loomed as heavily over the household as any parental figure, guiding decisions, shaping thoughts and, in some way, keeping Loghan in line. That silent pressure, that holy expectation, often felt like an invisible weight she couldn't shake.

Loghan cherished her family, but she longed for quiet - for room to breathe and to hear her own thoughts without the constant hum of voices and barking dogs and the occasional thud of a sibling tripping over a cat. Loghan wondered what life would be like without the pull of duty, or the familiar tug of tradition that had been instilled in her from birth. Maybe then, she wouldn't hold back as much and truly branch out to explore her world.

College offered Loghan the freedom to explore her independence, marking her first real breakaway from the religious teachings of her upbringing. Now, as a young adult, she considered herself spiritual but no longer tied to organized religion. Loghan's parents, though Catholic, leaned toward more liberal beliefs - her mother especially. Loghan loved that about her.

Loghan's parents worked hard and loved harder, giving her a foundation of love and support. During her teenage years, she went through what she considered rebellious phases - sneaking out after bedtime to drive around with her girlfriends or occasionally smoking a cigarette. Though mild by most standards, it felt scandalous to her. Lighthearted and easygoing, Loghan's world shattered after college, when reality came crashing down. Now she was anything but light-hearted.

The pain she held in her heart had become her constant and unwelcome companion. The loss of her boyfriend Ian, two years before in a car accident, haunted her. He was her first love and Loghan was still reeling from his tragic death. The emptiness around Loghan was suffocating, a vice on her heart made it impossible to feel anything. She longed to experience the lightheartedness that had left her since Ian's death - to feel normal again. His picture, still on her nightstand, a constant presence during the sleepless nights. Loghan held the framed picture close, eyes shut, trying to conjure his touch - his strong hands, soft whispers and the warmth of his breath against her skin. The pain and emptiness felt endless.

Loghan began each day missing Ian and did her best to keep moving forward. Today, she had something positive to anticipate. She would not allow the late start throw her off - it was a big day and she had to be on top of her game. Loghan was pleased with her finished article and she would be at her desk in just a few short minutes.

She wanted to be sure to deliver her article to her editor, John Campbell's desk before he arrived at work. She had emailed it, but he still liked to see the hard copy; and she would never let him think for a moment she couldn't handle this job.

Jesus, Loghan sighed loudly, as she printed out her article before heading to the office to place in his inbox. John's archaic ways were infuriating at times. Ok, *Boomer*. Loghan smiled and stifled a giggle.

Loghan remembered John saying he hired her against his "better judgment" in her final interview. The upside to the negative remark, was that it was followed by him saying he loved her enthusiasm and freshness.

John, a grumpy old-timer edging toward retirement, had a knack for spouting his unfiltered, politically incorrect views. While he said nothing extreme, his comments alluding to Loghan's age carried a paternalistic tone. Loghan wasn't fond of his outdated mindset, but he reminded her of a beloved uncle. She only wished he'd stop assuming she was inexperienced in her writing. Loghan knew she was skilled and one day, she believed John would come to see it too.

* * *

While rough around the edges, John Campbell had a soft spot for the young writers on his staff. He had a daughter roughly Loghan's age and knew sometimes all one needed was a break.

He thought Loghan was too young to carry a feature article spot on his magazine, but of course, he didn't say it to her directly. He understood he was too direct at times and tried not to use his 'outside voice' when speaking his mind. He knew Loghan wasn't naive and was confident she could read between the lines of his terse tone.

The damn politics of daily life and the endless human resources bureaucracy put a damper on John's outspoken nature. But truth, was truth and goddammit, he was going to speak it. For eight years, he had clawed his way through the thankless drudgery of newsroom life - rewriting dull press releases, ghostwriting editorials for editors who barely read them and nodding through staff meetings filled with corporate jargon. But it all led to this; owner of a successful, local magazine.

Loghan was fresh out of college when he hired her with only two years of internship at a local newspaper. She came with excellent references and John was in no position to be choosy. His feature columnist had taken a vacation to India on a whim to "find herself" and did such a damn good job of it, she never came back.

John had his fingers in everything he could at the magazine. Needing to fill a spot quickly, he began interviewing. While his competitors gave way to the 21st century and handed off many of these processes to managers and HR, John insisted upon being part of the day-to-day operation. There was no one on the current staff to fill the position as solid writers were at a minimum. So, after several interviews with Loghan, he agreed to hire her.

What the hell? She may turn out to be really good. John followed his gut. She worked her ass off for him, that was for sure. He liked her spunk and her writing was fresh and concise. She was building a good following as well and followers equate to the readership. He was impressed with Loghan's work and her ability to dig out an idea for an article, but he never let her know what he thought. He drove her and the rest of his staff hard, not letting up for a minute.

His theory: if you let anyone know you thought they were outstanding, they would get lazy and begin to have expectations or, they could become arrogant and the quiet accusations of favoritism could arise.

No, it was much more effective this way. John liked to keep a tight rein on all his writers. He called all the shots. What stories would be covered and who would write them. He was the last of the "dinosaurs" and the last of the tough, hard-nosed editors. This was not your dime-a-dozen, topical magazine.

John was unafraid to cover stories other editors thought would offend their readers and chase away advertisers. He hated the wishy-washy crap he read in his competitors' local publications. He had a hard edge and big bark, but those who knew him well would say he was fair and a genuine "renaissance man."

His magazine may be small, but it was known for having a gritty quality and winning many awards.

The base of readership leaned toward the liberal or younger generation, especially Millennials and Gen Z. John kept his fingers on the pulse of the world around him and was surprisingly in tune to Loghan's surprise. The magazine articles could be on hard-hitting topics ranging from Medical Marijuana, Transgender Teens to vacation spots on a budget. John wanted to reach his demographic while casting the net wider to entice new readers.

Loghan nipped at his heels to have more input over what articles she would like to write. John continued to hold her off and told her she needed more "seasoning." It was John's subtle way of letting her know she hadn't paid her dues yet.

Loghan didn't let John's apparent lack of enthusiasm deter her from her goal of landing a big lead. This is where Loghan could break out of the confines of being too cautious and stretch herself. There were so many exciting stories to report on and she wanted to be part of that excitement.

As part of her plan to wear John down, Loghan would finish one article and begin to circle his office with requests or emails on ideas she offered to cover. John knew the time would come and he would start to give Loghan more responsibility and take her off the soft articles, but for now, this is where she was gaining experience. This was his decision and he stood firm.

* * *

Loghan made the last turn to the parking garage and reeled her grey and white Mini Cooper into the garage, grazing the speed bump with the bottom of her car. The impact shot a numbing buzz from the inside out and resonated in her chest.

She parked quickly in her assigned spot and checked the time. It was 8:25 A.M. and she knew she could still beat John to the office with his daily arrival at 9:00 A.M.

Loghan walked briskly through the office, made it to her desk and dropped herself into her chair.

"Whew." She allowed an audible sigh of relief to escape her lips and opened her laptop. She continued to muse about beating John into the office, dropped her article off with his assistant and could now relax, pouring herself a fresh cup of coffee.

Moving through her following assignment lists from John, she deftly chose her next article and began her research. It certainly wasn't a "sexy" assignment: **Millennials and Real Estate: Changing the Way to Buy Homes with One Click.**

Whatever, she thought.

She would figure out how to move up the ladder, with or without John's full approval. This was her job and she'd write another damn good article.

She would never stop trying to impress him; one day he would see just how damn good she was at uncovering compelling, thought-provoking stories.

Even if it nearly killed her, she'd prove it - to him and to herself.

Little did she know, that moment was closer than she ever imagined.

Chapter 3

Deagan McGrath rummaged through his desk, lifting every paper, file folder and loose scrap in sight. His workspace was a battlefield of organized chaos, but he knew exactly where everything was - until now. With a frustrated sigh, he checked the floor, then the file cabinet and finally, the overflowing recycling box.

The janitors knew better than to empty it before Friday. That was the day Deagan submitted his articles and if he needed to rescue something he'd hastily discarded, it damn well better still be there. The last janitor who had the audacity to empty his recycle box early, had endured weeks of Deagan's grumbling. Not that he was quick to anger - on the contrary, he was even-tempered. But when it came to his writing, he had his ways.

His colleges still laughed about the infamous recycling incident, but they humored him. Deagan was, after all, the master of the written word in their eyes. If he needed his little eccentricities to work his magic, so be it.

Deagan, or Deag as he was called by most, was the head writer at **ForeFront** and everyone, including the hard-nosed editor, John gave him room to roam. Deagan was admired and well-liked. At thirty-two, he was one of the youngest and most awarded head writers in Northern California and he was damn proud of it.

"Jenny? Please...can you help? Where in the hell is the article about that murder in Virginia?" He called out of his office door. He had printed it out and placed it on his desk, right next to the pile of files and his organized chaos - so he thought.

"Damn it. Why didn't I file it on my computer or save the link?" Deagan ran his fingers across his brow as he continued to ponder.

Far from the typical millennial who lived purely in the digital realm, Deagan was more than just computer savvy - he was a rare breed who still valued the tangible. He loved the weight of paper in his hands, the subtle scent of ink and pulp, the act of physically turning a page. An oddity among his peers, perhaps, but he didn't care. While others relied solely on screens, he printed out his research, scribbling notes in margins, underlining key points and flipping through pages as he pieced together his stories.

In anticipation, Deagan stood up and looked out his office door to see if Jenny was on her way. Within moments, she appeared and instinctively went to the corner of his desk, lifted a stack of books and retrieved the article.

"You know, you can instant message me; or Google what you're looking for." She smiled at Deagan sweetly. Handing the print out to him, she exited as quickly as she had entered.

"Thank you." He grumbled under his breath. "You're welcome." Jenny shot back over her shoulder. It seemed Deagan couldn't find his ass with both hands if it weren't for his assistant. In his private life, it was never a problem; everything had a place and he knew where to find it. He was organized and kept a clean home, but when it came to his writing...well, it was another thing altogether.

He wondered if he relied on Jenny too much. She was terrific and it was easier to allow her to find things and put stuff away and he could move through his day without interruption.

He placed the printout next to his mail stack, USA Today and his steaming nonfat, triple espresso latte. He leaned in and began to read:

Charlottesville, Virginia - The body of a young woman was found in her home Tuesday; details of the murder have not been released by the police. The young woman identified as Rebecca Stills, 28, a designer for a children's clothing company was discovered by her roommate. Police have made no mention of suspects or a possible motive. Police stated her home appeared to be undisturbed with no forcible entry.

Deagan sat down heavily in his chair. His brow furrowed, drumming his fingers on his desk absentmindedly.

He knew he read something very similar to this recently and he couldn't place it. He began searching his computer files to see if he had saved anything there. One by one, he glanced over each file and still found nothing.

He mulled over the memory, then let it go, turning back to the pile of mail and *USA Today.* Jenny, noting his habit of pouring over the paper, made sure a copy landed on his desk daily. Deagan never corrected her, though like most his age, he got his news online. Most days, the paper went straight to the recycle bin - except today.

Deagan adjusted the chair to tilt back and the springs creaking their protest. Reaching for the paper he flipped the pages as his eyes casually ran down the page and then stopped on an item:

San Francisco, California - The death of a San Francisco woman remained a mystery Tuesday; said a San Francisco police spokesman. The body of Cynthia DuBois, 26, a professional ballet dancer, was found in her home by her parents, James Young, spokesman for the San Francisco Police commented.

Police were not releasing any details of the event at this time as further investigation is pending. The victim was last seen, Tuesday at 1:00 A.M. The police have no suspects or motives.

Deagan looked over both the clippings again, looking for any similarities. Maybe he was looking for something that wasn't there. Deagan knew there was another article similar from many months, or perhaps even a year ago.

Damn it, where in the hell did I see that? Deagan's brow creased as he continued to try and recall.

Always on the prowl for an interesting article to write, Deagan looked in the least likely places. He thrived on finding stories that would create conflict; conflict in one's mind or heart. It made for good story content and his readers responded with letters to the editor with praise or a well-founded critique.

His personal life was void of conflict. It was not his style to have disruption in his life. Conflict for the sake of good content was perfect and he welcomed it, but for his personal life...no way. He kept that shit at bay. No, thank you.

Conflict, of any kind, brought out the best information and the real side of the subject matter he may be writing about. He continued to rack his mind for the other news clippings he was sure he had read somewhere.

He frowned as he rifled through papers on his desk as he continued to search his mind.

It was the same damn thing, wasn't it? Several women found dead; same age range, no details from the police. Each of the young women located in their home? Shit, I know I have seen other articles on this same type of murder...

"Hey! Why the frown lines?" Loghan stood in his doorway, beaming her bright smile.

"Hey, yourself. Where the heck have you been? It's almost 8:30! Did someone die?!" Deagan teased. The two were good friends and Deagan knew all too well she was in the office every day by 7:00 A.M.

"Hmm...funny...no, just running late." Loghan flipped her wrist, feigning a casual air, but Deagan knew better. He knew Loghan was frazzled with her routine being out of sync. Her usually rosy cheeks had a significant flush to them. He grinned, knowing this about her, watching her nervously twist a rogue curl of hair between her fingers as she tucked it neatly in place.

Little did he know, just a few short minutes before bypassed the elevator and raced up the stairs, hoping to reach the office before anyone might notice she was late.

Deagan knew Loghan was easygoing about most things, but lateness unsettled her, she shared this secret with him over lunch one day. She never quite understood why, only that punctuality felt essential - something she'd always valued, even when others teased her

He enjoyed knowing these small things about Loghan. It added to the many attributes he appreciated about her and made her interesting and sweet.

"So, what are you working on today?" Loghan asked, looking down at the mess on Deagan's desk, ignoring the lopsided grin on his face.

"Oh, you know...The usual; death, crime, drama. Standard fare." Deagan's eyes twinkled with enthusiasm.

"No. Come on....really, what are you working on?" Loghan's genuine interest showed.

Deagan adjusted in his chair, his posture straightening as his easygoing smile faded. A more serious expression took its place, signaling the shift in his thoughts. Research had always been his refuge - a way to channel his energy into something meaningful. But having Loghan take an interest in his work? That was something else entirely. No matter how hard he tried to suppress it, the flicker of emotion in his eyes betrayed him every time she walked into the room. He reminded himself that the workplace was never the right setting for personal feelings - especially when it came to Loghan. He knew her history, understood her loss and honored both her and Ian's memory. So, he would continue to respect her space, appreciating the friendship they shared, even if, deep down, he wished for something more.

"Well, I'm trying to put something together, but...there isn't anything there. I can't put the pieces together yet, but I know there must be a connection." Deagan's brow furrowed once more. He rubbed his fingertips across his forehead, his tell that showed signs of frustration when he was thinking something through.

"I thought I was on to an exciting piece, but it hasn't panned out." His voice drifted off.

Deagan spent the next few minutes taking Loghan through his thoughts on the recent murders and mysterious lack of details. Loghan's eyes shined with excitement as she listened to the facts and the thought process Deagan used in his investigative journalism. She wanted to work on something that sparked her excitement like this, but listening to Deagan's story would have to suffice.

"Well, I'm sure you'll find something that makes the connection, Deagan. You always do." She smiled and Deagan couldn't help but return with a genuine smile of his own. Watching her leave, Deagan feigned sadness and remarked, "What? Leaving so soon?"

Turning to leave, Loghan playfully called over her shoulder, "Well, I have a *very* pressing deadline to get my 'Millennial's and Real Estate' article worked out." Loghan used air quotes and an exaggerated tone. "You know...the exciting use of computers to find your dream home without even talking to a person. Just point and click." Loghan winked over her shoulder.

"How about lunch today?" Deagan tried to be casual with his tone.

"I'll let you know, ok?" Loghan smiled slightly.

"Sure." Deagan leaned back in his chair and watched her walk down the hall, a weak sigh escaping his lips. *Damn... If only she weren't so intriguing.*

Chapter 4

She leaned back in her chair, staring at the dull computer screen... waiting.

She knew he was going to be here tonight. She had waited patiently for an hour, passing the time playing solitaire on a split-screen. After months of chatting online, tonight was the night she would suggest they take the next step: a face-to-face meeting via webcam.

Nervous butterflies fluttered in her stomach as she contemplated meeting him for the first time via webcam. What would his true impression of her be? Could she muster the courage to put herself out there? The thought of meeting him, even virtually, elevated her anxiety to a whole new level.

Her insecurities came flooding over her. Surely, he would be open to seeing her? She had thought it odd that he didn't press the subject of using a webcam, as that was the norm now. You couldn't be on the web and not expect to enhance the experience without the use of a webcam.

She thought it was a stroke of luck that he didn't seem to mind not using the webcam. She was always nervous when anyone suggested turning on the camera as it could go south quickly.

For men, it was a transaction and not a connection. And that was that. She loved that her new tryst was not that way at all. He seemed to love to chat and was soooo romantic! His way with words, the terms of endearment...oh yes, she could do this as long as he wanted.

She closed her game of solitaire and moved to Facebook when his message came across. She sat upright in her chair, looking at the screen waiting, her breath paused.

"Good evening, my love. How are you tonight?" His words continued to flow to the screen, *"I've been waiting for you."* Her fingers quickly tapped out the words.

Come on, talk to me, she whispered under her breath.

"Have you waited long?"

"No, only a few minutes. I just rushed into the room and jumped on Facebook. You're always very prompt." She lied. She was so adept at lying to him it was almost shocking.

The response came: *"I do try to insist on punctuality."*

She stifled a soft scoff. That was a joke. He made her wait often - telling her what time he would be online and not showing up for hours in some cases. It never mattered though, she always waited for him.

She began awkwardly. *"So, how was your day? I hope to talk to you about something important tonight."* She nervously shifted in her chair. How would she broach the suggestion for them to take this meeting to the next level using a video chat? How she wanted to see him and to know him more.

"Oh, let's not talk about topics of any importance tonight. I've had such a long day, darling. Tell me, what are you wearing tonight?"

She loved that he called her, "darling." Wistfully smiling, she pondered, who says that anymore? He was so polite and thoughtful. From his comment, she could see he was not in the mood for trivialities; he appeared urgent and insistent. Let's get on with it already.

She settled back in her chair, feeling warmth surround her.

Ok, yeah...I can do this. I have plenty of time to talk to him later. She had waited a long time for him tonight and she was ready to be swept away.

She hoped to draw him in more, perhaps closer to the *real world* but she remembered this was the basis of their connection.

She wriggled her fingers over the keyboard, offering a spell to the mighty word-sex gods. Yes, let's get right to it. Talk to me like only you know how to, Mr. Sexy... Excite me. Her fingers poised above the keyboard, she gently placed her fingertips to the keys and began.

"I'm wearing your favorite garter belt and stockings along with my red, Jimmy Choo heels. I picked them out just for you... I knew you would love them. I have

on a tiny, thin lacy black bra;" she paused and decided on her following words and typed; *"no panties."*

She smiled at how clever she was tonight. That will get his attention.

"Yes, my love. You sound just beautiful. Tell me, are you wearing your hair down? You know I love it like that."

"I am...I wore it like this for you, Derrick."

"Well, you are indeed a vision this evening. I want you to come to me now. Let me hold you in my arms so that I might caress you and feel your soft skin against my touch."

"Oh, yes, Derrick. I'm here. Only for you. Touch me. Do anything that you like. I'm yours." She thought it was lame, how he liked her to talk to him, but what the hell? This wasn't her first time at the rodeo. She believed herself to be a quick study of his ways. She learned that early into their "talks."

Derrick was polite, thoughtful and had such a way with words. Never had any man spoke to her the way he did; so artful and enticing. She read the words he typed coming across the screen and felt warmth come over her body.

"Yes, that is what I want from you. You must surrender yourself to me. I will please you in ways you've never known...but you must be mine. No others, only me."

"Oh yes," her tongue wetting her lips. Had the room suddenly become warmer? She felt her body tighten with anticipation.

His words flashed across the computer screen like sparks from a fire, each one striking with urgency. They were rapid and insistent - calling out to her.

"My hands gently grasp yours...I pull you toward me....my fingers entwined in yours...my mouth finding your neck....kissing, nipping, biting......you smell lovely."

"Oh, yes...Derrick, touch me..." The dance of words began and she could get lost in the moment yet still type her responses. He was magic with his words.

My God, what must he be like in person? She smiled at the screen.

He continued; *"My lips reach your ear...I nip and gently pull on your lobe...my tongue sliding in gently, my warm breath ....can you feel me, Dianne? Do you feel the warmth of my breath?"*

She was naive not to think he knew all their real names, yet he used many pseudonyms. He knew where they lived, what professions they held and all their intimate secrets. They never held anything back from him. Dianne was no different. She shared all her personal details and where she lived. She was foolish to think he was honest with her.

He never shared anything remotely close to his particulars, yet they all felt they knew him. He loved that part of the game. The feeling of control. How utterly exciting.

"Oh yes, yes...Derrick...I feel you...my body is responding.... your touch is so very warm."

"My fingers follow the curves of your body.... how does that feel, Dianne?

She typed quickly, *"It feels incredible, Derrick. I sense you, everywhere.... your fingers tracing the long length of my legs – the curve of my hip....my tight, firm stomach."*

She continued to type, trying to focus on the screen. She was able to respond to his words and feed into his fantasy. His words luring her into his world. What a wonderful place to be. She cared about nothing more than this time each week.

Meeting for their "scheduled" time to be alone. Often times he missed their interlude; he was so busy. Meetings, flights across the country, he was the owner of something huge, he told her but would share nothing more. He told her it would bore her to tears. It wouldn't though - she would have loved to hear anything he shared with her, but she would take him however he allowed.

Tonight was different, though and it was palpable... and he was here. That was all she cared about. He was here for *her* and she would do anything he asked of her...anything at all.

"Yes, Dianne, you must be entirely mine, no others.

"Yes, Derrick, anything...anything at all...I am entirely yours." She was enthralled with his words. She waited and hoped tonight would be the night he would go further. Make love to her with his words. She wanted to feel

him through his words. She knew it would be incredible.

She had been meeting him like this for months now, never getting much further than this. He was so unpredictable. She thought she knew what he wanted her to say, but then, for reasons unknown to her, he would react the opposite way and abruptly end their conversations.

Tonight, she would entice him and make him want her as desperately as she wanted him. He could weave such inviting scenarios for them each time they encountered one another online.

"I lay you gently on the floor...the fire warms your lustrous skin...my eyes drinking in your loveliness."

"Oh, yes...Derrick.... that's wonderful."

Today, while she was going about her usual day-to-day activities, she laughed about her dirty little secret of how much she loved sexting. She knew others would say she had lost her fucking mind, but Dianne was caught up in the freedom it allowed her and she didn't care how ludicrous it must be to the outside world. She returned to her computer nightly, closing herself off from reality and lost herself in the anonymity of her 'lover.'

She closed her eyes for a moment, allowing herself to be swept away in the delicious sensations of it all. It was so easy to feel his presence. She felt her body becoming warm, resplendent in the moment.

She took the fantasy further and envisioned herself lying before the fire, feeling the warmth of the flames licking her skin. His eyes devouring her body. She was there solely for his pleasure. Tonight, I must have him, she thought. I must find the right words to entice him further. She knew it was ridiculous to think of sexting as natural and tantalizing, but she did.

She wanted to move into the realm of using a webcam, but she grew concerned this was really where he might want her to be in the cloak of his fantasy. Derrick took her to places in her mind and body she never thought possible.

Tonight is the night - she basked in the warmth encasing her.

Her fingers poised on the keyboard, she pondered briefly what to write and began.

"I feel your gaze upon me...your eyes ravaging my body...I feel..."

She paused, trying to find the right words to express herself and failed.

"Yes, Dianne...are you ready for me?"

"I am...all of me...all for you, Derrick." She could hardly type as she was filled with excitement and lust.

Dianne knew she was on to something here with Derrick. He loved to control the situation from her previous interactions online with him over the many months.

Yes, I have him... I know he loves it when I say his name...I think I have him figured out, *finally.* She let her fingers dance across the keys, finding her courage.

"I find your belt and unfasten your pants....my hand sliding inside..."

His response was abrupt.

"Now, now Dianne. You simply must learn how to play this game. I'm afraid our little engagement is over this evening. Perhaps another night."

"Oh, no!" she said aloud. "I can't believe this...! Derrick!" She pounded on the keyboard. *"Wait, Derrick, don't leave...I want you...I need you...please don't leave me now!"* She waited and watched as there was no response. The button next to his name went dim.

"Shit." She leaned back in her chair and slammed the top of her laptop down. Sighing, she turned in her chair and looked across the room.

The night air hung heavy; thick with humidity as it slithered through the open window. It carried the distant hum of traffic, the sharp blare of a car horn and the muffled rise and fall of an argument from the alley below - just another jarring note in the city's restless symphony.

Dianne's gaze drifted across the room, settling on a crooked picture frame hanging askew. Opposite it, a dusty mirror clung to the wall. She stood slowly, drawn to the mirror's reflection. As she approached, the hollow gaze of a middle-aged woman stared back at her. The image felt unfamiliar, as though she was meeting a stranger's eyes instead of her own. Her skin, pallid and etched with lines of time, seemed to belong to someone else. Her hand swept over her dark hair with strands of grey and removed a rubber band that had kept it in place, letting the limp locks free. She wore no makeup, her face bare and expressionless, just like the over-sized t-shirt, worn, faded and shapeless.

For a moment, Dianne lingered there, caught between the woman in the mirror and the world beyond the window. The noise of the night continued outside, but felt distant now, as though she were watching from behind the pane of glass, unable to connect to the life happening around her.

"Oh, well... Maybe I should have dressed better." She said aloud in a tired, raspy voice.

She shrugged her shoulders and sighed heavily. Turning, she plotted over to the door, closing it quietly behind her.

Chapter 5

He leaned back in his chair, as a sly smile tug at the corners of his mouth. Her ignorance of the intricacies of the game and how it was to be played was painfully evident. He wasted entirely too much time with her and after tonight, he knew it without question.

He enjoyed enticing the women he encountered online for an undetermined amount of time. If he felt there would be the promise, he would invest endless hours, quietly teaching them what his twisted mind required. This particular woman was not the case.

He spent far too long trying to teach her his game.

It was, in fact, his game.

He had to be in control; that was the draw and the excitement. It was a necessity, just like the air he breathed. He guided them with his words; they needed to sense what he desired. He needed to dominate and they had to give themselves completely. When he took his game to the world of reality, there was no difference. He led his conquests virtually and into his reality.

He was disappointed in himself briefly. He could usually detect if they were suitable for his needs. He shook off the feeling immediately, running his hands through his dark hair. He must have been tired. He had so much going on right now; it couldn't be anything more. It could not have been his judgment or losing his edge. It must have been Dianne. She lied to him when she said she understood his needs. She said she was a quick study and he would have no problem in finding her arousing. Yet, he had grown tired of the game with her.

"Enough!" He yelled loudly, slamming a hand down on the desk and stood up. The chair swiveled around swiftly and snapped back. He quickly dispensed thinking of Dianne any further. She was a waste of valuable time, indeed.

He knew the game and the advantages it would present. He was not perverse or profane. He knew what women wanted and needed. He was the only man who could lead them to such passion - intellectually, spiritually and sexually. He knew how to guide women to the desire they would never admit. It was not merely sexual, as Dianne and the others before her may have thought. Sex was not the ultimate goal, although he was not one to turn it down.

For him, it was about control. He enjoyed how it made him feel when he was dominating them in conversation and in imagination. He could weave the most magnificent scenes to entice his encounters. They would fall into the rhythm of the story he unfolded and the conquests would unknowingly meet his needs. He never tired of this feeling but tonight was another matter.

Women could be so deceitful. One might not even know when they were lying. Except for him, he always knew.

He mused at his cleverness and rolled his head around, to ease his tense muscles. Women are so effortless to manipulate. So, easy to understand. He always knew what they wanted. He found them delightfully malleable in his hands and equally in mind as he wielded them in conversation. He knew the words to speak to them, how to touch them. Most importantly, how to make them entirely devoted to him.

This was a need in his life, his desire to feel powerful. At times, he felt he was riding the crest of a wave. The ebb and flow, the rhythm the waves allowed, he felt powerful and alive. Feeling something so exhilarating, he could almost touch it.

Dianne had not allowed him the luxury of indulging his hunger. The anticipation had curled in his gut like a slow - burning ember, but she had completely missed the mark entirely tonight. A dull headache coiled at the base of his skull, spreading discomfort through his temples as he pressed long fingers against the tension there. He knew what needed to be done as his thirst wasn't satisfied this evening.

His appetite demanded his attention.

He moved his observations back to his computer and sat back down. His fingers flowed gracefully across the keys. He knew where to look to feed his hunger. He searched for a brief time and found one of his favorite pages. He moved around the feed to see if anything of interest was worth his time this evening. He read a few responses to a recent post and found one name that gave way to his attention.

He hoped she would be online.

Despite his overseas travels and the time differences, he frequently stumbled upon her presence at odd hours. The unpredictability of her online activity added to the allure; one could never predict when a muse may appear and she was quickly becoming a favorite. Although he scheduled meetings with most of the pawns in his twisted game, he often found satisfaction in the spontaneous moments when he unexpectedly found them online, indulging his interests.

His admirers were so grateful for his attentiveness. He would engage them for a brief time online, searching out if they calmed the voices that tormented him.

At times the voices were so loud, he was certain others could hear them. They never did. When the voices became insistent, he moved from virtual to reality, allowing himself to be guided by the voices that whispered.

He tried his best to keep his behavior in line, but there were times he was filled with urgency. He was able to keep up appearances without fail. No one was ever the wiser that the voices within him were stirring.

Tonight, he could feel the rage quietly building. His few friends and colleagues never seemed to notice he was warding off an inevitable destiny.

His mother was utterly clueless about the demons that gnawed at him from within. Her only concern was how far he could rise within the family business and how much wealth he could generate. He knew she did not care for him, the way a mother should. She knew nothing about him. Never asking him what he wanted to do, only *when* he would do it. She wanted to only know when he would prove himself worthy of being part of this Juggernaut - this machine, just as his grandfather, now gone, had demanded. The old man hadn't cared for his happiness either – only that he was next in line for the throne.

Every time his mother's gaze fell upon him, he could see the glint in her eyes, reflecting her devotion to the virtues of wealth and power. They were the only things she valued. To her, his worth was measured by numbers and influence, never who he was – he was a vessel – a means to an end.

He shook off this memory and moved to one of his favorite message boards. He loved this antiquated method of communicating.

He was unhappy with the ever–changing technology since the advent of the invasive video chats that infiltrated the sites. He preferred the anonymity the internet once held in its early days; the chat rooms without using names or pictures. There was no thought behind who you were speaking to, just the excitement of live communication with someone from around the world you had never met. He would venture at times and use his webcam, but he found it to be less fulfilling.

He enjoyed the intrigue of mind, words and imagination. He found utter enjoyment in using words and language that only those of educated means or aptitude could appreciate. Ironically, he found most of his conquests online in the ancient means of message boards and Facebook sites and posts.

Many still communicated in this fashion. These days, however, he found his need to change with the times and venture to Facebook, Instagram, Snapchat and the like.

Tamera, from Kentucky; Rhyan, from Pennsylvania; Bethany, from Amsterdam – there were so many. At times, he found it hard to keep them all straight. His meticulous note taking was the only thing that kept him apprised. He knew each one intimately more than their own lovers or spouses.

The intimacy he found in each woman was beyond the obvious; it was his ability of them sharing their deepest desires. Each one told him secrets they never divulged with anyone else. He knew this to be true. Women rarely would share with their lovers, or spouses their needs sexually.

In the States, many were constrained by sexual repression, dictated by societal norms that expected women to be more reserved. In contrast,

Europe boasted a more progressive mindset and attitude towards embracing a healthy sexual appetite.

When he dealt with women in the States, it took hours upon hours of talking and showing interest in their world to get to those deep places. Most women were well-tuned to the social norms and unspoken propriety that was expected of them. Women who acted upon her own needs, often were branded as a whore or worse, if there were such a thing

It was his gift to extract this desire from women and have them perform to his needs. His prowess on the internet preceded him. He would, at times, receive a random message or chat request.

It appeared that some of his encounters shared information of his ability with vocabulary. They would try to engage him, but all could not have him. His need was of a particular nature.

His plan to entice, his plan to control the situation and outcome had to be his idea.

The name he hoped to see on the message board with tonight's timestamp wasn't there. He moved over to another page, used the chat function and typed her name to see if she was online.

"Of course, you're here, darling." He whispered out loud and softly chuckled when he saw the green button next to her name. His fingers swiftly typed...

"Well, imagine my surprise to find you here tonight, my love. I'd hoped you would be here." He hit enter.

He knew his wait would not be long. Her response came right back.

"I have been waiting for you."

He smiled. Ah, *yes indeed. She awaits me.*

His headache was a mere trace and the loud voices began to subside. Only a murmur was all he heard.

Soon, the voices would be gone. Just what was in store for her, she had no idea, but he knew it would quiet the voices.

He smiled, drank in a deep breath and a wave of euphoria swept over him.

He knew tonight, she would be his next.

Chapter 6

Loghan sipped her espresso and returned the small cup to its saucer. It made a quiet, clinking sound and Harry flicked his tail lazily as he slept. She gazed out her large picture window, overlooking the park. The moon was full and the duck pond across the way shimmered through the trees.

It was a quiet winter evening, the air still and crisp. Outside, the world seemed frozen in time, the only movement coming from a young couple who paused at the pond. Loghan watched them from her window, their silhouettes illuminated by the soft glow of a nearby streetlamp. They settled onto the bench, leaning into each other appearing to share a secret, their breath visible in the cold air.

Loghan mindlessly held the couple in her view as she mulled over the events of the past week. It had been long and exhausting. She had numerous meetings, a spirited discussion about her next two assignments with John and hours and hours of dull research for her latest assigned article. Loghan was ready to put this week behind her.

"TGIF!" she whispered as she sipped her wine. Friday nights had a different vibe altogether. All the stress that surrounded her week, along with the deadlines, fell behind her.

Loghan leaned back on the couch and stretched out her long, athletic, shapely legs and arched her back. Rolling her shoulders she tilted her head side to side, easing the tension. She let herself sink into the quiet, savoring the stillness.

"Ahhh, what a delicious night, huh, Harry?"

Harry, the big tabby, lifted his head, pretending to be interested in his human and settled down again in his warm kitty bed. Harry appeared to have no time to waste on his evening nap. Loghan smiled at him and shifted on the couch and mindlessly went back to her magazine, flipping the pages and sipping a glass of malbec.

Her article for the next publication had been approved by her editor, John. It wasn't her choice to write about real estate and Millennials, but she felt like she did a good job finding a story out of something she had no genuine interest in. John hadn't said it was great by any means, but he said, "It'll do, Loghan."

As far as compliments went from John, this was as good as they would get. Loghan hoped John would ease up on her soon, but she wasn't counting on it and would continue to produce the light-weight fluff, she was assigned. She wished he would provide more feedback on her writing but, she was just thrilled he did not kick the article back for revisions. He took it as is. That was a first and she would take that as a small victory. Loghan knew in order for her to make headway with John, she had to keep her head down and work; produce excellent articles and stay focused.

Loghan put the magazine down and returned to her thoughts. She gazed at the ducks and geese, now squawking and making a huge commotion as evening runners passed by the flock.

Her thoughts drifted to Ian, as they often did - Ian had always believed in Loghan. Her handsome, strong and attentive fiancé, Ian. He'd been there from the very start. She couldn't remember a time when Ian wasn't around. They had grown up together, went to the same grade school, middle school and then high school. When it came time to choose a college, they went their separate ways for a brief time. Ian, staying in California and selecting Sacramento State University. They couldn't tolerate being apart from one another, so Ian applied at Columbia and joined Loghan the following semester.

It seemed the two were meant to be together. Ian was so easy to be with and they rarely had to work at their relationship. They could just *be* and genuinely wanted to be in each other's space. She recalled Ian's strong arms around her, whispering in her ear he would be with her forever...love her forever.

How very much life had changed.

Loghan's eyes fell again to the young couple at the pond. She could see them in a sweet embrace, their arms around one another, heads tilted in a lingering kiss. Wasn't that how it was supposed to be for her and Ian? She thought they would be together forever. Even though they had never talked about forever, it was just implied. It was a natural pairing of surf and sand; water and wind; lovers and kisses. Ian and Loghan just made sense.

Now, everything was fractured and out of place.

That should be her and Ian down at the pond. She looked at the couple and felt the damn familiar feeling of loneliness engulf her. She closed her eyes and let herself continue to be swept away in the memories of Ian.

Loghan needed to let Ian go and move on, but it was so hard. She tried to work through her grief, read self-help books, research how to manage grief and looked into support groups. She found a grief counselor and went for several months. It helped a little, but even her counselor admitted it was harder for young people to deal with losing a loved one. They felt invincible and free from harm. Jesus, her counselor, couldn't have spoken more valid words. All of the feelings, anger, sense of loss, it all sucked. There was no easy way to get through the darkness, but one step at a time.

Ian had been there through thick and thin, encouraging Loghan with her writing. He inspired her to be brave and write what she loved and never give up. It felt too often that she was alone and her special someone, wasn't there to watch over her and give her that encouragement.

Loghan let her thoughts return to the present, shaking off the threads of memories and tried to stop feeling sorry for herself.

She tipped her glass back for the last sip of her malbec and walked down the hallway to her office. She may as well start researching her next article and there was no time like the present. She didn't have any plans and spending a little time researching would be a good thing.

Taking a detour to the kitchen, she grabbed the bottle of malbec and a plate of cheese. Dropping into her chair and opening her laptop; she deftly ran her hands through her hair, twisting its length on top of her head in a swift motion. Spying a pencil on her desk, she pushed it through her auburn hair; an instant top knot. In an absent-minded motion, she pulled the front locks down to frame her soft face. Loghan checked her email and opened the files that she sent home from the office, to begin her research. Her heart wasn't in to researching and it didn't take but a few moments before she was distracted and found herself on Facebook.

She smiled as she scrolled through pictures her college roommate Megan posted this afternoon. She could see the excitement on her face as she posted about her upcoming wedding. Loghan was genuinely happy for Megan and Conner and she couldn't wait to celebrate their special day. Megan was a dear friend and she wished they saw each other more often, but when Ian died, Megan didn't know how to support Loghan. As days turned into weeks, their once - constant communication dwindled to sporadic check-ins, each interaction tinged with an unspoken heaviness. Megan felt guilty that her life was going on and she was marrying the man of her dreams, while Loghan was left to bury hers. The two friends worked out their awkward sadness several months ago over a bottle of wine and a cascade of tears and, "I'm sorrys," and they picked up where they left off.

Loghan braced herself for the upcoming wedding, knowing it would be anything but easy. No matter how hard she tried, she couldn't silence the aching thoughts - the ones whispering that this could have also been her moment, her vows, her forever with Ian.

She clicked on the stream of pictures and the tinge of sadness left her. Smiles, laughter and photos of a fun-loving couple flooded her screen. Loghan smiled at each image; Megan and Conner sampling wedding cakes, looking at potential wedding venues and sipping wine on a ledge overlooking San Francisco Bay. Loghan's gentle laugh escaped as she clicked on the final picture of Megan and Conner, putting bow ties on their beloved Golden Retrievers, with a sign between them, announcing the wedding date.

Something caught Loghan's eye at the bottom of the page and she glanced down, seeing her chat box open.

"Hello there. Fancy seeing you here on a Friday night."

Unquestionably surprised, Loghan smiled softly and began to respond. Her graceful fingers tapped the keys.

"Hello. It's not that uncommon, actually. I should be working, but I find Facebook more interesting. The question for me would be, why are you here on a Friday night? What? No date?"

Loghan absently traced her finger around the rim of her wine glass as it quietly hummed. Harry followed her to the office and was intrigued by the high pitch, his head jerking toward the sound.

"No, no date. I'm not that good at the dating thing. I would rather spend time with someone that I know and not have that awkward feeling of finding things to talk about."

Loghan smiled and leaned forward, her turn to be intrigued and responded. *"Yes, dating can be awkward, that is for sure. I'm not a fan myself. Well, from what I remember. It's been a while since I dated. I'm surprised that you would ever have a hard time finding things to talk about."*

The response was quick: *"Oh, don't be fooled. I know I may come off well versed and articulate, but I get tongue-tied on dates; hence, why I prefer to go the route of knowing someone first before the date."*

Harry had made himself known and jumped on Loghan's lap, turning around a few times to find the most comfortable spot. Loghan shifted in her chair to accommodate Harry, scratching his furry head for a moment and then returned to the computer keys.

Loghan was enjoying this interaction as this *wasn't* a regular occurrence. She noticed her heart was lighter, happy at this moment. She smiled and poised her fingers on the keys:

"You aren't allowing yourself enough credit. I think you are bright and clearly charming. You must have several, if not many women you are comfortable with to go out on a date. Take your pick!"

Loghan smiled...waiting for the response and it soon returned.

"LOL! Many? You give me way too much credit! Of course, there are a few women I would be comfortable going out with, but..."

Loghan sat up again and Harry was not happy with her shift, jumping down on the hardwood floor. **Thump.**

Loghan brushed off Harry's annoyance and returned with interest to the computer. The response was coming as she watched the indicator.

"There is a woman...I am very comfortable in her presence. It's just not right, for many reasons."

Loghan's brow creased as she considered. *"Is she married? Is she with someone? What could possibly hold you back in asking her out?"* Loghan waited; the indicator was dim, she impatiently waited for a response. Finally, she could see the answer was coming.

"No, no, none of that. It's complicated. Isn't that the response someone says when there is too much to explain? Or, rather...you don't entirely know how to explain it?" There was a pause and the response continued: *"I think that is where I am currently. I hadn't really drilled down to the 'why'? Thank you for making me think about it; really...I appreciate that."*

There was another brief pause in their response.

"I know you're trying to work and I interrupted you. I'll let you get back to it. It was nice talking to you, Loghan. Have a great weekend!"

Tilting her head to the side, Loghan considered the response he had just made. They never had "chatted" online before. It was different to interact with him this way. Shaking it off momentarily, she returned to typing.

"Thanks... you too! Have a great weekend, Deagan. See you on Monday. :)"

"Hmm..." Loghan said aloud, "That was new, wasn't it, Harry?"

Loghan reached for the malbec and poured a splash and closed the chat window. Taking a sip, she settled back for another long night of research and her computer.

Chapter 7

The plane was dark and quiet as he strained to glimpse out his cabin window of first class. He had several fights in the US over the last three weeks on business, but it was nice to have a few days in his homeland. He found the travel exhausting but necessary to handle business deals and close on the most challenging clients. This trip would be grueling, but he knew once it was behind him, he would take several weeks off to relax and get some much-needed sun. His overnight flight was 8 hours and he would settle in for a few hours of sleep shortly after he put the finishing touches to email updates to his latest project. He enjoyed flying first class as often as possible, especially when he had a long international flight.

His seat's position was arranged so others flying in first-class couldn't be seen due to the seat/pod configuration. He appreciated the touch of added privacy it allowed.

His flight had been uneventful and allowed him to focus on last-minute business before his meetings this week, but he found himself getting tired. He decided it was a good time to settle in for some sleep and went to the bathroom to change.

Sifting through the provided amenities, he found the first-class pajamas and toiletry kit. Better than most, he mused as he brushed his teeth and looked over the garments.

Once he finished, he returned and settled back into his seat and pressed the button for the flight attendant.

"Can I get you anything else, sir?" Her tone, light and whispered.

The flight attendant leaned into him closely, reaching across to turn off the overhead light. "Can I make up your bed for you?" She continued; her smile lined with the most perfect teeth he had ever seen, glistening white brilliance.

Was her breast touching his arm? Indeed, it was. He considered this discreetly and watched through hooded eyes as she switched off the overhead light.

She was beautiful, lean and tan. She paid him quite a bit of attention throughout the flight. She engaged him in small conversations about art and even a theater performance she'd recommended to him on his trip.

"You must see it," she dreamily said to him as she took his tray and glass from him earlier.

He loved women who had the appearance as this lithe creature. It was such a shame when he saw a woman who chose not to look her absolute best. They were such beautiful creations.

Pausing, he looked at her with interest. "Actually, there is something else I would like."

"Yes, what is it?" she asked. Her smile again bright and sincere.

"I would like a nightcap before I retire, please. Cognac." His voice was low and husky.

"Of course, sir. One moment."

She disappeared from his sight and returned briefly with a snifter in her delicate, well-manicured hand. She leaned down and placed a white linen napkin on the side table and the amber liquid.

He reached for the glass and brushed his hand across hers. Her eyes flickered and locked on his.

"Excuse me." She let her eyes turn away and he sensed her slight embarrassment. He wanted to ease her concern and continued in a low, hushed tone.

"I would love if you would allow me the honor of having a drink with me after the flight?" He gazed into her eyes. They were pools of deep blue with flecks of gold, in the dimmed light.

"I...I would like that." She whispered discreetly. "It just so happens; I have a layover on this leg." She touched his arm gently as she spoke. He reached for his business card and handed it to her.

"Wonderful." His eyes grazed over her and paused as he found her name badge.

"I'll look forward to seeing you...Kari." Smiling, he picked up his cognac and tipped it in her direction. He paused, his eyes never leaving her as he took a sip and he returned the glass next to the linen napkin.

She felt a slight shiver run through her. His eyes piercing her soul.

Extending his hand to her, his voice in a quiet whisper, "I'm Aric; Aric Stanton."

*****

Loghan tossed the magazines on the restaurant tabletop and slid into the booth. The imitation leather groaning from years of age as she sat down. She was famished and the savory aroma of Mexican food assaulted her senses.

Loghan began to flip through the handful of computer and tech magazines she picked up earlier.

Over the last week, she was researching an idea for a story. She wasn't entirely confident what the story may be, but it was enough that she would continue to pursue the path. Her ideas danced around the internet; different search engines, dating sites, anything she could find. Everything had been done and covered, yet, she knew there was a story waiting to be tapped as she could sense it.

There had to be something new that hasn't been touched or covered. The years of Mac - iPhone, PC's and the internet had continued to change and grow through the years. One could hardly keep up with the latest and greatest. The great big world had become much smaller since the advent of the internet. The internet brimmed with knowledge and opportunities, but in the hands of those who knew its shadows, it became a tool for darkness.

Loghan knew she could turn over these stones and find a story that she knew was hiding.

In the process of her research, she stumbled into the old realm of chat rooms that were huge in the internet's infancy. She was surprised to still find chat rooms and not only were they still available, but they were also filled. The changes to those who loved the chat room's anonymity found they had given way to webcams.

She discovered you could still just "chat" and not have the use of the camera, but those who would interact with you were few and far between. While there were many *safe* chatters online, there were many creepy assholes as well.

Loghan stumbled onto a chat forum a few weeks ago in her research and was fascinated immediately. She became interested in the women occupying the rooms - why were they online? For fun, or trying to find romance? Maybe there was a story here.

She absently flipped through the magazines, making mental notes of ideas and tagging the placement with post-it notes.

Loghan also decided today she would approach her editor, John, with her article idea. She knew it would be a battle. Story lines most frequently had to be his idea or, no-go; that was John's modus operandi. She grew tired of his approach but still not ready to give in and start looking for work elsewhere. She needed to put in her time and gain more experience and she wasn't seeking *fame*, but she did want to know there was opportunity to grow.

Why in the hell did it have to be a fight with John? She needed a distraction in her life right now and working on an article *she* wanted to work on would be just the thing.

Loghan opened her notebook and attempted to concentrate, but her stomach was grumbling its displeasure and she glanced up to locate the server.

"Hi, what are you doing here?" Deagan was smiling down at her.

"Hey,! I'm stopping for lunch." Loghan was genuinely pleased to see Deagan. She had been putting him off over the last few days and was feeling somewhat guilty.

"Come on, sit down, Deagan." Loghan waved her arm toward the opposite seat.

"Are you sure? I don't want to impose." Deagan hesitated and stood still.

"Please, Deagan, join me." Her green eyes filled with warmth as she looked at Deagan and he immediately felt reassured.

He smiled and sat down across from Loghan. It was nice to see her smiling, he thought. She appeared a little stand-offish the last few days around the office. While he may have misread her response toward him, Deagan did not want to crowd her in any way, giving her space. He knew she was still struggling getting over Ian. He offered his support while allowing her the time she needed.

Loghan was skilled at hiding her emotions. Deagan knew she masked her feelings like a good hand in a card game, not allowing a "tell" of any sort to give her away.

Deagan sensed more distance from her lately and wanted to help if he could. He knew Loghan reasonably well. They had worked together on a several assignments, sat in on weekly editor meetings and always sought one another out for a laugh. They genuinely built a solid friendship and he knew when she was feeling down.

Deagan liked Loghan the moment he met her; from her easy-going and open demeanor and gentle laugh, to her wicked sense of humor. He respected her and Ian. He genuinely liked him and they met many times after work for drinks and dinner, even went for runs with Ian and Loghan occasionally. It was natural and the trio became solid friends.

Recently, Deagan felt his feelings change for Loghan from an easy-going pace of friendship to something deeper. He wasn't sure when it happened or what the hell he would do about it, but he knew it *couldn't* happen. Maybe it was his need to help her through this difficult time or the way he could see the pain in her eyes that no one else seemed to notice.

Deagan feared he was falling for Loghan and that was a position he wished not to be in. It felt wrong, a betrayal to Ian's memory. Deagan had never shown interest in any women at work; it was an unspoken rule he strictly adhered to. But Loghan was different. From the moment she walked into Forefront Magazine, her auburn hair framing her soft face and those iridescent green eyes, not to mention her confidence, he was drawn to her. She exuded professionalism - black skirt, heels, discreet form-fitting blouse and just the right amount of tasteful jewelry.

Deagan had to steady himself, resisting the urge to glance twice at

Loghan's effortless beauty. There was something striking about her - not in an obvious, attention - seeking way, but in the quiet confidence she carried. As John invited him to sit in on Loghan's interview, as he often did, Deagan pushed aside any fleeting, unprofessional thoughts. Instead of dwelling on the way she carried herself with grace, he refocused on the task at hand, tuning in to her resume' and the sharp, thoughtful way she answered each question.

Deagan was beyond impressed by her intelligence and savvy. Her resume' was spot on and the portfolio she provided of her work was excellent. He recalled thinking back to her interview, that she appeared too good to be true. But Loghan lived up to their expectations as a writer. She focused on her assignments, built a small, but loyal readership and proved herself to be a solid, new addition to the magazine. As time passed and Deagan worked with Loghan on a few assignments, they learned more about one another. Deagan found Loghan was in a serious relationship and he firmly, without question, took his place as her friend.

Deagan appreciated confirming Loghan to be a skilled writer. She had an uncanny ability to find a story in something that seemed so benign. He had seen many drafts from her that John would pass over. Deagan didn't understand why John would not allow her to present her own concepts, but John had other ideas for her. He wanted her to cover the *fluffy* side of journalism. Every newspaper and magazine had a writer who covered the soft side of events.

Unbeknownst to Loghan, Deagan went to bat for her several times with John, but to no avail. He found himself head-to-head with John soon after she was hired and boldly warned John he was on the edge of implicit bias with his attitude toward Loghan. John had some old-school ways that needed to be kicked to the curb. Deagan or, Loghan would be the one to do just that - he knew instinctively it would be Loghan. John needed to get his head out of 1979 and knock this crap off, but being the owner of a privately-owned magazine allowed John to hold on to old ideas.

Deagan sighed a deep breath and was jolted from his memories at the abrupt sound of clattering plates in the background.

"What have you got there?" Deagan motioned to the magazines on the table and Loghan's iPad.

"Some computer magazine references; I'm doing some research for an article I want to write." Loghan thumbed through the pages briefly.

"What's the angle? Deagan leaned forward in his seat to get a better look at the magazine.

"I want to go in a direction that is edgier for me than our readers are used to at ForeFront. I've been researching and I feel like I'm on to something..." her voice drifted off in thought." I'm just not entirely sure what it is. I know I want to focus on technology and how it's become a mainstay in our society. I know it's not new, but I find it fascinating how our society has everything at our fingertips with the Internet, Smart Phones, computers...all of it, Deagan."

She glanced up from the magazine, her gaze locking with Deagan's. A radiant, brilliant smile spread across her face, her eyes shimmering and alive, catching the light as they danced with fleeting joy. For a moment, something deeper stirred - a spark of life trying to break free from the shadows that weighed her down, whispering of the sadness that still clung to her.

Deagan smiled and reached his hand across the table. "Loghan, it's great to see you like this. You seem genuinely excited." His hand touched her arm lightly to emphasize his feelings. The moment Deagan reached for her, he knew he shouldn't, but he was already committed to his movement. Loghan looked down at his hand on her arm and he could see the slightest movement on her part. He moved his hand back as quickly as he touched her arm.

Concerned, Loghan took it the wrong way; he felt a dull ache in his chest. She was so damn protective of her feelings and surroundings. He meant nothing more than connection to a friend...damn it. Why did he do that? He cursed himself quietly in his mind and placed his scorned hand on the table.

Loghan smiled gently at Deagan.

"I am excited, Deagan. I know there is a great article in all of this. I feel there is something worth stating... I'm so close - I just haven't found exactly what I want to write yet...I will, though." Loghan held back some of her thoughts of the story she wanted to research further. Jesus, chat rooms and webcams. What would Deagan think of her? Why in the hell would she be in chat rooms? There is usually only one reason - sex. She looked down to ensure Deagan couldn't see her possibly blushing at the moment.

"I know you will, too. I'm just happy to see you smiling. I haven't seen that for a while." Deagan leaned back in the booth, his forehead creasing in concern. Loghan was aware of the vibe she was emitting of late; "stay back - let me be." She did what she had to do each day at work and moved through most days with a forced smile. Some days were easier than others and she felt if someone just scratched the surface, she would fall apart in tears.

Deagan knew better, she thought and he deserved a truthful response.

"I know...I know. I've been going through a rough spot lately. I'm sorry. I haven't been too... approachable." She paused and took a deep breath. "I have good days and bad days. Lately...the bad days have been winning." Her voice trailed off and the light in her eyes dimmed. She let out a long sigh and leaned back into the seat. She felt the coolness of the leather reach through her blouse.

"Don't apologize, Loghan. I just want you to know I'm here for you. Whatever you need. If you just want to sit in silence, or if you want to talk...whatever." His eyes held hers steady. Deagan knew this must be so hard for her. Ian was a great guy. To lose someone you had loved your entire adult life. It was just too hard to imagine.

At that moment, Loghan looked so vulnerable. He wanted nothing more than to take her in his arms and comfort her and tell her everything would be all right. He knew it was ridiculous to think that he could make Loghan forget her troubles by merely holding her. Loghan didn't need anyone to protect her. She was strong and resilient.

"Thank you, Deagan. I appreciate you - your friendship; I hope you know that." The last comment wasn't a question; it was a statement. Deagan did know Loghan appreciated their friendship and he quietly nodded.

There was a silence between them for a moment; each one slipping into their thoughts. There was no awkwardness, just ease to be in this moment with one another. Their friendship had grown during the three years since

Ian passed. Lost for a short time in their memories, both Deagan and Loghan sat quietly. They smiled at one another slightly; words were not needed to convey their thoughts and fondness for one another.

The server severed the quiet moment, by setting two glasses of water on the table, along with chips and salsa. She left the menus and trotted off with a promise of returning shortly. Deagan opted to lighten the immediate moment and pressed Loghan for more details on her article idea. She happily continued.

"Well, we all know that people have been meeting online for a long time. Nothing new, right? What I am finding, though, is people are still using the chat rooms, or just chatting in messenger to communicate." She leaned back and continued, "There is an entire "subculture" of people who are bypassing Tinder, Hinge, OkCupid, Bumble, Match...whatever method of meeting and going to these older versions of hooking up." She excitedly continued. "I mean...chatting was a big deal early on, but it seems to have found a resurgence again. It's really crazy." She shook her head, seemingly to clear the ideas flooding her. "Anyway, I've noticed a pattern with the people who are online and where they go, things like that."

Deagan listened intently. He liked where she was going with this idea. Loghan continued. "I want to talk to John and see if I can get his go-ahead to research this further." Loghan's shoulders dropped down, her well-manicured fingers tapping on the tabletop.

She knew what she was up against with John.

It would be the same argument from him. She could hear it now. *"You don't have the experience; why don't you cover Second Sunday?"* He would pose it to her as question, but they both knew it was his direction.

"Loghan, can I make a suggestion? Why don't you let me go with you? Maybe I can help persuade him."

"I don't know, I appreciate it, really Deagan. I just need to try and get John to come around to my way of thinking. Does that make sense?" Her brow was furrowed and her eyes searched his for understanding. Loghan regrouped and continued.

"I have to show him my ideas have value." She could feel the frustration building inside of her. The thought of another disappointment was not what she was willing to take today. Maybe she would put it off for a day or two.

Deagan nodded. "Well, you just say the word and I'll try to help, any way I can. It sounds like you're on to a good idea, Loghan." He smiled at her and she returned with one of her own.

The waitress appeared at their table and took their order. Loghan had almost forgotten her hunger. For the first time in a long while, she felt like she was awakening from a very long slumber. She hoped she was turning a corner. Excitement stirred within her; she was ready to start working on this pitch for the article.

Deagan was a great encouragement to her. She felt so comfortable with him. He had never made her feel incapable of doing anything but a good job. She liked that about him. He had faith in her and encouraged her - just like Ian.

When lunch arrived, they laughed and talked over tostadas and fajitas. It was delicious, not only to Loghan's palette but mind, body and soul. It had been far too long since she enjoyed anyone's company or laughed as much.

"Deagan, thank you." Loghan said quietly as they were walking to the parking lot to find their prospective cars. The sun felt vaguely warm on this Sacramento winter day as it strained to expose itself through thick, dark clouds.

"No problem...of course. Lunch was so good." Deagan patted his stomach to show his appreciation. He smiled lightheartedly; Loghan stopped walking and touched his arm gently.

"No...I mean it, really - Thank you." Her eyes met Deagan's with a warm acknowledgment.

Deagan was surprised by her touch and the candid, genuine moment she was showing him.

"Of course...anytime." Deagan nodded softly and smiled as they walked to her car.

"Sure you don't want me to talk to John?"

"No...thank you. I'm going to venture out on this one alone. I need to do this, Deagan." Loghan smiled at him.

"Just follow your instincts, Loghan...find the story." Deagan waved and headed the other direction to his car.

She smiled at him slowly and called after him. "I will, Deagan, I will."

52

Chapter 8

Kari smiled casually as she gingerly placed her hand in his. She immediately felt her cheeks gaining color and she tried to play it off, keeping her eyes averted from his.

He noticed how soft and warm her hand felt in his. Her French manicure, nails perfectly shaped and just the right length. Oh, how he loathed, incredibly long fingernails. They were too much and took away from a woman's delicate and beautiful hands, in his opinion.

Perfect, he thought; she was simply perfect.

Their eyes met and locked. Aric held her hand, perhaps for a moment too long and gently wrapped his free hand around hers. Kari couldn't help herself and she blushed and smiled invitingly towards him.

She discreetly whispered, "Aric, I'll look forward to seeing you later." She said his name slowly and deliberately; felt it roll off her tongue and lingered like a lover's kiss. She held her gentle smile and turned, walking away and slipped quietly into the galley.

His smile remained as he watched her walk away, leaning back in his seat, straining to follow her. He was reminded of how tired he was as his eyes were hooded and heavy in all the anticipatory excitement. He reached his long arms over his head in a delicious stretch and moved over to his pod, which Kari made up for him while he changed.

Climbing into the crisp and cool sheets, he stretched out, yawning and looked forward to a few hours of blissful sleep.

Kari noticed him the moment he boarded the plane. Dark, wavy hair, expensive black suit and Italian shoes. She watched him board, greeted him warmly and admired the confidence that exuded from him as he passed by her, walking toward the first class.

He was obviously a wealthy and successful businessman. His suit was custom-made as it fit him perfectly, showing off his trim, athletic physique. He worked on his laptop for much of the flight from London to Boston. He caught her eye on a few occasions, but nothing more than the everyday conversations on an international flight. Somewhere between Heathrow and midway over the Atlantic, she found every opportunity to engage him in brief conversations.

Kari rarely made it practice to flirt with passengers. It was frowned upon by management and obviously a well-placed regulation at best. Every now and again, she dismissed the rules and would have dinner or a drink with someone from the flight.

What could it hurt? She was discreet and no one was the wiser on the flights, nor the crew she flew with. She followed all the other regulations that were imposed upon her. Sometimes you just had to say what the hell and do what you wanted. It made her feel like she was living on the edge from time to time. Besides, what could a little dinner between two adults hurt?

Several hours later, she found herself lingering over the most delicious dinner, sipping Cristal champagne and sharing crème brûlée. Kari was impressed with Aric's captivating storytelling skills and ability to command her attention. He was attentive and polite and every bit as handsome as she recalled from the flight as she could now fully admire him across the table.

His stories were endless and engaging; his smile was intoxicating. Their conversation was easy and light as they made their way through dinner. She noted the way the warm candlelight flickered in his steel-blue eyes; they danced a seductive dance.

She knew where this night was going and she did nothing but encourage the evening's sensual feeling. Kari found herself drawn to him, a need to be in his presence.

Yet, during the course of dinner, something troubled her. It was a certain way he smiled at her that created an uneasy quiver in the pit of her stomach.

She dismissed it, telling herself she was silly, as she was doing something exciting and daring.

She freshened her lipstick when she excused herself earlier and paused at her reflection; *Christ - relax Kari, enjoy yourself.* She dismissed her worry and touched her finger to the corner of her mouth, ensuring her lipstick was perfect.

She was never one to jump into bed with a man whom she just met. However, there was a time for everything, she thought. She encouraged herself as she laughed at his quips and stories of travel. She could stop the evening's direction, thank him for a lovely evening and catch an Uber back to her hotel, but at this point, she was not sure that was what she wanted.

Aric was mesmerizing. The timbre of his voice was as lyrical as it was warm and rapturous. Kari felt the champagne doing its job and she felt a little tipsy but finally relaxed, allowing herself to lean into this glorious evening.

Jolted out of her thoughts by Aric's voice, she re-engaged herself in the conversation.

"Kari, tell me more about yourself. I have monopolized the conversation far too much this evening." His ice blue eyes searching hers. He continued to enjoy the crème brûlée, savoring the creamy and rich texture in his mouth.

Kari leaned into the table, picking up her glass. She pressed it to her red lips. Aric allowed himself the luxury of watching her full lips drink from the glass. She felt his gaze on her, knowing full well he was watching her lips and a slow burn came over her body.

"Aric, there is not much to tell. I've led a very ordinary life, really. I grew up in Detroit, went to college, then became a flight attendant. No broken home life or ex-husbands. I told you...very boring."

She set the glass down on the table, her fingers unconsciously tracing the rim. Aric's eyes held hers and he reached his hand across the table and touched her fingers. She felt a jolt run through her. His hand emitted a searing heat, or perhaps that was her skin responding to his touch. Her heart pounded in her ears; she was sure he could hear it. She tried to pull her eyes away from his, playing coy, but it was impossible. She left her will in the last glass of champagne.

"You are far from ordinary, Kari." His voice was soothing and gentle. His lilting accent entranced her. Then came his smile. She felt the same uneasy quiver deep inside of her. Something told her to run from him, to end this evening and to go back to her hotel alone, yet she could not gather the strength to leave his presence.

She felt alive and vibrant. She was uncertain of the feeling that simmered inside her breast. She could feel Aric's powerful sensuality, smell it and almost taste it. She'd never experienced this passion before and she wanted to explore it further.

She let his fingers entwine with hers and moved her leg under the table. She faintly touched his foot with the side of hers. She smiled at him, unable to stop the warmth that had begun to fill her.

Aric insisted on paying the tab as he gently reminded her; it was he who asked her to join him for dinner.

They made their way into the cold, Boston night. The leather was cool and supple as she slid across the limousine seat. Aric followed after her and the chauffeur closed the door, returning quickly to the driver's seat. The moon roof shade was slightly drawn and a slice of warm moonlight washed over the limousine seat. He casually leaned forward and tapped his fingers on the privacy window and the limousine lurched forward.

Coats and scarves were shrugged off quickly to make way for unmistakable passion. He pulled her close to him, drawing in her aroma, the sweetness of her scent. Her neck tilted toward him and Aric pressed his lips on her soft skin. A series of soft sighs escaped her lips and Kari closed her eyes and her arms, laced around his shoulders. They felt solid and muscular. She let her hands wander to his hair, thick and wavy. Aric's hands followed the curves of her body, his lips never leaving her skin. She was on fire and he could feel her desire. He seduced her with his mouth, taunting her, teaching her, making her succumb to his every touch.

She tasted sweet and salty as his lips caressed her. Reaching up, his hands deftly began to unbutton her blouse. Kari arched her back, allowing him the freedom to let his hands roam her body. A ripple of sensation coursed through her. Never had she felt such passion. She wanted him to take her, to command all of her and she knew that was precisely where this moment was heading...and she followed it to the end. The feeling of passion was tangible.

Soon they were entangled into one another, unable to know where one started and the other ended. There were shudders, gasps and moans that escaped Kari's lips that she had never heard before. His hands and lips brought her to the edge of passion and then, he would back off for a moment, his steely eyes watching her writhe in anticipation. When both could stand no more, he covered her body with his and both were lost in the steamy bliss of ecstasy.

All sense of time had escaped her in the heat and afterward, not knowing when, or how, she lay on top of him exhausted. Neither one had noticed the limo had come to a stop in a park. The night folded around the darkness with flecks of moonlight cutting through the clouds. Aric was the first to regain his composure and pulled himself upright. Kari followed suit. Both putting themselves back together.

"My, God...that was incredible." That was all Kari could muster to say. She opened her compact and looked around for a light to assess the damage.

She found a switch on the door panel and pressed it as a bright beam captured her face. She was somewhat taken aback at her appearance. Her face, red and blotchy, in areas from Aric's evening beard coming in. Her lips were full and moist. Her hair was mussed and absolutely out of place and she looked every bit the part of a woman well sexed. She reveled in every moment of this feeling.

Aric still appeared impeccably groomed, despite his actions. "Yes, that was delicious," he said with a smile, running his hands through his hair and pulling on his shirt and tie, maintaining his flawless appearance.

His demeanor was sexy and relaxed. Kari marveled how composed he was after that wild romp in the back of the limousine. She felt a brief, uneasy tinge stirring within again.

Primal, sexual and dangerous, he exuded strength and power. Maybe it was the way he looked at her. No - through her. Like he knew something about her she had not shared.

The moonlight caught his eyes and they shimmered, a smile escaped his lips, dispelling the unease she had felt.

Aric pondered taking her back to the hotel and make love to her properly, but time would not allow. He had an early morning meeting and was rather tired from his travel. Just as well, he thought. A good hot shower and clean, cool sheets sounded much more appealing. Strange, the voices that screamed at him during the flight had all but diminished. Must be the presence of a beautiful woman. Sometimes the anger within him would not quiet, no matter what he tried.

He never expected the evening to progress here. Rarely did he get involved with women as his travels took him. He found it cumbersome, dangerous and weary should he choose the women unwisely. They tended to cling and push for more attention than he was willing to give. His computer was often as far as he allowed himself to seek the company of women. He could speak freely and control the outcome and answered to no one. He loved to live his life online, primarily his sexual life. When he ventured into the real world...well, it rarely ended pretty.

He was becoming a bit unpredictable, he mused. He hoped he was not getting careless. This was the second time this thought crossed his mind and that would never do. He must be more cautious in the future. He never let his sexual appetite control him, nor would he start now.

Tonight, during dinner, he wasn't sure if he would kill her. He found her desirable and exciting. He was thankful she was a willing partner; it would have been terrible had she not wanted him as much as he longed for her. God knows the outcome would have been far different.

Aric tapped on the driver's window again; this time, it lowered.

"Yes, sir?" the driver tipped his ear toward the back seat.

"Where are you staying, Kari?" Aric's lazy and melodic voice surrounded her.

"Hyatt Regency – Boston Commons." she smiled.

"Driver." The single word, barely more than a breath, carried an unspoken command. The window slid up with a whisper, sealing the cabin in silence as the car glided forward.

Kari lay her head back on the seat and closed her eyes for a moment. That was absolutely amazing; she continued in thought. I can't believe I just did that...with a complete stranger!

She looked over at Aric; his smile was disarming this time.

"A penny for your thoughts, my dear?"

Kari left out a brief, nervous chuckle. "I was thinking how incredible that was and that I've never done anything like this before. I don't even know you and yet..." Her voice drifted.

"Yes?" Aric leaned closer to her.

"Well, you know...women...we need to be very careful about men." She nervously smiled at him.

"Of course, I completely understand." He left a slight pause in that moment and he continued. "There could be a - *killer* out there. "He stated it so, matter of factly, she nervously shivered. She looked up to his eyes and they were without expression and the lack of light now made his eyes look black.

Just as quickly as she noticed his eyes, they shifted and brightened with his smile as the moonlight illuminated through the limousine window. She felt at ease with his smile and shrugged off her ridiculous, ill-placed intuition.

He was endeared by her cautious demeanor and he knew all too well he could entice her to let her guard down. It was a woman's right to change her mind should she wish. It may be his right to do just the same. Who knows...the night was young.

He continued to smile at her lovely face, Kari smiled back, relaxing and shifted over toward him. There was still time before they reached her hotel, he thought.

"Lovely...so beautiful and sensual..." he whispered, pulling her on to his lap, she was willing once more... and his hand gently reached for her breast again.

Chapter 9

The light on John's phone continued to flash and interrupted John's train of thought. Deep into editing a new piece for the magazine, John was having difficulty piecing the article together. Slightly agitated, he picked up the phone.

"Hi, John. Sorry, but I've been pinging you on Teams." It was his assistant, Emily.

"Anthony Rice has been trying to reach you all morning and decided to call me instead."

John had his phone on send, so all his calls were going straight to voice mail. That was common for him when he was in his office and working on edits.

He looked up from his computer, rubbing his eyes. "Ok, thanks, Emily. Transfer the call, please."

Emily usually pinged him on Teams to let him know an important call was coming through. He didn't care for the constant interruptions with calls coming to him directly.

Once again, he found himself longing how things "used to be." He missed the old intercom on his phone. Emily said that was ridiculous. She took charge of the office phones being updated and many other areas when she was hired.

Emily continued to drag John into the 21st century with every change she could manage. John complained when she switched out his phone. Changing from the old intercom style to some damn fancy multi-button phone and he grumbled every step of the way. John said he wouldn't be surprised if eventually they created an implant in his head – a direct line, so he would never miss a call.

Over the years, John witnessed the manual typewriter, every writer's mainstay, going by the wayside. Along with endless hours of paperwork, stencil papers and waiting for letters of response from inquiries. All replaced – first by fax machines, then computers and email, cell phones and God knows what else. His desk had changed dramatically over the years; gone were the physical in-trays, pencil holders and ashtrays. His physical desk? No way was he going to change that. He held on to his large oak and mahogany desk. There was no way in hell he would let that go.

The rest of the office was replaced with streamlined and sleek furnishings. John had to succumb to other changes to become part of this century and be efficient. He was ok with his laptop and dock, dual -flat screen monitors and flat-screen TV hanging on the back wall. He wasn't going to be completely irrelevant.

John thought he adapted quite well to these new advancements for an old SOB. It did take some time to learn specific tasks over the years, but he was more than used to change by now. It seemed like the moment he managed to master something, it changed again.

John picked up the phone. "Tony! How the hell are you?" John's prominent voice filled his office. Formalities were long gone, only John and a handful of others used Anthony's informal moniker.

"Great, John – thanks. This is purely a social call, nothing more, so you can relax." Anthony joked.

Anthony "Tony" Rice was a friend of John's for more than forty years. They met in college, fraternity brothers, both majoring in communications. They spent hundreds of hours working on papers, sitting in shared classes and talking about girls.

After graduation, they ventured into the world seeking their dreams and aspirations. In the early '80s, Anthony stumbled into business on his own, publishing and writing articles for young travelers on a budget. He wrote about ways to save money and the best places to go. Anthony seemingly found a niche' and his business took off. Over the years, his business shaped his path and now he owned **Northern California at a Glance**, a popular tourist magazine.

Never following the "greed is good" concept through the '80s, Anthony continued to have the magazine distributed to all the major hotels and celebrated tourist spots. The revenue was generated by hundreds of advertisers. Anthony did quite well for himself and found it more than enough. He didn't sell out and take the deals offered him over the years, as they would have made him quite comfortable. Anthony was a man of simple means and found no reason to have more of anything. He had all he needed.

"Well, what's on your mind, Tony?" John leaned his husky body back in his chair. The aged chair creaked beneath his weight.

Anthony jumped right in. "Debbie and I are having a few people over for dinner this Saturday night. I'm going to pitch my magazine to Barrett Rohan. He's the owner of that new nightclub on the waterfront. A real Scotsman, he named it **'The Glasgow.'** Kind of clever – have you heard of it?"

John recalled hearing something about this new nightclub getting some attention. No one had built anything new like this on the waterfront of the Sacramento Delta.

"I've heard a little, but tell me what you're thinking?" John's interest was piqued.

Anthony continued. "I thought you might like to meet him. Maybe you can see if there is something to report on there, or an idea for some article. His place is creating some buzz and I think it might be worth your while to check it out."

"What kind of buzz?" John sat up and leaned on his elbow. Tony never tipped him off unless it was something that had possibilities.

"Well, I understand this place is expected to be a real hot spot. I keep hearing it mentioned in the field and other places." He continued, "It attracts all genres and age groups but, mainly the young adults – Millennials – Gen Z. "

"They just had a soft opening last weekend and the grand opening isn't for a few weeks yet.," Anthony's voice quieted. "I was told they are taking feedback from the soft opening and using that to make changes before the grand opening."

"Pretty damn smart." John offered. "Agreed." Anthony continued. "I also understand they're utilizing the space in an interesting way. They have different spaces in this building and rent out to organizations in the daytime. Things like large staff meetings, meet and greets and launch parties. I'm sure there are other options to rent out the venues, but it sounds pretty damn interesting. At night, it takes on a whole different path. It changes over to a nightclub.; no boundaries, you know? All-inclusive - Come one. Come all."

"Jesus," John responded. "Sounds like the owner may be on to a gold mine. Making money day and night."

Anthony laughed. "Yes, I think so too! Lucky bastard!" He added more details.

"There are four separate bars, each with a theme. You know, like, a jazz bar, dance bar, piano bar, techno, or trance club...Hell, whatever they call that music now." Anthony laughed again. "It's got all Gen Z and Millennials excited!" His laugh was rich and deep. "I understand all the young people can't wait for this place to open!"

"Good Christ, Tony," John questioned. "When the hell did you get so damn hip?" John's booming laugh sounded through his office.

Anthony returned the laugh. "I know, I know. It's actually Jodie who's tipped me off so much. I wouldn't know my ass from my elbow with shit that's happening if it weren't for my daughter!"

Both men laughed and settled into a few minutes more of catching up as old friends do.

John spun his chair around, wrapping up the call, looking out the window at the overcast and damp afternoon. Confirming details, he continued. "Sounds good, Tony. So, your plan is to talk to this owner....Barron? Bare?" John was snapping his fingers, trying to recall the name from earlier in the conversation. It wasn't a common name, but he still couldn't quite get it right.

Anthony helped him. "Barrett. Barrett Rohan."

John nodded. "Yeah, that's it. Barrett Rohan. Not the easiest name to remember." John would drill that name into his head now. He hated forgetting names and his wife chided him for that over the years.

John continued. "You want to see if you can get him to agree to advertise his nightclub in your travel magazine - that makes sense. You always seem to know what the "next big deal" is on the horizon. I appreciate you giving me a heads up, Tony." John was genuinely appreciative and he and Tony watched out for one another's business over the long years.

Anthony laughed again. "Oh, shit. I can't take credit for that, John! Jodie has been after me to start advertising and include a younger demographic. She's right. Time has moved on and just because I'm older doesn't mean my publication needs to follow my ideals. She is convinced that it will generate more income. She hasn't been wrong yet. She is the mind, behind the money!"

Anthony laughed. Jodie was his twenty-seven year-old daughter. He brought her into the magazine a few years back and profits had more than doubled. Anthony feigned his irritation by her competency to run the magazine's financial aspects, better than he. The truth of the matter was, he was filled with pride.

"OK, Tony; you talked me into it. Send me the details and time, what we can bring and we'll be there." John let his feet slide off the top of his desk. He knew his wife, Linda, would be happy to attend dinner with their friends, Tony and Debbie.

The two said goodbye and Anthony promised to email John later with the details and hung up. Staring back out the window, John wondered if there was something here. Was there a story or event he could explore by meeting the owner of this supposed hot spot?

John reached around absently, searching for a cigarette. Checking his desk and patting his shirt pocket. He stopped smoking more than ten years ago, but his routine remained unbroken. Whenever he had something on his mind, he would seek solace in smoking. It was a good thirty seconds before he realized what he was doing. "Shit," he muttered once he realized he was searching for nothing.

His fingers fell onto the pile of memos left on his desk throughout the morning from Emily. That was one damn thing he would not give up: "While you were out" messages. They were practical and he didn't give a damn that Emily said they needed to go.

He flipped through the memos: Call Bob at Anderson's copy; call Trisha to confirm your dentist appointment Thursday. He tossed that one in his wastebasket. He thumbed through a few more and set them to one side as he deemed worthy of return calls.

Glancing over to the side of his large desk, his eyes fell on familiar handwriting on the top of an inter-office memo: "John, would like to talk to you around 4:30 if possible?" It was signed in the firm and fluid handwriting of Loghan. He scoffed and smiled; Loghan knew how to play his game and wrote her message on an inter-office memo, not allowing her message sent via email to get dismissed as John was awful at email responses.

John knew what this meant. Another rousing bout with Loghan regarding her status as a writer at Forefront. It would be the usual argument; she was ready to take on more assignments on her own.

She was a good writer; John knew that without question. She was able to detect an article worth writing. He heard this all before, only to meet her with his usual retorts. "No, you need more time." "You need to work in the field a little more," or his best response, that may land him in hot water with HR, "You're not seasoned enough just yet," implying she was too young.

He knew the outcome would be the same. Loghan would be ticked off and leave his office with a false smile on her face, saying all was fine. John, would once again "win." But did he really win? John leaned back in his chair again, looking at the memo. Maybe he should re-evaluate his position with Loghan. Her last few stories had generated an enormous response from the readers, all positive reactions.

He knew Loghan was in her late 20s. She was very capable of writing excellent articles. Hell, that's why he hired her in the first place. She was on her way to moving up the ranks of staff writers when Ian had been tragically killed. After that, the spark left Loghan.

Everyone was affected by Loghan's grief. She was well-liked at Forefront and had the respect of colleagues in the field. Many at the office attended

Ian's funeral without ever having met him in consideration of Loghan. Being the father of three daughters close to Loghan's age, John showed a fatherly concern over Loghan.

He admired her and genuinely cared about her. He, of course, never let on to her that he felt this fatherly affection. She seemed to be coming back around again, he noticed recently in staff meetings and interactions with her. He truly hoped so. Loghan had so much to offer, so much life within her, to see the flame dim so prematurely.

John looked back down at the memo from Loghan, folding the paper over a few times in his large hands. Jesus, what would Loghan throw his way this time? She was something, that one. John leaned back again in his chair and this time smiled at the memo in his hand. He felt his eyes crease, making a considerable smile, considering a moment that he must be getting soft in his old age.

Shaking off the thought, he scoffed at this notion. His large hand began patting his shirt pocket, searching for the non-existent pack of cigarettes.

"Shit." John reached for his now cold coffee and returned to his editing.

Chapter 10

Deagan turned the key, hearing the familiar click before pushing the door open. His keys landed on the foyer ledge with a soft clatter, startling Max, his cat, from his perch by the window. With a flick of his tail, Max scampered down the hall towards the den, leaving a wispy trail of fur in his wake. Deagan chuckled, shaking his head.

Deagan left work early today, something he rarely did. He wanted to work from home the rest of the day and needed some downtime. The last few days were filled with tight deadlines and Deagan met each one, but was fighting off a headache and was tired.

He left for home directly after lunch with Loghan. He was quiet and contemplative, thinking about the time he spent with Loghan and turning their conversation over in his mind on the drive home. Something about her story, or the thread she wanted to pull around the online dating scene, didn't sit well with him. He loved the idea of the story and was so caught up in the moment when they were talking, he just ran with it. He was happy to see Loghan genuinely excited about this...hell, seeing her excited about anything was fantastic! He pushed the thoughts aside for the moment, knowing he would re-visit this area soon enough.

The mid-afternoon sun finally made its presence known as Deagan followed the muted sunlight into his kitchen. Winter was on its way, but the strains of autumn still clung, not willing to surrender. Fall was a brief season in Sacramento, transitioning quickly from the hot weather to mild temperatures and straight into winter. Deagan wished there was a more extended space in between the seasons but still loved the sunshine for which

California was known.

Opening the refrigerator, he grabbed a Blue Moon from the top and leaned against the counter, flipping through the mail. It was the usual daily spattering of bills and junk mail, nothing of particular interest. He tossed the junk mail in the garbage and pushed the few bills to the side. He would deal with those later, he thought dismissively.

Deagan picked up his beer and leather messenger bag and wandered down the hall, his shoes clicking on the dark hardwood floor. Deagan loved that sound. It reminded him of his childhood - running down the hallway in dressy clothes after family visits with his grandparents, Aunts, Uncles and cousins. He smiled at the memory, staying in the moment and was truly grateful for his home.

The late afternoon sun slanted through the window blinds, casting shadows across the floor that his feet broke with each step. The messenger bags' worn leather strap creaked softly against his shoulder, a comfortable weight he'd grown accustomed to over the years of travel and coffee shop writing sessions. His beer cold and grounding against his palm, he drifted in memories again - Sunday dinners at his grandparents' house had always ended the same way - the adults lingering over coffee in the kitchen while the kids raced through the halls, the patent leather shoes and tiny dress shoes creating a symphony of clicks and clacks on the hardwood. His grandmother would call out, "No running!" but her voice always carried a laugh beneath the warning.

Now, in his own home, with its crown molding and original hardwood floors he brought back to life, Deagan found himself recreating that satisfying click-click-click whenever he wore dress shoes. Sometimes he would take a longer route to his home office, through his wine room just to extend the simple pleasure. It was funny how such a small thing could bridge decades, could make him feel simultaneously young and older.

He bought his Victorian home 4 years ago, in what was called the fabulous '40s. It was a well-sought location in Sacramento, just east of downtown Sacramento. The streets were numbered from 40th avenue and above, lawns neatly groomed and landscapes and homes to envy. The home structures were English Tudor and Victorians and truly beautiful. Most of the houses were owned by families in Sacramento years ago. It was almost unheard of to purchase a home in the fabulous '40s. Some of the places were into the third generation of ownership in the families. Passing down the houses to children raised in them, now grown adults. A continuing cycle as each generation aged out.

Deagan found this house for sale on a Saturday morning during his run. He sprinted home, repeating the phone number over and over in his head as he left his phone on his desk that morning. Later that day, he was shown the house and fell in love with it. He made a full-price offer, which was accepted within three days of haggling back and forth with the owners.

Life was good for Deagan. He was well established in his job and had a small circle of friends whom he considered family. His parents were nearby in the beautiful surrounding mountains in Tahoe. His brother and sisters were settled close as well; his younger brother, Douglas, lived in Long Beach and his younger twin sisters, Hanna and Becca, were finishing up their studies at his alma mater; U.C Santa Barbara. He loved his family and spent as much time as he could with them. He enjoyed his free time and used it constructively, working around his home and considered himself pretty handy.

Deagan felt like he had it all. Well, almost...the only thing that Deagan felt was missing in his life was love.

He had a girlfriend through most of college and while he knew she wished for the "happily ever after" when they graduated, Deagan wasn't in the same space. They had a great time with one another, but something was missing and the relationship wasn't quite right. She knew it too. He remembered her saying, when they agreed to go their own way, she wished she could be mad as hell at him but thanked him for his honesty and helping her see the truth as well. She admitted she was enamored with the idea of being in love, but she too, wanted more.

A few years ago, his path crossed with Stephanie. A vibrant connection sparked through mutual friends. Their relationship blossomed on shared passions - music, fine wine and a mutual love for exploring new corners of the world. Together, they ventured far and wide, from the charm of Europe to the mystique of China, the serene beauty of Tahiti and the tropical allure of Hawaii – their favorite. Each destination brought them closer, their adventures filled with excitement. But when the whirlwind of travel faded and they found themselves back on familiar ground, the spark that once ignited their bond began to dim.

After that discovery and subsequent breakup, Deagan decided his next relationship would be quality. He would not venture into the water again unless he was confident of his feelings and, for that matter, hers as well. He would take his time and go slow – nothing to be rushed when the matter was about finding love. This thought brought a vision of the only woman who seemed to be on his mind these days, Loghan.

Deagan didn't realize he was attracted to her until about a year ago. He dismissed the feelings and thought he was just expressing compassion and caring for a dear friend. Loghan was still deep in her grief at that time and processing the loss of Ian. He questioned if that was the reason he was experiencing feelings for her and he recognized it may be out of place, or inappropriate for him to think of her beyond friendship.

Deagan recalled a time when he met Loghan for drinks. After he and Stephanie broke up, he and Loghan met up to talk things through. Loghan teased Deagan that the next girlfriend had to be more like her; grounded, invested and genuine. They had a laugh over it at the time and Deagan shrugged off the comment and didn't think of it again until now. Interesting, he considered, as he really hadn't thought about Loghan that way, but what she stated was true. She had all the traits that he considered essential in a lifelong partner. She was warm, vibrant, grounded and...he shrugged off the thought as quickly as it entered his mind and moved on.

His thoughts drifted to their earlier conversation. He hoped Loghan could meet with John to discuss her interest in writing her article. John would no doubt give her a hard time. He wished there were something he could do to help persuade John, but he understood her need for self-reliance. Another attribute he admired about her. She was an incredible woman and Deagan found himself drawn to her once more.

She was strong-willed and even-tempered. She was intelligent and had a way of framing her thoughts and ideas in ways that rarely crossed his mind. He appreciated that attribute in her and wished he had a tenth of that wisdom. Her beauty was unmistakable and Deagan knew she had no idea how beautiful she was. Loghan brought out the best in people and you never forgot her. She was soft-spoken, kind and compassionate and Deagan considered her many favorable attributes again. There was a time when her laugh came easily, a light that brightened even the dullest of moments. Loghan's joy had once been boundless and Deagan could vividly remember the sound of her laughter - a melody that seemed to ripple through every room she entered. But those days had faded, dimmed with the loss of Ian.

It was after Ian's death Deagan began to see the change in her. Joy, once so effortless, became something rare. The grief hung over her like a shadow and Loghan's eyes, once filled with light, grew dark with the weight of it all. Deagan watched her sift through the myriad of emotions that came with Ian's passing; sadness, anger, guilt and everything in between. It was like she was drowning in a sea of sorrow, with Deagan on the shore, powerless to pull her back.

Three years had passed since that dark day and though time had dulled the sharpest edges of pain, it was still there, lingering in the background of her smiles and the pauses between her words. Loghan was never quite the same. The woman she once was, a woman filled with joy and an easy laugh, was now a distant memory and Deagan mourned her too, in his own quiet way.

She showed some of the old familiar flicker in her eyes today over lunch and he would do all he could to help encourage that light from her once more. Their friendship was something Deagan was grateful to have and he would continue to respect their bond.

Deagan entered his den and moved to his desk. He loved this space and it was one of his favorite rooms in his home. Deep, rich oak shelves lined the walls, filled with a healthy dose of poetry, classics and mystery novels. The poetry and classics took hold from his years in college and he found he truly appreciated Cummings, Whitman, Frost and others.

A rich burgundy leather couch framed one wall and a matching easy chair sat next to a stone fireplace. Brushed nickel fixtures and wood made the room aesthetically warm and pleasing. His desk was a beautiful antique, passed down from his grandfather, a professor and gifted writer. He gifted it to Deagan with one expectation; he was to use it to write from his heart. Deagan loved his desk and honored his grandfather's memory by writing only truth and reporting with accuracy. It was a passion that had been passed down. Deagan dreamed of writing a book one day, just like his grandfather, but that would have to wait as his career took so much of his time and passion. He knew enough that his book would be in a familiar lane that he enjoyed – true crime and mysteries. He hadn't found the story he wanted to write just yet but knew one day he would. It had to present itself to him in a way only he knew and the vision and words would come to life. Until that day, Deagan would work from his desk and tinker with ideas and he could patiently wait for the story to make its way to him.

Deagan dropped his messenger bag on his desk and flipped the bag open. Max was sitting quite comfortably on his laptop keyboard. The keyboard was warm and Max's tail lazily flicked back and forth.

"Damn cat," Deagan feigned irritation with Max and grumbled under his breath. Max was unaffected and began to purr.

Deagan gently nudged Max over and checked his email. He removed folders and placed the bag on the hardwood floor. He hoped for some information he requested from the San Francisco police department. He was working on his next article and the additional information to move forward. He enjoyed writing thought-provoking articles. Unfortunately, sometimes they bordered on disturbing, as had his most recent acclaimed article.

Deagan won several awards for his work. His most recent expose' reported on facilities for the elderly and their abusive treatment toward their patients. His story broke open a significant investigation of Care Facilities for the elderly across the country. People continued to step forward to bring attention to this sensitive subject that had been going unnoticed and unreported for years.

The article was complete with photographs of emaciated, bruised and weary, elderly patients. Deagan wore a concealed camera in his hat, so the pictures captured were explicit. He felt strongly about the truth reaching people. Some of the facilities received write - ups and were heavily fined and the most severe were closed down. Deagan's coverage was lauded by his colleagues and readers.

Several large, East Coast newspapers solicited Deagan and tried to lure him away from "small-town media." There were promises of fame, money, travel accounts and luxury. Deagan wasn't interested in those things. He loved his quiet life and the serenity and hometown feel Sacramento offered. Nope, he wasn't leaving here anytime soon.

He returned his thoughts to the recent reports of a series of young women murdered without any traces or clues. He had no idea where this thought process might lead him, but he knew it was worth the research, hence waiting for the San Francisco police reports.

There it is, mused Deagan. His eyes darted to his email where several messages were waiting for him; one was the crime report and the other, the San Francisco police department logs. He requested information and knew they would provide little in advance. Deagan rolled his eyes in irritation, noticing that he had to wade through junk mail to get to his messages from the police department.

As he anticipated, the response from the police was brief; the crime was under investigation and there were no additional details at this time.

Wading through a few more emails, he located an email name he hadn't seen for a while, but he recalled it immediately. It was from a contact he inadvertently made around a year ago on another crime he reported on in San Francisco.

It was from Geyser1@gmail.com; it was from the creepy young guy who worked in the coroner's office in San Francisco with a self-given nickname of *Dexter.*

What the hell does he want? Deagan had made an odd connection with this assistant in the coroner's office when he interviewed the Medical Examiner for a story he reported last year. He emailed back and forth a few times for information and "Dexter" was his point of contact.

Deagan's brow creased and he rubbed his fingers across his forehead. He didn't understand why Dexter would be emailing him but, *I'll bite,* he thought. He leaned forward, moved his cursor over and opened the email.

You seemed like a cool guy and I thought you may be interested in this information. It didn't come from me if you know what I mean. D–

It only took a moment to download the information and Deagan leaned back in his chair, releasing the creaks and groans from the comfortable, thirty-year old chair. He flipped the switch on his printer and it came to life. The machine hissed for a moment, paused and pushed through several pieces of paper. He flipped through the documents and was surprised to see rough notes for the autopsy on Cynthia DuBois. He recalled immediately she was the young woman the police reported being murdered in her apartment recently in San Francisco.

Deagan sat up straight in his chair and looked around the room as if he were being watched. He didn't anticipate notes from the Medical Examiner and he shrugged off his foolish reaction, but the feeling of uneasiness continued to wash over him. He knew he shouldn't have this information yet it didn't stop him from reading. From what he could decipher from the somewhat illegible handwriting of the ME, there was nothing notable about DuBois' death. She was a healthy, active young woman who had no business being on the medical examiner's table.

He wondered if it was common practice for MEs to add notes of what appeared to be personal thoughts to cases they examined:

The victim, Cynthia DuBois, was found nude, lying on her bed. There appears to be no struggle. No visible bruises, cuts, or marks of any kind. Her clothes were tossed haphazardly on a chair in the corner. A blouse had fallen or was thrown on the floor. Photographs show the room was otherwise very neat. No forced entry. Everything in the apartment was neat and orderly. The body was found at approximately 9:30 A.M.

Off in the margin, he saw a scribble that stated: **Initial Observation– Suffocated?**

Deagan's fingers nervously returned to his brow, running them across his forehead for what felt like the hundredth time that day. There was a maze of cryptic shorthand - scribbled notations and abbreviations that might as well have been hieroglyphic for all he could decipher. After several futile minutes of squinting at the cramped handwriting, he set the document aside with a frustrated sigh.

The email was still open on his monitor and while the rest of his home was open and brightly lit. His office was dark, with rich wood and shutters that remained slatted to keep the muted winter light at bay. The blue light from his computer cast an eerie glow in his dimly lit office. His attention caught on the attachment icon he'd initially overlooked - a JPEG file, innocently labeled: IMG_2791.

His cursor hovered over it for a moment before he double clicked, the file taking what seemed like an eternity to load. When the image finally materialized on his screen, the blood drained from his face.

"Oh, Jesus." It was a photo of the victim's face; she was clearly deceased. All life drained from her body as her pallor was blue-grey. Obviously, there must be some reason why this close-up photo was taken, but Deagan, not being an ME, had no idea why. He was certain there were numerous other photos, but Dexter sent *this* photo. Deagan shook his head, muttering, "Creepy bastard." Other than her color being horrible, she just appeared to be sleeping. Peaceful, almost. This was too much for Deagan and he closed the picture file.

Still a bit shaken, Deagan scanned over the rest of the items attached. All standard information, it appeared, and he closed the email, settling back into his chair.

Why in the hell did Dexter send this to him was beyond his comprehension. He was a creepy "effer" for sure, yet having this inside information could be beneficial. He was bothered about the data being sent to him as he was a "by the book, kind of guy." His reporting instincts were strong and he allowed his thoughts to shift to processing the information.

Nothing of a proportionate matter was found in the report about how she was murdered. Was she suffocated? Deagan couldn't get his head around this at all. It was all so fucking wrong that a young and vibrant woman was dead. Re-positioning himself in his chair, he took a long pull on his beer and he heard the ping of a message coming across his computer. He glanced at the name and it was Loghan.

"Hey! Where are you? Get to work! LOL!"

Deagan smiled at her playfulness and was grateful to have his attention averted from the dark details he just reviewed.

*"Hi, Loghan! I **am** working, LOL! What are you doing? How's it at the office?"* He leaned back in his chair, smiling and took another swig of his beer.

"I'm taking a break and I'm browsing my friend's wedding registry. Wedding coming up, you know? The office...well...dull and dreary. I was heading into John's office to talk to him about the story I wanted to write. Unfortunately, he had to 'reschedule;' translation = 'I don't want to talk about it, Loghan.'

Deagan set his beer down and started typing: *"No, I'm sure he really had something else going on, Loghan. John's not like that. You know that."*

"Really? He said he had a dinner to attend. Sounds like I was dismissed. Since when does John run off to a "dinner engagement?"

Deagan smiled again and he banged out his response:

"I know this answer! LOL! John mentioned to me this morning he's having dinner tonight with Anthony. You know, Anthony Rice! Something about a meeting or talking with the new space/nightclub owner by the waterfront."

Loghan knew Anthony Rice as she was good friends with his daughter, Jodie. She and Jodie knew each other from familiar friends and the two hit it off. They saw each other frequently.

Loghan's response lightened with this news.

"Hmm...Ok, well then, I stand corrected! I guess John didn't blow me off! LOL! I'm used to him not listening to me, though, you know?"

She continued: *"I'm just anxious to talk to him, Deag. I have my idea all worked out. I know the story I want to do, the timeline and who I'm going to interview...I have it all carved out."*

Deagan smiled and loved when she called him by his nickname.

"Oh yeah? I'm all ears." Deagan leaned back and could see she was typing. He patiently waited for her response. Loghan was on a roll as the words flew up on his screen.

"I'm locked in on internet dating. Where women are trying to meet guys; What

are they looking for; what do they hope to gain? How do they know **who** *they are talking to? That is a significant factor here. Risk vs reward. I've read so much about people being cat-fished online, taken advantage of or blindly going along with someone. There is a lot of shady stuff that goes on out there.* Deagan leaned back in his chair, smiling at the constant steam of Loghan's message.

Finally, I want to uncover those women who are out there just looking to 'hook up.' We don't ever talk about this as it would be 'uncivilized.' Women are looked at negatively for wanting to have sex, yet, men? They can sleep all over and no one says anything but, 'Atta boy!' Present company excluded, she said smiling at Deagan."

Deagan was ready to respond but saw that Loghan was continuing to type.

"I've already started my research. Checking out dating sites and researching some of the sites...and you wouldn't believe the crap I've seen already, Deagan! It's crazy out there!"

Deagan's stomach twisted, as the thought of Loghan venturing deeper into dating sites weighed on him. Hadn't she mentioned diving even further into the web's dark underbelly for research? He wasn't aware of the crease deepening across his brow, but the dull throb of a headache made itself known, the kind that settled in when things didn't sit right. He knew too well there were players out there - twisted souls lurking in hidden corners. What might she stumble upon if she followed one of those grim trails? He was sure he was still feeling rattled from sifting though the information from Dexter, but this unease gnawed at him, refusing to let go.

He fought to keep his thoughts to himself and offered encouragement and maybe, just a little advice.

"That's cool, Loghan. Sounds like you're ready to pitch John with a great idea. I'm sure he will be interested in it. You're doing the work and it will show. He paused briefly, weighing the next measured keystrokes.

If I may say only one thing?"

Loghan's response came quickly:

"Sure! Go ahead!"

Loghan always appreciated Deagan's advice when it came to writing and how to manage John. She knew whatever he had to share, it would come from a good place. She was confident he would have some sage advice for how to best set up the discussion with John or frame certain words that land favorably on John for her best shot at this story.

She anxiously waited, shifting in her chair watching the typing bubbles appear.

Deagan hesitated, fingers poised above the keys, a strange weight pressing down on him. His mind raced, searching for a reasonable source of this odd concern that had crept up, uninvited and insistent. He couldn't quite name it, couldn't say what continued to gnaw at him, only the thought of silence felt heavier than the risk of sounding possessive, paranoid, or worse - vulnerable.

With a slow exhale, he forced himself to type three simple words. It felt strange to send them, like he was stepping out on shaky ground, revealing something even he couldn't quite understand. He pressed "enter" and leaning back with the same uneasy feeling that clung to him and he quietly uttered the words...

"Please, be careful."

Chapter 11

Loghan sat back and looked at Deagan's message. She reread it and shook her head dismissively.

"What the hell, Deagan?" Her hands dropped on the keyboard, spatting the words out loud. Her light mood instantly shifted to one of agitation.

She was used to John showing this behavior in some form, but not from Deagan. He always supported her and she was all too happy to share her story idea with him. What about when they were sitting at lunch? He seemed genuinely excited about her idea. Now, she was second-guessing herself and offended at Deagan's comment.

What did he take her for? She wasn't foolish. She'd been down this road before, carefully laying out her ideas and Deagan had been her biggest cheerleader, quick with praise and pushing her to reach higher. But today? Today, there was something different.

As she shared her idea for her article, she noticed it - a subtle pause, a hesitation that hadn't been there before. Right when she told Deagan about the dating sites and her idea to dive deeper. At lunch, his eyes shifted, the measured tone in his voice. And when he signed off tonight from their chat, it was absent of spark, but he gave her a gentle word of caution.

Loghan was tired of the soft words, the lingering looks and the cautious smiles that trailed her through every room. Three years had passed since Ian's death - long enough for her to confront the grief, wrestle with it and try to find her footing again. Yes, she had struggled, still did at times, but she had worked her way through most of the grief, piecing herself back together one hard day at a time.

She knew their concern was well-meaning; she never doubted that. Loghan was ready to be seen as more than the woman who lost her fiancé. She was no fragile thing waiting to shatter and frankly, she felt like a champion. She made it through the grief and kept her life intact, over-performing at work despite the ache she carried. She didn't need a medal for it–but a little recognition wouldn't hurt.

She put a lot of time and effort into her story idea. She spent the last few weeks piecing through timelines and details. Over stale coffee in her favorite morning restaurant, she put in long hours researching specific threads of her vision until it seemed time to plot it out. Finally, the story presented itself to her and she knew she was on the right path.

Her brow knit tightly as she sat, frustration simmering as she tried to unravel exactly why Deagan got under her skin so effortlessly. With a sigh, she spun her chair around, letting her gaze drift across the room as if the answer might be hiding somewhere in the noisy corners of the office.

The blare of the office created a vacuum of white noise. Loghan could hear talking and excitement surrounding today's deadline nearing for some, as the volume of discussions echoed around her. She tuned the noise out and returned to her thoughts. She wasn't going to waste one more minute trying to prove herself to Deagan. She told him all the details of her storyline at lunch, worked out the research plan and why she was focused on this particular topic; women seeking love in chat rooms and dating sites. She added more information for him regarding women meeting up with men, some trying to make a genuine connection and others...well, other women, just looking for sex. She told him all of that... didn't she?

Loghan's forehead was still creased in concern. An uneasy feeling clutched at her stomach, rippling through the rest of her body.

She knew deep down she didn't tell Deagan everything.

She didn't tell him about the "underbelly" of online dating she seemingly had found. She didn't mention to him about "talking" to a random guy who sought her out online a few weeks ago. She didn't tell him she was curious and filled with excitement she hadn't felt in a long time!

She felt a thrill, talking to that man…what was his name again? Tapping her pen on her desk in feigned recollection. His name was on her tongue immediately, David. David Rothchild.

Loghan knew she was lying to herself. She knew his name and there was a reason she hadn't shared all this with Deagan: it wasn't safe and certainly not like her at all. Loghan was the cautious one and most knew this trait about her. It was just like Deagan to presume there was more to something. He had an uncanny ability to perceive more in a storyline or a tale someone was sharing.

Loghan felt frustrated and anxious. She shifted in her seat, twisted her long hair into a bun and knotted it on top of her head. Whenever she had something on her mind, she had to expel her nervous energy and playing with her long hair seemed to calm her.

She struggled to focus on the computer screen and attempted a few different searches to re-engage her mind. She couldn't let Deagan's comment go and closed her eyes to quiet her mind and breathe. It was her respite - her use of breath when needing calm - she would always return to breath. It always brought her tranquility.

"Breathe in…one…two…three…and, out…one…two…three…in…." The quiet she attempted to create was lost in less than 10 seconds… "Be careful…" Loghan mocked the words out loud.

"Damn it, Deagan!" Loghan abruptly shut her laptop, grabbed her bag and coat and left for the day.

*****

His car rolled up to the curb at the Ritz-Carlton in the Boston Common. He adored this location and it was his usual layover for meetings with clients and a good halfway point to Europe, or Asia.

Two handsome, young bellhops approached his car, offering polite smiles as the driver held open his door. Aric stepped out, pulling his collar closer against the chill, his breath clouding in the brisk evening air. One bellhop stepped forward, a bit younger, fumbling briefly with Aric's overcoat before securing it around his shoulders with a quiet nod. The other bellhop, strikingly handsome and graceful in movement, seized Aric's luggage and whisked it towards the grand lobby. Aric's eyes followed the young man's fluid stride, noting the crisp way he stopped at the elevator, pressed the button and waited with a hint of poise that made him stand out. Aric watched from an angle at the door as the bellhop's gaze met his through the gleaming elevator doors, his dark eyes catching Aric's briefly - a subtle yet unmistakable hint of intrigue in his expression.

The bellhop smiled, a quick, knowing curve of the mouth, before the doors closed, severing their connection in an instant. Aric shook his head, amused by his own indulgent thoughts. Not tonight, he mused, suppressing the fleeting spark of temptation. He was still too worn from his earlier rendezvous with the flight attendant - an unexpected and thoroughly satisfying diversion.

Too much to do while he was here. It was not uncommon for him to whet his appetite with the attention of a handsome man. He did prefer women primarily but didn't allow his proclivities to be defined by something as dull as gender conformity. He was quite fluid when it came to his sexuality - whatever the occasion presented; he was a willing participant.

Aric strode confidently to the front desk, his gaze sweeping across the opulent lobby. Chandeliers glittered overhead, casting a warm, golden glow over the plush sofas and polished marble floors. The fresh scent of flowers mingled with a hint of leather and fine cognac - a signature fragrance he immediately recognized, evoking memories of every lush stay he'd enjoyed there.

The Ritz-Carlton was well-known for their ability to attend to each guest and their attention to every last detail of their *special* guests was unmatched. They never disappointed. Every detail catered to luxury and elegance, each staff member offering a subtle nod, the way one acknowledges royalty. For Aric, this wasn't just a hotel - it was a sanctuary where he was more than a guest - he was a distinguished presence, a name that commanded respect and familiarity. Here, he could savor the finer things in life, knowing his status and legacy were as much a part of the aged hotel, as the antique mirrors lining the walls.

The young bellhop knew Aric was arriving today and obviously was watching for his arrival. He smirked at the thought of the poor young bastard; he must have waited for hours as Aric was sidetracked this evening by the lure of the flight attendant.

A slow, lazy smile quietly stretched across his face as he recalled his recent tryst in the back of the limousine. He didn't give a damn about the bellhops and whomever else was "assigned" the task of waiting for him to arrive - even if they stood for hours waiting...it was well worth the delay.

Tomorrow would be most tiresome as he was scheduled to meet with his detestable mother. He wondered idly, when would this contemptible and voracious woman leave this earth?

Christ, how he loathed being in her presence. He walked down the capacious lobby toward the desk to check-in, admiring his reflection as he passed by the mirrors. His mind drifted to dealing with his demanding mother, Avery.

Avery Stanton was a strong, brilliant and savvy woman in the business world. But to him, he thought of her as nothing more than a waste of breath and his time. To others, she was vibrant, sexy and powerful. She appeared to be in her late '40s but was tapping on the door of 60. At least, that is what she would *admit*.

It was no wonder she was so well - preserved; she had invested a small fortune in staying that way. Between her meticulous diet, strict exercise and an occasional nip here, a tuck there, a bit of filler and Botox was magic when needed. She managed to keep herself looking as sharp as the day she took over the company.

As CEO and owner of their family business RHS Communications, an empire worth billions, Avery had taken the reigns when her father, Rhonert Stanton was forced to retire due to a debilitating stroke he suffered. With his passing in 2015, it was Avery who picked up every scattered piece and turned them into a thriving, multi-billion-dollar corporation, steering through storms and growth as it came their way. Power was her fuel and she was known across the industry as the woman who got things done. She loved reminding Aric, who was in charge.

The word, "charge" echoed in his head, her voice, a well-manicured hand squeezing the patience from him. She wore her power like an accessory, always with the intention to remind him and anyone else in the room that Avery ran the show, every spotlight perfectly angled her way.

He pushed the intrusive thoughts from his mind and tried to put his attention to the well-groomed man behind the counter. Aric's voice purred in a rich timbre. "Good evening; have I any messages?" His eyes, half lidded beneath the gleam of the lobby lights, still carried the haze of his earlier tryst. The warmth of her skin lingered on his fingertips, a memory mingling with the scent of her perfume. He shoved the ghost of his mother's voice, damn her, out of his head and sank back into the delicious memory of that delicate, seductive time with the flight attendant. Just then, a voice, deep and steady, broke through, yanking him from the thrill of the thought.

"Good evening, Mr. Stanton. Yes, two messages for you, sir. One moment, please."

The young man turned from the counter, retrieved two envelopes and handed them to Aric with a slight nod. He took them from the man's hand, slightly pausing, allowing his fingertips to linger on the man's hand. The man, try as he might, remained casual and hid his quiet panic, but Aric could see the slight flicker of homophobia in his eyes and he smiled. He slowly moved his hand away and read the first note; it was from his client he was in town to see, welcoming him to Boston and inviting him for dinner tomorrow evening. The second was from his mother, penned in her perfect, feminine hand. Why in the hell didn't she text him or leave him a voice mail?

So typical of her. It was Avery's way to further exude her control and insert herself into his life. He deliberately kept her at a distance. Precisely as he intended. Avery was astute and knew Aric avoided her as much as possible. He rarely would return her calls and she knew he would receive a message when he checked into the hotel.

A wave of quiet anger began to seep into his veins, slowly throbbing and emitting its way into his consciousness.

Darling–

So happy you've arrived in Boston.

Looking forward to spending time with you, although I'm sure
you've booked yourself solidly over the next several days.
We've many things to discuss with your work schedule.
Brunch tomorrow morning– 11:00 AM.
I'm in the Presidential Suite.
Love~
Avery

He scoffed out loud. "Avery" of course, never, *mother.* He quit calling her mother years ago, and she didn't seem to mind - or even notice. She was so damn pretentious, flowing through her life like she was starring in a film, where everyone had their role, but her lines were always prominent. She wasn't one for nurturing; the closest she'd come when he was a young boy was flipping her wrist dismissively if he wandered too far.

Every time she spoke to him, it felt like she was reading lines from a script, carefully rehearsed, perfectly polished. He clenched his jaw, her last words still ringing in his head, brittle and cutting. She had a way of turning their conversations over business into judgments and he could still feel the sting of her latest critique gnawing at him. He knew brunch would be a continuation of her voicing disappointment with him.

No surprise, she was in the Presidential Suite. He wouldn't have thought anything less. Everything about her he loathed. He could gain a faint hint of her perfume she must have bathed in. Its highly odiferous earthy scent wafting in the cool air of the lobby.

He thrust the messages in his jacket pocket and signed the open tab the concierge placed in front of him. The man seemingly had regained his composure and nodded at Aric with a forced smile.

"Thank you, Mr. Stanton. Enjoy your stay. Shall I send up a martini, sir?"

Aric's usual request each time he arrived. They never faltered with the impeccable attention of their highly valued guests. Aric allowed his smile to return and lazily turned toward the concierge departing from the desk to leave the lobby.

"Yes; please do." He knew it would arrive exactly as he enjoyed - extra dry, three blue cheese olives and dirty... filthy dirty.

He needed that damn martini like never before.

There wouldn't be enough Grey Goose to drown out the voices he heard tonight.

Chapter 12

Loghan's step was light this morning. The rest of her week went well and she was in bright spirits. She had an early start to her day and enjoyed a morning run through her downtown neighborhood. The streets shimmered from the evening rain and she didn't mind getting wet from some unavoidable puddles. Her feet found a rhythmic pace as cold rain splashed around her ankles. She returned home feeling invigorated, made a latte and showered to get ready for work.

It had been a long time since Loghan felt excited about anything. It was hard enough moving through life since Ian, but she felt the clouds breaking overhead and the sensation the fog was lifting.

Feeling a sense of accomplishment, Loghan was ready for her day to be filled with research and exploration on something she wanted to do! It was, at last, her choice ...her assignment.

Loghan met with John later in the week and he finally caved in. He gave her free rein to come up with her first draft on her idea for online dating and the women looking for love. Fortunately, Loghan knew to leave out a few parts, such as the women who were just like some of the men out there, looking to do no more than, "hook up," and some darker areas with the internet. She didn't think John was ready for that just yet but she would figure out how to introduce this storyline in her article. She would write such a compelling draft that he wouldn't even question the sultry details being added in the article.

Loghan was well prepared when she gave John her pitch. She stayed up late the night before, going over her notes, creating the timeline and capturing details and background on some of the more popular sites to meet people. Loghan presented a comparison between the use of dating sites to meet for well -intended reasons and in contrast, those not wanting commitment, but more casual contact. John allowed her center stage for 30 minutes and Loghan made good use of her time.

For the timeline of how dating has morphed through the years, she began with in the '50s and '60s and how men and women dated, meeting through friends, college, or church. As time moved forward and the country matured, society followed. Technology entered and propelled us forward. The '70s and '80s were geared toward business and the early beginnings of technology, not yet entering fully into our social aspect. Loghan continued to weave her story into a grand tapestry full of color and details.

She took John through the '90s, 2000s and to the current 'smart' technology that made life easier and brought efficiency to the forefront. This newfound technology made so many things accessible while allowing society to produce twice the amount of work in the same amount of time. While this success in technology is undisputed, she explained we've become busier and our social lives smaller.

She continued to layer the details brick by brick and finished with the psychological aspect to support the findings in her research and the human element. She had interviews lined up with sociologists and behaviorists about the benefits and negatives to the human psyche with the lack of social interaction.

Loghan wrapped up her pitch to John by adding the personal interviews and experience she would include in her article. What type of people/women used the dating sites and what were they looking for. It would present the human element and first-hand knowledge of women and online dating and allow the reader to connect with people through the story.

As the meeting ended, John remained silent and poker faced. Loghan couldn't read his position and she fought to stay quiet and allowed John to process. John's large, thick fingers drummed on his desk - he leaned back in his chair and Loghan almost jumped out of her skin with the loud creak the chair released. It was an excruciating 15 seconds of silence as Loghan sat quietly and allowed John to filter through his thoughts and make a decision. For a moment, she thought he would dismiss her, telling her he needed more time to think or just forget it altogether.

John leaned forward, clasped his large hands on the table and sighed. Loghan briefly closed her eyes. *Shit. Here it comes*, she thought; *You're not ready yet, Loghan.*

John started, weighing and measuring his words. "Ok, ok...I tell you what, Loghan, you got yourself an article of choice. Don't disappoint me." His big finger jabbed at the air.

"You have one week to give me a solid draft and timeline in writing and the direction you're going. It's one thing to hear the pitch, but another thing entirely to see it come together on paper. You need to make it translate to the reader first and foremost. *Translate*. He emphasized the word. "Does that make sense?" His bushy eyebrows lowered to convey his message.

John tried to look severe and firm, but it was pointless. Once he said, "Ok" Loghan lit up like a Christmas tree. Her smile was brilliant and John couldn't help but return it. She jumped up and shook John's hand while continuing his pointless speech in the direction and translating it to paper.

Loghan was up and out of his office with a stream of "thank you's," and "you won't be disappointed," trailing behind her.

John quietly chuckled and closed the door behind her. He remembered that feeling with his first article those many years ago. He recalled the feeling of excitement - euphoria.

Walking back to his desk, he couldn't contain himself.

"Ahh...good for her. Hot damn," John smiled. "I think we have Loghan back again!"

*****

The next day brought another semi-cloudy winter day, but Loghan was filled with light and happiness. She arrived at work early and almost ran to her office; she was anxious to start researching. Flinging herself into her desk chair, she spun around a few times with the joy of a child.

"Yes!" She threw her arms straight into the air and leaned her head back a moment to gather herself. Loghan felt vindicated and didn't waste a minute to get started on her article draft. She began work on the article, before John's approval, knowing deep down regardless of his decision she was moving forward. She wasn't sure how, but she decided manifesting her successful pitch to John was better than doing nothing and hoping.

Grabbing her notes from her meeting with John, she worked through several areas, but her mind drifted to Deagan. Loghan remained disappointed in Deagan's response when they messaged earlier in the week. She was so excited about her article and honestly thought Deagan would offer her tips or something helpful to her as she worked through some ideas. However, when he didn't and returned to the somewhat familiar role of "protector and guardian," she was immediately upset.

"Please, be careful..." Loghan could hear the words he typed to her over and over in her mind. Loghan leaned back in her chair and allowed her mind to wander.

She still wasn't entirely sure why Deagan's comment stung so much. After all it was just Deagan-the loyal friend who had been by her side through thick and thin, especially after Ian's death. But now, a flicker of disappointment gnawed at her, a feeling she couldn't quite shake. Deagan had joined the ranks of her father, her brothers and John, casting himself in the same, all - too - familiar role of protector. She had been down this road before: she was strong, resilient, self-sufficient and yet, men around her always seemed to slip into this pattern, assuming she needed to be shielded.

The more she thought about it, the more Deagan's actions of being her 'protector' came to light. She hadn't noticed it before, perhaps too wrapped up in her own grief to see it clearly. Yet, there it was, plain as day. He had self -appointed himself as her guardian, her watchman, as though she were something fragile. She hadn't been acting fragile since Ian's passing - had she? Now, she questioned herself. She didn't need another person trying to shelter her from the world or from herself. It was one thing for her family, even John, to take on this role - frustrating, but expected. But Deagan?

She realized his past behaviors were suddenly so glaring, the pattern so predictable. She quickly grasped how deeply it disappointed her. She had been fighting to keep moving, to rebuild a life without Ian and yet here was Deagan, enforcing the same storyline she had grown weary. She filtered through her thoughts rapidly to validate this new-found understanding of Deagan. Things like stepping in and offering to talk to John or speaking out in meetings, suggesting to John more accessible articles for Loghan cover. Then his reaction over lunch when she told him she was going to research darker areas of the internet, women who met up with men without expectations and now, his comment last night.

Once Loghan put her finger on why she was so bothered by Deagan's response, she found herself instinctively pulling back. Maybe it was a sign she needed a breather - a little space to clear her head. Deagan hadn't exactly made distancing herself easy, though. He texted her a few times, asked to meet up for coffee, even brought her a cup to her desk: none of this was out of the ordinary, which almost made it worse. He was so persistently himself, making her retreat feel even more noticeable. Still, Loghan had her excuses lined up - meetings with John, upcoming deadlines and stacks of research that, fortunately, all kept her just busy enough to avoid lingering conversations with him.

When the weekly all-staff meeting rolled around, Loghan slipped into a seat at the far end of the table, careful to avoid his usual spot beside her. She felt his questioning gaze, the slight tilt of his head asking what was up, but she pretended not to notice, fixing her eyes on her notes instead. They had always sat together, shared knowing glances and quick doodles when things dragged on, but not this time. Loghan focused on her article, her mind whirring with ideas about her new piece.

She was taking her writing in a different direction - her readers knew her for a lighter touch and her uplifting perspective, but Loghan knew this was her opportunity to show another side, one with sharper edges and a bit of grit. She wasn't trying to keep up with Deagan, but she wanted to show her ability to shrug off the warm and squishy articles she was known for - time to spread her wings.

The topic had been tugging at her since she stumbled upon it a few weeks back and her curiosity to run with this piece would not let up. It would take research, it would take focus and, maybe, most of all, it would take a bit of distance from the distractions that usually colored her day-to-day.

Deagan would understand that eventually, she hoped. For now, she needed to dive into this piece, let it consume her and see what kind of writer she would become on the other side.

Loghan forced her thoughts back to her research and panned over the stack of files and papers on her desk. There was so much to do and she had been side-tracked long enough. Loghan knew her article would include online dating and perhaps, the darker side of the internet, which included the men.

She intentionally left this area out when she was pitching John. She knew damn well John would have shut her down on the spot. Not because John was afraid of a bit of sex and darkness; he liked running articles that were edgy and unexpected. No, he thought she couldn't handle it, or the readers didn't want to see deep story lines from her; they wanted fluffy and brightness.

She recognized John treated her like her own father and the moment she brought a little sex and dark storyline idea into the mix; John would nix the idea. So, what's a slight shift in the storyline? What could it hurt? Once he saw how great this story would be, she knew John would jump at the chance for her to continue. She lied to herself and thought she wasn't completely misleading him. She had plenty of research to go over and the area of chatting and seeking sex online would be a minimal mention at best. Well, *maybe* it would be minimal.

Loghan made calls confirming appointments for interviews she lined up with experts in the field of IT and a professor who taught Digital Media. Her next interviews would be with actual users of the dating sites. She hoped to get some good content from those conversations to build out her story. Loghan enjoyed researching stories and content, so the hours went by quickly when she realized the time.

Justifying the need for a break, she turned back to her computer and opened Facebook. Just for a quick minute, she told herself, scrolling through her feed. She noticed she had a message and clicked on it.

"Hello dear, Loghan. How are you today?" The newly familiar name next to

the message was David Rothchild. A rush of excitement flooded Loghan and her face felt heat. There was a true excitement to see David's name and she noted her feelings - they felt like embarrassment.

Christ, she wasn't doing anything wrong. Why did she feel anything at this point? She was focused and working and not going to engage in chatting while at the office.

A resonating *THUD*, from behind, jarred Loghan's attention. Startled, she slammed her laptop closed.

"Jesus!" Loghan jumped at the sound of file folders landing on her desk from behind.

"Hi...., you're at this early today." A sheepish smile escaped from Deagan's face. He walked to the side of her desk and tapped his fingers on the stack of files he dropped on her desk. Seeing Loghan's reaction and look on her face, Deagan winced. "Damn...sorry, Loghan. I didn't mean to startle you."

Recovering quickly, Loghan turned her chair toward Deagan. "Hi, Deagan. It's ok. I was......I was deep in thought." She lied and covertly moved her notepad and files off to the side. She hoped he didn't notice how quickly she closed her laptop. Now, the earlier feeling of embarrassment she felt was validated.

"I was working on my research. John approved my story." Loghan heard the words coming from her mouth, devoid of the excitement she felt. Deagan smiled plaintively. He sensed Loghan's apprehension.

"Oh...wow... that's... that's great, Loghan." He wanted to jump up and swing her around in celebration. They had talked about this happening for her so much, but he saw the look on her face - strained and somehow-distant so he decided to hold back. Her behavior confirmed his thoughts with Loghan's evasiveness this week. It wasn't like her not to share this big win with him. What the hell?

"Congratulations, Loghan. I'm really happy for you." It was the best Deagan could do. Loghan leaned back in her chair, looking at all the files and papers around her. Trying to lighten the air, Deagan followed Loghan's eyes and surveyed her desk.

"Hey...it looks a little bit like my desk." He chuckled softly. "However, you still have some room for more papers and files over here." He pointed to the one neat corner of Loghan's desk.

Loghan's smile broke the tension a bit. "Yes, I do seem to have a bit going on here." Her hand waved over the top of her desk. "I just got everything together and I'm going to need to get organized... quickly." She reassured Deagan. "I feel ready, though. I sold John on the storyline, but I keep drifting to another area that I want to include in the story." Her voice trailed off somewhat and Loghan hoped it wasn't telling.

The silence between them stretched uncomfortably, thickening the tension hanging in the air. Deagan glanced at Loghan, catching her gaze just as she turned to him. Her eyes held a flicker or something - hesitation, maybe curiosity? He couldn't quite tell. The words slipped out before he could think twice.

"Ummm, look, Loghan, are we ok? I think I did something, or said something to you that I shouldn't and I...I... I'm not sure what I did. I just know...whatever it is, I'm sorry." Deagan's voice was barely a murmur, his gaze dropping to his hands as he spoke.

Loghan moved her chair closer to him, gesturing for him to sit beside her. He hesitated, then sat down, she pulled his chair so close he could catch the clean, rain-kissed scent that clung to her, like fresh soap and something else he couldn't name. The pale winter sunlight filtered through the window, casting a soft glow across her features, illuminating her in a way that made his breath catch.

Deagan's internal dialogue was firing on all cylinders. Christ, I have to knock this off. Pining over her won't change anything! Deagan tried to shake off the thought, focusing on her instead.

"Deagan, can I be honest?" Loghan's green eyes were unwavering, even tender.

"Sure, of course." He braced himself, feeling the weight of what she might say and if he could manage it, if her words cut.

"I ...I just feel like you and John, my parents - Jesus, anyone who is close to me is always trying to protect me. I just can't keep doing this and not have it affect me. I'm a grown woman; I know how to take care of myself. I need to move on... I'm not wild or irresponsible."

Deagan let out a long, quiet sigh and leaned back in the chair, the worn leather creaking under his weight. He couldn't help but let a wry smile slip. Loghan read him like an open book; though he'd been doing everything to close it, to keep the pages from turning. Now, he was left with a choice he didn't know how to make. He didn't want to pull away, not from her. The thought of losing her-even as a friend-sent a quick, instinctive ache through him, something he tried not to acknowledge. If she knew how he felt, that he's spent countless nights lingering on the edge of this feeling he couldn't shake, who knew what she would do? She was still working through her loss and he would never want to push her.

The risk was high and he knew it. If the only option was friendship, then he would take it, no questions, no hesitation. But he knew that pretending his feelings were nothing, just some passing interest, was a losing battle.

Gathering his thoughts, Deagan eased his expression and lowered his shoulders. He would keep his feelings close and find a way to express himself that didn't give away too much.

"Look, Loghan, I understand. I really do. Please, don't take this the wrong way. You're just so, so...." He searched for the words, failing to find them.

"Say it. Fragile? Weak? A girl?" Loghan sat upright and cocked her head to the side. She knew her voice sounded more stern than intended, but she didn't correct herself.

"No! No, I mean yes. A girl, a woman. Oh shit..." Deagan stood up, pacing in front of her desk and tried to express himself again.

"Loghan, you just bring out this feeling...Everyone cares about you and wants to protect you. John feels like you're his daughter. Of course, he would never tell you that, but I know that is what he feels. Your Dad and brothers? Well, they love you." He was rambling now and knew it but couldn't stop the words as they fumbled out.

"You've been through a lot with losing Ian and starting all over again. People just feel, feel...close to you. Protective. We just want you to be ok." Deagan's eyes filled with concern. Loghan's face softened and she looked up at him with genuine kindness and interest.

"What about you? What are *your* feelings Deagan?" Loghan's eyes were intent and sharp. Deagan felt his heart jump and hoped his face wasn't flushed - hoping his eyes didn't give him away.

Deagan's heart pounded so hard he thought Loghan might actually hear it. He shifted his weight, one foot to the other, willing his nerves to settle. Loghan's eyes met his, calm and cool, but he felt himself unravel under her steady, inquisitive gaze. She had that way about her, as if she could peer right into his thoughts, his secrets. He forced himself to look down, feigning interest in his hands, which suddenly felt foreign and clumsy.

The room felt warmer by the second or, maybe it was just the heat of knowing she glimpsed at something that was meant to be private. His eyes drifted to Loghan's desk - her notes penned in her exquisite hand, punctuated by delicate bullet points:

- *Finding love on the internet*
- *Dating-Tinder-Match-Bumble. Compare - Contrast*
- *Online Dating: What do women really want?*
- Interview users, experts, professors
- *Dark Web-where can this go? Find a path*
- *How to stay safe online*

Her notes drifted to a column and he continued to read: *It's ok to let go... it's ok to move on...David Rothchild. David. David Rothchild....*

Deagan stood up straight and took a quiet, deep breath.

"I feel...." He paused briefly and continued, "I feel like I need to let you do your thing," the lie was sour on his tongue.

Loghan's eyes followed Deagan's line of site and found her notepad. *Damn it.* Loghan knew that Deagan saw her notes. Just how much he read; she wasn't sure.

The mood shifted, subtle at first, like a barely - there tremor that ran just beneath the surface. It crept into the room, settling in the air, making it still, thick, almost tangible.

Deagan's mind raced. I'm such a fool! Why didn't I just tell her I wanted to spend time with her? Who in the hell is this, David Rothchild? Maybe that is why she's been so distant?

The silence went on for too long and felt uncomfortable. Deagan realized the moment was gone. It would be awkward now if he said anything more. So, he let the silence linger as he considered what may be happening. Well, I think I may have been delegated forever - to the 'friend zone.'

Deagan lingered just a moment longer, hoping his smile had masked the weight in his chest. Loghan met his gaze, her expression softening as if she saw straight through his bravado. He had always been able to hide his feelings well, but when it came to Loghan, lately, he felt his armor slipping. Everyone knew once you were in the friend zone, it was hard to get out. The lines between friendship and something more had blurred, but as much as he tried to deny it, his heart was already on the other side.

With an awkward tap of his knuckles on her desk, Deagan turned, the office air, heavy with the unspoken.

"Well, I should get going so you, can get to work," his finger lightly gestured toward Loghan, as he willed his best smile, but she could see right through it. His eyes held the message and told Loghan everything. There was deep heartache in his eyes as he turned from her and walked to his office.

Loghan watched Deagan as he left and leaned back in her chair.

She should be riding high and enjoying her victory with her first self-chosen article, but all she felt was sadness and she didn't know why.

Chapter 13

Drenched in perspiration, he climbed down from the elliptical, feeling every nerve struck, buzzing with the resentment and anger. For hours, he'd been pounding out each thought, each frustration in the hopes that the steady rhythm of his steps would drown out the voices in his head. He had hardly slept, had barely touched his coffee and arrived at the gym by 4 AM, hoping the early start would exhaust whatever storm he carried over from yesterday.

His eyes were clouded, now, fixed intently on the treadmill as if it were the source of all his rage. Normally, the view was the thing that kept him grounded - those sweeping cityscapes of Boston, the glittering skyline rising beyond the rosy walls of the club and the lush expanse of Boston Common stretching below.

Usually, he would find a strange peace, in seeing the city from such a height, apart from the chaos below - it assisted in quieting the voices in his head; not today. The view was wasted on him. Today, there was only the pounding beat of his feet and the tightness in his jaw, as he pushed harder and harder, letting his anger spill out with each step, his mind racing as fast as the treadmill beneath him.

He was fond of staying in shape and believed strongly that it helped him maintain his edge in all he acquired. He worked out six days a week without fail, allowing his body one day of recovery.

Physical acuity and awareness were a profound fact in his life. The need came from controlling his surrounding environment as much as possible. He could manage his diet and health, making sure to do so daily. It was a representation of his strength and willpower.

Even with all the travel, he never missed a workout. He preferred the hygienic environment of a gym over the filth of city streets; dodging park benches and the mindless, middle-class bourgeois. His status allowed his use of the gym facilities in most of the locations he traveled to and those hotels that didn't provide their own gym, offered a pass to any number of high-end workout facilities.

Today, he followed his workout with a game of squash with one of the instructors and beat him mercilessly at his own game. His ambidexterity allowed him an advantage to make what appeared impossible shots across the court. He switched from his right to his left hand quickly to make the final corner shot while the instructor turned his back foolishly, thinking his opponent wouldn't return the ball. Instead, the ball bounced within the lines with a deafening echo. The instructor quickly spun around to see the outcome. He saw the ball bounce off the back wall and his opponent with a smug look in his direction.

The club instructor shook his hand at the end of the game, feigning good sportsmanship. He shook his opponent's hand vigorously with his saccharine grin.

"Good game, Mr. Stanton. Well done!" *Bastard,* he smiled as he patted Aric Stanton on his shoulder.

"Better luck next time, mate," Aric declared with little sincerity as he made his way to the locker room, basking in his recent victory.

He loved to win and he won often. No matter the sport, business opportunity, or conquest, he was more than capable of holding his own.

It was time to prepare for his meeting and visit with his tyrannical mother. He needed this release of endorphins and sweat to ward off his ill thoughts of her. A steam bath, followed by a quick rinse in the shower, he headed back to his room to finish his morning grooming routine.

He woke early this morning with a dull headache and a feeling of dread. His one dirty martini turned into three and ended with a nightcap of cognac. He was not one to drink much, or often, for that matter, but his mother made him toy with the idea of getting lost in a bottomless martini pitcher.

Lately, the martinis were more frequent, as were the demands of his mother.

Returning to his room upon his workout, he showered again, taking his time and mulled over his day and expectations that would be pressed upon him. His mother was insufferable and never satisfied - a notorious, high type A personality. While she was magnificent in business matters, her affairs of the heart or close relationships, she failed miserably.

He found great satisfaction knowing this void in her life. On the other hand, he mastered this genre of people and relationships. He was able to hold court with all those he encountered; part of his charm, no doubt. This was one area he would find victory over the omnipotent, Avery Stanton.

He was sickened by playing his version of a loving son, perfect business-man and the closer of all large deals. Nevertheless, he would do whatever was necessary to continue the family business and honor his grandfather. His grandfather was the only person he had loved and admired. Rhonert Stanton was the last of the genuine breed of men, highly masculine, filled with passion and desire. He hoped to be a fraction of the memory of the man he loved more than his own life.

Tapping on the door announced room service. Aric was fully aware that his morning meeting was brunch; he ordered coffee and juice. He didn't want to disappoint the illustrious Avery. He was hopeful the coffee would ease the pounding headache.

Jesus, can't this meeting be over already? He wished nothing more than to move on with his day.

"Good morning, sir." The young woman tipped her head downward and smiled timidly.

Aric waved his arm widely to offer her entrance and she entered, holding a silver tray with coffee and juice. He noticed she was quite lovely; her mahogany hair pulled back with a whisper of tendrils slightly draping her face.

My... she moves gracefully and with ease, he thought as he closed the door.

"Good morning, dear." His smile curled softly as his eyes rolled over her body slowly in admiration. It seemed he was suddenly feeling much better and he found his appetite begin to stir.

"Yes, Mr. Stanton; would you like your coffee here?"

She gracefully moved past him into the sitting area. She stood at the window overlooking the city below and placed the tray next to the leather chairs and end table. He noted she briefly stole a look outside - a small indulgence, a glimpse of the luxuries she might rarely enjoy herself.

"Of course, my dear, thank you. It is a lovely view, is it not?" His voice was smooth, playful and entertained a brief mischievous thought of letting his admiration linger on her. He reigned himself in - he didn't want to tarnish his good standing at the Ritz-Carlton. They seemed to enjoy his business and he did bring them an incredible amount of it each year, not only with his visits, but his clients as well.

No, that would never do. He had far too many things to attend today. He dismissed the thought as quickly as it entered his mind.

"Yes, sir. It is a very nice view." The lovely young woman poured Aric a coffee from the silver service and tipped her head toward him again.

"Will there be anything else, Mr. Stanton?"

"No...thank you, my dear. You've done quite ...enough this morning." He lingered on his words intentionally and enjoyed her nervous reaction. He clearly could see this lovely maiden anxiously looking about the room to make her escape.

She left his room quickly, but not without a brief smile in his direction, wishing him a good day, the scent of her perfume lingering in the air.

He sat down on the leather chair facing the windows and sipped his coffee. It was a lovely and cold day outside, not that he really noticed. The early morning sun rose and reflected off the buildings brightly, sending beams of light, shimmering brilliantly like diamonds.

Gazing out the window, he eyed the dome of the State House across the city and surrounding buildings. He enjoyed Boston in the late fall and early winter and mused at the hundreds of people milling about the streets below. However, he loathed the numerous vacationers and avid gawkers this time of year brought.

He shook his head. He would have none of that today, he was sure. He detested crowds and avoided them at all costs. His occupation required merging business and pleasure on occasion. He had to entertain his clients in crowded locations numerous times and he tolerated it best he could. He much preferred the clients who dabbled in a bit of debauchery. Many of the male clients asked to be entertained by the likes of extraordinary ladies while their wives were none the wiser.

He noted his mood was already sour as he reached to refill his coffee from the silver service.

Pouring the steamy, dark coffee, he noticed a glass of water and aspirin in a packet next to the newspaper. He smiled slowly; they never missed anything here, now did they?

Obviously, they anticipated his health this morning after the martinis and cognac.

He tossed the aspirin back and washed it down with cold, refreshing water. Opening his laptop, he inserted his VPN token and logged in. He moved through some of his emails and glanced over preliminary closing documents of last week's large business deal he closed. All seemed in order and he moved the copies to his assistant for the final close.

I wonder...

Contemplating, he moved over to Facebook and looked her up again. There she was, smiling her lovely and brilliant smile. Her face was bright and full of hope and was that innocence? One could only hope she was beautiful and innocent as she appeared.

He loved this part of the game - he always did. Seeking out and finding one so lovely and open to his advances. There was a certain thrill in the preparation of this game and often, as the voices advanced, they quieted with each word he typed, watching the responses come forth.

He knew she would be perfect. There was no doubt - his instincts were never wrong.

Briefly, he recalled his last interaction with Dianne and how he'd not been able to teach her to properly play the game. He messaged with her numerous times and thought she would be perfect, yet she still didn't understand the game. His need to control the situation, the wordplay and his longing. No, she was stupid and unable to grasp the importance of it all and he wasted too much time with her.

"No!" He pushed the laptop aggressively forward and leaned back in his chair, the deep leather, creaking beneath him. It was *NOT* his fault. It was her! He was **not** losing his ability to read and control a situation.

He was more intelligent than anyone - even her...even Avery.

He must control himself today. The voices would not win and cloud his judgment with so much at stake. His meeting this morning, the impending deal he must close, or suffer the punishment of Avery. She would withhold money and belittle him with her words - threatening his lavish lifestyle...and his intellect. He gathered himself and sat upright. He smoothed his dark wavy hair, re-positioned himself in the chair and leaned over his laptop. The voices started up again, gnawing away at what little composure he held.

He knew what he needed to do.

He saw the button next to her name suddenly turn green as he moved over to his messenger. He glanced at his watch and made note of the time. Aware that she would likely be at the office, he saw an opportunity to gauge his influence over her by engaging her in small conversation while she was at work.

A slow grin stretched across his face and the noise in his mind quieted. His long and dexterous fingers brushed over the keys as he pondered for a moment and he began to type:

"Hello dear Loghan, how are you today?"

He waited for a moment and confidently knew the response would come. It was just a matter of time before the game would begin. He knew it. It was how the game always played out and he had nothing but time to invest. The chess pieces were in place and Loghan would become his pawn. He would wait.

Perhaps she hadn't seen that she had a message; maybe she was busy. Of course, there were many reasons, but he was confident she wasn't ignoring him. That much, he knew.

He sat watching the screen and detected the green light next to her name dimming, she was offline. He sat back in his chair, tapping his well-manicured fingertips. His left eye twitched slightly and he brushed his hand across his eye.

Was it impossible that she logged off without checking if he was online, right? Where in the hell did she go that she came online and suddenly left? The anger continued to rise and he fought to push it down. They never failed to seek him out and play into his game. He shifted in his chair breathing deeply and sought calm.

Quietly, he reached for the newspaper on the silver tray. He briefly thumbed through the USA Today copy and paused at mention in Nation News.

San Francisco, California – The body of a young woman, age 26, was found in her home; the victim of an apparent murder; a spokesperson for the San Francisco Police Department released this week. No further details are available at this time. The police state this is an ongoing investigation.

Sipping the last of his coffee, he folded the newspaper with precise care, straightening his posture as he rose.

Hmm...interesting. How utterly interesting. A glint of determination in his eye. With a final, thoughtful glance, he strode across the room, ready to embrace the day's challenges.

Chapter 14

"Hey!"

Jodie Rice leaped back, narrowly avoiding a full collision as a couple staggered off the dance floor, tipsy and giggling uncontrollably. She pressed herself against the wall hoping to slip past the chaos unnoticed. Luck wasn't on her side.

The woman, clinging to her partner for dear life, swaying like a leaf in the wind, a wild grin on her face. Her drink teetered precariously in her hand before, in one unfortunate swing, it tipped over completely, splashing a golden arc straight onto Jodie's blue top. Cold liquid trickled down and Jodie felt a shiver - not just from the drink but from the absurdity of the moment.

"Shit..." Jodie muttered, glancing down at her damp shirt with a mix of annoyance and resignation. Ironically, she had dodged the rain outside only to find herself soaked with a cocktail.

"Sorry, girl." The woman called sloppily over her shoulder, flipping her hair in Jodie's direction as the couple headed off in the direction of the patio.

Whatever... Jodie sneered, rolling her eyes in displeasure.

This place was packed. Jodie didn't expect this on a weeknight. Jesus, don't these people work? She at least had business here, for Christ's sake.

Jodie Rice was the Director of Sales and Marketing for her father's magazine, **Northern California at a Glance**. Her father, Anthony, "Tony," to friends and family had agreed that Jodie would visit a prospective customer tonight and try a cold call approach. This was not the average or standard approach, given that most clients expected a meeting, specs and agreement to their expectations.

Jodie was not easily intimidated and knew she performed best under pressure. She took her chances and arrived without an appointment and would work her magic. Jodie was very good at her job and loved meeting people and capturing, what was considered, unsecured advertising...and that was precisely what she was going to do tonight.

She decided to mix business with pleasure and invited her girlfriends, Tina Stoddard and Loghan Riley, to catch up while she figured out how she would gain some face time with the owner of this new night club, **The Glasgow.**

The venue had been advertising in local papers, Facebook and Instagram. Jodie discovered they hadn't signed with any ad agencies around town and wanted to get in on the ground floor. This was going to be something massive and she was focused on winning this client over, if she could just get in front of him. Jodie was confident she could sign them as a client. She knew when something would be significant and Glasgow was heading in that direction.

Whoever heard of a building with office space by day and a jumping dance club at night? No one within a hundred miles of Sacramento had anything remotely close to this idea. So, converting two side-by-side warehouses on the Waterfront into a revenue stream year-round was genuinely brilliant. Jodie researched and found they were booked out for eighteen months for use of the day space for meetings, training and smaller conferences.

She tried to convince her dad, Tony, about securing this account for their advertisements for months. Jodie may have been the Director of Sales and Marketing, but her dad still made many determinations on who they would consider for their magazine. The word was already out; while the 'daytime' activities would be mild-mannered, the nightclub would be open and free-spirited. Jodie didn't know if this was a rumor or someone on the inside trying to work up the anticipation of this new nightclub.

Jodie met with her father and the leadership team several times over the last 4 months discussing how important it was to secure this client. Finally, after a record-long account meeting, Tony relented and said he could make a few calls and see if he could interest the owner, Barrett Rohan, in a casual dinner at his home. Of course, anyone in the advertising arena knew about Tony and his "old school" ways. Tony made many a deal, during dinners at his home. He enjoyed entertaining and often joked; his magazine was built on his wife's fantastic cooking.

Jodie was slightly annoyed when she heard her father was able to contact the owner, but Mr. Rohan politely declined a meeting/dinner at Tony's.

Of course, he didn't accept! Jodie was not the least surprised.

The owner was a sophisticated businessman from Europe. He didn't know her dad from Adam. No offense, but he didn't have time for a small-town dinner at a magazine owner's house. Who does that anymore?

Jodie loved her dad very much, but his antiquated ideas made her crazy. The days of gaining business deals over a home-cooked meal were long gone. Nevertheless, there was no way Jodie would let this opportunity escape. She only hoped her dad hadn't blown it with the first impression of their magazine.

She called three times this past week to make an appointment with the owner, Barrett Rohan. He was quite elusive, she discovered, as each time she called, she was told he was "unavailable at the moment." She didn't give a damn that he was unavailable. She was going to, at the very least, drop off her card and specs for a layout. She knew this was a bold move, not having personal contact with Mr. Rohan, but she had no problem being assertive.

"Hey, Jodie! We made it! Been waiting long?"

Her friends, Tina and Loghan, arrived, appearing a little flustered. Shaking their coats, water drops cascaded to the floor. Tina took one look at Jodie's shirt and noticed it was wet. She tapped on her blouse as well, rolling her eyes in sympathy. They greeted one another with a hug and a quick buss on the cheek.

"You get caught in the rain too?" Tina yelled at her over the music.

"No! Some drunken asshole spilled a drink on me! She nodded her head to the side. "Here, let's go to the back where we can talk!"

They made their way through a series of hallways, first, passing a bar the size of a small kiosk. Jodie grinned at this little detail as she passed the booth. This place was something else, she thought.

The club was sectioned into several venues to attract a diverse crowd. They first passed by the fully decked-out dance club in the front, a full wall of floor to ceiling, perfectly placed, flat video screens. Dance music blared from the speakers and the wall of video screens projected a video of Ariana Grande singing her thanks to her exes for the lessons she's learned.

They continued to weave through the crowded hallways and to the left, a room filled with trance music and a dance floor, just as crowded as the first. Strobes flashing, pulsing music and fog misted through the colored lights. Nice touch, Jodie thought.

Midway, they passed a full bar and they continued a few more feet until they found their ears and senses were no longer under assault. They passed through a large room filled with cowboy hats, skirts, boots and everything in between. The Chicks pumped through the speakers and couples were two-stepping and "boot scooting."

The club had four theme bars; Trance, for all the metrosexuals; Dance; for the younger, hip and predominantly gay clientele; Piano/Jazz bar for those more intimate settings, or a place to talk without yelling; and Country; for those who enjoyed two-stepping and line dances.

The trio of friends finally made their way to the Piano/Jazz club near the back and settled into a booth by the fireplace. The club was cozy and intimate, with the scent of old wood and a hint of cologne drifting through the air. They piled their damp coats and their expensive array of purses, neatly in the corner of the booth. With a chorus of laughter and gentle nudges, they began the inevitable shuffle across the leather seats, awkwardly sliding in until they found a comfortable formation.

"Whew! I thought my ears were going to explode!" laughed Tina.

"I'll buy the first round; what do you all want?" Loghan, was at the end of the booth and easily stood up, smoothing her blouse and grabbed her wallet. Jodie smiled at her friend and was genuinely glad to see Loghan accepted the invite for a girl's night.

It had been some time since Jodie had seen Loghan and she hoped they could start to hang out again. She and Loghan had begun to build a friendship after a common friend introduced the two. They had a lot in common and enjoyed each other's company. They were meeting up frequently, before Ian's accident. It had been difficult for Jodie, being a newer friend, to know how best to support Loghan. Jodie and Tina still made an effort to connect over the months and now, years since Ian's passing and it was certainly good to see Loghan smiling again.

After giving Loghan their drink requests, Jodie leaned back to take in the atmosphere. It was nice and she was very impressed. The place was packed in the front clubs and they walked by at least two drink kiosks just on the way to the piano bar. Not to mention, it was a weeknight! Jesus - what must this place be like on the weekend? Jodie shook her head and continued to take in the sights and sounds.

The piano bar was decorated elegantly but was not overdone. It was re-markably quiet. The music played at just the right volume in the background; Jodie recognized the voice as Diana Krall. She loved her music and tipped her head back, enjoying the moment and plotting out her plan to meet the owner. Unfortunately, Barrett Rohan's calendar was next to impossible; scheduled out for two months and Jodie didn't have time to wait that long. Patience was never her strong suit.

"Oh, no, you don't!" Jodie jumped, startled at Tina's outburst. "I can see those gears going already, Jodie!" Tina laughed at her friend and smiled. "Well...this was strictly a business venture tonight! You know that!" Jodie winked and playfully swatted at Tina.

Loghan, with drinks in hand, joined the table and smiled at the banter. "Ok, what did I miss? What's the plan?" Loghan wasted no time getting to why they were together on a weeknight. Tina rolled her eyes at the two. "Jesus...you two are bad!! Can't we just enjoy a few minutes with each other? Always work! We never get to hang out that often anymore!"

"Awwww....do you need a hug?" Teasing, Jodie feigned a hug in the air. Jodie screwed up her face at Tina and then smiled, blowing her an "air kiss." It was followed by Tina's perfectly manicured flip of the middle finger. They all laughed at the playful antics of one another.

Settling into the booth, Jodie brought the glass to the air and the others followed suit: "Cheers to friends..." The glasses clinked and all three sipped their drinks. They smiled and settled into their places and Jodie started the conversation off.

"No plan, really. I have left three or four messages this week for the owner. His name is Barrett Rohan. I've tried to schedule a meeting, but he's booked out solid for months. I told his assistant I would be here tonight at 7:00 and I would love the opportunity to meet him. I guess we will see if anything happens. So, right now, I'm going to enjoy this drink with my friends and will determine when the time is right and I will walk right up to the front desk and ask for him."

The three ladies clinked their glasses once more and Jodie exclaimed, "To new business ventures and... "Loghan leaned in and ended the toast for Jodie. "To liquid courage!"

"To liquid courage," they shouted in unison, laughing.

Jodie sipped slowly on her Patron over ice and sighed. Courage in a glass, as they say – and she needed a little extra dose of bravery tonight.

Tina sat back and looked at Jodie thoughtfully. "I like that idea, Jodie. Just waltz up like you own the joint yourself and ask for him." They all laughed over the thought of this, although they knew damn well, Jodie would do that very thing. Tina wished she were as ballsy as Jodie. Instead, Tina quietly admired her friend and considered Jodie's outright confidence. She believed it took her far in this world and speculated it was one of the reasons Jodie was successful in her career.

The mood was light and the friends laughed as the conversation went from vacation plans to anything new and exciting and current movies. Sade was crooning in the background about a Smooth Operator and Tina looked over at Jodie.

"Speaking of Smooth Operator..." tipping her head toward the music, her voice drifted, leaving the comment to become a question. Jodie nervously shifted and glanced at Loghan.

"Ummm...Nothing to really talk about, Tina... let's change the topic."

Loghan looked back and forth between Jodie and Tina, shaking her head slightly and took another sip of her drink. Resigned, she squared her shoulders and took a slight breath before she began.

"Look...Tina, Jodie. Thank you for not giving up on me. Really. I'm ok. We can talk about anything. I've made a lot of progress these last few months and I'm even going to my college roommate's wedding in San Francisco that's coming up soon. That's a big deal, you know? "Her deep emerald eyes imploring. "I want to know everything…! What you've both been up to, who you're dating…your exes. All of it!" Loghan slid both her hands across the table toward her friends. "Really." Her eyes were sincere and full.

Jodie and Tina looked at each other, then to Loghan and placed their hands on top of hers. There was a gentle smile among the three friends, followed by a pause.

Jodie didn't miss a beat.

"Tina is just being nosy…" She smiled. "Tina knows I've been, ummm… dating a bit. You know, using apps and trying to meet, Mister Right Now.' They all bust out laughing, relieved for the light moment. Loghan sat up quickly, filled with immediate interest. "What?!…Is this dating…or…?"

"You got it…hooking up." Jodie leaned back and batted her eyelashes, feigning innocence.

"Are you really?" Loghan asked with enthusiasm.

"Well, well…*someone* is very interested!" Tina laughed toward Loghan, tapping her fingertips on the table. She continued. "Isn't it scandalous, Loghan? I love that Jodie is acting on what every man can do and not be made out to be…well…you know."

Jodie laughed out loud. "Yes, I know…slutty."

Loghan leaned over to Jodie. "Can I ask you a few questions?"

"Of course! You look shocked!" Jodie smiled at Loghan. "Ask away…but this seems more like an interview than just random questions, my friend." When Loghan was in her "reporter" mode, Jodie knew it. Her tone changed and definitely had that feel. She probed Jodie to understand her interest. "Ok, before I answer your questions, what is this really about?" Jodie sipped on the last of her drink, lifting her head, with eyes questioning Loghan.

Loghan sat up straight and smiled at her friends. "Well, I have my first article; one I chose and not my editor."

A loud "whoop" and claps surrounded Loghan and she joined in with their celebration of her big news.

"Thanks! It feels so good to finally feel like I'm writing something I want to write. Not someone else!"

"So....why do I know this is somehow connected to me and my "dating" proclivities?" Jodie made air quotes and smiled.

"Because it is!" Loghan's excitement was catching as Tina and Jodie looked at each other with large eyes and laughed. Loghan continued.

"My article is about how technology has propelled us forward, with work, school and...relationships." She paused for effect.

"Relationships? Or....hooking up?" Jodie cocked her eyebrow at Loghan.

"Well, that's the story I sold my editor on!" Loghan laughed. "I will cover, relationships, internet, dating sights, smart technology, etcetera, as part of my lead-in, but what I'm really interested in is what goes on within the dating sites." Loghan paused again, drifting into thought.

Tina noticed immediately. "Uh - oh...I know that look, Loghan. What are you thinking about?"

Loghan quickly re-engaged. "I have a hunch on a story and I'm going to follow the thread and see where it leads me. Loghan continued to fill them in on the details of her article and research she's started, along with the people she has lined up to interview. Jodie leaned back in the booth and nodded approvingly. "Ok, Loghan...ask away!"

Jodie answered Loghan's handful of questions. She wanted to know if she had the right dating sites, were there any others that came to mind; how do you meet someone; do you just talk to them online, or do you move to the phone? The questions were what most people wanted to know when venturing into the world of online dating, but Jodie was confident in Loghan's case it was pure, Reporting 101.

As the conversation wrapped, Tina returned with another round of drinks. Jodie's eyes perused the crowd of people coming and going through the clubs. The music was lovely and Adele's haunting, "Hello", serenaded lightly in the background.

Jodie sipped her drink and set the snifter down slowly. A man across the room caught her eye. Tina and Loghan were deep in a conversation about a recent bill that passed that both were on opposing sides, expressing their thoughts. Jodie was content with staying out of this conversation and continued to quietly admire the man across the room.

He wasn't looking her way, so she let herself take a long unapologetic look. Her gaze started at his polished shoes and traveled up the length of his well-fitted slacks, noting the quiet confidence in his lean build. Jodie savored each detail, her eyes lingering, until they finally reach his face. When their eyes met, she didn't look away. She held his gaze, bold and unflinching and he seemed to notice - lifting his glass in a subtle salute, a faint smile playing on his lips.

A waiter appeared out of nowhere, setting a fresh drink in front of her, its delicate ice clinking as it settled into place. She glanced up to thank him, wondering where he'd materialized from, given they had to go to the bartender earlier to get drinks. When she looked back, the mystery man vanished - her eyes moved about the bar and she noticed the handsome stranger was already making his way across the floor in her direction. Jodie felt a slow, confident smile spread across her face as he closed the distance between them.

"Holy shit..." Tina uttered under her breath. "Ummm...Two o'clock, coming this way."

Both she and Loghan had broken away from their verbal jousting to see this gorgeous man slowly walking toward the table.

"Good evening, ladies." he said politely, his tone warm yet smooth. As the words left his lips, his gaze seemed to hold, lingering - no, anchoring - on Jodie. There was a softness in his eyes, almost like he was seeing something that only she could show him. A heartbeat later, his gaze shifted, settling on Tina and Loghan with a polite nod.

With a respectful ease, he extended his hand to Tina, his handshake firm but measured, a greeting that left her feeling acknowledged without being overpowered. "Good evening," he said, then repeated the same to Loghan, his hand steady, his voice rich. In that moment, a subtle gesture escaped him - a slight bow of the head, barely perceptible but profound, as if he were in the presence of something rare.

With his attention briefly diverted, Jodie pondered. Was that a slight bow he just made?? Holy Mary, mother of God. She consciously made sure her lips stayed closed and her mouth didn't fall open in stunning silence.

"Rohan...Barrett Rohan," he offered his hand now to Jodi and she gratefully accepted it.' Jodie Rice, yes?" Barrett smiled at her and Jodie felt light-headed.

"Ummm...a...I...I...." Jodie stammered, failing miserably at regaining her composure.

"Yes, this is Jodie Rice... I'm Loghan Riley and this is Tina Stoddard. It's very nice to meet you."

Thank Goodness for Loghan. She pulled that off well, Jodie thought. Saving her from her stuttering and stammering.

Turning to him, she asked, "How...how did you know who I was?" That was the most coherent phrase that Jodie was capable of at the moment.

"Well, I make it a point to know all the interesting women who come to my establishments." Barrett smiled at all three of the ladies, but his gaze lingered on Jodie.

Perfect...he had "the look," and he certainly had a good line. Was it a line? She wasn't as sure as she initially thought.

Jodie felt her heart in her throat and her mind raced to pull it together. She had no idea how he knew her or found her, but this was her time to make the impression she had planned for weeks. She was not prepared for this feeling...it felt more than attraction. It was deeper, like she'd known him for ages, or had heard of him long before today.

She had to get her shit together - Fast.

When researching Barrett Rohan, she never found any pictures to recognize him. The most recent photo she found was a groundbreaking ceremony for another venture in Dublin. The picture showed a rainy day in Ireland and he was wearing an overcoat; head down over the shovel he planted in the soil.

No, this was not the man in the picture. This man was drop-dead gorgeous. Handsome and masculine. His clothing was impeccable and Jodie could not stop staring at him.

He had thick, dark hair with stunning blue eyes. His dress shirt was tailored and fitted tightly and Jodie could see the muscles under his shirt.

Jesus, she thought. *What is wrong with me?*

"I understand you're interested in doing some business with me, Miss Rice."

Loghan and Tina knew their cue and wasted no time. Loghan was the first to rise.

"Well, we'd love to stay -but morning comes early for us... Jodie, we'll talk to you tomorrow. It was nice to meet you, Barrett." Tina followed Loghan, grabbing their coat and bags in hand. Jodie had no time to think or pull them back.

"Ciao, Bella," Tina winked slyly at Jodie as each bussed Jodie goodbye.

"Ladies, it was a pleasure." Barrett offered his hand again to each.

Loghan silently mouthed, out of Barrett's view, "Call me." - thumb and pinkie finger-wagging. Jodie smiled slightly, arching her eyebrow wickedly and nodded absently.

Jodie watched as her friends disappeared into the midst of people, music and the rain-filled night.

Chapter 15

Rain pelted down on Loghan as she ran up her steps to the front door. Juggling her purse and umbrella, her cold fingers fumbled to locate her keys and rapidly entered the door.

The rain was relentless this evening and her Lyft driver, equally obnoxious. The driver talked the entire way and offered her an unsolicited rant about her life, her kids, her other job and that she was a devout Christian and hated the "F" word. "I can't believe how often young people use this word... it's like a noun or adjective!"

Then you don't want to be out with my girlfriends and me. Loghan smirked to herself.

Loghan sat in the back seat and rolled her eyes. She was not interested in listening to the drivers' stories and just wanted to get home without the commentary.

Loghan was always pleasant and polite but wished the woman would keep her focus on the road rather than her continued narrative.

Loghan thought it would be slightly humorous to find a way to work the F word into her responses, but she also knew it was the second cocktail that may have encouraged this consideration. Grateful the driver arrived safely; she couldn't wait to escape her chatter. Loghan jumped out of the car without opening her umbrella, offered a brief "thanks," and ran to her place.

Once inside, she dropped her things on the chair in the foyer and shook the rain from her hair. She had a lovely time tonight with her girlfriends and smiled at their antics. All the laughter and banter were good to be part of again.

She continued to muse about her night and hoped that Jodie was working magic on making a deal with the nightclub owner, but, Jesus, how could you get anything done with him looking like that? And that accent?! Stop it!

Loghan couldn't help herself and giggled at the recollection of Tina's response to her when she said Barrett was "good looking." What the hell did Tina say about him? Oh yeah, she recalled, "given the opportunity, she would climb him like a tree!"

Loghan was still laughing as she walked to her bedroom. Harry lifted his head to show remote interest in the sounds. The fluffy cat stretched his long body and released a yawn in the direction of Loghan.

"Oh, did I wake you, big boy?" Loghan scratched the big tabby under his chin; her reward was purrs and tail swishing. She changed out of her rain-soaked clothes, washed her face, slipped into her sweats and looked for the over-sized Sacramento State sweatshirt she wore at home in the winter. It was Ian's, from his short stint at CSUS and she had worn it for years. It had become a source of comfort for these long, cold winter nights.

Locating it in the top drawer, she traced her fingers over the cracked, fading letters on the sweatshirt, each one etched with a memory, a comfort she's turned to too many times. The soft fabric was warm, familiar and all too easy to wrap around herself like armor against the chill of the present. But tonight, she felt something different - a quiet restlessness she couldn't ignore.

With a sigh, she dug deeper into the drawer, sifting past her favorite shirts and worn-out sweaters. Then, her fingers brushed against the one she'd been looking for - a sweatshirt she hadn't worn in ages. It was plain, simple and unburdened by any memories or sentiments.

As she pulled it over her head, she felt a strange but exhilarating sense of lightness, like shedding an old skin. She glanced in the mirror, the unfamiliar sweatshirt staring back at her. It was time, she decided to step out of her comfort zone, let go of the memories of the past. Tonight, at least, her memories would stay neatly folded in the drawer, waiting. It was time for something new.

Loghan settled in at her desk and since it was a little early for bed, she opted to check her email and confirm her work schedule for tomorrow. So much to do to begin prep for her article and yet, she couldn't remember when she was so happy to have "too much work."

She responded to a few emails and moved through them quickly with practice efficiency. No, she didn't need additional information for her article on Millennials; Thank you, I completed that article and submitted it for print.

To the professor, she asked to interview for statistical information and detailed insight into digital media; Thank you for confirming; I look forward to meeting with you next week.

The next email, from the office assistant, was a familiar one. Checking in on her breakfast order for the weekly meeting. Without thinking, Loghan typed her response: "Ashley, thanks for confirming. Same order as the last three years, no changes. Thanks-Loghan."

She hit send and paused, Loghan winced at her response and it was too late, she was in the flow of responding to emails. Damn, she muttered under her breath, realizing it sounded curt. She decided she would talk to her in the morning and apologize. Leaning back in her chair and twisting her long, auburn hair in a messy bun atop her head, she reached for a pen and pushed it through to hold it in place. It was her tell-tale sign that she had something on her mind. She would fidget with her hair when she was alone or out of sight at the office. When Loghan showed up at office meetings with her hair piled on top of her head, the joke was that you might be in for some of her feisty "push back" as she was ready to banter.

Still feeling the effects of the fun she had with Jodie and Tina and in her last response to Ashley's email, Loghan decided work could wait until tomorrow before she said anything completely foolish.

Well, she could dabble on the dating sites a bit; that couldn't hurt anything. It is research, after all, she considered, as she casually opened one of her computer files with some of the early research for her story. She told herself she wasn't working since she was still a little buzzed and only perusing.

She toyed around on a few dating apps the last few nights and hadn't talked to anyone, even after she revealed she was a writer and researching for her article. She gave them the name of her magazine and would offer more, should anyone have accepted her offer to "chat." Sadly, no one did.

For her research, she planned to dive into the dating apps, reaching out to women to uncover their thoughts on finding "the one." Did they search with purpose, or simply let the dating app create the match? Did they meet many men in person, or did they meet them for casual hook ups? Yet, her attempts were hitting roadblocks. Most women ignored her messages, even as she identified herself properly. Often times they responded with a blunt dismissal, or blatant, "Fuck off, creeper." That was common in the venue of being online. Courtesy, it seemed, was unnecessary when no one knew who you were–unless you made a genuine connection.

She would have to find an alternate approach to speak to women directly. She decided she would work on that tomorrow.

Loghan had the outline of her article and was ready to start her interviews she lined up in the morning. She also had a promising lead on securing an interview with a well - respected professor who taught Sociology. They would add credibility to her article and she was excited to hear their take on the emotional and thought-driven aspect of looking for love. She knew her outline on dating and meeting the right person would hit a specific nerve in the readership. Women were always talking about how hard it was to meet someone. Everyone is so busy now it made meeting the right person beyond challenging. Loghan would weave into her article the time crunch of young professionals. The paradox of endless options leading to decision paralysis and the death of organically meeting people. But there was that darker undercurrent she couldn't ignore: the hookup artists masquerading as relationship seekers, the carefully crafted profiles hiding empty intentions.

She tapped her pen on the desk and circled a note she jotted at the bottom of her notepad; Dating apps: democratizing romance or digitizing deception?

That was the real story she wanted to tell - the one that she knew readers would connect and nod their heads in recognition, finally seeing their experiences reflected in print.

She recognized her article would include quite a bit of commentary on sex. However, she also considered John's response would be less than thrilled.

She hadn't included those details in her pitch to him about the sexual aspect, did she?

Loghan's brow creased. Why in the hell could other people, Deagan primarily, write about such topics but not me? But that is why Loghan had to make this part of her story relevant and enticing. She knew she was a good writer, but you write what you know; at least that is what Loghan learned in college, but how much did she know about sex and hooking up?

"Not enough." She dryly said aloud.

Loghan drifted back to her research files on her computer and opened her dating app research folder. She had already acquired hundreds of screenshots documenting the evolution of dating profiles, how the tone shifted from morning's earnest relationship-seekers to late night's more… "ambitious" proposals.

Tomorrow's interviews would help her understand why people dabbled on dating sites, but more importantly, they'd help her readers understand they weren't alone in this modern maze of love.

It was no secret that people were looking for long term relationships or, one-night stands, friends with benefits - you can paint it any color you wish, but it was all the same thing, sex without ties or commitment. Good old, down and dirty sex - and this would sell copy. She just had to research - ask questions - and speak to what was going on out there. She would have to rely on those she interviewed, that much she was certain. She hadn't been out there for a long time.

Hell, she had never been out there.

She'd been with Ian since she first started dating. Being with Ian was where she wanted to be. Of course, she had no control over how life turned out, but she knew she was entering in an area where she had little experience dating and meeting men. Let alone sex.

Harry wandered out of the bedroom and jumped up on Loghan's desk. He purred and butted his head against Loghan's arm, begging attention. She idly scratched the big, furry cat and continued to drift in thought.

Loghan knew she was feeling better about life since she stumbled on this idea for her article. It wasn't just that she finally had her own chosen piece;

she acknowledged she found all this discussion of sex and closeness had stirred something within.

The excitement of people trying to meet one another for good or "not so good" reasons was genuinely interesting to her. It was the excitement of being reinvested in something. Writing and creating filled her with life, it was the first thing she felt excited about in a long while.

Anyone who knew Loghan would tell you she was sweet, kind, loving and honest. It wasn't that she didn't appreciate she was all those things in the eyes of others, but she also wanted to be more. More of what? She thought. Edgier? Unpredictable? She chuckled at the thought.

She was slightly annoyed by those around her thought they knew her so well. She hated she was so predictable. She couldn't help that part of her personality, though. How do you change who you are in certain areas? Aren't we products of our environment? Our upbringing?

She returned her attention to Harry and absently stroked his shiny coat. She continued down the path of thoughts and had multiple questions. What else was creating these feelings? Did she feel a little uncomfortable? Was it the dating apps? Does John think she shouldn't write about the more "taboo" topics? Is Deagan thinking the same thing? Was it the undercurrent? The undercurrent of sex? Loghan's thoughts reeled.

Sex? Jesus, back to that again?

Loghan got it; she was not what anyone would call sexually free.

She experienced a great relationship in the bedroom with Ian, but it could be described as "vanilla." They were young and inexperienced when they first slept with each other. But as most young people are, they were wildly in love. She never experienced anything but love, as Ian was her first. Her first crush, first kiss, first love. Ian was her first everything.

She smiled at the thoughts and recalled that she was to put her memories on hold tonight...no such luck.

Loghan shifted uncomfortably in her chair, confronting the unexpected truth: researching romance and sexuality for her article awakened something in her. Despite her loving but vanilla relationship with Ian, these darker, unexplored territories fascinated her. The guilt crept in - was it wrong to feel this spark of interest when she was still deep in mourning? Between her Catholic upbringing and her complete inexperience with modern dating, Loghan felt lost in unfamiliar waters. Yet she couldn't deny the thrill that came with each new discovery.

She had struggled attending church since she buried Ian. Instead, she quietly stepped away from the Church, exploring new ideologies and questioning the concept of God after Ian died.

Life didn't make sense when Ian left this world. How could there be a kind and loving God that would allow his senseless death? Loghan struggled with her faith with Ian gone - now, she questioned everything. It filled her with uneasiness and made her apprehensive, to step away and question everything she was taught. Her grief counselor told her it was common to question faith in times of crisis. No kidding, that was an understatement.

Loghan was deep in her memories and she let them come. She knew she had lost her earlier pledge to keep them at bay, but there was no turning back. The memories came flooding in and she allowed them to run over her like a tide from the ocean.

When Ian and Loghan shared the news they planned to live together before marriage, it stirred a hint of scandal. Loghan's parents were taken aback, but her mother, Shawna, with her graceful presence, quickly smoothed things over. In her rich Irish accent, she reassured Loghan's father, saying "Times have changed; let them discover life together first. Marriage will come when it's right." Her words softened his worry and Loghan's father, despite his initial doubts, came to accept the idea. Loghan's father had always loved her spirited nature and it was clear she had never been happier than with Ian. Yet, when Loghan shared that she no longer considered herself a practicing Catholic after Ian's passing, it was that decision that troubled him most.

"How in the hell can that be, Loghs?!" Her father said incredulously. Loghan didn't try to make her father understand but offered to him she was finding her way with spirituality as it worked in her world. She continued to show up for church for a while on the "normal" holidays, Easter, Christmas Eve and Palm Sunday, but after she buried Ian, she put her foot down when her father requested she attend confession once a month.

She recalled her response to him that day; "Sorry, Da. I just can't do this any longer." Using his favorite name in Gaelic as she and her siblings often used when extending him love. It had been over two years ago, and she never returned to church after that day.

She moved to the sideboard her grandmother gave her and opened the doors. She converted it to a liqueur cabinet years ago, and reached for the bottle of brandy. She decided a nightcap would be appropriate at this time, as she was working through what she hoped were some of the long-held threads of loss. She settled back to her chair in front of the computer and sipped quietly on her brandy.

Even though Loghan felt herself making progress in moving on, she felt the painful reminder each day. Just this morning she instinctively reached over to the other side of the bed, only to find the sheets crisp and cool to her touch. It was months after Ian died before she realized that she cried each day before her feet touched the floor.

In those early months, she pulled herself together daily and would force smiles when needed. People around her knew she was grieving, but she never let on how much she ached, never validated their sad, soft smiles when they looked at her.

Change was hard for her, yet it continued to come slowly with her acceptance. It took a year for her to stop sitting at the dinner table each night - a place setting for one. She never thought the simple act of setting the table for one, would feel so unbearable. Yet night after night, she could only stare at the empty chair across from her. She just couldn't move to the couch as most people do when eating solitary. The table was where she and Ian laughed and talked about their day, a place they connected and shared thoughts and ideas about their future. A place they shared that had the feeling of "family" and closeness. Moving to the couch was another absolute reminder of Ian not coming home.

Never would he enter through the front door, sweep her into his arms and kiss her face and lips, as he did each day. Never would they sit close on the couch and watch television while Ian rubbed her tired feet. The milestones of grief crept upon her one by one. There were so many firsts without him over the years now - birthdays, anniversaries, quiet Sunday mornings. Each one held its own ache, like a ghostly reminder of his absence and yet, with each passing season, her heart learned to hold the loss alongside life's quiet moments. She found him in the simple things - the warmth of a cup of coffee on a cold morning, the way the sunlight slanted across the table, illuminating the chair he'd never again sit in.

Loghan set the empty glass on the desk, her fingers lingering on its smooth surface, her mind drifting to those early days after Ian was gone. In the quiet, when the ache became too much to bear, she would find herself standing in their closet, surrounded by his clothes, still neatly hung as if he might step back into them at any moment. She had pressed her face into the soft fabric of his jackets, breathe deeply and lose herself in the familiar scent that lingered like a ghost, half-expecting to feel his arms around her.

Sometimes, she'd pull a shirt from its hanger, clutch it tightly and sink to the closet floor, letting the heavy folds of his clothes wrap around her like fragile armor. She would stay there, memories crashing over like waves, sobbing until her strength gave out and finally, drained and trembling, she would lie still on the floor, the weight of grief and exhaustion pressing her down into silence.

Loghan shook her head to release the memories. Sometimes she felt so alone. She had people in her life who cared and loved her, but no one fully knew how she felt. Even though she told herself she wouldn't get lost in memories tonight, she thought it was a good experience. She had processed through some memories that allowed her to understand herself better. But it was time; time to permit herself to let Ian go.

Her counselor had told her she would arrive at this place in her own time and she would know when it was right. She had to let go of the guilt and know that she wasn't forgetting Ian; she was just allowing herself to live. She would hold on to his memory forever, but it was time to let the sunlight back into her life.

A flicker of light caught her attention and Loghan looked up briefly at her computer. She moved closer to look and she took in a shuddering breath.

How are you this lovely evening, Loghan?

It was the message window on Facebook that popped open. The hair on the back of her neck bristled. She smiled nervously at the name David Rothchild and she settled back and began to type.

*****

Aric found his morning meeting with his mother to be all he expected. Long, painful and tediously dull. Avery had business plans and her clear expectations were to be met. She lined his meetings up for the next several days and planned every detail. His expectation was to wine and dine and, if needed, find escorts and flatly have these gentlemen laid if that is what "duty" warranted. All of which was boring to Aric, but part of the plan if needed, Avery insisted. He knew all too well - what Avery wants - Avery gets.

Avery was manipulative, but in her subtle ways, only he could detect. Gwyneth, Avery's assistant, didn't seem to pick up on her employers' insistence at every turn. Avery feigned charming glances at Aric when "requesting" he perform this action or that request. She tapped her pen on the large walnut table when Aric didn't respond to her suggestions for their current clients and the deal she felt would be appropriate.

He knew every pointed and insinuated "suggestion" from Avery. Gwyneth continued to capture every note as the endless meeting ensued.

Aric was keenly aware that closing this deal with Vector Communications was needed. If they could not secure this client, their cash flow projections would be off track and the plans to expand in Asia would be on hold. He needed to land this deal, as it was the only way to get his insufferable mother off his back. For now.

Aric planned on meeting with the investors tomorrow for Vector and Avery insisted the deal be closed tomorrow. It had been months of flow charts, meetings, dinners and promises. He knew he was close to completing this deal; Aric would finalize it in his time, not Avery's timeline.

"Aric, darling. I know you will be able to manage this small request of me." Her saccharine smile made his skin crawl. She continued, "Our expenses these last few months have been excessive. Your appetite with your expense account has put our investors and me… on edge. So, close this deal tomorrow, Aric and we won't have to," Avery paused for effect, "renegotiate your expense account."

He quietly noted, her smile was sickening.

He knew it was time to leave the meeting and tell her what she wanted to hear, or the voices would start again. The constant picking at his brain, the noise it would make – the headache and feelings he loathed. Avery lorded her control over him about the money he was paid. She never made him feel as if he genuinely earned anything on his own. It was all her, the ever "powerful and financially perfect," Avery.

She needed to go straight to hell and he contemplated how delightful that would be. Aric stood up and smiled.

"Thank you, Avery. As always, a stimulating meeting and venture for us. I hear you and your expectations are top of mind for me." Aric's voice etched with the faintest hint of sarcasm. He could return her fake attempt at being courteous and warm.

Fuck off, he thought, as he politely smiled at her, slightly bowed his head, fabricating acquiescence. He turned toward Gwyneth and genuinely smiled, placing his hand over his heart. She sat at the table and captured the notes of this meeting on her laptop. She stopped suddenly and returned Aric's smile. Her blue eyes lifted, looking at him through thick lashes.

Foolish girl, he mused. He hoped Avery was paying her well. He turned and moved toward the door.

"Good day, Avery; Gwyneth." He bowed his head slightly and left the thick air behind him.

Upon leaving the meeting, he changed into his workout clothes and went for a quick run on the treadmill. His expensive running shoes found a rhythm that sounded like a metronome. Each footfall echoing his mounting frustration as he pushed the voices from his head. His mind replayed the meeting on endless loop – Avery's carefully manicured nails tapping on the table, her voice carrying that infuriating note of condescension as she questioned every recommendation he brought forth.

Five miles in, his legs burned almost as much as his resentment. Sweat darkened his shirt, but he pushed harder, as if he could outrun the shadow she still cast over his life in his early thirties.

Back in his suite at the Ritz - Carlton, he eased into the over-sized tub, for a long soak. The martini was perfectly chilled, three olives-just as he liked it. The steam rose in lazy spirals as Aric sank deeper into the water. He fantasized what life would be like without his dear mother, Avery.

How sublime it would be. Better yet, what if Avery were to have a terrible accident and perish? A slip and a nasty fall - it was quite easy, really. Accidents did happen. Tragic accidents that befell prominent business figures were hardly unprecedented.

He took another sip of his martini, savoring the clean, crisp taste of the vodka. He could already envision the press coverage: *"Aric Stanton Shows Remarkable Strength in Wake of Family Tragedy."* He'd wear his grief like a well-cut suit, perfectly tailored to public consumption. The board would rally around him, of course. The prodigal son, stepping up to guide the company through its darkest hour. He would gain complete control of the company, as it should be...there was still that one, nagging little thing he knew needed to address, outside of Avery. All in good time, he thought, as he continued to dream of life without Avery.

"Your mother would be so proud," they would say, not knowing how the thought made him smile behind his carefully constructed mask of mourning.

The water was growing cool, but Aric lingered, watching the last rays of sunlight paint the bathroom ceiling in shades of amber. Tomorrow was another day. Another meeting. Another chance to smile across the table at Avery while his mind and the voices wandered down darker paths.

He lifted his martini in a mock toast to his reflection in the gilded bathroom mirror.

" To family," he murmured, draining the glass and sunk under the water.

*****

Loghan re-positioned herself in her chair and smiled nervously. Her graceful fingers poised above the keyboard.

What to write - what do I say? She thought almost in a panic. Finally, her breathing escaping slowly, she began to type.

"Good evening to you as well, David. I'm fine, you?" She lied - only slightly.

She was nervous. David tried to message her the other day when she was in the office and Deagan walked in. What the hell would she have told Deagan had he seen his message? He would have wanted to know who was, David and how she knew him. The questions would have been endless. Deagan was already hesitant about Loghan researching dating sites and where it might lead. She brushed off the thoughts of Deagan and continued.

David's response came quickly as she could see he was typing:

"I'm very well this evening, my dear. I've had an extremely long week closing a deal and I'm so close I can almost taste the victory."

She smiled at this response. After the green light to write her first chosen article, she knew what victory felt like these last few weeks. She also came back quickly:

"What kind of deal would make you feel such triumph?" Loghan was slightly interested in hearing some details as she wanted to understand better who this man was. What was he about...was he for real? Why was he here online?

"My dear, I can't share too much as it's quite confidential, but I can tell you that I've been working on this deal for some time. It's been taking up much of my days and nights." He winced at the thought of hiring two high-end prostitutes to "entertain" his business clients this week—Jesus, how he loathed his work at times. The only redeeming factors were the travel and the means by which he lived from his success.

Yes, she recalled he had an "air" about him. How he spoke; words like, lovely and darling....it was interesting and certainly not familiar for her. She considered his response a moment. Hmm...A businessman, how nice...that's a little intriguing. Who is this man? What is he all about? She started to type again: *"It sounds exciting, David. I'm sure you must have something to celebrate then. So, what will you do once you've closed the deal?"*

The words returned swiftly as he typed. *"I'm sure I will celebrate by dining at some extravagant restaurant, surrounded by people I wish wouldn't be there."* He knew this would be true. Avery would be one of them and a handful of their investors all blustering about a job well done.

"Oh my, that sounds dreadful, David. What would you rather do? I'm sure you must have something else in mind that would be far better than what you described!"

Loghan smiled. This wasn't so hard, she thought. She never interacted online with anyone other than someone she knew. It didn't seem so strange or "scary." Why not? Why not just, "go there," and see what he has to say? Loghan wanted to gain more from this discussion. In her usual way, she tried to drive the conversation.

This is going to be wonderful, he thought. Sipping on a martini, he leaned back in his chair and stretched a bit.

"I would much rather be dining with a lovely lady. Well...perhaps such as yourself, Loghan. I do recall that you told me you were a lovely lady, did you not?"

Loghan felt her face grow warm and shifted in her chair.

"Oh crap, I thought I was driving this conversation?!" Loghan stated out loud and didn't care; there was no one in the room to hear. She paused a moment to consider her response. I'm only talking to someone online, she told herself. How in the world am I getting flustered? Loghan picked up her brandy and took a sip.

Gather your courage, Loghan thought, placed her glass back down and turned on Sade from her iPad. Music filled the room. She took a deep breath and began to type.

"Yes, David. I did tell you that. I have been told that I am attractive. I think I mentioned I was intelligent as well. I didn't know you were interested in that aspect of me and instead wanted to webcam, or cyber, or whatever."

"My, you are a fiery one, now, aren't you? I never said anything about those things, now did I, darling? It seems to me that you protest too much."

Loghan felt immediately annoyed. What is his deal? She couldn't believe that his response made her agitated, she didn't even know him! I'm not even in the same physical space as him! She leaned into her laptop and started again.

"No, you didn't mention cybering or web-camming – I just assumed you were interested in that. I mean, why else are you here talking to me?"

"To chat, of course. Meet interesting and intelligent people. Haven't you met a nice gentleman online and dated him?"

Loghan sat upright and scoffed, her fingertips hitting the keys with force.

Of course not! I had a fiancé that I'd known since grade school. I have no need or intention of meeting anyone online. Loghan questioned herself, why the need to tell him that? He doesn't need to know about Ian.

"Crap!" She spat out the words and Harry jumped off the desk at the interruption. Loghan shook her head and leaned back again in her chair for a moment. She knew what she would do; she would change the subject. She was good at doing this when it suited her or she didn't want to discuss something. Her slender fingers moved deftly across the keys.

"Do you date a lot of women online, David?"

"Not many, but I have found a few that I've found to be wonderful and entertaining. No one special, if that is what you mean, my dear."

"Where are you from? You call me darling and dear. Are you older? Please don't take offense to that. I find your way of "talking" to be very nice...refreshing."

Isn't she charming? He thought, drawing a long sip of his martini. He mused that his drink needed refreshing from how this conversation was going. He leaned over and poured the clear liquid from his pitcher.

He settled in again at the keyboard: *"I'm from Kent, a small town near London. I was born and raised there."*

Interesting, he mused; he had never disclosed that before. He kept his life private from those online. He found no need to share even one shred of his life, yet he shared with her without hesitation.

"That would explain how your "voice" comes out in your words. I adore that you speak this way. It seems so proper...old world. You didn't respond, though; are you an older gentleman?"

"Well, if you think being 33 is old and gentlemanly, darling, then yes." This brought a smile to him at the thought of her thinking he was "older." He paused briefly and decided it was his turn to shift the conversation:

"I must know something – all these questions. I would like to ask just a simple one. I'm not at all sure why I need to know, but what color are your eyes? Your picture online doesn't allow me to see."

Loghan paused. What harm was there in responding? *"Green - I have green eyes - the color of emerald - Well, so my father and fiancé told me."*

"Yes, yes, you did mention a fiancé, past tense? What happened, dear? How did the demise of your relationship come to be?"

Loghan tensed up momentarily. She hadn't shared with anyone in a long time. Most people knew Ian. She didn't have to explain his car accident. Ian left for work on Tuesday, just like any other day and never returned. The wreck was caused by a drunk driver falling asleep at the wheel and veering head-on into Ian's lane. But the officers, first on site told her that Ian felt nothing - he died instantly.

She would just be brief, she decided. *"He was killed in a car accident. It was long ago, and I don't like to discuss it, do you mind?"*

"Oh, of course. I understand. I'm sorry to hear of your loss. I can only imagine the pain of losing someone you loved so much. How old was he, if you don't mind my asking? Then, no more questions."

"He was 25." Loghan leaned back and dropped her hands to her lap. His whole life was ahead of him.... Our whole life, she thought.

He sat back a moment and was briefly stirred by a feeling, a tangible sadness for this young woman. He imagined her - felt her pain for a moment and settled into it. He immediately shook it off and re-positioned himself in his chair and responded.

"Please accept my heartfelt sympathy for you, my dear - if I were there - and you wouldn't mind, I would hug you and let you know you're not alone. I sense you feel that...alone, that is. Nothing is worse in life than to feel others don't see you or understand the feeling of being alone."

How in the hell does he know that? Did I say something about my feeling alone? How is he making me feel "something?"... It's impossible to feel a connection with someone you've never met...right? She pulled the pen out of her hair, allowing it to fall then pulled it back, twisted it and completed the earlier process. She chewed on her lip nervously and allowed her honesty to guide her emotions.

"Thank you, David...I would, well...I think I would lean into your hug and accept it willingly." She was startled at her response, yet it seemed natural and easy.

She watched again as his words came across the screen.

"I would reach for you then and hold you close to me – allowing you to feel. To cry...whatever it is you need. I will be here for you."

Loghan closed her eyes as she allowed her thoughts to continue to explore. *I would continue to lean into you as well...I would feel your warm body ...my eyes closing and allowing myself to be enveloped in your kindness...I may slowly lift my head and search for your eyes...*

Suddenly, her eyes flew open. She bolted upright, blinking as if waking from a deep sleep. She shook her head and glanced at the computer screen, her pulse quickening as she read the words the last words she typed: "He was 25."

"What the...?" Her voice broke the silence of the room, her cheeks warming as the reality sank in. She stared at the screen trying to gather her scattered thoughts. Had she really just been daydreaming...fantasizing?

Jesus...what the...?! She couldn't believe this was happening, what was wrong with her? This was not her. Or was it? Loghan had always been so buttoned-up, so proper. She would never talk to a stranger. Yet, here she was, talking to a man she had never met.

Loghan was always in her head, working things out. Looking for logical meaning in things that otherwise, didn't make sense. Why couldn't she just allow herself to "be." Just this once...what could it hurt? She reminded herself she had started her evening, saying she would leave her memories on hold.

She felt invigorated and alive... and David, whoever he was, felt real to her. This moment...connection, or whatever the hell it was.

"Hello? Are you there, darling...? Did I ask too much?"

"Yes... I'm here. I'm sorry – I have to take a call." She lied again. Little did he know the conversation she had just had with herself.

"Of course. I understand. Another time I hope, my dear?"

She rubbed her forehead, feeling a rush of embarrassment. Focus, Loghan, she thought. She agreed quickly. *"Yes, another time. It's getting late. Goodnight, David."*

"Goodnight, Loghan. Sleep well."

She jumped up at the chance to escape. Loghan closed her laptop and walked to her bedroom, with a sleepy, large tabby closely following her from behind.

He leaned back in his chair, removed the VPN token and smiled.

How very much he enjoyed this light-hearted conversation. Who was this lovely, Loghan? he pondered. Oh, I do like this one very much. She's delightful...delightful, indeed.

He settled back into the leather chair, poured himself another martini and closed his laptop.

Chapter 16

Jodie pulled her long, shapely legs into the passenger side of the Porsche 911 Carrera. Finally, there was a break in the weather and she and Barrett made the most of the opportunity. She did consider staying in bed the rest of the day as the two of them lazily made love all morning long. However, they reluctantly decided they required sustenance if they were invested in a command performance of the mornings' activities. Jodie was interested and the way Barrett looked at her as she slid into the car spoke volumes.

Pulling away from their hotel with a lurch, Jodie pulled her scarf around her tighter to ward off the chilly air. The convertible top was down, the sun shining, as they whisked through the city streets. Jodie looked at Barrett and smiled as the muted winter sun bounced a glare off his dark sunglasses.

Barrett caught her smile and returned one, equally promising. Jodie smiled and tipped her head back on the seat, thanking her good fortune. She didn't know what she did so right, but she was certainly glad that seemed to be the case. She was utterly caught up in her unexpected romance with Barrett. Life was good, she thought and settled back into the seat to enjoy the ride.

The last several weeks swirled around Jodie like a whirlwind, her thoughts spiraling back to that fateful night of meeting Barrett Rohan. Their impromptu meeting, set against the backdrop of his nightclub, had been more charged than she expected. Smoldering glances and flirtatious exchanges filled the air as easily as the jazz music that filled the bar. Though Barrett's magnetic gaze and exceptional good looks made it almost impossible to leave, Jodie somehow managed to compose herself, thanking him for the drink and setting up a formal time to discuss business.

A few days later, with nerves steeled and a clear purpose in mind of securing his business, Jodie returned for their formal meeting and discussion. The meeting did not disappoint. Barrett, sharp and direct with an edge of European charm, listened as she laid out the vision for **Northern California at a Glance**. By the end, not only had he signed the contract securing his advertising business, but he placed a hefty advance on the work she promised would follow. Jodie's pride surged - not just in landing the deal but in holding her own under Barrett's intense, roguish gaze.

Her father, Tony, was thrilled when she walked into his office to share the news, though she couldn't resist a playful jab, "Well, there you go, Dad...I landed the deal!" Waving the signed contract in the air. His smile said it all, a hint of pride woven into his words. "You nailed it, Jodes. Congratulations!" Jodie playfully punched her dad on the arm. Jodie laughed, shaking her head. Securing Barrett Rohan's business was just the start. She left the meeting with more than just a contract, a new date with Barrett was on the horizon - she knew then, whatever whirlwind had started wasn't about to slow down anytime soon.

She and Barrett hit it off immediately and Jodie, always the pragmatic one, tried to hold back as she knew he had no plans to stay in Sacramento. Why would this successful and handsome man stay here? She continued to hold back her interest each time they exchanged emails or calls over the next several days. She didn't want to jump into his bed and have it be nothing more. Yet, something about Barrett was different. She contemplated briefly, in the back seat of her Lyft home that night, that she could hook up with him - what harm could that be?

Jodie was a sexually liberated woman and if men could sleep around, why in the hell couldn't she? She was discerning when she took a man to bed, which wasn't often. Just when she was " in between" boyfriends. No, Jodie mused; Barrett was not that kind of guy. Well, he didn't come across that way. He was kind, intelligent, engaging and, holy shit...gorgeous.

In the following days, Barrett was quite intent on pursuing Jodie. He called her every day, asking her to meet for coffee, to which she replied,

"No, thank you." She told him that she didn't date her clients, which wasn't entirely true, but she knew it wasn't good practice. She continued to justify dismissing him and told herself he would leave and go off to another location for work. She would feel terrible. He would be that heartache, or at least that five pounds she may gain from eating ice cream to drown her sorrows.

She put him off the first few days and then she did what every red-blooded, heterosexual female would do...she said yes. She could hand off his account to someone else's parents should this date work into something more.

After that, she said yes to every other invite that followed. The first date turning into an entire day.

They met for coffee before work, lunch that afternoon and rounded the day off with a lovely dinner at The Firehouse Restaurant in Old Sacramento. They lingered over an elegant meal of seared scallops and summer truffles with baby squash tortellini. Barrett enjoyed an herb-crusted rack of lamb and they shared dessert, Grand Marnier Souffle.' Barrett reached across the table and gently held the spoon to her lips with the rich delicacy. Jodie was surprised at her own behavior when she returned his long gazes and smiles over the candlelight. She lost herself each time he spoke with his rich, Scottish burr.

She told herself over and over during dinner to get her shit together and stop behaving like a teenage girl, swooning over "the cute new boy." It was pointless and after dinner, cognacs arrived; they were headlong in conversation, sharing stories, laughing and diving deep into their backgrounds. There were no barriers, no awkward moments, only genuine interest and intrigue as they began to learn the story of one another. Each felt free and open to sharing their memories of families and growing up. It was a fantastic starting point for what seemed to be the date of a lifetime.

Jodie learned Barrett was an only child and was adopted when he was just a few weeks old. His parents, older than most, were well-off, and had everything they ever wanted except a child of their own. He grew up in Glasgow, Scotland, where the sun rarely shines, but the people are strong and resilient. He came into his parents' lives and they wished for nothing more. They showered him with love and dedication, as parents will. He shared that he was a good child, obedient and curious. He had everything a child could imagine; a large garden to run about and play, toys and bikes and as he grew older, horses and scooters to fill the adventurous life of a young, adolescent boy.

He was doted over, loved, cared for and he recalled many wonderful trips and adventures with his parents. Jodie loved hearing his childhood stories those few short hours over dinner.

They quietly strolled out into the calm winter night after they finished dinner on what felt like a marathon first date. Barrett lightly put his arm around her waist gently guiding Jodie toward the walkway; she acquiesced and leaned into his shoulder.

"How about a walk down to the waterfront. Not by my nightclub, but the riverboat..." He searched for the name, "Umm...the Delta King?" Jodie smiled at his recollection of the name of the riverboat.

"I would like that very much." Jodie smiled and thought, *what a perfect night...hell...what a perfect day this had been.* She spent every free moment she had during her busy workday to be with him. Barrett also made the time to be with her; he put a couple of meetings on hold he shared with her earlier and said he could make them up tomorrow.

Today was here and now.

They sauntered arm and arm through the quiet streets and Barrett was a perfect gentleman, wrapping his strong arm around her that made her feel protected and safe. Jodie leaned into him and looked around at her city, taking it in through fresh eyes this night.

Jodie loved her city of Sacramento; the capital of California had much to offer. Parts of the town were still small and quaint, while the downtown area provided just enough atmosphere, great food and ambiance. The surrounding areas were filled with suburban neighborhoods, tree-lined streets and warm, sunny weather for 8 months of the year. It was a wonderful place for active people and the Sacramento River was filled, every year, with kayakers, jet skis and boats trolling up and down the delta. She had lived here most of her life except when she went to college back east and struggled to think of herself being anywhere but here - Sacramento was home.

At Jodie's request, Barrett offered more details about his family.

His extended family was relatively small, with aunts on both his parents' sides. Barrett recalled his aunt on his mother's side, Betsy. She was lovely, warm and smelled of honeysuckle; Barrett smiled at the memory. Sadly, his parents were no longer alive and Betsy passed the previous year at the ripe old age of ninety-eight.

His other aunt, his father's sister Katherine, was still alive, but he hadn't seen her recently. She came and went in his life in fractured visits, but he always enjoyed seeing her. His father was rarely forthcoming with sharing information about his aunt, but he chalked it up to them not being close. He knew her to be the "eccentric" one in the family and she traveled the world, never staying in one place too long. She would send cards and letters and was very generous with her gifts and money. Barrett would have preferred to see her more frequently, but those occasions when she visited were special memories. She had planned a visit for the last few months, but Barrett knew she would come at the least expected time.

Barrett revealed to Jodie that he was educated in the finest schools in Europe and was not boastful about this; it was just a fact. Boarding school is common among the affluent in Europe. After boarding school, he went to Edinburgh University to major in business. He was fortunate to have a large trust fund and didn't have to work through college. It allowed him more time to focus on his studies and he was forever grateful for that opportunity. He graduated with his degree and obtained his Master's in International Business at the prestigious St. Andrews in Edinburgh.

The air was crisp and cool and Jodie pulled her coat closer around her neck. They walked down Old Sacramento's wood plank streets and made their way to the Delta King riverboat. This charming, old vessel certainly had a home in Sacramento and hundreds of people visited the beautifully restored riverboat daily.

The old riverboat deserved her retired state following her heyday back in the '20s when she first entered service. She ran transportation between San Francisco, Sacramento and San Joaquin Valley. In the '40s she was commissioned by the Navy to receive naval reservists and in the '50s, she served as home to men working for a large aluminum plant and needed housing. In 1981 the Delta King sunk in Richmond, California and to this day, the reason is unknown. As fate would have it, the damage was minimal and it was decided to raise her back up and restore her. She sits on the Sacramento Waterfront along Front Street, in Old Sacramento, in her renewed glory as a floating hotel and fine dining restaurant.

They found their way to the back of the riverboat, overlooking the large, red paddle wheel and sat down on the red velvet cushioned wrap-around bench. The view was lovely on this unseasonably calm winter night. The golden Tower Bridge glimmered to the left and the Sacramento riverbanks were lit and inviting to the night.

Barrett shifted slightly, letting a sigh escape. His deep, rich burr resonated quietly.

"This place, here, Sacramento and its unassuming charm. This is why I wanted to own a business here. I love the feel of this city, so much to offer and so many people aren't aware of its allure." He continued, "I've traveled to many places and met many people, but here, it's - he swept his arm to indicate the expansive view and his piercing blue eyes settled on Jodie. "Incredible, it truly is...incredible."

Their eyes met and locked and Jodie stopped breathing for a moment and felt a slight tremor in her body. There was acknowledgment in her eyes and Barrett leaned over and gently put his lips on hers. Jodie leaned into his kiss and allowed his lips and the darkness of the night full reign.

Chapter 17

Deagan dropped his worn leather bag in the foyer; his car keys rattled loudly as they landed in the ceramic bowl, one of his twin sisters made him years ago, on his table.

His eyes quickly surveyed his living room to be sure he wouldn't be embarrassed by some mess he didn't pick up. Then, relieved to see all was good, he moved toward the kitchen, with Loghan following behind. "Come on in, Loghan. Make yourself at home."

They left the office early that afternoon, headed to The Bank on J Street and had a great lunch. It was as if nothing ever happened between the two of them. Laughing and talking through lunch, they caught up and discussed everything. It was old times, friendship and ease, laughter and chatter. Deagan was happy to have somehow moved through their last several weeks of awkward detachment. Loghan appeared to be as well - she was all smiles and seemed more relaxed in her mannerisms toward Deagan.

"Can I get you something to drink? Wine? I have a great bottle of that malbec we like."

Loghan smiled, "That sounds delicious...I haven't had malbec from Myka Estates for a while. I love that wine."

"Me too...I always have a bottle or two tucked away in my wine fridge for special occasions or, just because." Deagan shrugged off his last comment of 'just because,' and smiled at Loghan. He moved to the sitting room that he converted to a sultry and inviting wine room. He reached into his large wine refrigerator and pulled out the bottle of wine.

"A perfect fifty-nine degrees of velvety delight," Loghan stated as she moved closer to peer into the wine refrigerator. "It's been a while since we've shared wine, Deagan. So, what else do you have in there? Anything new?" She smiled at him and her fingertips brushed over the wine bottles.

"Hmm...nothing that I can think of. Oh, wait...I have a great bottle of Cotes de Cruz from Myka Estates. Oh, and I have a Petite Sirah from Gwinllan Estate Winery in El Dorado County. Not to mention my new affinity for their port."

"Oh my, Cotes de Cruz?? Isn't that the wine with a smokey taste? Mmmm... Chewy rich berries and perfect tannins?" Loghan briefly recalled how she and Deagan shared a love of the grape and could talk about wines endlessly.

"Yep... I remember you loved that wine. Right up your alley." He smiled and laughed, exhibiting gentle laugh lines around his eyes and mouth. "Let's have that one the next time." Loghan returned the laugh and they entered the kitchen again through the archway between the two rooms. They talked briefly about the wineries they enjoyed and Deagan brought her up to speed on Gwinllan, as she hadn't been there yet.

"Great atmosphere, people, wine cave for the tasting room and not to mention amazing wines." He lingered on the word '*amazing*' and rolled his eyes to show his appreciation.

"Sounds fantastic, Deag...we should go sometime." Loghan realized the words came out so suddenly that she paused briefly and looked at Deagan. It was their first awkward moment and Deagan helped her recover and popped open the cork at just the right time.

Pop...! The sharp, tinny sound broke the awkward moment and they laughed.

The wine was poured and a cheese and fruit tray was quickly put together by Loghan; they moved into the wine room and settled down.

Deagan selected music from his phone and the perfectly placed speakers on either side of the room came to life. Deagan had a wide variety of interests in music but opted for a more relaxed playlist tonight and started with Blue by SG Lewis. The ethereal music surrounded the room and Deagan turned it down low so it would not distract. They relaxed into the conversation; it was easy and light. Deagan enjoyed being in this space with Loghan; he noticed she was checking her phone and her brow furrowed.

"Everything ok?" Deagan tipped his head in question.

"Oh, yes...sorry," she placed her phone back in her newly acquired, Kate Spade bag and turned back to face Deagan, with a meek smile. "My reminder on my calendar just popped up. I have a wedding to attend this weekend and I'm so last minute about the whole thing."

"Same one you mentioned a while back? College roommate, right?" Deagan smiled gently at her.

"Yes...Megan," she said quietly as she looked at Deagan and measured her response.

He had that sad look in his eyes. Loghan had seen it for the last three years now and knew it all too well. She knew Deagan was worried about her attending this wedding. It was that painful reminder that Ian was gone - there would be no wedding for Loghan to plan. No future to look forward to with Ian. She recalled briefly how she shared this loss with Deagan one night when she was in tears. She returned his gentle smile, pulled her chair closer and put her hand on his arm. He was warm and his flesh was taught and muscular beneath her hand. She noted the contrast between his strong, tan arms to her soft, fair skin. She looked him in the eyes and spoke softly.

"I'm good, Deagan. I've thought about this for a while now. It's more than time for me to step back into the world," her voice soft, "I can't allow my feelings to interfere with Megan and Conner's wedding." Deagan nodded but he couldn't mask the pain he knew was showing in his eyes.

He broke his gaze with Loghan and looked down a moment, trying to shield his feelings. He knew this was a massive step for Loghan to attend a wedding...and not just *a* wedding. It was her friend from college and they had both talked about planning their weddings together one day.

Deagan looked up as soon as he felt he had recovered and gave her a weak smile.

"I just want you to be ok, Loghan. I can't imagine how hard these last few years have been for you," his eyes were filled with compassion. "If you say you're good, that's all I need." His smile and eyes became warm and Loghan could feel his genuine care and concern. Deagan held Loghan's eyes for a moment and nodded slightly.

This is nice, she thought. She didn't mean to notice, but in that instant, something shifted. She looked at Deagan, really looked at him, as if the familiar lines of his face held something she's overlooked before. A strange warmth crept up her neck and her heart quickened in a way that left her both surprised and flustered. She didn't know, but in that moment, it was as if she was seeing him anew. Their eyes met, lingering a beat longer than usual and in the stillness, a silent understanding seemed to pass between them.

She caught herself, leaning back - breaking the gaze. Her cheeks warmed as the moment unraveled, slipping through her grasp like silk. She forced herself to look away, scanning the room, searching for a distraction. But the feeling lingered, a whisper against her skin, an imprint she couldn't shake - and maybe didn't want to.

Deagan sensed her change and shifted in his chair, reaching for his glass of wine and popped a few grapes in his mouth.

"OK...Tell me where you are in your article?" He shifted the subject so quickly that Loghan hardly noticed as he wiped a small bead of sweat from his forehead. He continued, "Every night I leave work, you're buried in your computer. I've never seen you so focused. It's great." Deagan smiled and tilted his head in anticipation.

Loghan placed her wine glass on the end table and crossed her shapely legs. Deagan tried not to allow his eyes to linger, watching her shift in her chair, raising her skirt slightly to allow her legs to cross easily. He looked away and took a sip of his wine. Jesus...he thought and hoped she didn't see him steal a glance.

" Well, I'm deep in research...talking to women online and asking questions of what they are looking for; be it a relationship, companionship, or sex, I have found one common denominator; the women want to feel desired- appreciated - sexy - made to feel like a woman." Loghan thoughtfully took a sip of her wine, her eyebrows raised with appreciation and she nodded slightly. She leaned over and tipped her glass toward Deagan. She continued her thoughts, "I've also found a darker side out on the internet. You never know who you are really talking to..." Her words drifted, making Deagan uneasy as he watched her process what she was about to say.

"I've had interviews with a few psychologists and a professor who teaches Digital Media at Sac State and it's been eye-opening, to say the least. There is an entire science behind us all - what motivates us to the sexes, why we respond to faceless words and how they can draw us in...we all want to be recognized and hiding behind a screen, we; at least women...we are braver, we can be forward and open - talk about anything and not feel..." she was looking for the right words again and paused until she found it... "vulnerable."

She picked up her wine glass again, tipped it toward her full lips and sipped. Deagan gathered she was deep in thought as her eyes drifted and seemed unfocused. He broke the pause with a gentle clearing of his throat.

"That is really great, Loghan. I mean...really great! The thread on not knowing who we - collectively, are talking to; I guess, as a man, I don't really think about that. We just "assume" we know we're talking to whomever they say they are."

"Exactly, I mean, no offense, but men don't have to think about that... I mean, by and large, men don't feel vulnerable and exposed. It can be dangerous out on the internet. For everyone, but especially women. On the other hand, we must be cautious as we are "out there" trying to meet Mr. Right...or, as someone I know says, *Mr. Right Now.*" She chuckled.

Deagan held back again, knowing better than to ask her anything too personal. The last time he shared his concern about her investigating and moving around in chat rooms - they had a problem. Nope...he wasn't going to say anything this time around, he thought. He didn't have to ask more questions as Loghan offered more detail.

Loghan took a quiet, deep breath. "I have been talking to someone online, a man. I mean, of course he is a man. It isn't someone acting to be a man or a boy, he's too knowledgeable...worldly." She was on a roll now and needed to tell Deagan everything.

"He is...interesting and articulate and I think I'm interested in what more he has to share." She looked up at Deagan and they locked eyes for a moment. Deagan felt the gut punch when she said, *"I've been talking to someone online...*" He heard the rest of what she said, but he was quietly reeling from her sudden admission.

Deagan's mind raced. He didn't know why she told him this. Did she know he was interested in her now? Did he give something away a moment ago when they were talking? He felt like they just had a 'moment,' when they locked eyes, but he must be way off. He had too many questions and needed to calm down. He was impressed with his recovery and feigned a relaxed response.

"Very cool, Loghan. Is he part of your research?" Something told him otherwise, but he didn't want to give it away should she not be aware of his feelings.

"Yes, he is." She lied. She knew this interaction between David and herself seemed a bit more, but just what? She didn't know.

She continued. "He seems to know his way around the ladies, literature, business and many other areas. He tells me, though, I'm "different," not like any other women he's had the pleasure of speaking to." She gave a slight sassy smile at Deagan. Again, her playfulness showed and this confused Deagan again. He didn't know what she was trying to convey, but he went with her mood.

"Oh yeah? Different? And is that what he said...? That you are a *pleasure* speaking to?" Deagan chided her and smiled. "He sounds old..." He said flatly.

Loghan returned his laugh and agreed. "He does sound old, but he tells me he's not. In his early 30's, but he's English."

"Oh...that explains it then!" Deagan laughed and thought this was a good time to segue into his news. They enjoyed the light moment and the conversation surrounding Loghan's article slowed.

"So, can I tell you what I'm working on now?" He didn't wait for her response, knowing she would be interested, so he reached for his laptop.

Deagan threaded the needle and brought Loghan up to speed on the women murdered in different parts of the country. They had discussed this topic a few times, but they left off weeks ago when they weren't really connecting, so Deagan filled her in.

"Dexter?" You heard from that creepy, greasy-haired little man in the coroner's office??" She replied incredulously.

"Yes...he is a creepy little bastard, that is for sure. But I did hear from him and it's freaking weird. I don't know why he's reached out to me, but whatever...he contacted me. He sent me a receipt last week that was found at the murder site of Cynthia DuBois in San Francisco. I can't figure out exactly what it is, but it looks like a bank receipt, but not entirely." Deagan moved his cursor over to his email and Loghan shifted her chair closer to him to get a better look. Deagan fought off how appealing she smelled, sweet and earthy, as her shoulder brushed against his.

"Here..." He clicked on the email from Dexter; Loghan quietly read it aloud and whispered the closing words of the email, "As always, you know it didn't come from me?" She inflicted the question at the end of the sentence. "What is his deal?" she asked with almost alarm in her voice.

Deagan shrugged it off and clicked on the attachment. The receipt opened up and Loghan leaned across his lap and pulled the laptop closer. Deagan moved back slightly. "Sorry." Loghan sheepishly grinned.

She continued to look at the image and the smudged lettering that was difficult to read.

"I know what this is, Deagan. I recognize the image. It's a receipt, all right. It's from a bank here in Sacramento. It's a safety deposit box receipt."

They both leaned back in their chairs and looked at one another.

"Why would there be a safety deposit receipt from Sacramento in her apartment in San Francisco?" Deagan and Loghan picked up their wine, sipped and considered.

*****

The rain pelted down in sheets, blurring her vision as she ran down the darkened street, her heels hammering against the slick pavement. Water sprayed up in cold bursts, soaking her legs, but she couldn't stop.

Her breath tore raggedly in her throat, each gasp cutting her chest like knives. The blaring lights of taxis and ride shares streaked past, indifferent to her frantic, outstretched arms and desperate cries. She was a blur, a ghost in the night, ignored and nearly invisible.

"Stop...Anyone!"

Finally, a yellow cab screeched to a halt and she didn't slow down, lunging at the door with trembling fingers. She stumbled into the back seat, barely managing to pull the door shut before banging her hands on the back of the driver's seat.

"Anywhere...just, **GO...GO!**" she gasped, her voice raw with panic. The driver, a middle-aged man with a kind, but puzzled face, stared at her in the rear-view mirror, his eyes wide with confusion. He hesitated, his foot hovering over the gas pedal, but she wasn't having it. She slammed her hand against the seat with desperate force.

" I said go, goddammit! **GO!**"

That seemed to jolt him into action and the car lurched forward, the tires skidding on the wet road before finding their grip.

She leaned back, every muscle trembling and let out a shuddering, relieved breath, though her eyes flicked constantly to the window, searching the shadows for any sign of pursuit.

Her hand dove into her purse, rummaging until her fingers closed around her phone. She let out a breathy, half-crazed laugh, a spark of hope amidst the terror.

When she raised the phone to her ear, her voice faltered, stammering and broken.

"Hello? Hello....? My, my...My name is Jenny...Jenny Harper...and I...I ...I just escaped from...from..." She swallowed, her throat raw, forcing herself to steady, to speak, to get the words out.

She gathered all she had and cried out the words into her phone.

"I - I ... was almost murdered tonight!"

Chapter 18

The sun continued to shine as Barrett and Jodie sped down the highway and turned onto Highway 1. The brisk winter wind whipped through the convertible and the air was invigorating and crisp.

Jodie took deep, cleansing breaths of the ocean air and admired the beach as the car sliced neatly across the highway. Barrett mentioned he had a special place in mind for brunch and was looking forward to treating Jodie to the views he knew would be waiting.

The Cliff House was a favorite venue for Barrett with its spectacular views, California cuisine and a staff that knew him by name. Parking could be challenging here as it's first come, first served, but Barrett had a close friend who managed the National Parks Service, which oversaw the restaurant and had an "in" most people would not possess.

On one of his many visits to the restaurant, he was offered by the manager to call ahead any time and was told they would be delighted to provide a little "special treatment." Barrett appreciated their recognition of his loyalty and, God knows, how much money he tossed in their direction and today was the first time he took them up on the offer.

As he pulled up to the restaurant, he found they blocked a spot up front for him. A nicely dressed young man ran out of the restaurant and Barrett smiled as if on cue. The dark-haired young man moved the cones to the side and Barrett sheepishly grinned at Jodie as she lifted an eyebrow and gave him a wry grin.

"Oh, really?" She said as she looked at him and unbuckled her seatbelt.

"Ummm... it's not that big of a deal. I called in a favor." Barrett said as dismissively as he could but failed miserably, given the look on his face.

Barrett spent quite a bit of time in San Francisco as he had numerous restaurants and bars around the city and the outer region of the Bay Area. Barrett had many irons in the fire and recently opened three high-profile venues, including The Glasgow. He was glad the last few weeks had been what he considered downtime. He was in between deals and openings and with his new nightclub/venue in Sacramento taking up much of his time, it allowed him the opportunity to spend time with Jodie and get to know her.

That was precisely what he planned on doing.

Barrett hopped out of the car and his stride had barely hit the pavement when he noticed the young concierge - a Gen Z kid, eager and quick on his feet - already hurrying toward Jodie's door. Barrett felt a surge of instinct, that gentlemanly urge that had become second nature over the years. Before the young man could reach the handle, Barrett's hand quickly shot out, his fingers wrapping around the cool metal first.

The young man stumbled to a halt, his eyes widening slightly at the unexpected hand-off.

"Excuse me, Mr. Rohan. I'm sorry."

Barrett gave a polite nod. "Not a problem, Robert," he replied, glancing down at his name tag on his freshly ironed shirt. "I'll take it from here."

Understanding flickered across the young man's face and he offered a slight, knowing smile, his shaggy hair falling into his eyes as he tipped his head. This wasn't the first time he'd been gently redirected by a gentleman who wanted to make his own impression. Barrett discreetly placed a folded $20 bill into the young man's hand and his grin stretched into a lopsided, appreciative smirk. With a nod, he stepped back, watching as Barrett opened Jodie's door with a calm confidence that spoke volumes.

"Thank you, sir." He tucked the bill in his pocket and trotted ahead of Barrett and Jodie.

Barrett placed his arm around Jodie's waist and they walked in sync to the front door. The door was opened for them and Jodie stepped inside and immediately her eyes were drawn to the sweeping views of the Pacific Ocean and Ocean Beach below. Before she realized it, her feet propelled her toward the bar where she could continue to see the ocean waves crashing against the rocks.

"The view is magnificent!" Jodie's bright green eyes opened with wonder. She couldn't believe she'd never been here before, but she was happy to share this experience with Barrett. She experienced many beautiful venues and traveled a bit herself; maybe it was just being in San Francisco with Barrett, but it all felt new. Jodie dismissed her thoughts - all she knew was -it didn't matter. Jodie felt radiant - like a woman who had been adorned from dusk till dawn. Her body felt languid, her skin tingling with the memory of Barrett's hands tracing over her body. She demurely smiled as if she had a secret as the maitre d' showed them to a corner table in the bar.

As they walked by others chatting and sipping cocktails, she could feel all eyes on them as they were seated at the best location in the bar. All the surrounding tables were crowded and they walked past customers waiting in the lobby.

"I'm so happy we're here, Barrett, but I feel almost... guilty!" Jodie leaned across the table and whispered discreetly.

"Honestly, I've never done this before. I mean, lass, I've never come here and pulled the *"I'm important"* card. I feel funny about it, too, if I may be honest." He smiled at her, scooted his chair closer to her and whispered, "I don't feel too badly, though." He smiled a wicked grin and a wink followed.

Jodie laughed with Barrett and couldn't recall the last time she felt so free and thrilled. Could this be happening? She turned the thought over in her mind and decided to stop worrying and "what if'ing" every detail. Instead, she would lean into this time with Barrett and enjoy every moment.

The two made small talk over the menu and enjoyed mimosas as they looked out the vast windows overlooking the San Francisco Bay. The waves crashed and lunged angrily against the rocks and the views were breathtaking. Seagulls danced in the wind as they fought for their place on the jagged rocks and pecked at one another for the meager food findings.

Barrett and Jodie settled into a late brunch and commented on the beautiful weather the day had unexpectedly provided. A contrast from the night - the weather was cold and rained much of the night and Jodie reflected on being all too happy being warm and snuggled in the lush bed last night.

The evening was the most incredible night for Jodie. She was fairly certain Barrett felt the same. She almost drifted off while waiting for him to arrive, which would have been a perfect shame. Instead, she arrived at the hotel early and had time to settle into the room. Barrett had a meeting in San Francisco that started at 5 P.M., so they agreed to meet at the hotel later in the evening. That worked out perfectly for Jodie as she had work that kept her occupied until 5:30 at her office.

She wrapped things up at work and planned to call a Lyft and head to Richmond to take BART into San Francisco. She preferred not to deal with her car; besides, she didn't want to have two cars once Barrett arrived.

Her phone chimed and she smiled. Barrett was checking in on her status to leave and she quickly caught him up on her progress for their weekend, mentioning she was just getting ready to call for a Lyft.

"Lyft? Oh no, lass." Barrett's rich voice rumbled through her phone. "That is why I was calling you. It's my fault that we're not going together, because of my late meeting tonight. My clients changed the time on me... damn them. So, I'm sending a car for you." He made it so simple, she thought and she was quiet on the other end of the call.

"That's ok, isn't it, Jodie?" Barrett's voice held traces of concern. He hoped he didn't overstep or just assume.

"It's wonderful." Her voice was higher than usual when she responded, but it wasn't every day that she had a handsome man make things happen for her. Who knows? Maybe they will play hooky on Monday and carry the weekend over, she thought casually.

The details settled, Jodie walked outside the office and there was a car waiting for her, just as Barrett said. Incredible, she thought as she slid into the sexy Town Car.

The drive to San Francisco was uneventful and rained most of the way. Winter in Northern California was always the same; cloudy and rainy, with a muted sunny day from time to time. It was hard to focus at work today with her weekend plans ahead, so Jodie made use of her time in the car.

She responded to emails and made a few more calls and once she felt her tasks were complete, she texted her group message to her friends, Tina and Loghan.

Her friends knew the protocol - when they were out with a new guy or, on an "adventure," as on occasion with Jodie, they let each other know where they were.

"Safety Girls," Tina would laugh, referring to a line in Pretty Woman.

Tina was the first to respond to Jodie's group message, making them aware she was heading to San Francisco with Barrett for the weekend.

'OMG! Is this it? You know...the first time for you two?'

Tina didn't wait for the response as she knew it to be true. There had been plenty of "girl chat" in text messages over the last several weeks. So, the trio knew exactly where Jodie and Barrett were in the trajectory of a new relationship. *'Have fun! Don't do anything I wouldn't do...much!'* Tina's response came immediately.

Jodie replied: *'Thanks! I will have fun! Don't worry! He's amazing! I'm sitting in the back seat of a black Lincoln Town Car. Plush leather seats, music surrounding my ears and San Francisco just coming into view.'*

Loghan's response followed right behind: *'Sounds terrific, Jodie! Be careful and have so much fun!'*

Tina couldn't stand the civility a moment longer: *'Careful my ass! Climb him like a tree!'*

Her message was followed by the trio of friends with crying, laughing faces and a few more sassy comments.

'Love you, ladies!' Jodie signed off and told her friends she would be in touch a few times during the weekend. There was nothing better than good girlfriends you could count on in life and Jodie considered herself very fortunate in this area.

The sleek black Town Car eased to a stop in front of the iconic, Mark Hopkins Hotel, it's polished brass doors glinting under the warm glow of the grand entryway lights. Jodie stepped out, her heels clicking against the cobblestone driveway as she craned her neck upward, marveling at the regal stature of the 19-story landmark. The top floor seemed to kiss the heavens, promising luxury as lofty as its perch.

Inside, the air was infused with the soft sent of fresh flowers and the quiet hum of piano music coming from speakers discreetly hidden in the tall ceilings. The marble floors gleamed beneath the ornate crystal chandelier that created a constellation of lights across the lobby.

At the front desk, Jodie was met with smiles so polished they could have been framed. The concierge addressed her by name even before she introduced herself and within moments, her reservation was confirmed, her key card handed over with an almost ceremonial reverence.

"The Penthouse Suite is ready for you, Ms. Rice," the desk clerk said, as if unveiling a crown jewel. The bellhop - a young man in an impeccably tailored uniform-handled her luggage as though it contained treasures. The elevator's surprisingly tight quarters were mirrored and golden accents gleaming, he pushed the button for the 18th floor, but Jodie was too captivated by her surroundings to notice.

The suite was everything she had dreamed of. The moment the door swung open, she felt her breath hitch. Three massive windows dominated the far wall, framing a panoramic view of San Francisco that could silence a symphony. The city lights glittered like a thousand diamonds scattered across black velvet, their glow reflected faintly on the dark waters of the bay. Above, the sky brooded with dark, swirling clouds, adding a dramatic contrast to the scene below.

The furnishings inside the suite were a masterclass in elegance. Plush sofas upholstered in velvet invited her to sink in and the dining table, set with crystal glassware, was crowned with an arrangement of white roses. A bottle of chilled champagne waiting in a silver bucket, a single note tucked beside it:

Welcome to your home above the clouds: Barrett xo

He didn't miss a thing, she smiled and slipped the note into her bag, for safekeeping.

The bellhop showed Jodie the amenities, the bar and the view and ushered her into the sitting room. Jodie was impressed with her acting skills as she was polite, yet blase' as if she'd been here many times and was no longer impressed. She thanked the bellhop, offered him a sincere smile and handed him a generous tip.

She opted to save the champagne for her and Barrett and made herself a drink, showered and picked out something "comfortable" and sexy to greet Barrett when he arrived. She was tired as the long week ended and Barrett suggested they go to San Francisco to relax and unwind. She loved the idea of the two of them running off to the city for a romantic weekend.

He promised her more of getting to know one another and she agreed it would be a perfect weekend. She loved the early stages of a relationship and becoming familiar with one another.

Barrett was unexpected, that was certain.

A few hours passed and Jodie relaxed on the opulent, king-sized bed. She considered its comfort, leaned back on the billowy pillow and dismissed the thought as she knew tonight would be spent doing something other than sleeping. Jodie was a little nervous while contemplating this thought, which she found interesting. She had to acknowledge she felt differently about Barrett and quietly cautioned herself. Still concerned about being swept up in romance, as Barrett lived so far away. She would remain practical and she knew better but told herself this was just for now.

Jodie flipped through a magazine passing the time and closed her eyes for just a moment when she heard the door click. She sat up quickly and slid off the bed. She smiled at Barrett sheepishly wondering if he thought she was sleeping. Barrett came to her immediately, scooping her in his arms and nuzzling her neck. She felt her legs turn to water and leaned into his warm whispers and deep burr.

"I'm so sorry, lass. I'm later than expected. Did you get my message?" She loved that he called her "lass" or, darling and smiled each time as the words rolled off his tongue with a lilt. She loved his sense of decorum and old-world manners. Her eyes were hooded from sleep and nodding in response to his question, she dissolved into his strong arms.

"Mmm...hmm...I did get your message. I was just passing the time and relaxing." She mused and wondered when she would stop swooning over him? She brushed off the thoughts and returned his nuzzles with a warm, deep kiss.

He smelled of rain and musk, his overcoat slightly damp; he tossed it over a chair, without thought.

His face was slightly damp as she kissed him. "You're wet," she murmured when she paused between kisses.

He kissed her neck and his breath danced lightly on her skin in whispers. "Yes...a bit. I left my damn brolly at the meeting." She smiled as she had recently been submerged into Scottish slang since meeting Barrett. She knew brolly to be "umbrella," and she laughed as she reached to tousle his dark, wavy hair.

"Mmm... I've got a good mind to take you straight to bed, lass." She reluctantly pulled herself away from his warm mouth, sauntered to the bar and poured him a scotch.

"Well, what's taking you so long?" She smiled at him and handed him the drink.

"Oh, thank you." His eyes showed appreciation at the drink and locked on her long and lean body. His voice drifted as he eyed her seductively.

"I've already had a drink tonight with the clients for the new location." He continued with a lazy smile as his eyes rolled up her long legs and admired her flimsy nightie.

"I think I may hold off on that drink, I see something that looks far more inviting." He gently ran his hands down her waist and his eyes shimmered a dark, impossible blue filled with want and need.

The apprehension Jodie was feeling fell away like dust. She allowed herself to fold into the night and found safety in Barrett's arms. The rain tapped against the window throughout the night and they were unaware. Surrounded by the warmth of twisted sheets and responsive skin, they created their own heat during the drizzly night and drifted off in a sated slumber.

Brunch was delicious and Jodie shared some of the other large accounts she was working on currently and how she plans out her meetings and angle to capture the interest of her clients. Barrett listened intently and had several questions about how she manages so many clients at one time and, more importantly, how did she find out about his nightclub, The Glasgow.

Jodie smiled and stretched her long legs under the table just enough to place her high-heeled foot next to Barrett's foot. Barrett arched his eyebrow and smiled at her.

"My, my... now...I didn't take you for a 'footsie playing' lass..." His response was deep and resonating and his eyes crinkled at the edges with a smile. "I'm just....keeping you interested." She replied seductively and returned the most beautiful smile he thought he'd ever seen. They both laughed and found themselves comfortable in one another's space. They talked over eggs Benedict and mimosa's as their waiter paid them considerable attention.

"Mr. Rohan, is there anything else I can get for you now?" Barrett looked at Jodie and she shook her head. "No, thank you, Nate. I think we'll take the check now." The waiter left the bill and Barrett slid a few large bills inside the leather holder. He leaned back a moment, turned his attention to the large windows again and noted the clouds were rolling in again.

"What a lovely morning and brunch. Thank you, Barrett." Jodie smiled and ran her hand gently across the side of his hair. Barrett turned to her and smiled. Jodie's brows creased in concern.

"What's this? I didn't notice this last night." Jodie traced her fingers across a scratch mark on Barrett's jawline.

Barrett ran his strong fingers over the mark dismissively. "Ahhh, you appeared to be preoccupied last night," he winked, "Tis' nothing, lass. I scratched my face last night by accident."

Jodie leaned over and kissed the mark gently. "Well, I hope it doesn't hurt."

"No...no, it doesn't at all." He winked and smiled at her tenderly. Jodie leaned in once more and gave Barrett another gentle kiss. She thought better of their plans to go to Union Square for a stroll and afternoon shopping. Barrett seemed to share the same notion, casting a knowing look glance her way with a determined expression in his deep blue eyes.

He is simply amazing, she marveled as Barrett stood from his seat and offered her his hand.

Chapter 19

Jenny sat with a blanket pulled around her in a small room in the back of the police department.

"Here, Miss Harper. It's a poor excuse for coffee, but it's warm and will take the chill off you." The kind-eyed detective, Charlotte Kinder, handed her the steamy paper cup. "Careful, it's hot as hell," she gently warned.

Jenny gratefully accepted the coffee, shivering and took a small sip. The bitter taste ran over her tongue and jolted her senses alert. She had been sitting in the room for several hours now, providing descriptions of her night of terror. She offered every sliver of detail and specific characteristics of the man she met who called himself, Aidan.

His accent, his eyes…Jesus, she thought. She recalled those incredible, piercing blue eyes of his, thinking they were initially memorizing, but they turned gray, filled with mania. She shuddered at the memory. She went over everything she could remember multiple times to ensure nothing was missed. She was rattled and still feeling the shock from the horrifying events of her evening.

"Take your time, Miss Harper. We don't want to rush you. We know this has been an excruciating event for you."

Detective Kinder was in her third year as a detective in the San Francisco police department. She was 7 years out of the academy and finished number two in her class. She surprised most, as her stature was diminutive, but she held her own during grueling physical agility sessions as well as everyone agreed she ran like a gazelle. She was described as intelligent and keen and had the tremendous mental capacity her fellow officers longed for and she quickly moved up the line. She was a sharp detective, friend and well respected. Pretty and petite, her eyes the color of amber, slightly almond-shaped and glinted with kindness. She sat down next to Jenny and patted her arm gently. Jenny accepted the show of compassion and decided she liked Detective Kinder very much.

Jenny was in rough shape and overwhelmed. She was bruised and had a few minor cuts on her face, cleaned and dressed at the hospital earlier in the night. They didn't need to complete a full rape kit, but they did scrape her finger nails for debris and ran lint rollers over her clothing for possible hair and fiber. She felt well enough to return to the police station and answer questions.

She knew she was damn lucky to have escaped her horrific night and she recalled the details repeatedly. She couldn't get his voice out of her head. Angry that she allowed herself to be coaxed to his room and let her lust almost get her killed. She dropped her head down on her chest and gathered herself again.

The kind eyes looked at her across the table. "I want to go over the next steps with you and if you have any questions, please ask. I know we asked earlier, but is there anyone you want to call other than your friend, Erin? Detective Kinder opened her notepad again and clicked her pen, the sound echoed in the cramped room.

Jenny, still visibly overcome, shook her head back and forth. "No, no one that I can think of right now." She adjusted herself in the chair and took another sip of coffee. She wrinkled her nose at the taste again.

"I know, I'm sorry," Detective Kinder eyed the simmering coffee again, nodding her head in agreement. "We have a coffee run every morning at 7:00 A.M. I'll make sure you get a decent cup of coffee. We should be just about done with all this around that time." The detective smiled softly and she looked back down at her notes, pointed to them and Jenny nodded.

The detective continued, "I think we have everything needed for the composite drawing and it should be completed shortly. Our sketch artist starts with the computer software and then draws a composite. We should get really close to your description. Once that is complete, it will be posted everywhere and released to the press." Detective Kinder looked up just as the door to the small room opened. It was Detective Thornton, her partner on the case as well. The detective had three cups of steaming Pete's Coffee and a bag containing something that filled the room with the warm scent of vanilla and cinnamon.

Jenny looked up and nodded at the detective as he handed her a coffee and the bag. His large, beefy hand dropped the bag on the small table. She pushed it aside and cupped her hands around the coffee.

He shrugged, "I thought you might be hungry and I know damn well that coffee you're trying to drink is crap."

Jenny sighed again. "I just feel so - so foolish. I thought that was his picture on the app and I was ..." she sat back in her chair, tears trailing down her cheeks,"...I was so caught up in the night and being at The Mark Hopkins and going to, The Top of the Mark. Her voice quivered slightly as she recalled. "When I met him, he looked a bit like his picture he had online, but not really, if that makes sense. I mean...he looks really close to the photo...," her voice trailed off in a whisper. "His eyes are wrong...totally wrong."

The tears came in a constant stream and Detective Kinder pushed the box of Kleenex close to Jenny. She reached out and grabbed a handful, wadding them in her lap.

"It can happen, Miss Harper," Detective Kinder reassured." Please don't be so hard on yourself. We're going to do everything we can to find this suspect."

Jenny nodded, "I just thought I did everything right - you know?" She wiped her tears with the back of her shaking hand and blew her nose. "We texted and talked a bit before we met up. I met him at a public place. Can't you see if there is footage on the surveillance cameras? They must have something!" Jenny's voice elevated.

Detective Thornton, a large man with 20 years as a detective, looked at his partner and took his cue from her seemingly imperceptible nod.

"We're reviewing the footage now, Miss Harper," he moved his chair closer to her and folded his thick fingers on the table. "I'm sorry, but I can tell you the preliminary results show he's not in full view at any time."

"We can see him at the front desk, checking in. We see him walking down the hallway and going around a corner. We can see him in all areas with security cameras, but he clearly knew the locations as he made himself out of view of the cameras or turned his face away."

Jenny pulled the blanket around her tighter and rocked slightly. "This can't be." she whispered.

Detective Thornton's voice grew quiet. "I know it's frustrating and unbelievable, Miss Harper. This happens sometimes, but we're still reviewing. He's made it difficult, but we will continue to review every bit of information. He knows what he's doing. He paid in cash at the front desk and the card he put on file is tied to the false name he used."

The shrill ring of the phone cut through the brief silence like a blade and Jenny jumped in her seat, her hands clutching the coffee, nearly crushing the paper cup. Her chest rose and fell with shallow breaths, her wide eyes darting toward the offending noise. Every sound, every movement seemed amplified in the oppressive atmosphere of the small interrogation room. Every nerve she had was frayed.

The kind detective looked at her with empathy and reached for the phone.

"Yes?" her voice surprisingly stern and professional. "Bring it in, please."

Detective Kinder hung up the phone, turning to Jenny. "That was the forensic artist. He's completed the rendering of the suspect. He's coming right in."

Jenny sat upright and placed the coffee on the table, spilling some with her unsteady hands.

"What if it doesn't look like him? What if no one recognizes him?" Jenny's questions came in a rapid pace.

"Miss Harper. It's best to let us take one step at a time. We have to go through a process of steps to make eliminations." Detective Thornton scooted his chair back and the sound vibrated through the tiny room.

"The renderings are usually very close based on previous history and experience," Detective Kinder took over, to soften the information. It was how they worked so well together - yin and yang. "That's why it's best to sit with the victims early and get as much detail as possible. You know, yourself, having spent more than 3 hours describing your attacker." Her kind eyes made Jenny feel a sense of understanding and compassion.

The door shot open and all three in the room stood up.

"Christ, James...," Detective Thornton boomed. "How many times have I told you to tap on the door and not bomb right in?!" Thornton was clearly agitated and took the folder from James. His thick finger jabbed at the door showing James the way out.

"Sorry, Detectives...Miss..." The young man nodded and left the room, quietly closing the door behind him.

"God damn, kid..." Thornton grumbled under his breath. He looked up and noticed both women were looking at him with anticipation. "Sorry," he shrugged and they all sat down.

Sliding the thick paper from the folder, Thornton placed the drawing on the table and slid it across to Jenny. She sat at the edge of her chair and whatever composure she had earlier found for those few moments was now lost.

She picked up the drawing with shaking fingers and fixated on the drawing.

"That's him...that is **him**" her shaky voice found volume and strength.

"Jesus...." Jenny sat back again in her chair. "Well, then...now, what?" exasperated, she released a huge, shuddering sigh. "How do you catch this fucker?"

Detective Kinder looked up with determination in her eyes. "We will...I promise you. We will."

Chapter 20

Loghan walked into the kitchen and dropped the mail on the counter. It had been a long day and she was exhausted. Day drinking with Deagan left her famished and she didn't feel like cooking. So instead, she headed straight to the refrigerator and grabbed leftovers from her favorite Thai restaurant of Drunken Noodles and Jasmine Rice.

She moved fluidly through the kitchen and dished up the food, placing it in the microwave and grabbing a bottle of Barbera from her wine refrigerator.

Harry greeted her in the kitchen with his soft, furry body and lapped around her legs a few times. He was starved for attention and rolled over on the kitchen floor. Loghan was always pleased to see Harry and ready to oblige his request for attention.

"Oh, big boy... you're getting hair all over my skirt," Loghan brushed her hand across her A-line skirt, "Naughty, boy," she playfully smiled and gracefully bent down to reward him with a pat and tickle on his furry belly. Harry purred, settled into the attention and relaxed for a few moments until the microwave timer sounded off. He jumped at the sound and scampered out of the kitchen in a flash and Loghan stood up and smoothed out her skirt.

"Well, that was a quick visit," she called after Harry and laughed gently at his skittishness. She took a moment and debated her hunger level and if her heels and skirt could wait to be removed. It was not a hard decision and Loghan made her way to the bedroom, where Harry was already settled on her bed. Loghan stepped out of her heels first and placed her Kate Spade bag in the shelf cubby, in her ample closet.

She smiled for a moment as she admired the organized and spacious walk-in closet, turning a memory over in her mind.

She was thrilled when she and Ian found this cute apartment downtown on 8th street. It was right across from Southside Park, with its running trails, large duck pond and local artwork nested throughout the park. It was a Victorian house that was refurbished and turned into an apartment and was completely updated with new appliances, flooring and heating and air. When you lived in Sacramento, you depended on air conditioning in the summer with the many hot and sultry days and nights.

The final touches on the apartment were just completed before she and Ian moved in and Loghan knew they were fortunate to find such a great location. They joked it was bonus points for all the updates, urban neighborhoods and running trails so close by. Ian, the more reserved of the two, held back his initial enthusiasm and pretended he wasn't completely sold on the apartment. However, when he saw Loghan's bright green eyes light up over the large walk-in closet, he dropped his shoulders and shook his head, "Where will my things go?," he playfully teased as they signed the lease.

The memory tugged at Loghan's heart, a bittersweet ache that made her smile faintly as her fingers brushed across the fabric of her clothes. Soft blouses, skirts, tailored jeans and jackets. She recalled Ian saying he only needed a sliver of space and the rest he could put in the hall closet. She paused, her hand hovering over the section where Ian's things had once hung. She held on to a few shirts and suit jackets of Ian's. She remembered how he'd laughed, insisting he only needed, "a sliver of space," and relegating the rest of his wardrobe to the hall closet. His compromise had been more than practical - it had been his love language.

Her fingers grazed the edges of the few remaining shirts and suit jackets, tucked in the corner like relics of a life once lived. Ian had always wanted to make her happy and she hoped she'd done the same for him. The thought warmed her, but she felt the now-familiar sting of grief creeping in.

Loghan closed her eyes and took a deep breath. She wasn't pushing Ian's memory aside-far from it. She was choosing, deliberately, to move forward.

Last week, for the first time in three years, she thought about calling her old counselor. It had surprised her how the thought hadn't brought dread, but rather a tentative sense of hope. Back then, her counselor had been a lifeline, helping her find footing after Ian's passing. Now, Loghan felt ready-almost-to revisit those conversations, to open herself to advice and let go of some of the weight she still carried.

She hadn't made the call yet but the decision was taking shape in her mind. That was progress. More progress than she'd managed in a long time. I'll call her soon, she thought. For now, she lingered a little longer in this quiet moment, running her fingers along the fabric, letting her memories settle like the hush of calm evening breeze.

Loghan was astute at holding her feelings back and putting on a brave face. She was weary of this facade at this moment. She considered that progress is curious; it comes when you least expect it and Loghan was comfortable knowing more change was coming to her. She smiled softly and re-engaged her attention back to her beautiful walk-in closet.

Loghan was not a materialist woman, but she did have one extravagance; her heels and purse collection. She kept her spending within her means and attended a yearly shoe and purse auction with her girlfriends to sell and buy new. It was her way of managing her "obsession" not to exceed a reasonable amount and rotated out her Jimmy Choo's, Malano Blahnik and her current favorite, Christian Louboutin. She justified her need for beautiful heels and bags as a passing phase and knew one day she would no longer wish for such things, but that wasn't anytime soon, she mused.

Loghan felt lighter after meeting up with Deagan that afternoon and spending quality time with him. The wine they shared was outstanding, just as Deagan stated and it was so enjoyable to share wine with someone who also appreciates it.

She giggled at the two of them with their lofty wine vocabulary as they swirled, smelled and sipped. Deagan enjoyed the wine as much as she and they drank and nibbled on the cheese and fruit tray Loghan made from rummaging around in Deagan's refrigerator.

Deagan was such a good guy, she thought and why she became so angry with him a few weeks ago, she still pondered. She told herself she was tired of the men in her life treating her with exceptions, being "gentle" with language, topics and, God forbid, the subject of sex. Loghan was a grown-ass woman with plenty of ideas and could discuss dark issues. Well, maybe not entirely on the dark side, but damn it, she could discuss heavier topics and didn't need to be protected.

She sighed, her breath escaping like a whispered secret and pulled a comfy sweatshirt from her drawer. The fabric was soft, worn from years of use, a small solace in the chaos of her mind. Moving to the dressing area, she brushed her long, auburn locks, the motion rhythmic and familiar and gathered it into a high ponytail. Her reflection in the mirror held her gaze longer than usual.

Tilting her head from side to side, she traced the contours of her face with her eyes. Her cheekbones, sharp and regal, were her mother's. She could see her in every line, every shadow and she smiled faintly. Her complexion was something she'd always taken for granted-smooth, freckled and glowing with an Irish undertone. It was a gift, one she hadn't fully appreciated until recently.

Loghan wouldn't call herself beautiful. She wasn't one to revel in vanity. But the late-night discussions she'd been part of lately had her questioning her self-perception. Anonymity had been her shield as she explored these virtual conversations, delving into the lives and vulnerabilities of strangers while sharing fragments of her own. Her work for the article had taken her to places she hadn't expected-places on the internet cloaked in darkness, where identities blurred and desires spilled out like confessions. The threads she unraveled were tangled with raw honesty of those seeking connection, pleasure, or escape.

She leaned closer to the mirror, her breath fogging the glass as her thoughts lingered on the paradox of it all. Strangers had seen parts of her she'd never dared to show in person and yet they didn't know her at all. She had touched the forbidden area of talking about peoples' hidden desire when it came to sex...

The fine lines between research and self-reflection were starting to blur.

"Hmm...yes," she considered out loud and wincing slightly, "I didn't really get into that detail with Deagan, did I?" Stepping out of the dressing area, she looked at Harry and he, in turn, rolled over, stretched and emitted a long, lazy yawn. She creased her brow, thinking how she suddenly saw Deagan in a different light tonight. Of course, it was just a brief moment, but it did happen and she felt somewhat confident that Deagan was considering her in the same light - she thought their eyes connected when she was gazing at him considerably.

All these damn feelings and changes the last few weeks had Loghan exasperated. She wasn't one to give in to emotions or, back-and-forth feelings, but this is where she was of late. She wasn't going to put a lot of energy into this thought stream and moved on.

She gave Harry a rub and padded down the hallway to grab her warmed dinner. Dinner by the computer was nothing new for Loghan as she had work to do to finalize her draft of her article to turn in to John this week.

She was so close to completing her article last week and then things, well... things, got a little complicated.

Loghan let those know in advance she was interviewing for research for an article, but interviewing online was very different from in person; the formalities and decorum of introductions were next to non-existent, so you may get someone coming in hot and start typing things that quite frankly, make Loghan uncomfortable, or, you would get someone very pleasant and willing to take time to respond to questions, open and honestly.

Loghan wasn't quite prepared for the onslaught of 'heat' and wildly inappropriate invitations she received, let alone the 'dick pics'. She learned quickly how to weed out those trying to lure her into nothing but 'sexting' exchanges, to those truly offering insight to help her article. She experienced a short setback, while she learned the ropes.

Loghan planned on sharing everything with Deagan this afternoon about the final touches for her article. She had ventured more into the dark history of sex on the internet than initially expected. She didn't plan on taking that hard turn, but the hours she spent online for her research helped determine the path she now carved.

She talked to psychologists, digital media professors and interviews with random people she sought out online and it became clear there was more to this story.

There was more sex and debauchery available on the internet than she could even consider. Loghan was a quick study, she quickly found you start out as most people do when dabbling online - looking for someone to date and possibly fall in love. She didn't anticipate some of the stories she heard from women firsthand and her research.

Some women she spoke to had average, everyday experiences with online dating; others found a dark and frightening side to dabbling online. Some people were not safe online, sharing information about their private lives and they were hacked or taken advantage of emotionally or, financially. She found others wanted to see the dark side of sex and meet men anonymously online, or in person. Several of the women she met face - to - face for her article, told her they wanted to meet only for sex. Loghan considered how sheltered she was concerning sex, dating and some of the less savory sides of sexual inclinations.

She was no longer concerned with John's response to her going rogue with her article, as she knew this had the potential of an excellent copy. Sex sells and everyone knows that. The twist would be to have this article come from Loghan Riley, an all-around local girl who covered soft topics; it would be unexpected.

Once again, however, when Loghan shared with Deagan where she was in the final leg of her article, she barely broached the subject she met someone online "unexpectedly." Loghan recognized the pattern she was falling into with Deagan. If she wanted to be treated differently and looked at as a mature and confident woman, she had to present herself in this way. She had to speak what was on her mind and, over the last three years, Loghan drifted into the background.

She allowed her voice to be muted and it was her own doing.

She settled into her office chair and continued her soul searching. She thought again how far she had come in these last few months and weeks. Her progress in moving forward and letting part of Ian go had allowed her to be honest with herself. Not always a great feeling to acknowledge she was the cause of how others perceived her.

Hell, she didn't give a damn what others thought about her; she cared about what John thought and would accept from her. She cared about what Deagan thought, she considered him a good friend; he had been there through the good and bad times. He knew her reasonably well and tonight, he showed that again.

Deagan had always been there for Loghan. Even before the horrible accident, Deagan was around - with Ian or with her. She looked at him as a dear friend and her thoughts drifted again tonight. She noticed Deagan had been acting a little strange lately when she was around. She brushed it off to his protectiveness of her and thought nothing more of it. She did recall he seemed to blush today when she walked into his office without notice. Maybe she caught him off guard and he was in the middle of something. But Deagan was always solid and Loghan knew it was nothing to worry about.

She sipped the Barbera and placed the wine glass gently on her desk. The day drinking having caught up with her, as she opted to put the cork back in the bottle and set it to the side. She leaned back in her chair and crossed her long legs, stretching them slightly under her desk. Tracing her thoughts in this lane, she closed her eyes and considered.

She mentioned to Deagan when they were sharing wine that she was talking with some man online. She was surprised when she started to share with Deagan that she met someone, but when she started to talk, she corrected herself knowing she would withhold many of the details.

Why did Loghan hesitate to tell him more about David? She acknowledged she created this perception of herself as not being strong emotionally or capable of handling too much. In doing so, the men in her life and her friends wanted to protect her.

There was certainly no harm in them doing so; it made her realize how fortunate she was to have this tribe of dear friends protecting her from harm. Loghan had to own her part in creating this perception and thank her friends more for their help as she moved through her grief. She didn't know where all this self-realization was coming from, but she gave credit to her progress of late and she jotted down this critical revelation and added this to her list of things to discuss with her counselor.

"Progress..." she smiled and whispered.

Her thoughts continued about the afternoon with Deagan. Her article draft was close to complete and they discussed it at length into the second glass of wine. They made tentative plans to connect tomorrow afternoon and brainstorm the last details. But what didn't get discussed, was the truth in the matter that Loghan's research had become more than words on paper...she had a personal perspective now.

For the last several weeks, Loghan had been "meeting" David online, talking to him at his discretion. Loghan found herself looking for excuses to be "accessible" at different times of the day and night. So, she moved her schedule to chat with him for a few minutes or hours. It started out innocently enough as her interest was piqued and she found him fascinating. He initially sought her out, what seemed like years ago now, as introductions started slowly and progressed to in depth conversations. So much had been shared, that Loghan had an understanding of how women felt so connected to those men they met via the internet.

She recalled the first night they met online and how quietly curious she had been with him. After that first day, he messaged her a few more times and she ignored him. She smiled, thinking of when Deagan entered her office and David was messaging her. Loghan jumped out of her skin when Deagan walked in and was horrified at what Deagan might think. She deliberated if she would respond to David again, but she was drawn to his words like a moth to a flame.

She messaged with David that night when she arrived home and while it had been brief and nondescript, the seed of curiosity was firmly planted.

She initially was interested in obtaining information from him about his reasons for being online and meeting women in this manner. However, it worked out perfectly that her research was in this area and the story she kept telling herself that this was the only reason she was making time for him.

Loghan asked if she could quote him on some of his earlier disclosures of the "interactions" he had experienced with meeting women online. He was more than willing to oblige. She found him charming and his manor of expressing himself spoke to her intellectually. She worked his comments into her article and it made perfect sense that she continued to converse with him online for the sole purpose of her research as that was all it was until a few weeks ago...

"How are you tonight, darling?" His words pulled at her in ways she couldn't explain.

"I'm doing just fine, David. You?" Loghan found she was becoming more comfortable with the idea of talking to a man she didn't know. She felt fearless and capable of saying and asking anything she wanted without fear of judgment. David had a way of making her feel strong and invincible.

"Tell me about your day, love?"

David had taken the liberty of using endearing names to address her of late. Loghan didn't correct him.

She spent the last few weeks playing coy and unreachable, but somehow David had broken through her walls. She knew it was the night they spoke for hours about her loss of Ian and how difficult her world had become without him. Every day they messaged. Over time, it became something Loghan looked forward to. It had been so long since she had anything to look forward to and hiding behind her computer, made it easy with no real commitment.

Loghan, being in the business of investigating and researching for her field, found it somewhat bothersome that she couldn't find anything on David. She didn't want to blurt it out, but at the very least, she wanted to see photos of him.

David rarely posted on Facebook and what photos were on his page were of scenic and majestic locations. So, when she asked him about the lack of content on his page, it made perfect sense; he was a businessman and didn't have time to scroll and post on Facebook, but he did enjoy browsing and chatting as time allowed. He had very few friends on his page; when she clicked on their pages, they were private. Loghan decided she would let it go for the time being, as they were only talking.

She shrugged it off each time she thought of what he may look like; what did it really matter? She enjoyed talking to him and found him fascinating - so what if he didn't have any pictures posted?

David was kind and didn't pry. Instead, he took his time and allowed her to talk it out. She hadn't really noticed how their relationship morphed into sharing ideas and her deepest feelings, but it had made that shift in the last couple of weeks and it felt natural. That pivotal night she spent hours talking online to David, he somehow knew she was struggling and sad.

They both shared thoughts that night and David expressed his troubles about his relationship with his domineering mother. He didn't go into considerable detail, "a family business and all," he had said, but he told her enough to determine the deep problems and she couldn't believe a mother could be so cold and distant.

They shared a bottle of wine that night, figuratively speaking, but she found it exciting to use her imagination to simulate the two of them being in the same space. She felt odd at first, talking so deeply about her feelings and loss, but the anonymity of it all or, perhaps, the wine made the environment safe for her to share.

Once she told him about Ian's death and her fears of moving on without him, the dam broke wide open. She hid very little and found security, surrounded in her dark, cozy office at home. Loghan went against all reason and bared her soul that night. David interjected with his questions at the appropriate times and she could sit back and read his words. It allowed her time to think about his questions and think clearly, something she wasn't used to as, in everyday conversation, one had to respond quickly.

Her reasoning told her David didn't really know her and she knew that to be true, but hiding behind the veil of the screen of her computer provided courage. It was just as the women she interviewed told her; now, she was experiencing it firsthand.

She shared how her friends and boss treated her gently since Ian died. It had been three years and she felt ready to move forward. But she was tired of trying to prove herself.

"What do you have to prove, Miss Loghan?"

He asked so properly of her that night. It was such a simple question, yet the question gave her pause that she took a good minute to respond. This was the beginning of her change - the shift in how she thought about her life. Loghan considered herself thoughtful self-aware, but the last few years were dull and without light. She moved through the world and went through the motions but wasn't living. She was on autopilot.

"*I have to prove I'm more than the whole of my sadness;* she dug deeper and continued, *I'm stronger than everyone knows. I'm an independent woman and I'm capable.*"

Just writing those words made Loghan sit up and take notice of herself. Loghan had to admit now that she was playing a victim of sorts and wasn't speaking up to those around to say she was capable - that she was ready to move on and live again...perhaps, love again. She worried others would think she was disrespectful to the memory of Ian. She was still wearing her grief as a shield, using it to protect herself. She considered her residual "Catholic guilt" time and time again.

"*What are you trying to say you're capable of, darling?*"

Without hesitation, her long, manicured nails glided over the keys and responded:

"*That I'm not someone who needs to be protected - sheltered.*"

She answered every question David asked and found she was asking more questions of herself that night.

'*No, I don't believe you are one who needs to be protected, dear, Loghan. On the contrary, you're a strong and competent woman. I wish to hell I was in the room with you now and we could toast to your new found vision of yourself!*'

She smiled at his words and the use of the exclamation point. She couldn't have agreed more. It would be nice to have him here and toast to her proclamation. She continued to smile and watched the small dots appear on her screen, indicating he was responding.

"*May I share something with you, Loghan?*" His use of her name, not a term of endearment, made her take notice.

"*Of course, you may, David. I've shared too much with you tonight. I've entirely monopolized the conversation.*"

"*You've not shared too much with me, my dear. I've very much enjoyed becoming acquainted with you on a more personal level.*"

"*I have as well, David. Thank you...really. I've shared thoughts, feelings, with you tonight...I've not shared with anyone else since Ian died."*

"Well, you're most welcome, Loghan. I'm happy I could help in some small way. I find what I have to say rather delicate and embarrassing, but I'm going to as you've shown such bravery tonight sharing yourself."

Loghan sat back and realized she was holding her breath as she watched the tiny dots on the chat box continue.

"I'm aware this is new to you – connecting online and speaking at length, but I've never had this happen before. I'm very drawn to you and I hope you feel the same."

Loghan exhaled and considered his words for several moments. She hadn't realized until he said these very words that she, too, was experiencing a closeness to him that she couldn't explain. All reason told her this was ridiculous, but there was a draw and she couldn't deny this fact.

"Loghan...? Did I speak out of turn? I'm so very sorry if I've done so. Please..."

Loghan didn't wait to see what else David was writing but tapped the keys as quickly as she could.

"No, no! You're not off base and I feel something too. Is that crazy? I mean, we haven't even met! I don't even know what you look like!"

"Does it matter, darling? Do you think the connection has to be validated with your eyes or...with your heart?"

David needed nothing else to say that night, as Loghan found herself drawn to the words and kindness behind the screen.

Chapter 21

Deagan cleared the wine glasses and plates and placed them in the sink. Turning up the music, he stood at the sink and washed the dishes, playfully shaking his hips and tapping his toe to J-Lo singing, Love Don't Cost a Thing. He continued with his solo dance and completed the song with a spin. Laughing at his own antics, he smiled and noticed Max, his cat peering at him from the doorway.

"What?" Deagan shrugged his shoulders at Max and dropped the kitchen towel on the counter. A smile tugged at his lips. His time with Loghan had been productive, refreshing even. His mood reflected in his smile and he made his way to the living room to relax. He dropped onto the couch and his hand reached instinctively to the notepad on the coffee table that he and Loghan jotted notes on earlier. They spent some time discussing different reasons or scenarios of how the receipt was left at the murder scene.

"It's obvious, Deag," Loghan was enjoying her glass of wine and feeling good," it's the murderer!" She stared at Deagan, intentionally emphasizing her green eyes and lifting her brows for emphasis.

Deagan laughed. "It's never that easy, Loghan. If only it were! Let's get the address for the bank and we'll go there on Monday."

"Really?" her voice raised in excitement, "I thought you were a solo worker...solo writer. Solo..." She dipped her long, feminine fingers showing air quotes. "I have no idea where that came from," Loghan laughed at her antics and Deagan smiled, gently taking the pen from her. Their fingers touched briefly and Deagan looked up to catch Loghan's eyes. Her eyes flickered and was that a blush he saw in her cheeks? He pulled his hand back and quickly recovered, jotting down the address for the bank and dropped the pen on the end table.

"OK. We will go to the bank on Monday and see if someone will talk to us. They won't, of course, there are laws and regs they have to follow but sometimes you get someone who says, 'too much'." He copied Loghan's earlier air quotes and smirked. "I love those people," he smiled wryly at Loghan.

"Hey, what time are you leaving for the wedding this weekend?" Deagan looked at Loghan as she pulled the laptop over to her.

"I'm going to head out around 2 PM tomorrow. The wedding isn't until Sunday afternoon in San Francisco but I have a room and wanted to get down there without rushing. Time to relax, kick back, you know?" She shrugged and grinned sheepishly at Deagan. She knew most of her free time would be spent messaging David.

"Sure, I totally get that. I don't like to be rushed when I need to be some place." He rubbed his fingers across his forehead and Loghan saw the crease in his brow. He wasn't the only one who knew something about her; she knew when he rubbed his fingers across his forehead that Deagan was deep in thought - he had something on his mind.

"What are you thinking about, Deagan?" Puzzled, her eyes fell on the notepad with Deagan's handwriting.

Deagan continued to tap the paper. "I think I want to go and talk to Dexter. He knows something or, has a reason for sending me this information, right?" He didn't wait for her response. "I think if I go down there and get a face-to-face with him, I can get more information about this receipt, the crime and maybe see if there were other notes." His voice hammered away and he suddenly stopped, realizing he was overly excited about this prospect.

Loghan laughed, her green eyes bright and glinting from the lights. "I think that is an amazing idea!" a buzzing diverted her attention and she reached for her phone in her bag. "Excuse me, Deagan. I'm expecting a message." Deagan nodded and watched her face as she looked at a message. She had a small smile and tapped out a quick response. Curiosity got the better of Deagan as he watched her place the phone back in her bag. "Everything ok?"

Loghan sat upright and gave a slight stretch. "Oh, yes. Everything is fine. Just a friend I've been waiting to hear from." She smiled coyly and Deagan, as much as he wanted to ask, let it go.

Looking at her watch, Loghan stood up and Deagan followed. "It's been a great day, Deagan," she reached out, touching his arm. Thank you so much for the wine, conversation...," her voice drifted slightly and Deagan helped her finish. Gathering himself, he returned her touch by placing his hand on top of hers.

"No problem at all. It's been a good day; productive and fun." He smiled and this time he noticed how Loghan was looking at him. Her eyes were soft and warm and she returned his gentle smile. There was something different this time. He didn't know what it was, but he knew he liked how she was looking at him.

"Can I help clean up?" Loghan continued her gentle smile and Deagan noted his legs weren't doing him justice in standing firm as he walked her to the door.

"No, really – there are just a few things and I know you want to head back home to finish up your article." His hand reached for the door handle and willed himself to be steady.

"Thanks again, Deagan," she leaned in and embraced him gently, noting the lingering scent of his cologne, unexpectedly, she caught her breath and left him standing at the door with smile.

*****

Loghan allowed herself to drift back to present and inserted herself back to her article. Pushing her dinner plate aside, she pulled up her notes for the final touches to her article. She was pleased with the progression of her writing and talking it through with Deagan tonight was helpful. She wanted him to read through the entire article to get the rest of his feedback and would see if he could do that soon. Once that was done, she would be ready to send it to her editor, John, in both hard and soft copy.

She looked at the time on her phone and knew she only had a few minutes before she would hear from David. One thing she knew about David; he was prompt and somewhat expected her to be as well. Something he'd mentioned to her recently when she was 'late' for one of their meet ups online. No, she didn't want to disappoint David again, so she was mindful of the time.

David messaged her when she was at Deagan's, saying he was just finishing up with something pressing and would contact her in about a half-hour. She wanted to be home when he reached her and her time with Deagan seemed to be wrapping up.

They messaged through WhatsApp and since they exchanged their initial contact information, it was easy to stay connected with one another. There was something exciting about David being able to message her - it had the feeling of a secret; one she would not share. She did feel a little hesitation when she added him to her contacts, but quickly let the guilt go and smiled each time she received a message from him.

Sometimes it would be just a smiley face or, lately, a "Thinking about you..." message. The two would message during the day, being considerate of the time difference. Loghan was exceptional now at knowing the 8-hour time difference between London and Sacramento.

"Bong..." The notification sound went off and Loghan shook her head from side to side and smirked. Right on time, she noted...right on time.

"Hello, darling. How was the rest of your evening?"

Loghan turned in her chair and made herself a bit more comfortable. Then, smiling, she began to type.

"Hi David. It was very nice. As you know, I left work early today and went to my friend's house." She continued to write; *"it was so lovely to spend time with him. We went over my article and I've almost completed it."*

She momentarily leaned back in her chair and basked in the thought of nearing the end of her first feature article. It was an exciting feeling and one she hadn't stopped to really consider.

"I'm so glad you had such a lovely day. Which friend was this, darling?"

"Thank you, David. Me too. It's been a long time since I went out with friends and enjoyed life. I know you're aware of that." she continued to type, her

fingers gracefully touching the keys.

"It was my friend, Deagan. Do you remember me telling you about him?"

"Oh yes, of course, I do, darling. He seems like a true gentleman, from what you've described." Loghan laughed at the top hat emoji and David quickly related to being a gentleman.

"That was very clever on your part, David. I like the, top hat emoji, LOL!"

"Did you now? I thought it was wildly clever myself. LOL."

"Deagan helped me with some feedback on my article and you know how much I admire his writing. He's our most established and awarded writer in my office and Northern California."

"Well, that is wonderful he's able to help you, darling. You mentioned the other day he's working on a big story. Is that right?"

"He is, David. Deagan has this incredible ability to hunt out stories. He's working on piecing together these murders of women in different parts of the country, Boston and San Francisco, so far. He says he knows they are connected somehow. I am curious to know how he does it. Primarily by reading newspapers, talking to people and having a sense, you know?" Loghan picked up her wine glass again, allowing David time to respond and took a sip.

"Yes, he does sound brilliant. Always lovely to surround ourselves with brilliant minds. I hope you aren't smitten with this gentleman? I would hate to have to interject myself."

Interject himself? That was an odd thing to say if David was trying to be playful and show some jealousy toward Deagan. Seems aggressive... Loghan felt uneasy with his use of phrasing and pushed the feelings away. Maybe it's a common expression in the UK.

"Interject yourself? I think you mean you may be jealous of Deagan spending time with me. LOL..." Loghan smiled brightly to help ease her feelings of discomfort.

" I know exactly what I said, my dear and I meant it." David's response was quick and followed by no smiling emoji's to lessen the intensity of his reply.

He continued: *"I don't like to be corrected, or questioned, Loghan. I'm a man of my word and you and I have something truly wonderful happening and I dare not allow for anyone, or anything to come between that."*

Loghan sat still, staring at the screen. She didn't know how to respond but this wasn't sitting right with her. She took a deep breath before responding.

"David, I don't know if your tone or intentions by that comment is being lost in the messaging but I wasn't correcting you, nor was I questioning you." She took another deep breath and continued.

" I have never heard anyone use that phrase before, so I thought you may mean something different. I told you, Deagan is my friend and I too, am of my word." She didn't know why she felt the need to defend herself but here she was. Shouldn't she be put off by David's directness about her spending time with Deagan? She was more invested in making it 'right' with her and David. This was a misunderstanding at best, she rationalized. She was sure to fully explain herself as tone or intent, is easily lost in texting or chatting.

There was no response from David for what seemed like minutes. The dull light from the cursor remained silent. Finally, the light came to life.

" My dear Loghan, I want you to know I feel strongly about you. I merely was stating I don't want anything to come between us."

Loghan sat with his brief response and rolled it around her mind – was she being too dramatic? Maybe he was just 'playing,' and we all know Brits have a dry sense of humor…right? She continued to push the uneasy feelings aside and pressed forward. She wanted to make this 'right' and not upset David in any way, so she changed the subject hoping to lighten the direction of the conversation.

"David, I think I understand your meaning. I feel strongly for you too." Her fingers poised on the keys, she closed her eyes momentarily willing away the uneasy feeling. She opened her eyes and focused on the need at hand. She hoped her feigned acknowledgment of David's comments were enough to move forward.

" Tell me about your day, David. How did it go?" The pause was excruciating waiting for a response from David. The cursor light dull and lifeless as she continued to wait until finally, she could see he was typing. Loghan felt an odd sense of relief to see a response was coming.

" If only my day where as good as yours today." Loghan detected the "tone" in David's response.

"Oh no. What happened today, David? I have yet to ask you how your meeting went with your mother. Your weekly meeting with her, right?"

"Yes, that is right. Every week I must sit in with her and the board members. It's perfectly dull and dreary, but today was of particular irritation."

"Please...go on. Tell me what happened?" Loghan's green eyes clouded at the thought of a mother being so hard and unreasonable with their child. David was a grown man in a position of power within their company, but his mother liked to remind him she was in control, not him.

"Nothing new to share, darling. Just another meeting with her throwing her weight around. She quickly mentioned that I hadn't closed any deals in the last three weeks and she was none too pleased."

"I'm so sorry, David. It's terrible how she belittles you in these meetings. Can't you talk to her and let her know how it makes you feel?" Loghan knew that was a simplistic suggestion, but she didn't know how he could continue to allow for her ill behavior week after week. It must be challenging, but she understood it was the family business and he was next in line when she stepped down. She knew there must be more to the story, but David was such a gentleman and didn't speak poorly of his mother, only matter of fact in how she talked to him.

"It's fine, darling. Really. I shouldn't have said anything. It's impolite to speak negatively about anyone, especially one's family. I'm actually getting tired. I would appreciate it if you would be mindful of the time difference."

Loghan looked at the time and, flustered by his response, she began to type. *"It is late for you, David! I'm so sorry! It's almost 2 AM in London! Of course! I'm usually better about watching the time. I have to pack for this weekend, too."*

One again came a long pause in his response. This made Loghan uneasy again and she grew concern she had offended David. I know better and need to be mindful as he stated about the time difference...how thoughtless of me. Loghan winced at her shortfalls tonight with David. She continued to wait for his response and was relieved to see his typing.

"Yes, my dear Loghan. Thank you for acknowledging the time difference. I don't want to keep you from packing for your weekend away. It sounds like a lovely time attending your friends' wedding."

"Yes, it will be. I'm excited to see Megan. I love being in San Francisco too, so it's a bonus all the way around."

"Well then, I'm off to finish something and then head to bed. I wish you a lovely evening and rest, dear Loghan. Talk soon."

* * *

He closed his laptop and removed the VPN token. Looking about the space, he was satisfied that all was in place and well. He was satiated and remarkably relaxed.

The voices in his head tonight were insistent and non-stop. He tried with all his might to quiet them, but he was familiar with the pattern and once the voices showed their insistence, he knew what needed to be done.

The silence in his mind was immediate. He felt the peacefulness surround him in the room and allowed himself to rest at that moment. Closing his eyes, he rolled his shoulders to relax the ache of his muscles. He glanced at the clock on the wall and noted it was still early; 7 PM and plenty of time to get back.

He made excuses this afternoon to avoid questions that he needed to run off. He chuckled at how easy it was to make a quick escape.

He stood up and drained the martini they had shared earlier. It wasn't the best one he had, but right now, it tasted delicious. He gently wrapped the glass and placed it in his briefcase.

"Well darling, thank you for such a lovely evening." He continued across the room and found a mirror. He admired his reflection and ran his hands through his wavy dark hair.

"Striking, if I do say so myself, wouldn't you agree, love?" His smile stretched slowly and laboriously across his face, showing admiration. He thought back to when they first met those months ago. He just knew it would be perfect. Perfect for helping him in all ways. Sexually, mentally and most importantly, covertly.

Tonight was so simple, so incredibly easy to make the voices stop in his head. The screaming in his mind made for a quick end to the poor soul.

He walked to the bed and tilted his head as he looked down, patting the lifeless figure in the bed gently and continued to smile.

"Yes, I do believe you agree…thank you for a delightful fuck. Sleep well, dear, dear, Dexter."

Chapter 22

Roger Murphy was a handsome man. In his youth, he was often told he strongly resembled the famed old actor, Burt Reynolds - he never saw the similarities, but the comment always made him chuckle. Roger was lean and fit with thick, wavy hair women loved and men envied. He was in his early 70s, appeared ten years younger and still had his share of women visiting his bed. So, what if Roger had a little help over the years to maintain his appearance and vitality? He ate well and worked out and Grecian Formula was one of his secrets to maintaining his looks.

Roger moved to San Francisco right after he graduated from law school and his friends thought he was out of his mind. It was the mid - '80s, the height of gay pride. Thousands of young men flocked to the city to escape the confines of forced conformity, creating a haven of liberation that Roger admired but had no personal stake in. Roger wasn't here to escape, instead, he was chasing success - and San Francisco promised it in spades. Roger interviewed with some of the top law firms in San Francisco and the draw of money and city life, was one he couldn't turn down. While his friends joked about the abundance of men in the city, Roger knew that gave him a quiet advantage. It wasn't lost on him that women, particularly professional women, often found themselves in short supply of successful, good-looking straight men. Roger, with his broad shoulders and easy smile and sharp sense of humor, would have his pick.

Never marrying and living life to its fullest, Roger was active and thriving. After settling down and going into business on his own, he had an abundant cash flow, purchasing his law firm in 1991. He never looked back; his law practice continued to thrive, he was known as one of the top five attorneys specializing in estate planning and acquisitions.

Living in San Francisco in one of the most luxurious apartments on the 39th floor, he lived like a king. He happily dropped seven grand a month for his three bedroom, Jasper apartment with every amenity one could imagine. He never aspired to own the house with the white picket fence, wife and children that went along with that particular American Dream.

He was a stud in the stable and may have sired a few foals, but none to his knowledge. He was quite happy and had no intention of slowing down in his later years.

Roger knew it might not be the sexiest business in estate planning, but his docket, office hours and bed were filled.

He leaned back in his chair and swiveled around viewing the break in the weather, to a beautiful, day on the San Francisco Bay from his office window. His phone rang and he pressed the speaker button. "Yes?" His voice was rich and robust.

Parker, his beautiful and young assistant's voice was light and youthful; "Mr. Murphy, your 2 o'clock is here."

"Thank you, Parker. Send her in, please." Roger swiveled back around, put his feet on the floor and straightened his tie. He stood up with anticipation to greet his next client.

"Roger, darling. How very good to see you." Avery Stanton glided into the room in her customary manner, class, style and the slightest fragrance that made his knees weak.

Roger immediately took Avery's, perfectly manicured hands into his. "Avery - Jesus... you look stunning." He leaned in and bussed her left and then right cheek. He held her hands, leaned back and his eyes swept over her with appreciation and hunger.

"Roger, you're terrible," Avery tossed her head back with a throaty chuckle and exposed her neck. Being no fool for an invitation, Roger leaned in close to allow her fragrance to assault his senses.

"You haven't changed one bit, darling. Still, the strong, virile man I've known for years." Avery's proper English accent always affected him in the best way. He never wanted to be 'appropriate' with her when he was in her presence, but today he needed to keep his wits about him.

Avery stepped back and returned his knowing smile. Perhaps later, she would have a tumble with him in bed, but it was all business for now. There was much to settle and discuss.

"Avery, please...please sit. Can I get you anything? Coffee? Water? Tea? You must be exhausted from your flight from London." Roger swept his hand to the overstuffed leather chairs in the corner of his office. The view was spectacular, showcasing the beauty of the San Francisco skyline to one side and the other filled the large, floor-to-ceiling windows with sailboats, Alcatraz and sweeping views.

"Thank you, Roger," Avery's voice purred. "I would love a cappuccino if it's not an imposition?"

"None at all, Avery," Roger moved purposefully to his desk and picked up the phone. One quick request to Parker for two cappuccinos and he returned to settle in next to his number one client.

Roger met Avery years ago when he was a young and eager lawyer helping finalize the paperwork for a significant acquisition for the company. Avery was impressed with his ability to help her father close this particular sale, as he was not one of their usual attorneys. She worked to help build the business after her ailing father was in and out of the hospital before his final stroke. He inevitably stepped down from the company and Avery continued to work to show him she was capable. Avery guided the communications company in their transition over the years and it was not easy.

The ensuing years continued to bring technology fast forward and shifted to the present cloud-based platforms. As a result, Avery's company provided state-of-the-art video conferencing, web conferencing and cloud technology.

Roger adored Avery and knew her to be a complicated, strong woman. Her rise to success was built on tenacity and her complicated past. He appreciated that she trusted him implicitly, as her acting lawyer and with her many indiscretions. He was fortunate enough to be her lover for a short time, but that seemed like a lifetime ago. He knew he must have filled that "father figure" for her and he preferred to hold the title as her lover.

He managed all her business dealings worldwide and helped make her the success she was today with his skill in closing acquisitions. Avery had made him a wealthy man over the years.

Avery was solely responsible for the recent success of RHS Communications, as they were the first to offer cloud and digital technology to the masses. They made millions in their first two years of Avery taking the helm. She was brilliant at predicting marketplace trends and was at the front of the wave of technology as it roared into the 21st century.

While Avery was every bit the success in the family business she now held, she was aware she was born with the proverbial silver spoon in her mouth. She still had to prove herself in a man's world as she took the seat for her father's business.

Her father, Rhonert Stanton, came from means and used his resources to build himself into a millionaire by the time he was 34 years old. Although he was a strong and self-built man with a thick Irish accent, he worked hard to disguise his brogue as a proper English accent. He was proper in every way and presented himself in this manner to all. He was far from a saint, but Rhonert learned early on that his behavior resulted in many treating him respectfully, so he maintained this perception to his benefit.

Rhonert found his first job assisting in a large factory that made copper wire and cables for telephones. As the industry grew and changed, so did the demand for telephones. The need for research and innovative ideas to move from analog to digital helped Rhonert make a name for himself. He jumped into the market with Bell Systems in 1961 and tripled his money when they unveiled their touch-tone phone in 1963.

Avery followed her father around at every opportunity as a little girl, marveling at his large office and importance. She wanted to be "just like Daddy," when people asked her what she wanted to be when she grew up. Avery wanted for nothing, being "Daddy's little girl," and Rhonert showered her with lavish gifts and equally lavish attention.

Her mother, Elizabeth, was a lovely and gentle spirit. However, she was purely ornamental to her father, Rhonert, parading her at the country club and theater when necessary to keep up appearances. His prowess with women was well known and he had numerous mistresses over the years. Unfortunately, it was an ill-kept secret and those close to his circle turned a blind eye to his carelessness.

Except for her mother. She was brokenhearted over his indiscretions and sadness was her constant companion. Avery loved her mother purely as children do. As she was so young, her memories of her were fluid and soft as silk, filled with the sweet scent of vanilla and cloves. Her mother was kind and loving and carried a delicate touch. Avery remembered her mother as a fragile woman, suffering from the complications of a 'nervous breakdown,' as explained to her at a young age. Finally, her father told Avery her mother had to go away, explaining she was ill and needed care.

Through the haze of years, one memory remained sharp as broken glass in Avery's mind: that cruel autumn morning in London when her mother was torn away. Standing frozen on the front steps, young Avery could only watch as her mother was escorted to the waiting car - the black car swallowed her mother whole. Behind the cold window pane, her mother's trembling hands reached out, her lips forming "Avery" over and over like a desperate prayer. But no sound penetrated the glass, no warmth could breach that final barrier between them. The terror etched on her mother's face - eyes wide with disbelief, tears streaming unchecked - would haunt Avery's dreams for years to come, a portrait of heartbreak preserved in perfect, painful clarity.

She took away a lesson that sad day and while it didn't make sense entirely in her young heart, she knew one thing for sure - she would never allow weakness in her life.

Life went on rather well for her father. He carried on with his business and affairs and there was little, to no talk of her mother. Instead, there were empty promises of visits to her mother, replaced with excuses for business meetings or trips her father needed to attend.

Avery knew not to question or ask her father about her mother. At first, he was kind and gentle about her questions, stroking her hair and wiping away the tears she cried. Avery felt secure and loved in her father's arms as he comforted her.

As the years went on, her father grew weary of Avery's questions about her mother. His answers became short and harsh, showing exasperation with Avery's constant questions. Finally, she stopped asking questions and it appeared her father never noticed.

Avery learned to live without her mother as a cavalcade of other "mothers" drifted in and out of her life. She grew resilient and strong and eventually became quite shrewd at masking her feelings of resentment. Her feelings toward her father evaporated from love, to bitterness.

Avery pretended to be the doting daughter of Rhonert Stanton and everyone spoke highly of her. She went on to finish her education in the finest private schools and graduated with honors from Rutgers with a master's degree in International Studies; she was fluid in French, German and Italian languages. Avery Stanton was every father's dream of a daughter.

He was so proud of her accomplishments and showed her off at every cocktail and dinner party to the eligible young men. Avery was not the least interested in marrying and still had her eyes on working next to her father in the business. She was ready to break the stereotypes of women working in traditional positions men held.

Her father continued to show his pride in Avery until the day she moved home from college and disclosed she was pregnant. Her father was beyond angry and followed the old traditionalist way of thought, demanding she marry the father. Avery would have none of it and would not disclose the father's name to keep her privacy and the father's knowledge at bay. The thought of being married off was not in Avery's future, nor would she ever marry unless it suited her purpose.

Rhonert continued to demand she marry or, have an abortion. He didn't agree, nor approve of abortion but foolishly felt her carrying a bastard child was worse. Avery scoffed at her father's hypocrisy suggesting she have an abortion-so much for his catholic beliefs. While Avery was not interested in being a wife, she was very interested in becoming a mother and this caused her father to continue to rage. He used every threat he could imagine and stated he would cut her off from the money and the family business. His concern was she would "soil" the family's good name and sent her off to a private location in Switzerland, before she was showing signs of pregnancy to remain out of sight. He would deal with Avery when he needed to and not a moment sooner.

Rhonert Stanton was not a man to cross and Avery knew this too well.

He played his hand better than Avery and knew she had grown accustomed to her lavish lifestyle and working alongside her father. Rhonert made clear that without going away to have the baby, married or not, Avery would not step in and take over RHS Communications. She felt she had no choice but to follow her father's orders.

She left London quietly under the guise of her yearn to travel and explore, for some much-needed rest after graduation and ready herself to work alongside her father.

Avery had a traumatic delivery, but with her father's lack of interest at that time, she was grateful to be away from prying eyes and maintained her privacy. She remained in Switzerland a few months after the birth and Rhonert began working on the *next* fabricated story to bring her home.

Rhonert would never warm to an illegitimate grandson she knew he didn't care to try. He held his head high and deemed his indiscretions far less than siring a bastard child. Avery didn't care what her father thought and merely laughed at his hypocrisy as women continued to come and go in his life and her mother withered away and died in an asylum somewhere.

Avery returned to London with her five-month-old son and a story of painful circumstances. Rhonert was pleased with his story and shared it with all the right and important people: Avery met and married a man she met abroad - but, tragically, he was killed while hiking in Switzerland and heartbroken Avery returned home to be with her father and infant. Avery thought the story was ridiculous, but no one seemed to press her for more details, allowing her to "mourn" quietly over the next few years.

Avery mastered the art of sorrow. In public, she wore her grief like an exquisite gown, draping her every word and gesture in a solemn elegance that turned heads and hushed voices. Her father insisted on it. "Let them see the pain in your eyes," he would say, his voice as sharp as the angles on his face. "It's what they expect, what we need them to believe." And so, Avery played her role. She cast down her gaze at the perfect moments, offered tight-lipped smiles that hinted at inner turmoil and carried herself with a fragility that made her untouchable.

Behind closed doors, however, the mask shattered with a single breath. In the privacy of their sprawling estate, Avery spoke freely, her voice rich and melodic, devoid of the weight she feigned. She dove headfirst into learning the family business, soaking up every lesson her father taught with a voracious appetite of someone who refused to be confined by pretense.

Rarely, did Avery step beyond the confines of her carefully curated world in those early years. On the rare occasions she did, the whispers followed her like shadows. "Have you seen her?," they would murmur behind their hands at the cocktail parties. "Poor girl, the sadness in her eyes is palpable." Avery almost smiled at their pity. The truth was far more satisfying than their gossip: she was no fragile bird, but a hawk, waiting for the right moment to spread her wings. Her father's ruse was a cage, but behind its bars, Avery was anything but broken.

As the years waned, Avery grew into a brilliant and strong business woman and carried her father's appetite for sexual conquests and indiscretions. Time passed quietly and Avery built her life and career around her obligations and son, Aric.

Aric was a willful child and demanded much of Avery's attention. She did her best to give him what he needed but was left bitter and resentful. During those first ten years, Avery would leave Aric with his nannies once a month and go off for business in Scotland. She loved the busy, bustling city of Glasgow, but the lure of the quaint island of Great Cumbrae spoke to her heart. Avery built a small, quiet life in the countryside of Millport, Isle of Great Cumbrae and had a tiny circle of friends. It was here she could be herself and as with any young, single woman in her thirties, she would meet and have brief encounters with men willing to remain untangled.

It was in Millport she met up with Roger Murphy who was on the island vacationing for a few weeks. She thought it was a coincidence to have stumbled upon Roger here, but he knew she was vacationing here and hoped to entice her to his bed. Avery didn't need much convincing. She loved his strong sense of style, mannerisms and handsome ruggedness. Roger was drawn to her obvious beauty, grace and sex appeal. They both needed one another for different reasons, but it made no difference to either of them.

They ran about the Isle of Cumbrae and were never out of sight from one another. They both knew it would be a short-lived affair, as he was twenty-five years her senior and his business and heart remained in San Francisco. Roger learned much about Avery during those weeks and their lifelong bond was formed under her cottage's soft, cool sheets. Little did they know their paths would cross again when Avery inquired for Roger to help her with a delicate, personal matter. From here, their business relationship grew; Roger was re-introduced to Rhonert again and soon became the sole attorney for every point of business, not only for Avery but for Rhonert as well.

Roger was the closest to a father figure in Aric's life, as he was the one most present next to Avery's side. Rhonert had grown fond of Roger and often would mention the two making it official - a merging of a significant business venture. Still, Avery and Roger appreciated their friendship and occasional tryst far too much to complicate it with marriage. They remained close over the years and Avery's visit today was serious.

They finished their cappuccino and moved to Roger's desk to discuss business. Roger's tone changed from friendly - to serious.

"Avery, I have all the paperwork here. We have a few details to go over, but I want to ensure you know where we go from here." He leaned forward, brows creased in concern and continued, "Just as you've asked, I've put everything in your son's name. He will be the sole owner of your business, the estate in London and all holdings for RHS Communications upon your death."

Avery leaned back and crossed her long and slender legs. She was aware of her intentions and lifted an eyebrow at Roger.

"Roger, darling...please. We've been over this a hundred times. There is nothing else to go over. It is the right thing to do and it's long past time. You're an estate attorney, for God's sake! I'm fully aware of the implications. Father has been gone for years and he will be none the wiser." She scoffed and flipped her wrist in the air dismissively.

"I know *exactly* what I'm doing and we have years ahead to discuss this if needed...although, I will not change my mind." Avery opened her purse and pulled out her gold cigarette case and lighter. She looked at Roger in a questioning matter and he waved her on.

"Christ. How I wish you would give up that nasty habit, Avery," Roger walked across the room and turned on the air purifier. It let out a soft hum and the room filled with a quiet, white noise. "You know," he continued, "I work hard to protect my health and physique. It wouldn't hurt you if you gave those up." He lectured her each time he was in her presence and she lit a cigarette.

Avery stood and walked over to Roger and smiled as she ran her long and delicate finger across his cheek. "Whatever would we quarrel about then, darling? Her smile was warm and seductive. "Let's get on with it, as I would like very much to take you to bed." she smiled coyly at Roger. "Now, where do I sign?"

*****

Aric held the card to the door lock and waited for the light to turn green. He walked into the spacious room and dropped his laptop case on the couch. He found the room was recently cleaned as he could smell the furniture polish and the floors were shining.

He removed his jacket and tie, hung them neatly in the closet and continued to remove his clothing with the precision of a man methodically shedding the layers of the day. Finally, he walked, naked, to the well-stocked wet bar - a shrine to his vices - and made himself a pitcher of martinis, the clinking of ice against glass the only sound in the room. The drink wasn't for pleasure. It was a numbing agent - to anesthetize the voices in his head that whispered their demands. He knew it was just a matter of time. They would start getting louder, as his meeting with Avery was tomorrow.

Jesus, how he hated her. She was worthless to him and with his recent spending spree on more Italian suits, shoes and time in the South of France, he knew she would berate him.

"Fucking, Avery," he quietly whispered as he poured the martini. The first sip, was warm and sliced through his lingering taste of regret. He poured a second before the first was even empty, watching the liquid settle, cool and clear - a false promise of calm. He lifted the glass and stared into it, as if it might reflect something other than his own shadowed eyes.

He stood at the large windows looking over the cityscape below. He didn't care if anyone saw him naked, standing there with his martini. They should be so lucky to see him in his utter masculinity and desire. He continued sipping his martini and walked to the large bathroom to draw a hot bath.

He was in the second largest suite at the Mark Hopkins and his room enjoyed panoramic views of San Francisco, a wet bar and a large Jacuzzi tub. He appreciated this location almost as much as the Ritz - Carlton in Boston. He stayed at so many luxurious hotels that it was hard to stand out. Still-San Francisco, New York, Boston and a few European locations held standards that accommodated his taste. He appreciated the finer things in life - clothing and shoes, cars, locations and sex.

He knew there was a time and place for all things and of late, his acquired taste for sex was showing up more than usual for him. He was a healthy and virile man with many tastes for his sexual proclivities, but he was always able to tamp it down and not let it get in the way of business. But unfortunately, it was proving a problem of late and he needed to get a handle on this area.

He dismissed these thoughts and basked in the knowledge he was more intelligent than those in his business circles. He was undoubtedly more intelligent to those women with whom he chose to entertain himself while online...and he was certainly more intelligent than his damn mother, Avery. She thought herself to be so fucking brilliant, he mused.

He stood at the mirror in the bathroom and admired himself. He was striking and fit and noted he needed to tan more often. His English heritage was evident, with his skin a shade of pallor he didn't care to hold.

The hot water steamed the mirrors as the large bath filled, transforming the suite's bathroom into a misty sanctuary. A slow grin tugged at the corners of his lips as he topped off his martini. He admired the faint clink of the glass against the counter before stepping toward the bath, the soft, golden light catching the rising swirls of steam.

Sliding into the water, he let out a sigh of contentment as the heat embraced his body. With a causal flick of his wrist, he scattered a generous handful of Epsom salts into the swirling water, watching the grains dissolve like the whispers in his head. Then, with a moment of indulgent deliberation, he plucked a musk-scented bath bomb from the tray and tossed it it. It began to fizz and swirl, painting the water with muted tones of amber and gold.

He slid under the water and allowed the warmth to ease his aching muscles. He was stiff and sore and hoped the bath would help. The musk aroma crept over him, rich and warm, mingling with the steam in a way that felt both grounding and luxurious. The scent enveloped him, conjuring images of dark wood paneling, leather bound books and faint memories of his younger years at the estate. He closed his eyes and allowed his mind to continue to wander. He was pleased he was several steps ahead of Avery. He anticipated her anger tomorrow and then she would try to make nice by taking him to a lavish meal and spending thousands of dollars to appease her guilt.

He recalled when he snuck into her office at their estate. It was a long time ago, yet he held his own secrets. Not just Avery.

He used to be a quiet, caring young man. There were no voices then - only riding lessons, poetry readings and boring dinners with his mother. He knew she was distant and didn't seem to care for him, but it was all he knew. He had no fundamental understanding of her behavior toward him. He knew he was supposed to love her - she was his mother, yet he stopped calling her that while in his youth. She certainly didn't seem to mind.

He was treated like a second-class citizen even by his grandfather, Rhonert. Aric loved him very much and it didn't matter that his grandfather was cold and distant. He learned all he could from him when opportunities arose. Rhonert begrudgingly helped Aric learn the business and seemed to be warming up to him, but the stroke hit him and his grandfather became like another man; angry and bitter, biting comments and seemingly not wanting to spend any time with Aric. Rhonert's health continued to worsen over the years and Aric was left in the dark to learn the business and fall to the whim of his mother.

She held Aric back and stepped into the limelight firmly - never discussing that one day, he too, would be leading the company where he should have been. His reason for venturing into her study that day was simple; he knew he might need to hold something over her one day. He knew she had secrets. Of course, everyone had secrets, but something told him Avery had many.

Avery was unaware that Aric carried her secrets and he loved the knowing she was blissfully ignorant. She was an awful woman and she continued to treat him like a stranger...an employee instead of her son. Her heir to the family business. She was such a hypocrite, a cold-hearted, two-faced bitch.

He sipped his martini, watching the droplets of condensation trickle down his glass and could hear the voices start quietly again. They began as a whisper and would insist on his attention - his direction and decision. If he didn't, they would grow louder until he found a way to make them stop. He placed the glass down and balled his fists to his throbbing temples - willing the voices to leave him.

He remembered walking into her study and looking at all the leather bound books his grandfather lined the walls within the dark oak, silver and gold room. There were paintings from the 18th century, on two walls and floor-to-ceiling bookshelves on the other walls. He walked around the room, undetected, as Avery was getting ready upstairs. He didn't know what he was looking for that day, but he knew there was something that may assist him down the line.

He ran his fingers across her elegant office chair and allowed his eyes to dance across her desk filled with papers and folders. He recognized most of the documents - legal reports from the last few deals for RHS Communications, invitations to parties and art openings. He scoffed when he saw the invite to upcoming Royal Ballet season, as Aric knew he and Avery would attend to keep her lofty appearances up, while he knew she loathed ballet. Such a hypocrite and charlatan, he thought. His eyes continued to scan her desk and he noticed an envelope peaking out slightly, tucked under a folder. His glance darted to the office door and listening, he determined the estate wing was quiet and he was in the clear. He pulled the envelope out and saw it was Avery's sickeningly sweet penmanship addressed to Roger Murphy.

"Well, well…what have we here, dearest, Avery," he whispered. His fingers trembled as he opened the envelope, unfolding the crisp, legal documents within. His eyes devoured the words, each sentence a revelation. He couldn't believe what he had read, yet it all made sense - every lie, every omission, every shadowy detail he'd questioned for years. The puzzle pieces he thought lost forever, had fallen into place at last, that night of discovery.

This finding was too much for Aric and the voices that now haunted him, became permanent part of his life.

The paperwork was all he needed to validate his thoughts and to put the missing pieces of a lifelong puzzle in place. He was so glad he found them years ago, but now it was time to do something.

He needed to quiet the voices for the time being. If he got back to his computer, it would help. Hiding behind his screen always helped. It would soothe the voices before they got too loud. He was feeling frenetic tonight and longed for calm. He couldn't wait any longer to get to his computer, to talk and guide the night. The anonymity appealed to him, but he was getting attached this time. That wouldn't do, but he was drawn to her. He couldn't continue to be sloppy. That happened tonight with that needy and gullible Dexter.

"I shut him down," Aric said aloud. He recalled how lovely the night was and how Dexter looked so incredibly shocked as the life left his body. A sickening smile teased at Aric's lips as he recalled the memory. The time was coming close.

He allowed himself to be guided by voices and willingly listened to their persistent chants.

"You're next - You're next - You're next-," Aric whispered quietly in a rhythmic monotone, quietly chanting until the voices stopped.

Perhaps, just a brief chat online with his favorite subject at this time. Yes, that would calm the voices. She had such a way with him that he didn't fully understand, but this would be an unexpected contact from him. I can truly see how devoted she is to me if I contact her unannounced. Aric smiled and knew, no matter the time of day or, night she would answer. This much he did know.

Twenty minutes later, after reaching her, the voices were quiet now. Just as he knew, she quickly responded to his pings and he felt at last, satisfied once more. He returned to the bath, topping it off with steamy, hot water and turned the jets on in the tub. Bubbles and warm scents filled the steamy room once more and he slipped again under the warm, dark water.

*****

The rain started to fall, tapping against Loghan's bedroom window. It was early Saturday morning and she stretched and groaned as she wasn't quite ready to awaken. Harry decided otherwise and butted his head against Loghan's arm.

"Oh...silly boy. I know, I know. It's time to get up." Loghan threw her legs over the bedside and headed to the bathroom.

Harry followed her from the bathroom to the kitchen, hopeful it was time for breakfast. It was and he rewarded Loghan with a loud meow and rubbed around her legs while she filled his bowls with food and fresh water. She remembered she left her phone by the bedside and went back to retrieve it. It brought a slight blush to her cheeks as she recalled her brief interaction online last night. She surprised even herself lately with her online escapades. Shaking her head she reached for her phone.

There was a message from Deagan;

"I know it's raining. It won't kill either of us. Let's run off that wine from yesterday. I'll be there close to 9 AM. Sound good?"

She smiled at the message, looked at the time and saw it was 8:40. She shrugged and replied, *"OK. See you then."*

Five minutes later, her face scrubbed, hair pulled back in a ponytail laced through her favorite ball cap, Loghan was ready to go. She flipped on the TV for the local news and hit the button on the Keurig for a quick cup of coffee. Sipping from the large, warm cup she looked out the window and it appeared the rain was slowing down. She was glad for that, while she didn't mind running in the rain, she didn't feel like having soaking wet feet and this would be a given with the state of the day.

The knock on the door made Harry run like lighting down the hall and

Loghan laughed. Harry was a big boy and anything remote to running for him was like watching a ball with fur roll away from you.

Continuing to laugh, she opened the door to Deagan and he smiled back.

"What's so funny?" He smiled again and there were those great laugh lines around his eyes, she thought.

"Oh. Nothing really," she waved her delicate hand toward the hallway, "It was Harry. He jumped and ran like lightning down the hallway when you knocked. It's always good for a laugh," she smiled and opened the door wide for Deagan to enter.

"Thanks. Yeah - I know what you mean. You've seen Max. He's a roly-poly these days. downright, 'chonky.' I need to get him on a fitness plan." Deagan laughed and nodded at her coffee.

"Oh, sure. Come on. Let's get you a cup before we head out." They sipped on steaming cups of coffee and Deagan contemplated not running and thought breakfast with Loghan would be much better but opted out, knowing a run would benefit them both.

"Hey, turn that up a sec?" Deagan nodded to the TV in the family room and they both walked closer to the TV. Loghan hit the clicker button and the volume filled the room with details about an attempted murder in San Francisco.

"...Police say there is no immediate danger in the area and the victim identified the man as one she met on a blind date earlier in the evening. The victim identified is in her early 20s and not from the San Francisco area. Police have released a sketch of the man and are asking anyone that may recognize this person to contact the San Francisco Police..."

A loud crash jolted Deagan from the television and he turned to locate the source of noise, quickly spying shattered glass on the floor. Loghan stood ashen-faced and looked down at the floor with her coffee pooling around and her mug in pieces.

"Loghan! Loghan...are you ok?" Deagan jumped over toward Loghan and helped her sit down on the couch.

She gathered herself and looked at Deagan with eyes filled with terror.

"Deagan...I know that man," she whispered hoarsely. "I met him a few weeks ago. His name is Barrett. Barrett Rohan."

Chapter 23

Deagan ran to the kitchen and poured a glass of water for Loghan. He returned to the couch and handed it to her as he sat beside her. She was still visibly shaken as her hands trembled slightly when she took the glass from him. Deagan's brow furrowed in concern as Loghan was still pale. She took a deep drink of the water and started to stand again. Deagan gently guided her back to the couch. "Hang on for just a minute or two, Loghan. You look shaky still - rest a minute." Deagan's deep blue eyes were filled with worry.

"I need my phone, Deagan." She looked around frantically, trying to place her eyes on her phone. "I'll get it, Loghan. Just rest another minute, ok? Where is it?"

"I think it's still in my bedroom - on the nightstand." He was up before she finished her sentence and located the phone beside her bed, resting on the charger. He looked around her room quickly and noticed her suitcase was out and she was packing for the weekend visit to her friends' wedding.

Deagan handed Loghan her phone and it was ringing; it was her girlfriend, Tina Stoddard. "Hello? Tina?" Deagan could hear the quiet desperation in Loghan's voice. Loghan put the phone on speaker as she stood up to see if her legs would support her.

"Loghan! Are you sitting down? Have you seen the news? Have you talked to Jodie?" Tina was just as upset as Loghan and peppered her with questions. Deagan was still unsure what was happening but knew he needed to get up to speed quickly. "Yes - I just saw it on the news! I can't imagine, this can't be real! I haven't heard from Jodie! Oh my God, Tina, what if ?" Loghan sat back on the couch and picked her phone up again. "I'm going to text her right now; I don't know what to say, but I'm on it." Loghan texted as quickly as her fingers would allow. Tina continued to talk while Loghan texted." That's him? Right? That's Barrett! Jesus, Loghan. I have to call her - you're texting, one of us has to get a hold of her!"

Loghan looked at Deagan as she completed her text to Jodie; *'Hey - It's me. Checking in-are you alright?'* Loghan kept it brief to get a message to her as quickly as possible. "I am checking 'Find My Friends'... Oh, my God! It shows, her location is at The Mark Hopkins, but that was hours ago!"

Loghan looked at Deagan. His eyes were filled with questions and concern. She realized Deagan had no idea what was going on as their eyes locked. "Tina - I have Deagan here with me. You know, from work? You're on speaker and I need to catch him up with what's happening."

"Yeah - yeah - sure!" Tina was quiet on the other end while Loghan filled Deagan in on record time. "Let's call the police, Tina." Loghan gathered her wits about her and stood up, taking the phone with her as she and Tina wrapped up details. They agreed both would contact the police in San Francisco and Loghan reminded Tina she was heading to San Francisco today. Desperation entered Loghan's thoughts. Jesus...what if she didn't hear anything back from Jodie. What if...

"Wait...Tina!... She's texting me back! I see her typing!" Loghan stopped in her tracks, turned to look at Deagan and grabbed his hand. She held her breath while she continued to wait for her response.

*****

Barrett pulled the chair out, smiling at Jodie as she slid into her place. She looked around the restaurant and sighed. Jodie could not believe the weekend she was experiencing with Barrett. She loved San Francisco and considered herself well-versed on the city, but Barrett knew all the places to go and the best restaurants for ambiance and food.

They were dining at the Waterfront Bar in the Bridge Tower Room. It was elegant and the sweeping views of the San Francisco bridge were breathtaking. The room offered a panoramic view of the bridge and being only two stories up, you felt as if you were on the water and experiencing the aquatic life.

They found time today to leave their room after more lovemaking and a much-needed nap. Jodie was thrilled how the weekend was progressing; they never tired of conversation. There was so much to learn about one other that it felt like a crash course. They smiled and laughed about this comment several times over the weekend as they both seemed to feel the same and had much to catch up on.

The afternoon was spent walking around the shopping district, taking in the sights and sounds of Union Square. Jodie, like most women, enjoyed shopping and never had a boyfriend or, male acquaintance seem to care about this pastime. Barrett was different in so many ways, she noticed. He was kind and caring, loving and funny and let's not forget how utterly handsome he was. Barrett took her breath away with his strong, masculine form and mannerisms and knew his way around her body without a doubt. She was still swooning over his accent and the pet names he would call her.

They walked arm and arm in and out of shops and found their way into Neiman Marcus. It was fun to walk the rows of glass display cases and look at the fine jewelry, perfumes and colognes. Jodie walked around to the side where the handbags were displayed and casually admired the expensive variety; YSL, Versace, Prada. They were lovely, but she didn't need anything over the top. She felt she had spent enough on her favorite line, Kate Spade, as she considered all the beautiful, lush, leather bags lined up.

Well, it was just about time she purchased a new Kate Spade bag, she justified as her eyes landed on the large, red leather tote. Divine, she thought. I should have something to remember this weekend and this is just the thing. She smiled slightly as the salesperson approached, following her eyes to the Kate Spade bag.

"It's lovely, isn't it?" The elegant older sales woman stated as she nodded at Jodie. She smiled at Jodie, reached for the leather bag and handed it over the counter. "Yes, it's beautiful. Just like her." His voice was deep and purred in his richly layered burr. Barrett quietly came up behind Jodie and noticed that she admired the leather tote. He discretely nodded at the saleswoman and she returned with a knowing smile.

"It's a fine choice, sir." She smiled and put her hands out to Jodie to take the tote from her. Jodie obligingly handed the tote over to the saleswoman and smiled. The saleswoman walked to the side of the counter, taking out the tissue paper and gently wrapping the bag when Jodie realized Barrett was planning on purchasing this for her.

"Barrett - please. I planned on buying this for myself." She smiled at his deep, resonating eyes and felt a jolt run through her body. Christ, she thought, I wonder when that will stop each time I make eye contact with him. She felt her body melt as he pulled her into his strong arms.

"Now, lass, please. I saw you from across the counter looking at this bag with such admiration. Please allow me to buy this for you." his eyes were full of light and glistened as he looked down at her. He squeezed her against him a moment and continued, "Consider it a gift to remember this weekend and I hope there will be more of us together every day." He gently pulled her hands to his lips and kissed them, his lips soft and breath warm against her cool skin. How in the hell could she resist?, she thought.

She was not a woman who allowed men to wine and dine her, purchase gifts for her, or treat her in a way that appeared she was a woman incapable of paying for herself and worse yet, not strong and financially independent.

"Thank you, Barrett. I feel funny about you buying it, but how can I deny your compelling request and... those eyes?" She laughed and decided there was a first for everything. Acquiescing, she chuckled and kissed his cheek.

Walking through the restaurant, she loved every bit of this day, she recalled as she turned once more to look out the window at the bridge. She watched Barrett as he took his place at the table and noticed several women and men were looking at him. He was a striking man and she couldn't blame them for admiring him. She turned back to take in the beautiful view of the San Francisco bridge and Barrett took a moment as well to enjoy. The late afternoon sun, which made a brief appearance after the rain, glinted off the water.

"Barrett. Thank you for such a wonderful day." Jodie smiled at him and placed her cool, soft hand on his. She found it easy to show affection toward him, look at him and get lost in his eyes. How was it possible they found one another in this crazy, busy and hectic world? What were the odds? She reflected quietly, watching him look at the beautiful scenery. Barrett pulled his eyes away from the view and noticed the look on Jodie's face. "What is it, love?" he looked at her intensely and creased his brow. "You look as if you've something heavy on your heart." He reached down, placed his hand on top of hers and gently patted.

"It's nothing, Barrett," she tried to deceive him. "I was just thinking about how funny life is sometimes. How we met – how we seem to connect. This..." she looked about the restaurant and took her hand away from his, gesturing to indicate the view gently. "I'm – I'm just having the most wonderful time." There. She said it. The world didn't shift and he didn't blink or run away. She didn't tip her hand too much, as she couldn't believe she may be falling in love with him. That would be impossible. It would be ridiculous. That, she knew, was crazy. However, she did know that she felt something deeply for him and it wasn't just lust. She was falling for Barrett Rohan.

He smiled across the table at her and she noted again how weak he made her feel. It was how she felt when she looked at him. It was beautiful and she needed to relax and enjoy the ride. Stop processing and asking herself all these damn questions. Jodie just needed to enjoy it.

"I'm having a wonderful time as well, darling. But the day isn't over and the night young." His voice lifted and she could hear a little excitement in it. "We have tomorrow, too and I know we can find more things to experience." He laughed and she returned his smile.

The waiter came to the table, took their drink orders and returned quickly with a glass of Cabernet for Jodie and a martini for Barrett. They laughed, chatted over their drinks and recapped the day's adventures. Jodie settled into her seat and took a sip of her Cabernet. "Tell me more about your family and life, Barrett. It's simply fascinating."

Earlier, Jodie had filled the afternoon with pillow talk and details of her family, job and career. She spent the last several hours in his arms and in the warm afterglow, they whispered and shared more about their lives. He laughed, showing his perfect, white teeth and took a deep breath.

"Well, love...what to share...? Ah, well.... I'll tell you more about my memories of my family." Jodie knew Barrett was adopted, an only child and had a small family, but she wanted to know more. Who was this beautiful man and where did he come from? What were his memories? His values? "I know I told you about my small family. I really only remember good things with my parents and aunties. Betsy, mother's sister, was lovely. She made me feel loved and special. That was everything to me as a small child. Knowing I was adopted created feelings of doubt about my self-worth when I was young, but Aunt Betsy and my parents told me over and over that, I was special because I was chosen." He smiled at the memory and took a thoughtful sip of his martini.

"Go on, Barrett." Jodie gently urged. She loved learning about his life and his family. His experiences were so different than hers, growing up in America and having a bigger family with cousins, aunts and uncles. It was different, yet some things, like the love of family and the special memories they held, were similar.

"Yes - well, Katherine. My father's sister - she is something to consider. She is strong, brilliant and feisty. She's the eccentric in the family and I wish I had seen her more. She doesn't visit often but she came to the important parts of my life; school promotions, graduation from college and grad school. She travels all over the world and never stays anywhere very long. My father always said she was a "restless spirit" and needed to move around."

"She sounds like an incredible woman, Barrett."

Their early dinner arrived and the conversation continued about Barrett's memories of his life as a child.

"Katherine has always been in the background, it seems, throughout my life," he continued as he made work of the Kobe New York steak in front of him. "I can't thank her enough, as she has helped contribute to my success as a businessman. She supported me with her words and ensured I had money as I neared graduation. She insisted I use it to help fulfill my entrepreneurial spirit."

"Barrett, it is incredible that you've had such support with your passion as you started out." Jodie finished her Alaskan Halibut and placed her napkin back in her lap. The light was fading outside and the rain started again. Jodie accepted another glass of wine brought to the table and thanked the waiter.

"Do you mind if I check my email quickly, lass? I'm expecting the final paperwork for the new restaurant and I need to be sure I'm timely in the review of it." The waiter had returned and picked up Barrett's plate as he held up his martini glass to the waiter, nodding, indicating he was ready for another.

"Oh, of course, Barrett. Please do. I think we've both been remiss in looking at our emails for our business." She laughed gently, reached inside her bag for her phone and then thought better of it. She enjoyed being disconnected from the world and would check her phone later tonight.

Barrett quickly perused his email and saw the email from his lawyers and was just about to return his phone to his pocket when an email caught his eye. "Well, now - look at this, lass." He smiled and leaned back in his chair. "Is this kismet, or what? It's an email from my Aunt Katherine. She's in San Francisco and plans to see me next week in Glasgow. She obviously has no idea that I'm in the city."

"Oh my gosh! How ironic, Barrett. We were just talking about her! Talk about coincidences."

"It is incredibly ironic, lass. I would love for you to meet her. Would you mind if we met her for a drink later tonight if she is free?" He looked at her and smiled. She could see the anticipation in his eyes.

"Of course, Barrett. I would love to meet her."

"Fine then. It's settled. Let me email Katherine to her know I'm here in San Francisco and we can meet up." Barrett tapped out his response and leaned back in the chair.

"I also have one quick visit I need to make for business. I'm sorry, it will just take me about forty-five minutes. I will drop you off at the hotel and you can relax for a few minutes and then we will meet up with my Aunt Katherine."

"Of course, Barrett. It's fine." She could use a few minutes to herself to catch her breath. Jodie felt so relaxed after dinner and settled into her second glass of wine. She was so happy right now. She was full, satisfied and quietly smiled, knowing she had made love for the last 24 hours. Nothing could take away the sheer joy she was experiencing now. Absolutely nothing.

*****

He arrived at the bank with just a few minutes to spare. He called ahead and they made an exception for him to come past the regular banking hours. He was, after all, one of their best customers and placed millions of dollars into their banks each year. So, they wouldn't dare give him any grief for keeping the bank open for his special appointment.

He dropped off the other documents last week at the Sacramento branch and when he was late, they didn't ask one single question. When he called today on the way to the bank in San Francisco, they grilled him and he didn't appreciate it. He decided that when he returned from his trip, he would contact the bank manager and talk with him about his concerns. He understood how vital timelines were with most business documents, but sometimes he found it frustrating. He raced across the top of town, but the traffic in San Francisco was relentless.

He parked on the side of the building in the "Employee of the Month" spot and headed to the front doors. A paunchy guard was standing inside the vestibule and his attention was elsewhere, as he didn't notice him standing at the door. Tapping on the glass gently to get his attention, the guard looked up, nodded and opened the door.

The guard glowered over his thick, caterpillar eyebrows. "Yes, sir?" He placed his card in his beefy hands and the guard looked over his glasses that edged down to the bottom of his nose. Satisfied, he stepped aside to allow entrance. He walked over the shiny tile floors, his footsteps breaking the silence as they echoed inside the cavernous building. Finally, he neared the desk and was greeted by a friendly smile from the woman seated behind the large mahogany desk.

"Welcome, sir. Nice to see you again."

"Thank you, Miss Evans."

He pushed the papers across the desk and removed his wallet from his jacket pocket. He sifted through the contents, found his driver's license and gently guided it across the desk next to the papers.

"Thank you, sir. It will be just a moment. They have to open the vault for the safety deposit boxes. I hope you don't mind waiting." She smiled at him and reached for his license. "I need to make a copy and get you a receipt. I'll be right back." She gave him another smile, this one showing, what appeared to be an invitation.

She stood and he smiled at her with gentle appreciation. He watched as she walked away, noticing her dress fit like a glove. Tight and form-fitted in all the right places. Damn, he wished he had more time, but he was in a hurry tonight. He had to get back. He continued to watch her walk and her body moved in a beautiful rhythm. She leaned over to the shelf on the side of the copy machine, knowing he was watching her as she grabbed a ream of paper.

He didn't disappoint her and maintained eye contact each time she glanced over her shoulder. Finally, she picked up the phone near her and he couldn't hear what she said, but she held his eyes with a pleasant and professional expression.

She walked back to the desk, slinky and stealthy, like a cat on a narrow fence. One perfectly beautiful high-heel in front of the other. She got his attention, worked her walk back to the desk and slipped back into the leather chair.

She crossed her legs off to the side and slowly, methodically pushed his license back over to him.

"Thank you for waiting, sir," she smiled and pushed her business card and his receipt across the desk. "We certainly appreciate your business. They are ready for you downstairs now."

He took the receipt and tucked it inside his jacket pocket and his license. He reached over, picked up the documents and slid them back inside the folder. Looking at her business card, he gently brought it to his nose, picking up the subtle fragrance of her cologne she had left behind. He locked his steel-blue eyes with hers.

"Thank you, Miss Evans. It's been lovely seeing you again. Let's meet at another venue sometime?" He smiled and she felt her knees go weak. Those eyes, she thought. Mmmm...those eyes. "Of course, it's been my pleasure serving you today, Mr. Rohan."

Chapter 24

"What is she saying?! What is taking so long?!" Tina's voice was loud, filled with panic.

"Tina, I don't know yet! Wait a minute - please! I'm waiting!" Loghan was every bit as worried and realized she yelled at Tina. "I'm sorry, Tina. I'm just…"

"Scared?" Tina finished her thought. "Me too. I'm scared shitless|"

Loghan squeezed Deagan's hand again and turned toward him, her eyes filled with concern. He squeezed her hand in return and gently guided her back to the couch to sit down. "Why isn't anything coming across? She was typing!" Loghan blurted out to no one in particular. Tina couldn't take one more moment without a response from Jodie. "Loghan, I can't do this anymore. I'm calling the police right now."

"Of course, Tina. Yes, you call the police and I'll wait a few more minute for a response. Sometimes there is a delay with text messages. I'll call the police too. Let's connect in a couple minutes. If anything changes, call sooner!" Loghan set her phone down a moment and stared blankly out her window.

She realized she was holding her breath when Deagan put his arm around her. "It's going to be alright." His voice calm and steady. "Take a few deep breaths, Loghan. You want a clear head when you call the police." Loghan drew in several deep breaths to calm her nerves, one…two…three…. She felt her head clear and pulse return to a reasonable rate. "Damn it…still, nothing coming across. She was typing…at least I thought she was." Her shoulders dropped and she tipped her head back in exasperation.

"That happens sometimes, Loghan. I see it all the time when I'm messaging someone and I think they are returning the text. I see the bubble...or, dots...whatever the hell they are called...then, nothing." Deagan shrugged his shoulders and gently smiled at her. "I guess." She looked down at Deagan's cell phone he was holding. "Do you have the number to the police in San Francisco?" She noticed he was searching for the number earlier when she was talking to Tina. He recited the number to her and Loghan tapped in the numbers. They answered quickly and she took a deep breath and gave out the initial information so they could determine where to transfer the call. She was placed on hold and Deagan placed his hand on her shoulders, gently rubbing between her noticeably tense shoulders.

She gave him a tentative smile and silently mouthed the words, "thank you," while he continued to comfort her and ease her tension for a moment.

"Hello. This is Detective Kinder. Who am I speaking to, please ?"

"This is Loghan Riley. I believe I have information for you regarding the composite photo that was on the news today - about the attempted murder."

"Please continue. I'm working on the case with my partner. What can you tell me?"

Loghan ran through her story and gave the detective as much information as she could remember. She told them about her friend, Jodie Rice and how she thought she was with the man in the sketch in San Francisco this weekend. She only met Barrett one time, but she remembered how handsome he was, so that was easy. She told the detective she was almost certain the drawing she saw was Barrett Rohan and her friend, Tina Stoddard believed this to be true as well. Detective Kinder said her partner was on the phone with her now and there were other calls and leads they needed to attend.

"Oh, I already checked Find My Friends and it showed her last ping, hours ago, at the Mark Hopkins." Loghan stood up abruptly and moved about the living room. "She is still not answering her phone! I know they are staying at the Mark Hopkins...surely someone has some information or has seen them." Her voice edging up again and she closed her eyes, breathing deeply. Don't panic, Loghan, she reminded herself.

The voice on the phone was calm and steady. "Ms. Riley; we will do what we can. We have other leads and will follow up with the information you've given us and the hotel. Rest assured, we're on this."

Loghan's phone pinged and she jumped. She looked quickly and noticed it wasn't Jodie. The detective paused. "If you hear from Ms. Rice, please let us know right away. We'll be in touch." The call disconnected and Loghan dropped her arm to her side.

"Damn it..." Loghan sighed. Deagan moved to the kitchen for more coffee and Harry was purring around his legs. He dropped down on one knee to give the big tabby a rub and allowed Loghan a moment to gather her thoughts. Loghan seeing he was preoccupied looked back to her phone and opened the message. It was David.

"Hi Darling. How are you today? Thank you for not being late for our scheduled chats. I've looked forward to talking with you all day." She tapped back a response quickly before Deagan noticed. *"Hi David. Not just now. I have an emergency. I'm ok, but I can't talk right now. I'll fill you in as soon as I can."*

She closed her message to David and checked her texts again to see if anything came from Jodie. Nothing. Damn it, she thought, where is she? She does this from time to time and doesn't respond until she can, or says she's busy and will talk to her later. This time, it was different. Jodie would usually let her know she was "going off the grid."

Deagan punched the button to the Keurig and asked if Loghan wanted another cup. "Yes, please. Thank you, Deagan." Her voice was soft, almost apologetic, as if she were speaking to herself more than him. She lingered in the doorway to the kitchen, one hand gripping the frame, the other absently twisting a strand of her ponytail. Deagan couldn't help but notice how the muted morning light made her look ethereal, like a painting he'd seen once in a dusty gallery. Strong, yes - but in this moment, a quiet vulnerability danced in her eyes and it stirred something protective in him. He smiled, hoping to ease the weight she carried, if only a little. Her beauty wasn't just in the way she looked, but how she carried herself, even now, standing in uncertainty.

"I thought this might help," he said gently, extending the cup of coffee toward her. Its rich aroma curled between them like an unspoken promise, "Thought it may help to clear your head, while we wait...or come up with a plan." For a moment, she hesitated, her gaze dropping to the cup. Then, slowly, she reached out, her fingers brushing his as she took it. The warmth of the cup spread through her hands and maybe, just maybe, through her heart. Her lips parted as if to speak, but she stopped herself. Instead, she glanced up at him, her eyes searching his face for something-answers, comfort, hope. Whatever it was, Deagan didn't know if he could provide it to her, but he'd do everything in his power to try. "It'll be ok," he said softly. "We'll figure it out."

"Deagan, I need to finish packing. I'm heading out earlier than I anticipated to San Francisco. I've got to find Jodie." Deagan nodded, "Sure, of course. Let me get going. Is there anything I can do to help?" Setting her coffee cup down on the counter, she took off her ball cap and undid her hair. Shaking her auburn tresses loose, she looked at Deagan, her green eyes serious. "Yes, there is, Deagan. Will you come to San Francisco with me?"

*****

He stood looking at the message from her with a puzzled look on his face. Did she just dismiss him? Impossible. That never happened with any woman he made contact with. Ever. He wouldn't allow for this type of treatment from anyone...even the beautiful and naive, Loghan. He drew in a deep, labored breath working to keep his temper tamped down. The voices began their fervent whispers. With gritted teeth, his fingers tapped urgently and with fierce dexterity. *"I'll reach out in a bit, my darling. I do hope all is well. I'm sure we will talk in a short while. Please let me know if there is anything I can do to help."*

He needed to have the last word with her. It was important that he made his intentions known. Loghan wasn't going to dictate how and when their conversation would take place. It didn't work that way. Hadn't she learned that by now? It didn't matter if he was late to the arranged times he made with all his "contacts." They waited for him without hesitation and without question.

This was the game of his choice. His control and doing. When they didn't follow, consequences must be paid. Some consequences were more serious than others, but all would be dealt with swiftly.

Some, he may never contact again. He would leave them wondering if he would ever show up again in their messages. Others, he would chastise and help them learn the game if he felt there were possibilities. The others, well, they appeared to know the game – venturing into his world in person if he felt they were fit to do so. If they didn't follow through with his needs or were unaware of his need to control how the game played out once he had them in person, there were serious consequences indeed.

He would play with them, like a cat with mouse – toying, teasing and taunting, until it was too late for his prey to know they were in danger. It was not his fault. Not his fault at all. Some women were unable to meet his needs and they had to pay the price. They lied to him. Told him they understood what he needed; offered their body to him for his taking. They were foolish. They thought it was all about sex and thinking he was in love with them, Christ, women could be so easy to manage.

His agitation was increasing by the minute. His concern about his recent sloppiness in his affairs flared up once more. Rarely did he miss any details with the women he talked to online. He always covered his bases – left no traces.

He reserved his encounters with men for bars, dimly lit corners where anonymity was both a cloak and a thrill. He adored those fleeting moments of opportunity. But women were his main "soup du' jour." So easily manipulated. Their trust a simple game of charm and deceit...and control. He took great care and consideration, teaching them his needs and he realized at this moment he overlooked this area with Loghan as well. She got under his skin so quickly and with ease – he didn't understand how this happened. All he knew was he had to have her. There was something about her innocence, her mind and way of phrasing her thoughts. She was lovely in all ways; he knew this to be true. He kept her very close to him, without her knowledge. There was something different about Loghan. Something he couldn't figure out, but he wasn't concerned. He was ahead of her in all ways.

He was able to track her calls and movements. He knew her email, text and ping conversations. Nothing was sacred. There was something to be said about working closely in communications. He had the knowledge of what was needed and he had contacts. Some people worked for him within the outer edges of their company who managed these "details" for him, or looking outside the company, in this case. He was pleased with himself for going outside his contacts within the company for this *assignment.* He reassured himself he wasn't being sloppy in all areas. He made a good choice here.

It didn't take much to find someone desperate to make money, or wanting something Aric could provide. In this case, on one of his recent trips to San Francisco, he looked for someone online. He was in the mood for a man who would not only be interested in a sound fuck, but one who could help Aric with a special request. Dexter was perfect for this job and it was so simple. He had his fingers in things that were illegal and was motivated by money and sex. A tech nerd that took his expertise of gaming and perverse interest in voyeurism to new levels. Aric found him easily upon one of his many business trips to San Francisco and chatted him up in a men's bar off Castro.

Dexter rattled on with casual arrogance, oblivious of the silent scrutiny of Aric. The pulsing lights of Badlands on Castro, painted shifting shadows over his sharp features, giving him the look of prey, to Aric's amusement. "All it takes is the right tools and knowing where to look. Most people don't even bother with basic security on their phones." He leaned closer to Aric, his words barely audible over the pounding bass. "You'd be amazed how many people hand you the keys to their life without even knowing it."

Dexter enjoyed Aric's questions on how to track someone. He foolishly assumed Aric was interested in getting to know him. Dexter shared his knowledge of wiretapping, tracking phones and how easy it was to run code or location programs with only having a cell number. Aric continued to recall their 'chance' meeting at the bar on Castro. "Is it really? I had no idea such things were available." Aric lied and smiled, pushing another whiskey toward Dexter. Aric knew he found the right person to manipulate. "You must be very good at solving...puzzles," Aric's lips curled in a polite half-smile, his tone measured and calm.

Dexter laughed, a short, barking sound. "Oh, hell yes. I can track anyone on their phone. It's kind of my thing - you know? It makes me feel powerful. There are all kinds of locator programs that run behind the back door - no one knows, not even the Feds." He smiled, exposing a row of crooked teeth, then took a long sip, his eyes flickering with pride, "So, who's the lucky target? Or are you just curious about the dark arts?"

Aric chuckled softly, swirling his own drink. "Curiosity," he lied, leaning back on the bar stool with a casual ease, "and, well, I do believe I have some work for you, my friend." Aric couldn't believe how easy it was going to be to manipulate Dexter. Dexter was overly eager and ready to please, Aric. The homely ones always were, he sneered. Aric tipped his glass toward Dexter, the corners of his mouth quirking up an almost imperceptible smirk. "To power." he said, his voice steady and cool.

Dexter raised his glass with a cocky grin, "To power." Dexter felt uneasy for a brief moment as he stared back into the cold eyes, "Where exactly are you from...umm...what did you say your name was again?

"David - David Rothchild." He extended his manicured hand to the young man. It was so easy for him to lie. It rolled right off his tongue and into the ears of those around him. They never questioned or believed anything other than what he fed them.

Fool, he thought. "I'm from London. Across the pond, as you yanks say." He smiled brilliantly showing his perfectly white teeth and moved in closer to the young man. He didn't want him to wonder if he was interested in him and leave with someone else. Aric scoffed at this thought as if Dexter would not spend time with him...please. He smiled at Dexter and took a thoughtful sip of his cocktail.

Dexter was mesmerized by Aric's eyes and held his gaze for a brief moment. The uneasy feeling came again, but shrugged it off, as Aric placed his hand on his thigh, gently teasing his fingers toward Dexter's crotch.

"Ahem... Well, I can track whoever you want... and as many as you want, David."

"Delightful. Why don't we go someplace where we can...work out the details?" Aric's hand continued to tease. His eyes rolled over the young man's body. He was a little too thin and he hated his hair, but he was certain this, less than an attractive man could suit his needs. He may get what he wanted without even having to pay him, only *service* him on occasion. He could certainly do that from time to time.

Dexter couldn't believe his luck with this fucking hot guy interested in him. Hell yes, he would go with him -*anywhere*. Do whatever he needed. Tracking someone on a cell phone was chicken - shit easy. He was more interested in leaving and getting right to it. So began their brief, but lurid affair. "David" provided Loghan's phone numbers - cell and work and Dexter retrieved the IP address and provided the links for him to access her location. It really was quite simple. Right from his phone he could see where Loghan was and whom she spoke or texted. Technology was truly lovely.

Dexter turned out to be quite helpful and Aric had extended his use to provide information on Avery's whereabouts and cell phone activity as well. Aric was leaps and bounds ahead of Avery now. He was able to locate Avery at a moment's notice from his phone and he plotted his next steps to deal with her easily. It was not Aric's intention to kill Dexter, but it had to be done.

Dexter talked too damn much and it was his fault he was dead, certainly not Aric's. He was a fool and shared too much about himself. Aric found it fascinating he worked at the coroner's office and was surrounded by poor, hapless victims. Victims of circumstances they may have otherwise controlled but weren't smart enough to do so. Dexter talked and talked one night after a rousing romp in bed. Aric couldn't believe that he still had it in him for "pillow talk," but he talked non-stop of his case this week and it was too close for comfort.

Dexter had blathered on and on about the cases that came in. In the endless stream of talking he shared, he sometimes would tip off writers from different news agencies or papers with information. He was so proud of this disclosure as he lay naked that night, staring at the ceiling. He told him about this writer - someone who came to interview him about a year ago for a story he was writing. "He is hot. Not hot like you, David...hot, in a different way. You know?" He had stretched across Aric's lap for a cigarette on the nightstand, lighting it with an unsteady hand. "Whew...I'm still shaky from all the...fun," he paused as he took a long, deep drag from the cigarette.

"Yes, of course. I know what you mean. Please continue?" Aric had to show some amount of interest in his lame stories, but this one seemed to be going to some place of particular interest to him. Dexter let out a perfect stream of smoke, "Well, I enjoy helping out the "underdogs" and sometimes, the cops don't let out enough details to help the public identify if they know something about a case," he rolled over and propped up on his elbow. "I like to help them along when I can," a look of smugness came over Dexter's face - a sense of superiority. "So, I chose this writer to help along the path. He writes really great articles and I think there is something about this murder case I'm working on this week." He was clearly so proud of himself, Aric recalled the details from Dexter's story from last night.

Aric knew another quick romp in the sheets would satisfy Dexter to continue to provide details on his findings on Avery and anything else regarding Loghan, so it was all an "act of service."

"Do continue, dear Dexter." His fake smile, undetectable to Dexter. Dexter went on about the writer he decided to help and how "dreamy he was."

"Did you just say, 'dreamy?'"

"I did! I know, I know...I sound like a girl!" Dexter lay back down and stretched his legs out, placing one on top of Aric's thigh. "I'm fangirling over him, but he's sexy. Even his name. Rugged and maybe Irish. McGrath-Deagan McGrath."

Aric ran his hands up and down on Dexter's thighs and he stopped suddenly. "Really? Deagan McGrath?" The name immediately resonated with familiarity. What a coincidence, this had become too close for comfort, he thought. This called for a change of plans and he quickly considered his options. "I think I may be getting a tad jealous of this "rugged man" you continue to speak of Dexter." He could care less really and grabbed Dexter's legs and sharply pulled them around him.

"Oh my...! I do like it when we play rough, David!" his eyes glistened with anticipation. "Honestly, it's always a surprise coming from such an English gentleman." Dexter laughed and handed his cigarette to Aric, giving him a nod to go ahead with whatever he was going to do to him. Aric placed the cigarette in the ashtray and smiled at Dexter.

Oh, he had no idea how rough it was going to be, poor soul as he reached for a pillow.

Shrugging off the memory of Dexter, Aric rolled his shoulders and head from side to side. His struggle was quite brief, not at all a fighter. He had all he needed now.

Aric spent his time the last 3 years zig-zagging his way across the continents, seeing women, spending time with some and allowing many to go about their daily lives. Some were not as fortunate, he thought dismissively. It wasn't his fault if they didn't understand the game. His temper was coming fast and he thought again, he hadn't the time to teach lovely Loghan everything he needed. He was, quite frankly, running out of time as the voices were challenging him. He had to hope she would be a quick study and come with him willingly. It would be a shame for her to go the way of the others, like the last few who refused to play. He knew he needed to be in her physical space - to touch her velvet skin and take her at least one time before he decided what he would do with her.

He needed to stay on track and be sure he was covering up his steps along the way. Now was not the time for errors. He made a few of late and he acknowledged he must re-engage and not allow these fucking voices to direct this part of his plan. He still had work to do and then...there was Avery.

*****

Back at his hotel, he paced the room. The pain was sudden and harsh. "Fuck!" He placed his fingers on top of his eyes, pushing back the pain and throbbing in his head. He forced himself to sit down and stop the manic pacing. It only aggravated him and the voices were stirring now. They were coming more frequently and he didn't know why they continued to press him. He tried to do what he could to manage them, feeding that 'want' the voices required, but nothing seemed to help stop the noise in his head.

The pain began to subside and he felt his shoulders relax. He took in a few deep breaths and looked out the window, musing about his text with Loghan.

Whatever could be the emergency? He kept considerable tabs on her and was certain she told him everything. She even mentioned to him about the writer, Deagan McGrath she worked with closely. He knew damn well, this, this miserable fuck, was interested in her. He would not have any opportunity to get to Loghan, he would need to figure that out as well. He knew Loghan was interested in him, not this, Deagan. He was taking it slow with her. She was educated, smart, but she was also skittish, like a young spirited filly. She shared much with him these last many weeks and they drifted off to sleep on the phone a few nights back. He was setting the pace to not deter her and it was surprising the other night when they chatted on line and described how they wanted one another sexually. It was unexpected to him that Loghan took the bait and 'gave herself' to him.

He was truly touched that she gave into her needs. That was a first for him having such feelings. He found that he was unusually attracted and interested in Loghan Riley and he needed to get a hold of himself. He had to make the best of impressions with her. She was different. Different than all the others and he cared for her. He didn't know what to do with these emotions, but he wanted more than anything to put his hands on her. To touch her and feel her warmth beneath his fingertips.

She was not like others, but maybe...maybe she would see how perfect he was. He knew he must step carefully with her. He wasn't sure what he would do with Loghan, but she needed to see him. Meet him and then...then he would see where the moment took him. He was unpredictable these days and he was aware of this, but the yearning for her sweet, young and vibrant body was more than he could contain. He shook his head slightly as if to shake the thoughts.

He moved away from the window and walked to the wet bar. It was early, but he needed a God damn drink, now. Too much was happening and he needed to slow things down. He still had the meeting with Avery to prepare for today. He was angry with an early text message from Avery. *"What time can I expect you today, dear?"*

He could read the sarcasm in her text message. Heard that tone so many times in his life. If something weren't going Avery's way, he would know about it immediately. "She's a vile human being," he whispered through gritted teeth. He knew today was the day, Avery wanted to speak to him. She made it very clear she wasn't pleased with his spending habits from his expense account for work. She wasn't happy with the money he pulled from one of the joint business accounts to help support his lifestyle. It was just fine that...that shrew to flew off to Aruba, or Portugal when she wanted to impress a client or new lover, but for him to try to win over a client, or perhaps fly to the states to see one of his "lady friends"...no. She wouldn't hear of it.

Aric knew the time was nearing for him to drop the boom on Avery. He was privy to information that he held for many years. He snuck into her study years ago, and found documents that opened a world of secrets and falsehoods that made the story clear for Aric. He never understood why Avery and his own grandfather, Rhonert Stanton, treated him so poorly. Aric made himself a martini and placed three large, garlic stuffed olives on a stainless-steel pick and dropped it into the glass. The sound was so satisfying as it softly tinged against the sides. He would have coffee later, just as soon as the vodka martini took the edge off his nerves.

He poured the clear liquid into the glass after a suitable shake and smiled at his reflection in the window. The fog wrapped the Mark Hopkins like a damp shroud. From his perch twenty floors up, he watched the umbrellas bloom on California street, black petals against the gray morning. He pressed his forehead against the cool window, his breath ghosting the glass and continued to turn the plans over for the next steps in his fevered mind.

He was smarter than anyone, he knew. Even the damn voices taking over his thoughts. His head was throbbing, and he hoped the martini would help numb the pain, but he knew he needed to stay clear, reminding himself not to drink too much today. His day depended on his plans. Everything had to go right.

He looked out the window, watching the cars pass by on the street below, his eyes swept the streets and neighboring Noe Valley. He allowed his eyes to continue to brush across the views and locked on the building across the street. Multiple voices in his head were making themselves known last night and this morning. One voice was the most persistent of them all. He pulled his focus from the building across the street and his reflection in the window came to his view again. His normally handsome, confident appearance was not looking back at him, but one of questionable concern.

He didn't like what he was seeing and set the martini glass down quickly, some of its contents spilling on the wet bar.

"DAMN IT! ENOUGH! IT WILL GO AS PLANNED!"

His fists balled up, he held them to his temples. The pain was excruciating, and the voices were hammering in his head like a machine gun. He would not allow them to dictate how he would plan out his next steps. He waited for years to pay Avery back for her hidden secrets. Avery, thinking she was so fucking smart. She was no match for his brilliance, for his aptitude in business. That is why she called *him* in to close the big deals, to make the clients come to his way of seeing the value in their acquisitions. He was always able to close the deal and make millions for the company.

Just one more perfect aspect was needed to make his plans fall into line. He knew once he had it all in place, maybe the voices would quiet down...perhaps, stop altogether. Yes, that would be nice to not have their constant interruption. He controlled all things in his life, and this would be no different. He needed to control and banish the voices and, he knew what needed to be done to make them stop.

*****

Barrett drove across the top of town making his way back to the Mark Hopkins. He hated when business interfered with pleasure, but sometimes he knew it was unavoidable. Deals were always in the making and didn't wait for reasonable times. He was glad that one was behind him, and he could go on with the rest of the weekend with Jodie. He received an immediate response from his email to his Aunt Katherine and made plans to meet at Bourbon and Branch on Jones St. It was a swanky, speakeasy with reservations only that held up to its theme of the prohibition days. He visited this location on his last trip to San Francisco and enjoyed the ambiance, decor and the "house rules" that all were required to follow; no cell phones, no photography and to "speakeasy," while in the bar. He tapped on Jodie's name on the screen console in the car. The phone rang and she answered on the second ring.

"Hi there, handsome." He could hear the smile in her voice.

"Well, hello there yourself, lass. I hope I didn't take longer than I stated?"

"No, not at all. I freshened up, put on a new, sexy dress just for you and I'm ready." Barrett smiled at the thought of her putting on something lovely, just for him. "Well then, I'm just about 3 minutes away. Let me drop off the car and I will come up and get you."

She laughed. "Don't be silly, Barrett. You don't need to do all that. Please... I'll come down and meet you in front."

He veered onto California street and dodged a pothole. "I'm a gentleman - and a gentleman escorts a lady. I'll split the difference. I'll meet you in the lobby, lass. See you in a few moments."

How in the world did she find an old-world gentleman in this day and age? She didn't think about that for one more minute and grabbed her wrap and headed out the hotel room door.

*****

Jenny tapped on the number on her cell phone and waited for the call to connect. She looked around the apartment and smelled bacon and eggs from the kitchen.

Her friend, and previous roommate, Erin, was making breakfast for them. Jenny was exhausted from her frightening encounter this weekend and Erin told her to stay. There was no need for her to go back home, just yet. There was no one there for her and she was safe with Erin.

She adored her friend, and Erin took off the rest of the weekend from her hair show that she had done nothing but talk about with Jenny for the last three months.

"You'll do no such thing, Erin!" Jenny was shocked that Erin wasn't going to finish the weekend hair and fashion show she entered.

"Jenny, are you kidding me? You're more important to me than a stupid - ass hair show! Besides, you said you aren't calling your parents and there isn't anyone to go home to. Stay here with me for the weekend - better yet, take another day, or two."

"I have to work, Erin. I need to get back to Sacramento. I'm ok, really. I just need..." She paused and wiped away the unexpected tears that filled her eyes.

Erin grabbed the box of tissues from the counter and handed one to Jenny. "You just need to rest and sleep. I'm here for you, Jenny. Call your boss - let him know you're taking a few days off."

Jenny pulled the throw blanket up around her and settled back deeper on the over-sized couch, surrounding her with a sense of comfort. She considered her options for a moment. She didn't have anything pressing at work and sure as shit didn't want to call her parents. Christ...that would do her mother in, and the sanctimony and preaching would never end.

No, she would not call her parents and tell them what happened. She *would* call her boss, Deagan, though. Deagan would understand she needed time off and she hoped he didn't think less of her for asking for time off so unexpectedly. She wasn't sure if she was going to tell him everything, but she would figure it out once she called him.

"Ok.," Jenny acquiesced to her friends' request. "I will call my boss and ask for a few more days off. You sure, you're ok with me being around and all?"

Erin jumped on the couch and hugged Jenny tightly. "Fuck yes, I'm sure! I will take good care of you, my friend!"

Jenny felt a small smile cross her lips and realized it was the first time since the attack she felt "normal." She was certainly grateful for her friend, Erin.

"Hello? Jenny?" Deagan answered the phone, and she could hear the slight curiosity in his voice. Jenny rarely called Deagan, she texted when she needed anything or had to communicate for work.

"Hi, Deagan...thanks for taking my call. I'm - I'm sorry to bother you on the weekend, but I need to ask a favor?" She felt her stomach tightening up and the feeling of panic settle in again. The recollection of her attacker and what she had been through this weekend welled up in her voice.

"Jenny? Is everything ok?"

Jenny's emotions got the better of her and she told Deagan she was alright, but something horrible happened to her the other night. She was so embarrassed to tell him she met a strange man for drinks, but she respected Deagan and he deserved the truth. She finished telling him and Deagan responded with total empathy and concern. "Oh my God, Jenny. Is there anything I can do for you? Can I call your parents, anyone?"

"Oh, no, Deagan...thank you - no." She watched as Erin set the plate of bacon, eggs and toast on the coffee table in front of her. "I - just need a few days to get my head together. I'm sorry. I hope I didn't disappoint you." Jenny closed her eyes and leaned her head back.

"Disappoint me? No! Of course not! I'm so grateful you're ok. Please, take as much time as you need, Jenny. I'm actually on my way down to San Francisco today with...," He paused. Deagan kept his business separate from his personal life and even amid this terrible news, he had his wits about him and didn't mention Loghan's name. "...with a friend. I have some investigating to do for something I'm working on," he continued, "are you sure, there isn't anything I can do for you?"

"No, thank you, Deagan. I appreciate you more than you know. Thank you for letting me take a few days. I'll be here in my old apartment. I'm staying with my ex-roommate, Erin."

"Please take care of yourself, Jenny. Call me if you need anything. Anything at all."

Jenny put the phone down and Erin nodded at her with a brief smile. "Eat," she nodded at Jenny's plate.

Jenny's phone rang again. "Shit...," Erin jumped, startled by the ring. "I guess my nerves are a little on edge. Sorry." Erin picked up her plate and pushed the scrambled eggs around with her fork.

Jenny looked at the number but didn't recognize it. She looked at Erin and answered the phone and tapped on speaker, so Erin could hear.

"Hello? Jenny's voice was hesitant.

The voice came through with a gentle, but authoritative nature. "Jenny Harper? This is Detective Kinder. We think we have a very strong lead."

Jenny and Erin locked eyes and froze.

Chapter 25

Barrett put his hand on the small of Jodie's back, guiding her to the discreet, nondescript door nestled in the shadows of a faded brick building. The dim glow of a single light barely illuminated the street number etched beside the entry, the only indication that he was in the right place. Barrett glanced at it, silently confirming the address: *this was the place.* Bourbon and Branch-infamous, elusive, and just as mysterious as he recalled his Aunt Katherine had described.

The Tenderloin district hummed around them, the sounds of muffled laughter, echoing footsteps and distant sirens weaving the soundtrack of the city's underbelly. Barrett's eyes flicked to passing strangers, scanning their faces with a casual wariness. No one seemed to take notice of them, still, his hand stayed steadily on Jodie, a subtle reassurance against the backdrop of uncertainty.

"It's not much to look at," Barrett murmured, glancing down at Jodie with a smirk.

"You'd think a place like this would be a dive," Barrett continued, his voice low. "I enjoy it, and Aunt Katherine swears by their cocktails. Said it's her favorite stop when she's in the city." Jodie arched a perfectly manicured eyebrow. "Your Aunt Katherine knows her way around speakeasies?"

Reaching for the unmarked door, he pulled the handle - it was locked. Remembering her email, he chuckled and pressed the buzzer next to the door, adding, "She knows her way around most things."

He recalled that he needed a password to get in, and the entrance would not have any indication it was a bar of any sort. "All part of the atmosphere, my dear, it's a 1920s themed Speak-Easy. You will love it," not realizing he had already experienced the bar's mystique. She signed off on her email, leaving him the address and password, and her usual, "Love you, forever. Aunt Katherine." For as long as Barrett could remember, this is how she always signed off on her cards and emails.

He smiled at her choice of location and thought it perfect as his Aunt Katherine was known for her lofty sense of self and mystery. Her email included what time to meet, and she was looking forward to seeing him as it had been far too long.

Barrett couldn't agree more. It had been some time since he'd seen her last; he was happy to meet up with her and tell her more about his life and business adventures. It was, after all, her help over the years that allowed Barrett to stretch his wings and lean into his entrepreneurial spirit. He owed her so much for his success and he could never thank her enough for her belief in him and financial support over the years. Even when he was in college, she would drop him a postcard from some exotic location and there was always mention, she "added to his trust" and for him to use it wisely.

He was sorry he didn't get to see her more as a child, but she did come around for the big occasions and a holiday dinner or visit from time to time. Now, as an adult, their paths crossed on the rare opportunity and he promised himself, he would take every opportunity to see his aunt more frequently. His parents passed long ago, and he missed the blessings of having a family. No time like the present, he thought.

Barrett learned very little from his father about his aunt, but he loved her spirit. Katherine was a world traveler and had business dealings in the art community and other businesses that kept her from settling down. He'd known this since he was a child and he learned from his father, Katherine was a wanderlust and invested well. Barrett's parents were financially stable and well-off, he lived a very privileged life. His Aunt Katherine was all too happy to help Barrett maintain this lifestyle, as she was quite generous with her wealth.

"Are we sure this is the place?" Jodie looked around the dampened streets and up at the sign outside the building. It read: Anti-Saloon League. She smiled as she took in the sign and looked back at Barrett, they continued to wait for a response to the buzzer.

"This really is something, Barrett. I can hardly wait to see inside." She reached into her purse and stopped suddenly.

"Something wrong, lass?" Barrett looked at her and noticed a slight strain in her eyes.

"Well, nothing terrible. I feel silly telling you this. I didn't mention it at the hotel, but I think I lost my phone. It's not a big deal, but it's odd. I have never lost a phone...misplaced it? Yes - I have not responded to texts for a while - guilty. But lost?" She waved her hand dismissively.

"Do you need to use mine, lass?" Barrett reached into his pocket. Jodie waved her hands away. "Oh gosh, not right now, Barrett. It's not a problem. I just don't lose things - especially my phone. It's so odd that I did," her eyes met with his and she relaxed immediately. "Let's go meet your aunt."

Her beaming smile lit up the misty night air, and Barrett tried once more, pressing the button next to the large, wood door. This time, a large man cracked the door and stepped outside, closing the door behind him.

"Good evening... May I help you?" His voice was smooth yet firm. His attire was meticulous - a black dress shirt with sharp creases down the arm, suspenders taut over broad shoulders, black tailored slacks and a fedora angled, just so, lending an air of quiet authority.

Barrett straightened, instinctively pulling Jodie closer to his side and held her hand in his. "Yes, please. We have 7 PM reservations, they are under Rohan - Katherine Rohan." The pause stretched and Barrett's confidence wavered. When no sign of welcome came, he leaned in, his voice dropping to a near whisper as he murmured something into the man's ear.

The man's lips twitched - perhaps a smirk, perhaps approval - and with a curt nod, he stepped aside, holding the door open just wide enough for them to enter. The bar was dark and even though they entered from the night, their eyes took a moment to adjust. They were met with the sounds of Billie Holiday, and a young, beautiful dark-haired woman met them with a small flashlight in hand.

"Good evening, welcome. This way to your table, please." She was very chic, and her dark black hair was slicked back into a bun with a sparkling hair net holding it in place. She wore a black skirt, heels, a tailored blouse and deep red lipstick. Jodie loved everything she took in - her eyes swept around, adjusting to the dimmed lighting. There was a long hallway going to the back of the bar that piqued her curiosity. "What's back there?" she asked the waitress.

"Oh, that is for customers that don't have a reservation. There is a secret passage into the library room," She smiled at Jodie and continued; "your table is right here."

In the darkened bar there was a small booth, made from oak, topped with a small Tiffany lamp and a stunning woman sitting, looking at a menu. She heard the waitress approach and looked up with anticipation.

"Oh, my darling, Barrett!" She rose from the table and the waitress stepped out of the way to allow Katherine out of the small booth. "I'll give you a moment and come take your cocktail orders." Katherine smiled sweetly at Barrett, "Let me have a good look at you. Handsome as ever, isn't he?" She smiled at Jodie as if the two were friends sharing the most obvious statement.

"Aunt Katherine. So good to see you," Barrett kissed her on both cheeks and pulled Jodie closer to his side, "this is Jodie - Jodie Rice. She is...well, she's my...special friend." He smiled awkwardly at Jodie and pulled her close to him. "She's a wonderful woman and very special to me. I wanted my special ladies to meet one another." He continued to beam at Jodie and turned his attention back to Katherine.

They embraced in a long, welcoming greeting. Jodie detected Barrett's eyes glistening, and he closed his eyes tightly. Katherine was first to break away and placed her hands in his. A single tear trailed down her cheek and she blinked it away. There was no time to be proper and withhold feelings here, she withdrew her hands and reached up and held Barrett's face.

"Please let me say this," her eyes filled with emotion, "I'm so sorry I've not seen much of you over the years, lad. I wish I could have been with you more...spent more time with you. It was just - it wasn't always possible." She brushed away tears as if they were a nuisance and pulled him in again.

Barrett returned her hug and kissed her once more on the cheek. "Oh, Auntie…what's all this?" He smiled at her with deep affection and glanced at Jodie who stood off the side, trying to be discreet at this heartfelt reunion.

"It's fine, Aunt Katherine…really. I'm a grown man now. I know you were so busy with your traveling and career. I was very young and didn't question it…really." He looked at her with genuine concern. Barrett didn't know where this sadness was coming from, as he was quite happy, he was finally getting to see a family member. His family was so small, and since his parents passed, he lacked the feeling of completeness that only family can offer. Katherine regrouped and smiled through her wet lashes. Jodie admired Katherine and realized suddenly how elegant and beautiful she presented herself.

Barrett had not really told her much about her appearance, or how she held herself, only that she was mysterious, strong and very well off in the family. He really didn't know more details of her as he'd liked, but their bond was strong, regardless.

"Please – let's sit down. We have much to catch up and discuss." Katherine waved her arm to the seats and Jodie slid in first and Barrett sat next to her. Barrett looked around the bar as his eyes had adjusted to the lighting. "What a spot, Aunt Katherine. How did you find this place?' Katherine slid the cocktail menu to Jodie and placed her hands on top of Barrett's.

"Oh well, you may know, I'm always looking for something different and fun." She winked wickedly at him and chuckled, "This place checks all the boxes, and I love the ambiance. Can't you almost feel the way it must have been back in the '20s when one couldn't get a drink to save their soul?" She laughed and her head fell back slightly to expose her necklace covered in diamonds and a perfectly placed emerald at the base of her throat. Jodie couldn't help but notice the brilliance of the beautiful necklace as it picked up a glint, even in the dimly lit bar. She had never seen such elegance or an emerald that large. She really is something, Jodie mused as she looked over the cocktail menu.

Barrett smiled and agreed with his aunt. The place seeped of the atmosphere of the prohibition days. Deep, dark mahogany wood, oak tables,

Tiffany lamps and the bartenders were decked out to the nines. He watched as one bartender created a cocktail and shook the silver shaker above his head, all the while smiling. He poured an amber liquid through a strainer up high to make an impression. They certainly didn't miss a beat here, Barrett mused.

Their small chat and greetings continued a few more minutes as they settled in. They passed the drink menu around and when the waitress returned, they placed their orders. Vodka Lime Gimlet for the ladies and a classic, Old Fashioned for Barrett. "The Gimlet is the best I've ever had, Jodie...and I've had plenty." Katherine winked slyly at Jodie and the two laughed.

The night was lovely and filled with Katherine reminiscing about, "young B," and how she remembered him as a child. Jodie laughed at the nickname his aunt referred to him and leaned back, smiling at the conversation. She loved learning about Barrett and meeting his Aunt Katherine was the icing on the cake. The cocktails arrived, and the mood shifted to a lighter tone.

The conversation drifted to Jodie and Katherine had many questions, but none she considered prying. Jodie didn't mind at all, and responded to Katherine's questions regarding her work and career. It was just a matter of time that Katherine would ask how she and Barrett met. Jodie shifted nervously in her seat. She blushed when she mentioned they had only been dating for a short time.

"Now, now, darling. There is nothing to be embarrassed about at all!" Katherine had noted Jodie's blush even with the dimmed lighting. "There is nothing more exciting than meeting someone to whom we're wildly attracted....a moth to a flame." Katherine smiled brilliantly. "It's all part of this exciting life we are blessed to lead." Katherine patted Jodie on the hand reassuringly and smiled.

Jodie liked Katherine very much and instantly knew she was a worldly and sexy woman. Barrett may not know much about her, but this -Jodie knew intrinsically. His Aunt Katherine was stunningly beautiful and appeared to be in her mid-to late 50s. Barrett never mentioned how attractive and vivacious Katherine was, but then he wouldn't necessarily, as she was his aunt. For some reason, Jodie thought she would be much older and smiled; it seemed Katherine was perhaps the age of her own mother.

Katherine turned toward Jodie and reached for Jodie's hand. "Do you mind, darling if we shift our conversation to something quite dull for a short while? She smiled at Jodie and lifted her perfectly shaped brows to indicate her question.

"Of course not, Katherine. Please do!" Jodie smiled at Barrett and thought this may be her quiet cue to visit the ladies' room. "Will you please excuse me? I'm going to find the ladies' room." Barrett scooted out of the booth and Jodie slid across the bench, following him. He offered his hand to her, she took his hand, stood and pecked his cheek; then he watched her walk away.

"Oh, my darling, B...you've fallen hard. I can see it all over your face." She smiled at Barrett and tipped her head to the side, looking him over and showing her approval of his apparent feelings.

"Oh now, Auntie..." Barrett's burr was quiet and he smiled a slow, lopsided grin. "I am quite taken by her, I cannae lie," his Scottish brogue thick, taking Katherine a moment to register he was saying - 'he cannot.' She chuckled and watched him lean back against the seat and let out a quiet sigh.

"I can see that, lad." Her voice quiet, making her accent more noticeable. "It makes my heart so very happy to see you light up as you are. I hope this time is appropriate, but I want to get to it. I have a tiresome meeting in the morning and won't be able to stay too long, but I have some news - very good news for you, indeed."

"Auntie, what is it? You said good news, so I can assume you're alright? In good health?" Barrett's eyebrow creased. Katherine let out a large smile and patted his hand. "Oh my, yes...there is not much that would keep this old, girl down, Barrett." She laughed and Barrett couldn't help but return her laugh. She seemed relaxed and at ease. Shifting in her seat she reached for her large bag and lifted out a large manila envelope.

Katherine caught the eye of their server and motioned for another round. "I hope I'm not being presumptuous?" She smiled at Barrett and he shook his head. "I think from the sounds of it, Auntie, I may need this next drink."

Katherine smiled as Jodie appeared at the table and took her place once more. She reached for her glass and held it up to toast, Barrett and Jodie followed suit and paused as Katherine took a deep breath.

"To love - success - honor and...forgiveness." Their glasses clinked and Barrett looked questioningly at his aunt. "Cheers," he nodded as he held Katherine's sparking eyes, and took a sip of his Old Fashioned.

* * *

Deagan nodded and offered a reassuring smile as Loghan peeked her head out her front door.

"I'll be right down." She called down to him. He was standing outside his car and opening his trunk to make room for her luggage.

"Hold on," he said as he ran up the stairs, two at a time. "Let me get that for you, Loghan." He bent down and grabbed her suitcase. She smiled at him and pulled the front door closed.

She had a garment bag draped over her arm and a small overnight bag. "I think I have everything. I left Harry a lot of food and water; my neighbor downstairs will look in on him over the weekend."

"That's good. I know that's always a concern - I did the same with Max." Deagan reached for her overnight bag and without thought, Loghan handed it over to him.

They arranged the luggage in the trunk; Deagan lay the garment bag across their luggage. "Did you bring something fancy?" Loghan gave Deagan a small, somewhat teasing smile.

"You told me we may be going to a fancy wedding, so I brought my tuxedo." He shrugged nonchalantly and closed the trunk. Loghan smiled and climbed into Deagan's Volvo. He was such a practical man, she thought, her gaze lingering on the clean, understated interior of his car. She didn't know why it surprised her that he had a tuxedo, but he did, certainly. Just as he could drive any vehicle he wanted, but Deagan chose safety and subdued luxury, over a flashy vehicle. He was unpredictable and she liked that about him and smiled slightly as she settled in for the short drive to San Francisco.

The rain was still coming down, but it wasn't too cold. That was the thing about Sacramento, even in the winter, the weather could be comfortable.

Loghan rarely found herself cold, but when she did, she opted for a cardigan or light winter coat. She wished she could wrap up in thick scarves and boots and a classy winter jacket, or coat, but that didn't happen often in the Sacramento climate.

She checked her messages again and still nothing from Jodie. She tried to keep her nerves in check and reassured herself that Jodie was smart, she wouldn't get herself into something she shouldn't. She was a great judge of character, but she was sure the drawing she saw on the news was Barrett.

Wasn't it?

She didn't want to second guess herself, but she thought that it must be common when you don't want to think the worst.

She had called the police station once more before Deagan arrived and this time was told unless something changed, they would be in touch with her. Jodie was an adult and until twenty-four hours had passed, there was nothing they could do. They were working on the leads and nothing in that aspect had changed.

Loghan checked in with Tina and she didn't have any updates either. Loghan filled her in on what the detectives told her and Tina confirmed she was told the same. They agreed they would remain calm and Loghan would let Tina know when she arrived in San Francisco.

She didn't know what she was going to do about her friend Megan's wedding, but she continued on as if she were in fact, attending. She took her dress, makeup and everything else she planned for the weekend, with exception to Deagan. She was certainly glad he was available and coming with her, but he was unexpected, for certain.

She would take it one minute at a time and if all turned out well, she would see her dear friend getting married tomorrow.

She shook her head - If? - If everything goes well?? What in the hell was she thinking? Way to be positive, Loghan, she thought sarcastically.

She looked down at her watch to note the time as Deagan pulled out of the driveway. She leaned her head back and closed her eyes.

"Hey, it's going to be fine - I just know it. I don't know how I know that, but I feel it." Deagan reached over and placed a gentle hand on her shoulder.

"Thank you, Deag," she smiled at him weakly through tired eyes. "I kind of have that sense too, but I won't rest until I hear from her, you know?" Her green eyes, though tired, were filled with hope. He smiled at her once more and started down the street. They stopped at Starbucks for more coffee and pumpkin loaves and made their way to the freeway.

Loghan looked at her phone and noticed David was trying to reach her, again. She found a few minutes to contact him as she was preparing to leave this morning, but she noted a change in his otherwise, cheerful and warm demeanor.

He seemed short with her and pressed for details about what was going on and why couldn't she talk to him now? She was slightly put off how he responded to her but dismissed his behavior. She knew he had a terrible meeting recently and mentioned it was with his mother and he was "simply dreading it," as he put it.

Loghan felt empathy for David, but she had too much to do and didn't have the time to spend at her computer chatting with him. His responses were short and she felt again, that nagging concern this may not be the best decision to continue with David. She didn't want to stop talking with him and the thought entered her mind, she wished there were something more tangible between them. She was not doing anything wrong talking with him - these were small steps for now, she justified and shook off the thought. Everything was just fine, she considered and once Jodie responds, everything will be back to normal.

She stared straight ahead, her eyes fixed on the highway as cars blurred past. The roar of engines echoed in her ears, while the slick pavement sent up sheets of water from spinning tires. The world outside seemed distant, a rushing torrent of speed and spray, yet she remained still, lost in the rhythm of the rain-soaked road. Deagan sensed her need for quiet and kept his eyes locked on the road and concentrated.

Loghan continued to think about David. She didn't quite grasp what was going on between him and his mother, as he limited what he shared, but she knew it wasn't good at all. This was something else she found unsettling about him, as family meant everything to her, a cornerstone of stability and trust. From what little he did share with her about his mother, he said she was horrible and powerful and, "filthy rich," as he plainly put it. He helped make her millions, but her complaining was relentless anytime he spent a dime that wasn't rationally accounted for in her opinion. Loghan considered a moment what it would be like working with your family, it would be difficult enough even if all got along well, but put in the mix a fractured relationship...? It must be hell.

She found herself inexplicably drawn to David, even though she hadn't met him in person. She continued to push away the uneasy thoughts of this morning with his response and 'tone' with her - it poked at her though - something, not quite right. She once again, tamped down the uneasy feelings he left with her.

She spent so much time talking to him, sharing details of her life, work, day to day, and she was remarkably comfortable with him. She reminded herself of the "intimate" evenings they spend with one another - typing away passions and desires. There was something more intimate in expressing herself through means of writing. In the quiet stillness in her home, she found comfort in the rhythm of typing, the soft click of each key pressed and slow emergence of words. It felt as if the words were drawn from the deepest recesses of her heart. She found David interesting, sincere and passionate in his expression. They both agreed, it was different than talking on the phone, where words can tumble out too quickly, lost to the noise, or in her case, the emotions would not come as easily. Typing allowed her to be deliberate, to choose each word with care, to craft sentences that held the weight of her feelings...to show a side of herself she never knew existed.

She didn't dare share any of this with Tina or, Jodie. How utterly out of character for her! They would tease her and then shift straight to worry. No, she would keep this as her little secret. The interactions started out innocently and then, it began.

The night it started, she was feeling vulnerable and broken. David happened to be in the right place at the right time. The article she was working on allowed her to drop her guard, to be part of the stories she heard from others as she researched. Yes, she fully understood she and David weren't in the physical space with one another, but she felt otherwise. It felt 'real,' as if he were in the room with her. He knew what to say and made her feel safe, strong and sensual. David had such a way with words that she felt enveloped in them and let her mind wander and be open. She never felt this way before; it was the first time she allowed herself to feel deeply intimate, other than with Ian.

She blushed at the memories and looked out the window so Deagan wouldn't notice.

Loghan and David continued to spend this 'special' time with one other these last many weeks now and she felt it was nearing the time for them to meet in person. She didn't know where it may lead, but she knew she was feeling something and David helped her move forward in more ways than he knew.

She appreciated feeling like herself again, as well as feeling like a beautiful, sexy, vibrant woman. It's not that Ian didn't make her feel beautiful, but they were so young when they met, so innocent. Their relationship remained sweet and inexperienced over the years. She didn't know any different and she assumed Ian was the same. They shared everything with one another and were happy as a couple.

She considered a moment, what was the phrase...? Oh yeah, "You don't know, what you don't know." The phrase made sense to her now. Loghan wasn't aware she was a sensual women, until she met David. It was freeing to be able to express yourself behind the safety of a computer screen. Loghan found a freedom she never knew she craved. The walls she usually kept so tightly guarded began to crumble, piece by piece, until that first night, and then, there was nothing left of the walls but dust. She discovered a desire that stirred within her, the things she longed to do to him and the ways she wanted him to make her unravel. The screen became her confessional, her gateway to unbridled honesty, where her deepest cravings could spill out. Her words allowed a closeness that transcended the physical distance between them. She imagined David reading her words, feeling the same flutter in his chest, the same connection she was feeling. It was the shared moments, a silent conversation that spoke louder than any spoken word could. Loghan felt seen and truly understood in a way she knew would not have happened, should they have been on the phone, or visual chat. She was safe behind the screen and this allowed her sensuality to escape. She conceived this may be crazy to think this way, but what harm could there be in all this?

She wasn't about to share with anyone she was "sexting" and meeting online for "dates." Her girlfriends wouldn't believe her! Hell, she couldn't believe what she was doing! It was so out of character of her, but she couldn't seem to stop herself and why should she? She was a woman - a sexually active woman. Right? She winced and held back a smirk, as she still wasn't sure she thought of herself as a "sexually active women."

David helped Loghan moved forward from Ian and step into her newfound sensuality, in addition to unknowingly helping her write her article. She tapped into areas she didn't know she had and, allowed her mind to open to the sex that was happening all around her as she researched and wrote her article. Her newly discovered freedom and sensuality allowed her to ask questions of those she interviewed, she wouldn't have known previously to ask. She was experiencing the same interactions many of these women were online; falling for men, having intimate experiences and, finding their voice and strength. The story she hit upon was striking a nerve with her and she knew it would with those who read it. Who would expect Loghan Riley to write a titillating article about online hook ups? No one.

She recalled the evening when everything changed and she ventured into territory unknown to her - sexting. She and David spent the first hour talking and Loghan shared with him how lonely and shattered she felt with her loss of Ian. David was kind and gentle in his questions - he allowed her all the time needed to express herself with words. She recalled her typing that night, frantic and fractured at times once the words started to fly from her fingertips. At some point, she felt herself begin to pull away, when she tapped into the painful memories of getting Ian's affairs in order after the funeral.

"What is it, darling? You've become quiet - almost still, it seems."

Loghan sat back against the pillows she propped against her headboard. A long sigh escaped her lips as once again, David instinctively knew she pulled back. It wasn't just the flow of words slowing down, it was the lack of tone. She felt herself exposing too much of her story of Ian. As she would often do to protect herself from the pain, she artfully 'stacked' the bricks higher on her figurative wall to keep people at bay.

"Darling, I can only imagine how difficult this must be for you – allowing your feelings to come out and perhaps, overwhelm you. I assure you, I'm here for you. A safe place for you to land. I would protect your heart at all costs...will you allow me, dear Loghan?"

Loghan pushed a stay tear away with her sleeve, hesitating as she reached for the keys, fingers trembling. *"Yes, David...I will. I don't know exactly what that looks like, or means, but I think I could welcome you to care for my heart."* She recalled when she typed these words, she wasn't certain where it would lead, but she somehow knew a door would be opened. David must have known this as well, as he immediately walked through the threshold.

" I'm reaching my hand out to you – do you see that? Sense the feeling? I'm here..."

Drawing a deep breath, Loghan committed and began to type. *"I'm reaching for your hand – feeling the warmth and strength of your hand as you lace your fingers through mine."* She stopped typing and curiously awaited David's next words. The wait was not long as she watched the curse blink to life.

"I step into to you and fold you in my arms – you're warmth and softness ...I feel enraptured by your delicate perfume...it's quietly taking over my senses. You wrap your arms around me and I feel you surrender to me as your body releases tension...your shoulders relax and you tip your head to look into my eyes. I tell you – It's alright, that I am here."

Gathering herself, Loghan poised her fingertips on the keys and thoughtfully and with deliberation, she typed.

"Your eyes find mine and we are locked in a gaze – I feel you studying my eyes, reaching into my soul – finding secrets I've never shared. My head tipping further to the side...slowly moving toward you." She paused a moment considering her next move – her fingers hovering above they keys, heart racing with a

mix of anticipation and uncertainty. Her whole life, she had been the good girl-reliable, steady, never stepping out of bounds. But now, as she stared at the screen, an unfamiliar thrill coursed through her veins, igniting a part of her, she dared yet to explore.

The excitement was intoxicating, a dangerous allure pulling her closer to a choice she'd never imagined making. She could feel her pulse quicken and the flush rising to her cheeks. One simple string of words and she would be crossing a line, stepping into a world of sensuality that she was unfamiliar and distant, so far from who she thought she was.

She drew another deep breath, her mind a whirl of thoughts and possibilities. The keys beneath her fingers felt like they were burning, a gateway to the unknown. Her next few words would define her path - she could dive headfirst into this new, thrilling world, or she could pull back, continue to stack the bricks of her imaginary fortress. The choice was hers and in this moment this new power felt exhilarating - she knew what she would do.

She gave into her desire and stepped onto the path before her and discovered her heat.

" I close my eyes and gently part my lips – leaning closer and closer into you as I seek to find your kiss. Following the warmth, our lips gently, shyly find one another...the heat of your lips as they barely touch mine, is almost too much... intoxicating. You begin to sense my lips, as you gently, but firmly press your lips against mine. Your cologne lingers close to me...a heady mix of spice, leather and oak, complimented by your natural, masculine scent. You pull me deeper into our kiss, allowing us to be caught up in the moment."

Loghan stopped typing and gently shook her head, jarring herself from the physical feelings she was experiencing - every nerve in her body was alive and tingled. She looked back to the screen and saw the words appearing on the screen in a rapid, fluid cascade, each letter he typed materializing as if, by magic, filling the blank space with sudden life. She had opened the door and allowed this new path to take hold - she read his words as quickly as the sentences unfurled like a ribbon unraveling at breakneck speed, shaping the screen with purpose and urgency.

David left no room for lack of imagination, leaving behind a trail of raw, unfiltered descriptions of his touch–Loghan matched his heat as the words she too typed, found life and she described all of what she wanted to do as she described exploring David. The descriptions for each started slowly, as they built the story line of their first time with one another. Loghan eagerly kept up with her part, until she could no longer hold back the feelings - her head falling back to her pillow as her fingertips traced her now, bare skin, seeking the warmth he elicited with her words.

The car's gradual deceleration shifted the rhythm of the world outside and snapped Loghan from her daze of memories. Her body jolted upright as if pulled by an invisible thread, eyes wide and senses suddenly on high alert.

"Whoa... you alright, Loghan?" Deagan smiled gently at Loghan and touched her shoulder. "You looked like you were deep in thought, so I just let you be. Hope the music isn't bothering you?"

Music? She was completely unaware of any music these last, however many miles she was lost in thought. Loghan re-positioned herself in the car seat and hoped she wasn't blushing. "No, no...I'm fine." She was clearly flustered and continued, "I - I - I was just thinking about work and my article ...trying to keep my mind occupied," she lied as she looked over at Deagan. She noticed the San Francisco - Oakland Bay Bridge off the right and knew they were getting close to the city. Deagan didn't appear to notice anything out of sorts with Loghan and they shifted back into conversation about work and tried not to worry incessantly about Jodie.

Grateful for the interruption of steamy and scandalous thoughts, Loghan settled into a far safer topic with Deagan. She shared the article was almost complete and she was to send to John in email and have the hard copy on his desk early next week. Deagan offered to look it over and while she was nervous about his input, she welcomed it. She would worry about what Deagan thought about the content later, as she knew the questions may arise when he read the article. For now, she would keep her sexual "secrets" to herself and would find out what in the world was wrong with David, later. There were more important and pressing things to be concerned about at this time.

Loghan sat up and smiled at Deagan and he returned her smile. "How about some light music? Something quiet and easy?"

"Sure, Deagan. That would be good. Keep my mind occupied. Sorry I was a little quiet there."

"No worries at all." He tapped the button for, The Coffee House on Sirius and Rickie Lee Jones spilled over the speakers and lazily sang, Chuck E's in Love.

The music was just what they needed to ease the tension in the air, but Deagan needed to share the details with Loghan about his assistant, Jenny Harper. Loghan worked with Jenny directly, even though she was Deagan's assistant. Jenny was well-liked at the office and everyone had nothing but a kind word about her. Deagan took a breath and began.

"I've been stalling a bit to share with you, but I'm afraid I have some more unsettling news. I got a call from Jenny today."

"Jenny? Your Jenny?" Loghan turned her body toward Deagan in considerable interest.

"Yes, my Jenny...I mean...not 'my,' Jenny...yes. Jenny Harper."

"Yes?" Loghan reached over and turned the volume lower. "What's going on?"

Deagan went over the details Jenny shared and Loghan was horrified at the news. "Is she alright? What can we do? Do we need to go get her?" Loghan peppered Deagan with questions and he helplessly waited until there was a break for him to speak.

"I know - I know...it's awful, but she says she's ok. She's still in the city and staying at her old apartment with her previous roommate, Erin." The rain began to pelt on the windshield with more urgency. Deagan turned the speed up on the wipers and glanced upward to the sky.

"Geesh...must be going through a rain cell." He gripped the wheel tighter and continued down the freeway.

"Oh my gosh. There is so much going on, Deagan." Loghan glanced at her phone again, to no avail. "I don't like this at all. Worried about Jodie - now, Jenny?" Loghan chewed on lip a moment, her mind racing.

"Hey - you don't think there is some connection here, do you? I mean, to the drawing of that man we saw on the news today? You said Jenny was

meeting a man for drinks...the news said the victim was out on a blind date."
She blinked rapidly jabbed at the air as she recalled the details from the news.
Visually trying to connect the dots.

Deagan's eyebrows lifted in great consideration. "Wow...I didn't think of
that, but what are the odds of that being case? There must be many attacks
in San Francisco in one day...right? I mean, that would be crazy if there was
a connection?" He looked over at Loghan briefly to connect and turned his
eyes back to the road.

"Well, she did say she was 'OK' and that was a relief to hear. I told her if
she needed anything, anything at all to let me know. She's a great person
and I can't imagine what she went through. She didn't give me a lot of
details, but I could hear in her voice, she was still shaken."

"I'm sure, Deagan. We can check in on her when we get down there, if you
like? Maybe it will settle her as well?"

"That's a great idea, Loghan. I'll text her when we get into the city."

They tried their best to shift the conversation to other topics to ease their
minds. Deagan mentioned he was anxious to read Loghan's article and he
knew it was going to be great. She smiled at him and appreciated how he
encouraged her. He always had been like this with her and maybe she didn't
notice it before because she was with Ian.

"I'll check my emails when we get to San Francisco. I want to see if Dexter
responded. I asked to meet with him tomorrow evening. I want to see what
else this guy knows and why is he contacting me." Deagan ran his hand
through his hair and Loghan noticed it looked thick and wavy. His hair didn't
even get messed up when he ran his hand through it. Funny, how she was
noticing more about his lately. She accounted for it in part of coming out
of the fog and being part of life again. It momentarily made her smile and
relax. Her phone pinged and she jumped at the sound.

"Oh my gosh! It's Jodie! Deagan! It's Jodie - she says she's alright and
lost her phone!"

*****

She removed her heels and placed them neatly inside the hotel closet.

What a wonderful night this turned out to be, seeing Barrett and his lovely young lady. He was so surprised by her news that it pleased her so. She recalled the look on his face again and it filled her with warmth and delight. To be able to give him so much more for all the lost years, she knew it was the right thing to do.

There was a response of disbelief initially, but she explained it all perfectly well and in the end, Barrett was taken aback, but happy and joyful. There would be more time to fill in blanks, but for now, it was purely celebratory. They made plans to see each other in a few weeks at her estate in Scotland.

She was deliciously tired and the gin cocktails certainly helped add to her state. She moved into the large bathroom and drew a bath, tossing in some fragrant bath beads.

Returning to the dressing area she reached for her laptop to quickly checked her email and upcoming confirmations. All seemed in order. She checked her calendar for tomorrow and messaged her assistant.

"Hello, dear, please block my calendar for 11 AM and have brunch sent up to my room for two. Perhaps the idea of brunch will encourage him to arrive on time, although I doubt it... Thank you"

She didn't wait for the response as it was late, but she still knew her assistant was awake and waiting for her boss to confirm tomorrow's calendar. In the 6 years she employed her, nothing had ever changed.

She returned her attention to the mirror in the dressing area. Taking off her silk blouse and placing it on the chair. She knew the cleaning staff would take her clothing to the dry cleaners, all part of their exceptional service for those so inclined to use. She smiled at her reflection and pondered again about what an exceptional evening with Barrett and his soon to be, bride.

She scoffed at this thought, but she knew it would be coming sooner, rather than later. She may not have spent much time with Barrett over these years, but she could see the look of love in a young man's eyes. He may not know it yet, but he would ask for her hand in marriage. She couldn't wait for the announcement. Something lovely to look forward to, instead of the dull and dreary meetings she had on the calendar these upcoming weeks - and tomorrow - well, tomorrow would be the most difficult and challenging of them all.

This was a conversation she was not looking forward to, as she knew it would not go well.

She reached up and unclasped her necklace and placed it in the black velvet case. It shone brightly in the lights from over the dressing area. It glinted and sparkled and she admired it again. It was one of her favorites and her delicate fingertips traced the diamonds and landed on the opulent, large green emerald.

She closed the black case and walked with purpose to her awaiting bath.

Chapter 26

Detective's Kinder and Thornton stood as Jenny and her friend, Erin, entered the small interview room. Jenny was hesitant to go to the station, but Erin offered to go with her as moral support. While it had only been a few days since the attack, Jenny hadn't left the apartment and was still trying to get her nerves under control. She decided to stay with her friend Erin a few days longer after talking with Deagan, but she also didn't want to take advantage of his kindness.

"That's ridiculous, Jenny!" Erin scoffed at Jenny when she mentioned she was going back to work as soon as possible. "Don't put expectations on yourself," They were sharing a mirror in the bathroom, just like old times and putting on makeup. Erin brushed her hair out and applied a small amount of lip gloss in the mirror. "Besides, you don't know if the detectives will need you to hang around longer." Erin stopped applying the lips gloss and looked pensively at Jenny in the reflection.

"I know - I know..." Jenny sat down on the edge of the tub. "I don't know what to expect today. What if the photos they have... don't look like...," she paused, picked absently at her fingernail and continued. "...like him." She continued to look at her nails and tried not to think of looking at those eyes again. His eyes. The eyes she initially thought were so sexy when she hit on his profile; Aidan. She thought, perhaps, that wasn't his name, after all, she gave a false one. It was what you did when you were looking to hook up. At least, it was what she did. She never gave her real name when she was "trolling" for hookups. She just felt stupid at her choices...and for what? To have gratuitous sex? She sighed and her shoulders slumped. She knew better but damn it, lots of people hooked up with those they didn't know. Nothing happened to them!

She chatted with Aidan several times on the app and he seemed cool. She was just going to hit it and leave. Now, everyone who knew her would hear about this incident and realize she was...well, to be frank, slutty.

Why could guys sleep around and no one thought or said anything, but if women did the same, they caught hell? Such crap, she thought disdainfully. She shook her head to discard thinking about the attack...she wanted this behind her, but the likable detective said it would be some time.

Detective Kinder reassured her when they spoke, she would only have to be there a short while. They had some photos they wanted her to view and see if the man who attacked her was in any of them. She was initially relieved to hear they may have a strong lead, but as she walked into the stuffy little conference room, she felt her stomach tighten and lurch.

Erin must have felt her tense and reached down and grabbed her hand. "You ok, Jen?" She whispered and she looked at her friend gently. Jenny nodded, squeezed her hand back and stepped into the room. The contrast of the stark interrogation room was the utter opposite of the beautiful city of San Francisco. The drive over to the precinct, Jenny pretended all was right in her world, as she watched the colorful and bustling city filled with life. She knew this meeting with the detectives would be hard, but she did her best to remain calm.

The interrogation room was a small, a space where time stood still. The walls were dull, institutional gray, lined with scuff marks from countless tense encounters. A single, fluorescent light hummed overhead, casting harsh shadows across the room's only furniture: a battered metal table and several mismatched chairs. The air was thick with the muted scent of perspiration and lingering anxiety. A soft, fragrant scent of lavender cut through Jenny's anxiousness and she inhaled deeply, letting the lavender's soothing essence wrap around her, allowing her to make the next steps toward the table and chairs.

"Hello, Ms. Harper. May I call you Jenny?" Detective Kinder extended her hand to Jenny and nodded at Erin.

"Yes, that's fine." Jenny heard her own voice and it was quiet and raspy. She cleared her throat and tried again," Yes. Sorry. I prefer it if you called me Jenny." She turned to Erin and back again to Detective Kinder. "This is my friend, Erin Winters."

Detective Kinder and Detective Thornton glanced at each other briefly and nodded in agreement. Jenny picked up on their non-verbal actions and added to her introduction. "I'm staying with her. I think I mentioned that the other day. She's my old roommate and yes, it's fine; she is here with me." Jenny jutted her chin out a bit and felt some of her fire returning. She wanted Erin here and stated what she needed and it felt good. She didn't know if the detectives cared but wanted to make her voice known.

"Of course, Jenny. That is fine." Detective Thornton, a big man, reached his hand over to greet Erin. His massive hand clamped over Erin's with surprising gentleness. He continued in his deep, authoritative voice. "We wanted to be sure you were ok with your friend being here. We have some additional details for you and wanted to inform you." He waved his hand to the two chairs on the opposite side of the table and Jenny and Erin took a seat.

The tension in the air continued to fill the room and Detective Kinder sensed the uneasiness. She smiled at the young ladies and offered her hand to Erin across the table.

"Hello, Erin. I'm Detective Kinder and this is my partner, Detective Thornton." Her eyes were filled with compassion and kindness. "Hi, nice to meet you, detectives." Erin sat back in her seat and removed her coat. Jenny and Erin settled in their seats and waited for the detectives to begin.

Detective Thornton began first, his large, meaty hands were placed on top of a file folder. He appeared comfortable in this setting and his broad thumb repeatedly rolled the folder's edge. The rhythmic sound breaking the deafening silence of the surroundings.

"Jenny, as Detective Kinder told you on the phone, we have a strong lead." He moved his chair back to accommodate his bulk. "We had a few calls that gave us the name of someone and they corroborated the information provided by another. It's just a preliminary beginning to the investigation and it may go nowhere, but we check out every lead as we shared with you earlier." The chair creaked as he leaned back and like a dance, Detective Kinder knew it was her turn to lead.

She smiled slightly to reassure Jenny and continued, "We have several photos for you to review and let us know your thoughts." She rested her delicate hands on a manila envelope and slid three sheets out, face down. Jenny looked at Erin, reached under the table and grasped her friend's hand.

Detective Kinder tapped the papers gently, "Are you sure you're ok to move forward, Jenny? Are you ready to look at the photos?" She waited for Jenny's response and squared her shoulders. Jenny slipped her hand from Erin's and placed both hands on the table. Taking a deep breath, she replied, "Yes, I'm ready," she nodded at Detective Kinder.

Detective Kinder turned two of the thick, glossy papers over and placed them in front of Jenny.

"Take your time as you look at each picture." Detective Kinder stated gently and leaned back in her chair, looking at her partner.

There were twelve pictures in all, six photos on each sheet. Twelve men that all slightly resembled one another. The air in the room felt thick and warm as Jenny quietly looked over each image. She sat upright, pulled the pictures closer and leaned over to get a better look. Her internal dialogue was in full swing as she looked at one photo, then another.

The first three were not him, right off the bat. They had longer, scruffy hair and their eyes were not right. Jenny moved on to the bottom row; the man had powerful features in the first picture and his nose wasn't right. You could tell he had broken it at some point in his life. It was crooked and off-center. No, this wasn't him.

She moved to the fifth photo; the handsome man seemed out of place in this mug shot, but it wasn't him, either. Suit and tie, they were getting warmer. She took another breath, looked over the last picture and promptly dismissed the photo and pushed it aside.

"No - none of those are him." She looked up at the detectives and they nodded at her to move forward.

Jenny pulled the second sheet of glossy paper over and slowly examined each photo. She continued to eliminate each man as she moved through the images. She let out a large sigh and leaned back in her chair.

"Now what?" Her brows were creased and her shoulders fell. "None of these guys are him." Erin put her hand on Jenny's back and rubbed it gently, offering her reassurance.

"Well, we have one more for you to look at, Jenny." Detective Kinder's eyes fell on the sheet in front of her. "These photos won't be from a line-up, but the quality of the photos is good." Detective Kinder pushed the thick paper across the table again and Jenny pulled it forward the rest of the way. Jenny slowly turned the photo over and froze, color draining from her face.

The detectives looked at each other and knew they hit their mark.

*****

Loghan wasn't aware she'd been holding her breath as she read the message, but she sighed and her head fell back on the car seat. She quickly righted herself and looked at the text again. There was a strange phone number Jodie messaged from and she explained it was Barrett's phone she was using as she had misplaced her cell phone.

"Wow...that must be a huge relief for you, Loghan!" Deagan checked his rear-view mirror, glanced over his shoulder and changed lanes. "What did she say?" He reached over and placed a hand on her shoulder, smiling brightly. Loghan smiled back and turned back at the message. "Well, she says she misplaced her phone and is using Barrett's...she paused, "Wait... someone is typing something else. It's a group message to me and Tina." Loghan patiently waited for the message to come across and now she was able to clear her head and relax. Thank goodness, Jodie somehow remembered our phone numbers, Loghan thought.

"I hate to say this, but...," Deagan had stolen the thought from Loghan's mind. "How do you know it's her? I mean...well...you know?" Deagan looked over briefly at Loghan.

"I know... I think that as well..." Loghan looked back down at her phone, read the message and smiled.

I know you two must be worried sick. I'm fine. Really! I don't know where in the hell I misplaced my phone, but if I don't find it today, I'm heading to Apple. Oh...! Wait! Can one of you try to locate my phone with Find My Friends? I think it will still show the last place it pings, even if the battery is dead! Oh...and may I say, Apple pie. My, my, my!"

Loghan let out a short laugh and absently wiped a small tear from her eye. "It's her. I can tell you this much - she certainly knows us all too well, Deagan," she momentarily set her phone on her lap and reached for a tissue from her bag. "She knew we were worried and used our "code" to let us know she was ok." Loghan pulled the visor down to check her mascara in the mirror. She quickly checked, Find My Friends, once more and texted Jodie the last location was the hotel.

"The code?" Deagan's eyebrow shot up and he looked over with a quizzical smile.

Satisfied her mascara hadn't run down her face, Loghan flipped the visor back up.

"Yes, the code. Most women do this, Deagan. I'm surprised you don't know this."

She laughed and Deagan instantly felt the atmosphere around them lighten. Loghan shifted slightly in her seat. How would she let Deagan know that most women, before venturing into the unknown territory of a first date, women often felt the need for a little extra reassurance - call it an insurance policy for the evening. Loghan took a deep breath and began to explain 'girl code' to Deagan.

"Sadly, women need a code to let their friends know all is well. Before stepping out the door, there is always a pre-date conversation with the squad. The game plan is simple but crucial: if a date starts to drag, or worse, gives off uncomfortable vibes, a discreet message is all it takes. We have a prearranged signal and a quick, discreet text triggers a perfectly timed "emergency" call from a friend. "

Loghan used air quotes and smirked at Deagan. She continued, "In this case; when one of us may be in trouble, or we just need to let someone know we're ok, we made up this random code; she smiled sweetly at Deagan and in a dramatic, Southern accent, she stated, "Apple pie - my, my, my." She fluttered her lashes for effect and Deagan laughed. "That's another story behind the phrase and accent, but it's her!"

Loghan smiled and laughed at the silliness of the phrase, but in this case, it worked. She felt such relief that Jodie was alright and she knew it.

The phone buzzed again and Loghan read the following messages to Deagan. It was Tina with her usual antics and peppering Jodie with more questions; *How could she not let them know sooner? How did she lose her phone? We already tried, Find My Friends, when are you coming back? Was everything really ok with Barrett?* Jodie responded with LOLs and said she was sorry, but she was having such a wonderful time with Barrett she lost track of time. She didn't know where she had misplaced her phone, but she would look further in the hotel room. She didn't know when they were coming back, but most likely, Tuesday. They had been all over San Francisco and in each other's arms the entire time. She added that she didn't want this trip to end and, she met Barrett's aunt last night.

Loghan assumed, based on Jodie's responses, she hadn't seen the news. She must be overreacting. Clearly, Jodie was fine, and Loghan and Tina were wrong. Jodie said she and Barrett hadn't been out of each other's sight. Loghan thought a moment. Wasn't there a saying that everyone has a doppelganger? A close resemblance? Maybe this was Barrett's. At any rate, she was satisfied her friend was safe and having an incredible weekend.

After a few more back-and-forth messages, Jodie signed off with the promise she would text soon and, if they needed anything, to message Barrett's number in the meantime.

Loghan reached over and turned the music up again and rolled her shoulders back. The tension she was holding slowly released and she could feel herself begin to relax.

She questioned how she could have thought the man in the composite drawing was Barrett. Clearly, it had to be her mind playing tricks. She was too invested in her article and the darkness she had discovered in her research had tainted her perceptions. She had pulled Tina into her illusions as well.

Right? She tapped her fingers on her phone, absent-minded, as she rolled through the thoughts.

Deagan broke the brief silence. "I'm sorry that you and your friends, well, hell...sounds as if, women in general, need a code to keep themselves safe from men." Deagan's face was serious as he focused on the road. Loghan could see he was truly bothered by this notion and reached over to him, placing her hand on his shoulder. "Hey, it's ok, Deagan. I mean... it's not ok that we need a code, but I mean... it's not your fault. No one needs a code for you." She smiled gently and reassuringly at him.

"Well, I guess I knew somewhere deep down that women don't always feel safe around men. This situation with your friend, Jodie, made it very real." He shook his head slightly and reached up and touched Loghan's hand. Her skin was cool and soft. He smiled at her briefly, "Guys can be assholes; there is no doubt about it. I'm beyond happy that everything is good with Jodie."

"Yes - that is for damn sure!" Loghan smiled. They had more time to reach San Francisco if the rain and traffic held, as the bridge always backed up on weekends. Loghan was happy that Deagan was with her, and she looked over at him once more, smiling.

"What?" Deagan smiled back at her, and she noticed his creased laugh lines around his eyes again. "Nothing, really. I just wanted to say thank you for dropping everything and coming with me. You didn't even hesitate."

"You're welcome," He glanced at her and their eyes connected briefly.

Loghan discovered at the moment she really saw him...saw the truth in Deagan, not just his presence but the essence of who he really was. Suddenly she understood this kind, strong and selfless man who sat beside her. She felt an odd stirring in her heart as she tipped her head slightly, studying him with this new awareness.

Damn, she thought. I feel like I've had this thought recently...He really is such an incredible guy. Loghan allowed the realization to settle. Feeling considerably more relaxed, they settled into conversation, plans for the weekend and the rest of the drive.

Chapter 27

J odie's eyelids fluttered slowly as she woke to the muted light reaching through the curtains. Sleepily, she rolled over and snuggled up to Barrett. He was warm and smelled of soap and sleep. She kissed his back and followed his neck, nuzzling into his warmth.

He stirred and rolled on his back, pulling her into his shoulder. "Mmm... Good morning, lass." His voice, deeper than usual, was slow to warm up as he chuckled at its throatiness. "Oh, it seems my voice hasn't woken yet either, lass." He cleared his throat and smiled at her, kissing her head. She frowned and stretched her neck upwards to kiss him.

"I have morning breath, love." He offered her only a peck and she giggled. "I do too, but you can do better than that little, pitiful peck." She smiled and gave him a soft kiss, her lips slightly parted.

"Mmm...well, that is better, don't you agree?" She smiled at him, closed her eyes and stretched her languid body.

"Absolutely. Just as long as you don't judge me for my whiskey, morning breath." His chest reverberated as he chuckled. "I still can't get over last night with Aunt Katherine." His face was suddenly serious. Jodie rolled her head toward him as she finished her stretch.

"I know. How do you feel today? That was a lot of information to take in one sitting." Jodie stretched her arm out under her head and touched his arm gently with her free hand.

"I guess I feel alright. I didn't see that coming, though. Aunt Katherine has always been so generous with me over the years. She has no family to speak of except me and maybe she wanted to make amends since she is getting a little older?" His steel-blue eyes locked on her.

Jodie was absently trailing her fingertips over Barrett's arm and chest. "I know you don't feel she needs to make amends, Barrett," her fingertip trailed his chest. "I think she just wants to pay forward her kindness more - show you she is here for you."

Barrett smiled gently at her and placed his hand on top of hers. "I suppose that could be true. I just feel funny about it. I know it's coming from a place of love and she is insistent, so I won't deny her kindness." He noticed she was trailing her fingertip on a small scar on his chest.

"What is this from?" Jodie gently rubbed her fingertip across a small, raised scar.

"Oh, 'tis nothing, lass. It's an old scar from surgery many years ago." He re-adjusted his head on his arm, taking his hand and guiding her fingertip across the scar. "I had a birth defect when I was born. My parents told me I had a hole in my heart and was quite sick." Jodie leaned in closer to examine the scar. She hadn't noticed as it was camouflaged under his soft chest hair. Her fingertip gently traced the raised line, "It's very discreet." She smiled at him. "All the things we've shared with one another in such a short period. I feel like I've known you for many years." She leaned in and kissed his chest where the scar lingered.

"I do, as well, lass. It was a long time ago, and you should know I still see a cardiologist who keeps track of my heart health." He looked at her with slight concern. "I recovered from the surgery, but it took years for my health to maintain. I was a small child. I had several surgeries and here," he turned his side toward her so she could see another small scar. "This is the other scar from the surgeries." He took her hand and kissed it. "I'm healthy as a mule now. Nothing to worry about, my love." He smiled and his eyes filled with light.

"Now, I'm hungry...how about you, lass?" He stretched on his side and propped up with his cheek on his fist.

"I am too. I think I want coffee more than anything. Let's call down for something." She rolled over to face Barrett. She felt so comfortable with him; she didn't mind she didn't have on any makeup. He had no false pretenses, and she was surprised how easy it was to be with him...anywhere. She considered the story of his health when he was a child. So many things they had yet to share with one another. She smiled at him as he gently tucked a loose tendril of hair behind her ear.

"I will go to the corner and get some proper coffee and bagels. What do you say? I can get there and back faster than room service." He jumped up from bed without waiting for her response.

"I think that sounds wonderful. If you don't mind? I will text the girls to let them know I lost my phone and all is well." She looked around the room and spotted Barrett's phone.

"Of course, love-1857, that's my code," he unplugged his phone from the charger and handed it to her. He reached for his pants and walked to the bathroom.

Jodie could hear Barrett brushing his teeth and getting ready. She tapped out Loghan and Tina's cell numbers and smiled at her cleverness for recalling their numbers by heart.

She knew the girls would be worried and tossed the covers off the bed and sat up. She momentarily allowed herself to be sidetracked and set the phone down to open the curtains. Curious to see what the morning held for them, she was surprised to see it was only misting. There was muted sunshine and the mist rolled off the street below. She noted a few bellhops hustling to open the car door of a Mercedes that just pulled in.

She took another lap around the room, looked under the bed and pulled the drawers out, seeing if she absently placed her phone in one of them. She sighed as she found nothing and walked into the adjoining suite. She thought that she left it on the bar or the end table.

She again found nothing and had to admit she lost her phone. It wasn't misplaced - it was gone. She contacted the restaurant they were at for dinner the night before; The Waterfront. There was a chance she left it there, but at the very least, she needed to go to Apple today and get a new phone. She had a lock on her phone and everything was backed up to the cloud, so she wasn't worried about that, but she didn't like the idea of her phone possibly being found by someone that would not turn it in.

She returned to the bedroom in time for Barrett to walk out of the bathroom, freshly showered and smelling amazing. "No fair!" She laughed as he wrapped his arms around her.

"All is fair, in love and the need for coffee." he smiled at her and kissed her gently. "I'll be back in just a few with hot coffee and fresh bagels." He smiled and walked out.

She returned to the phone again, entered Barrett's code and let the girls know she was okay.

*****

He reached his hand out and knocked on the over-sized, double doors. His head still felt thick and foggy and he hoped running on the treadmill would help. It didn't. He recalled the martini he tossed back this morning didn't help either. Drinking so early was not his habit, but he prayed the martini would take the edge off and keep the voices still.

Anything to help prepare himself for the meeting, with the almighty Avery would do.

The door opened and Avery's assistant, Gwyneth, smiled at Aric. She was long and lean, wearing a lovely rose-colored silk blouse with white, high-waisted slacks. She looked gorgeous this morning, Aric noted.

"Mr. Stanton," her chin dipped slightly to offer her greeting, and she took his leather bag.

"Please come in. Ms. Stanton is waiting for you in the dining area."

Gwyneth stepped aside to allow Aric entrance into the large Presidential Suite. She moved out of sight momentarily and returned to lead Aric to the dining area.

Aric's eyes swept over Gwyneth's length, and he offered her a smile of appreciation when she caught his ravenous gaze. Aric didn't mind that she saw his appreciation and touched her arm gently.

"You look positively stunning today, Gwyneth. What has you looking so..." his eyes rolled languidly over her once more, "so sumptuous?" He knew he was making this sweet, young thing nervous, and he rather enjoyed it.

She shifted her weight and he detected a break in her feigned confidence.

"I'm not sure what you mean, Mr. Stanton. This way, please." He followed her down the hallway and allowed his eyes to rest on her ass as she glided before him. The moment of enjoyment was broken when he heard Avery's lilting English accent.

"Aric, darling. Do come and sit." This morning, Avery Stanton was in complete form, filling the room with her elegance and style. She stood as Aric walked into the room. Avery wore black, high-waisted flared pants and a crisp white blouse with the collar pulled up high. She wore Jimmy Choo, black high heels and a diamond encrusted necklace with a shimmering emerald at the hollow of her throat. She oozed confidence and kissed Aric on each cheek.

"Hello, Avery. I would ask how you were doing, but I can see you're quite well." Aric tried unsuccessfully to hide the snideness in his comment. She grinned at him and looked over to Gwyneth. "I think we're settled here, my dear. I know you have an appointment; please don't let me keep you." Avery waved her perfectly manicured hand in the air.

"Thank you, Ms. Stanton. Is that all then?" She smiled thoughtfully at Avery and bowed her head slightly. "Of course, dear. Have a nice day off." Avery smiled after Gwyneth as she left the room, then moved her attention back to Aric. She noticed the look in his eyes as he watched her assistant leave the room. She frowned at him. Once again, Aric was off on his usual pursuit - chasing anything with a pulse. Avery knew of his antics and loathed his inability to show discretion.

"Now, Aric, really. You're far too old for her. You look at her like a lecherous, old man." She scolded Aric, her words cutting through the room like a knife. His weaknesses were all too easy to spot and she could no longer ignore them. This was just one of the flaws her son carried and today she decided it was time to confront them head-on. She would help him face his shortcomings and guide him to the changes needed for the future success of the business.

Aric quickly scoffed at her and took a chair at the large, ornate table. The table was set lovely for brunch. Fresh scones, fruit, scrambled eggs, bacon, hot coffee and tea for Avery. Avery never acquired a taste for coffee, the

American tea equivalent. In her mind, nothing was as civilized as a proper cup of tea. She poured another cup of tea for herself and offered Aric coffee. He gratefully accepted and forced a smile for Avery.

"Well, Avery," Aric settled in his chair and took a warm scone. "let's get to the business at hand, shall we?" He layered a generous dollop of creamy butter on top of it, placed it back on his plate and waited for her response.

"My, my, Aric darling. You certainly don't hesitate to start a meeting now, do you?" She returned his fake smile with one of her own. She controlled this meeting, not him and she would remind him as she settled into her scrambled eggs and fruit. She would not entertain him with moving forward until they had completed breakfast, and pretended to be interested in one another outside the office.

She took a small bite of her eggs and placed the fork on the plate. She allowed herself to take in her son's appearance. He was always put together; she did have to admit this to herself. He was not unlike her in this area; he loved fine clothing, shoes and jewelry. She admired his dark grey Armani suit, cobalt blue shirt and red silk tie. His shirt matched the color of his magnificent eyes and she smiled at the family trait of striking blue eyes. She noted, though, Aric's eyes were always on the "cool" side. Never showed warmth or affection, but then, he was a cold-hearted bastard, thought Avery, another family trait she was all too aware of. She hated admitting this about her son, but it was the truth.

Aric was ruthless in business and his personal dealings. He closed deals with little compassion as they bought out small businesses for their company. Avery was behind the scenes of the agreements but wasn't always aware of how Aric secured many of the transactions. She would receive updates from Aric or, someone on the board that a critical deal was completed and she left it at that. Avery never thought about the ruthlessness Aric would impart upon his dealings. She was the face of RHS Communications and her name and reputation were upheld to the finest standards. Avery was respected in her line of business and she valued that aspect very much.

She experienced his will at several board meetings and Aric was thoughtless and rude. Many of the mergers included the sellers and Aric would announce RHS Communications would strip their business to the bones, leaving nothing recognizable. While this may be partly true, Avery didn't appreciate Aric's callous behavior in the final signings with these purchased businesses.

"Good God, Aric," Avery chastised him privately in the last meeting, "there is no need to state such things to our partners." Avery believed in working closely with the businesses they were working to purchase. Calling them "partners" allowed RHS Communications their continued good name in the marketplace. Aric may know how to close a deal, but he has no idea how to maintain good relations. This last acquisition was Avery's final straw regarding what needed improvement. It should have been taken care of long before; deciding was challenging.

No, thought Avery, the time had come to change the direction of RHS Communication and Aric's path of destruction.

She patted her lips with her linen napkin and placed it on the large table. "Come, darling," Avery rose from the table, "let's adjourn to the living room by the fire. We have some important dealings to discuss."

It was time, thought Avery. While Aric had made RHS Communications millions of dollars over the years, he had grown complacent. Squandering millions of dollars on trips, private planes, clothing and not to mention the complaints she'd been receiving. Complaints from shareholders, insiders and recently, soured relations from two large businesses they were in line to purchase. They fell through at the last minute due to Aric's behavior and the humiliation of the sellers in the final signing meeting. Avery had seen it too many times and was ready for a new direction.

She sat on the large, overstuffed sofa and reached for her leather bag. Inside her bag, she held information that would change the trajectory of RHS Communications, her life and Aric's.

She smiled up at Aric and patted the sofa next to her. "Please, darling - sit next to me. It's time we had a talk." Aric strolled in causally behind Avery, coffee in hand. "Oh, I'm sure we do, dear Avery. I have a good idea what you may be considering." He sat on the couch beside her and moved the pillows off to the side. He crossed his legs and sat back on the deep, comfortable couch.

Avery sniffed at Aric's comment and dismissed it. "What is this, darling?" Avery reached across and touched his cheek. There was a scratch or scratches she couldn't quite tell. Looking at him closely, she noticed he was a little bruised in the same area.

He pulled his head back slightly to deter her touch. His fingers traced the cuts on his face. He fabricated the lie on the spot. "Oh, that? Nothing, really. I had a rousing game of racquetball this week and let's just say, I had a run in with a..." he paused for effect and looked into her eyes; she noted his eyes were accusatory, "...sore loser."

Avery felt a chill run up her spine and considered this was not the first time her son had given her an uneasy feeling. She brushed it off, knew that Aric most likely lost the match and didn't want to discuss it further.

When Avery looked deeper into his eyes, she could see the lies. There was no game, it was something more, but one thing was true: she certainly knew who the sore loser was in this story.

"Well then, let's get started, dear." Avery dismissed her previous question of Aric and pulled out the papers from her leather case. Aric looked over at her and tried to determine her mood, but Avery was astute at hiding her emotions well.

"Darling, I don't think it's any surprise to you that I say I'm not pleased with your performance these last many months." Avery positioned herself and her back was razor-straight. She crossed her legs at the ankles and tucked them to the side. "I have spoken to the board and met with my attorney; you know, Roger?" She casually mentioned Roger's name and knew Aric would understand the direction this meeting was going quickly. Avery tipped her head to the side to survey Aric to see if she could read him.

Aric knew Roger as Avery's personal attorney and was also aware his mother and Roger were lovers once. He pondered a moment and wondered where she was going with this conversation. Avery pressed forward with the discussion.

"Aric, there is no sense in mincing words. I think it's time for you to step down from your position. I'm quite prepared to give you 25% of the full worth of RHS Communication and 8% invested interest in anything upcoming for the lifetime of RHS Communications." Avery let the words linger in the air. Her eyes narrowed as she watched Aric closely. She knew this was the moment of truth. "You will be a wealthy man and can maintain much, not all, of course, of your expensive lifestyle. It would behoove you to accept this offer." She placed her hands in her lap and continued to eye Aric.

Aric sipped his coffee and placed the cup on the saucer. Taking a deep breath, he jutted his jaw slightly and turned toward Avery.

His voice was even and deep. "Avery, surely you jest. Do you honestly think you can pay me off with a mere pittance? His eyes locked on hers and he was seemingly calm. "I've made you millions of dollars over the years. Do you think you can just write me off? Write me out?" His voice began to rise. "I've **never** been treated well in this miserable excuse for a family. You, grandfather...**never**!" He was angry now and stared her down blatantly, "What in the bloody hell is this all about?" He bore down on her with his eyes and she noticed the vein running down the middle of his forehead. His jaw clenched and unclenched.

"Aric, let me finish," She snapped at him. She feigned to compose herself, ran her delicate, slender hands down her slacks and gathered her composure. Aric continued to rage on and she would listen for a moment further and then stop him. His responses seethed through gritted teeth. He contributed more than she would ever know; how could she do this to him?! Her son?!

"Are you quite finished?" Avery was done with his arrogance and attitude. It was her turn to let Aric know her thoughts on this matter. There was one president of this company - period. **She** ran RHS Communications and never thought for a moment, Aric would run the company one day. He was irresponsible and careless with money and with people. She wouldn't stand for him to run the family name and business into the ground.

She set her jaw, turned directly to Aric and continued, "You will hear what **I** have to say, my son and when we're finished, you will sign the agreement I have offered."

She returned his glare and doubled down with her confidence and attitude. She reached for the papers and turned them over.

Aric stood up and glowered over her. "Before you go one step further, dear, *Mother...*" his fists were in balls at his sides, "I think there is something you should know." He smiled now and reached into his jacket pocket, pulling an envelope out. "I have information about you that I don't believe you know I hold," He began to pace in front of her and Avery sat silent. She had never seen Aric in this state; he was manic. "I've had this information for years. I found it in your study... I know about everything...I know...I know about **him**...I know he was always here...**I know...!**," his voice raised with each unfinished sentence. He was across the room and came directly toward her now, papers clenched. He tossed them on the coffee table in front of her.

"You think you're so bloody smart..." He spat the words out directly at Avery. "You don't know...**ANYTHING!**" His hand slammed down on the papers in front of Avery, startled she looked at his insistence. **"Look!"** He insisted once more, his finger pointing to the documents.

"Aric! Stop this at once!" Avery began to stand up and Aric pushed her back down on the couch. Reaching for the papers, he held the papers up to Avery's face, forcing her to look. "You will take nothing from me!," his lips snarled as he spat out the words.

Avery's eyes focused on the papers and she froze. She took the forms from his hand and sat back on the couch in disbelief. Her eyes fell on the top of the papers as she recognized a birth certificate from Switzerland.

Aric sat down next to her and for a moment, Avery thought the dust had settled, the secrets were now out and there would be finality... a conversation, discussion and consolation...but that was not the case.

Aric reached behind him and his hands found a pillow, his salvation. Avery didn't have a moment to tell him what happened - not one moment to explain how things came to be.

In a heartbeat, he was on her, moving with a speed she couldn't believe - Aric, her own son. She barely had time to register the madness in his eyes before he pressed the pillow over her face. Her mind struggled to comprehend the horror of what was happening as she heard his shouts of anger and then, eerily calm, the words in her mind repeated over and over, "I love you forever," and then nothing as the world went black.

Chapter 28

SWITZERLAND:

The young woman was weary and exhausted from the long travel. The small Peugeot dropped her off at the end of an isolated road. The early evening sun dipped behind the mountains to the east and the mist gathered around the mountain tops and drifted down into the valley. She climbed out of the car with her hastily packed bags and pressed money into the driver's hand. He tipped his hat, waved and turned the car around to follow the same path.

She traveled lightly and carried only a medium suitcase and a small overnight bag. She knew she wouldn't need much for the time away she was forced to take. She must be out of sight from judgment and gossip; she heard this over and over as it was constantly recited to her.

Glancing upwards, her eyes trailed along a wall in the foreground and followed the rock wall up to a large clock tower. She squinted her eyes and continued to survey the grouping of structures that surrounded the area.

Clearly old but well-kept, she reached down to pick up her suitcase and made her way to what appeared to be the front doors.

A smaller door to the side opened as she approached the large doors and a slight, elderly woman greeted her.

"Güten tag." Her head nodded slightly and she smiled, her weathered skin showing the expectations time had its way with her. She reached for the smaller bag and continued in a deep accent, "Do you prefer I speak in English?"

"Ya, bitte. I do speak German, but I prefer English." The young woman returned the smile, her nerves briefly soothed by the warmth in the bright blue eyes. The soft crinkles at their corners spoke of kindness and perhaps a hint of mischief.

"Very well," came perfect English. "I'm Sister Margarite. Welcome, to St. John Mustair. We've been expecting you, "the nun said gently, her tone as welcoming as the smile she wore.

The young woman nodded, her voice caught somewhere between her throat and her unease. She managed a quiet "Thank you," as Sister Margarite gestured toward the towering double doors ahead. The doors creaked open with effort, revealing a dimly lit foyer with vaulted ceilings that seemed to hold its breath.

Several sisters greeted her once inside, their faces as varied as their whispered introductions, yet all cloaked in serene politeness. Sister Margarite led her past them, down a seemingly endless hallway where echoes of their footsteps mingled with the faint smell of candle wax and aged wood.

Finally, they reached a small, neatly kept office. Sister Margarite turned to her with a smile that hadn't wavered since their first meeting. Without a word, she gently took the suitcase and overnight bag from the young woman's cool, trembling hands. Before she could muster a protest, two other sisters appeared from the shadows. Silent and efficient, they whisked her belongings away like ghosts, leaving behind only the faint rustle of fabric as they disappeared down another corridor.

The young woman swallowed hard, her eyes darting toward Sister Margarite, searching reassurance. The nun only gave a calm nod.

"Please - make yourself comfortable. Reverend Mother will be with you in just a moment." Sister Margarite patted the young woman on the hand and left her in the cold, barren office.

The walls were sparsely decorated with only a few critical items. A large crucifix was poised behind the desk and a painting of Jesus at the last supper was on the opposite wall. She swept her eyes around the room and folded her hands in her lap and shook her head in resolve. She accepted the arrangement she agreed to with her father. She was young, unmarried and pregnant. In his opinion, all were unacceptable and she could not return home until after the baby was born. She had no idea what story her father would concoct and what the hell difference did it make? She was pregnant. End of story.

She knew all too well what difference it made to her father as he made it very clear. If she wouldn't divulge who the father was, nor would she marry him, he would not have an illegitimate child ruin his name. She didn't care initially that her father was so damn angry. She spoke her mind and had plenty to say about her pregnancy. She was going to have the baby and doing so should have no bearing on her status, let alone her father.

Her plans didn't go as anticipated and her father made it perfectly clear of his exceptions. She would go to Switzerland, out of sight and the gossip, to have the baby. He would come up with some story of why she was gone and only then could she return. He demanded she put the baby up for adoption, but she dug her heels in and disagreed.

It was up to her father if he would accept her with a newborn. She was an only child. Wouldn't he want to have a grandchild? Someone to carry on the family name, tradition and business after they were gone? It wasn't something she wanted to gamble on, but she knew she wanted this baby and could see no other alternative but to go away to Switzerland. She didn't know if her father cared if she never returned; she could only hope he would come to see her way.

A knock on the door interrupted her thoughts and she turned with anticipation to the sound. It was Sister Margarite and she entered with a smile. "I'm sorry, my dear. Reverend Mother has been detained for a while and asked me to show you to your room." She swept her hand toward the door and the young woman stood to follow again.

The hallways were long and cavernous, resonating with footsteps and Sister Margarite's robes swishing. The surroundings were quiet and serene as she passed several rooms where she saw other sisters sweeping, reading, or doing whatever nuns do.

She sighed and caught herself before she bumped into Sister Margarite. The sister had stopped quickly and opened the door to a room at the end of the hallway.

"Here is your room, dear child," she led the way into the small room. It had all that was needed: a bed, a small wash basin, a bookshelf, a nightstand and a desk. She looked to the other side of the small room and found a dresser. She looked around and her suitcase was nowhere in sight. Sister Margarite continued, "We have unpacked your suitcase and your toiletries are in the bathroom, down the hallway to the right." She smiled at the young woman reassuringly.

"I'm sure you will find all you need here, dear. I know this must be difficult for you, but I assure you we will take great care of you." She smiled again with her kind, bright blue eyes. "I'll call for you when Reverend Mother is ready." She quickly left the room and closed the door behind her.

The young woman looked around the bare room and sat on the bed. The springs beneath her creaked and she lay back on the feather pillow. She just wanted this to be over. She wanted to go back home and be with her things, her familiar spaces and even though she didn't have many friends to speak of, anything would be better than what appeared to be confinement.

Her thoughts were filled with a frenetic pace of questions of what would come next. How long would she have to stay here? What would her pregnancy be like? What kind of mother would she be?

There were too many things to think about and she was exhausted. She still had business to attend to with meeting the Reverend Mother. There would be paperwork to be signed and rules to go over, but for now, she closed her eyes, draped her arm across her eyes and allowed sleep to finally take her over.

The early months moved slowly and she settled into a routine, up at 4:30 AM, praying and reflecting until 6:30 AM and then a small breakfast with the other sisters. There was light work for her in the kitchen and around the grounds and she didn't mind. Afternoon prayers were followed by lunch and she rested until early afternoon. She may gather vegetables from the garden or read in the large common area until dinner. The routine helped her remain active, making the days go by quickly. She enjoyed the company of the sisters and found them to be caring and thoughtful. Her time at the convent was nothing like she'd thought it would be. They doted over her, asked how she felt and ensured she didn't exert herself. The sisters enjoyed her being there and anticipating the baby's arrival added another layer of promise.

She was surprised she enjoyed the solitude, quiet walks in the morning after prayer and helping in the garden. Reverend Mother was also kind to her and offered counseling and thoughtful conversations about life and the future. She felt her affinity grow with the genuine sisterhood and compassion of the women she witnessed daily. It was certainly not life for her, but she appreciated how they worked together and found peace in their quiet devotion and simple life.

Her pregnancy went on without incident and the later months passed quickly. She noticed in her last trimester, she gained more weight than expected, but her monthly visit from the village doctor didn't show concern.

There was not much to her exams from the doctor on call: he would measure her stomach, take notes and listen to her heart with a stethoscope. Being in the deep recesses of a small village, there wasn't an opportunity for advanced medicine or technology in larger cities. During this visit, he listened to her stomach, arched an eyebrow and jotted down in his weathered notepad. He nodded at Sister Margarite, indicated all was well and left the room.

Knowing her delivery day was nearing, she couldn't help but wonder if her father had shown any interest. "Has my father called this week?" she asked Sister Margarite.

"No, we haven't heard from him, my dear." Her expression soft and filled with compassion and she reached out to pat her hand. "Have you thought any more about adoption, Miss Stanton?"

Sister Margarite and the Reverend Mother were the only two who would ask her decision on occasion and her response was always the same: "I will not be giving the baby up for adoption because my father wants me to." Her response was always received with a slight nod and Reverend Mother and Sister Margarite quietly accepted her resolve.

She heard from her father only twice during her months there and grew more bitter each day. Sister Margarite would ask her to search her heart and find forgiveness for her father, but she chose to hold the anger inside. How could he not call to see how she was doing? She was holding up her end of the bargain, but he couldn't bear to talk to her and see how she felt. She may be young, but she knew this behavior from any parent was unacceptable.

The night she went into labor was unexpected. She was 8 months along and her last visit from the doctor stated she was on track for her delivery in a few weeks. He poked and prodded her more than her previous visits from him, but he seemed satisfied with her progress. She was happy the days were drawing near for her to meet her baby for the first time.

She woke with a start, her body jerking awake from the depths of sleep. Groggy and disoriented, she blinked into the shadows of her room, her bladder sending urgent signals that couldn't be ignored - *bathroom*, she thought groggily, reaching to rub the remnants of sleep from her eyes. She fumbled for the bedside lamp, its dim light spreading little warmth into the small room.

As the room came into focus, she swung her legs over the side of the bed and her bare feet met the cold floor. That was all it took for the pressure in her abdomen to intensify, the need now a sharp, insistent demand.

Before she could even think twice, she stood abruptly, ready to make a beeline for the bathroom. Halfway through her first step, the urgency shifted - an unmistakable, startling *pop* followed by a rush of warm liquid cascading down her legs and pooling to the floor beneath her. Her breath hitched as realization dawned, it wasn't just her bladder.

Her water had broken.

The next several minutes were filled with the sisters scurrying about and attending to her. There was excitement in the air, as they helped her along and took her to another room they had prepared for her birth.

They helped to settle her into bed and brought warm water, blankets, hot water bottles, towels and a basin. Reverend Mother entered the room and announced the village doctor had been contacted and that he should be there within the hour.

She labored long and hard throughout the night and into the early morning. The doctor requested all the sisters leave, with the exception of Sister

Margarite and Reverend Mother. Sister Margarite never left her side and soothed her forehead with a damp cloth and whispered encouraging words and prayers in her ear.

When it was time to push, she gave it her all. She was tired and perspiration gathered on her brown, but she was determined with one goal in mind.

Sister Margarite mopped her brow and she felt the Reverend Mother take her weak hand in hers. "You can do this, dear." She whispered as she leaned into her closely. She felt the next contraction and moaned through gritted teeth. Bearing down and pushing with all her might, she felt the baby make its way into the dimmed sunlight that now filled the corner of the room.

"It's a boy! Congratulations!" Sister Margarite announced to her as she tried to catch her breath.

Thank goodness it was over, she thought to herself. The doctor quickly cut the umbilical cord, wiped the crying baby with damp, warm cloths and handed him over to Sister Margarite to dry him off. The baby was quickly swaddled and Sister Margarite placed him in the arms of Revered Mother, who immediately cooed to the crying infant.

"Shh...ttt...ttt...there, there, Kleiner...Wilkommen..." She switched to Swiss German and continued to bounce and speak softly in German to the tiny crying infant.

The doctor smiled slightly and moved his tray closer to him once more. "Well, I see another contraction coming." He spoke to Sister Margarite and she moved closer to assist if needed.

Another sharp contraction came and she cried out and felt the need to bear down again.

What in the hell is going on? she thought. The pain was equally as intense as the birth of the baby. Wasn't this just the afterbirth? Why did she feel such pain? She winced and began to bear down once more.

"Oh!" she heard sister Margarite exclaim and continued her outburst.

"She's crowning... it's... it's another baby!"

She was in the throes of pain and otherwise preoccupied to ask, what in the hell was happening, but she certainly thought to herself, what *the hell was happening*?! She just delivered a baby! What the hell did Sister Margarite mean, "She was crowning?" The sounds around her faded as she focused and pushed again against the pain.

The doctor glanced up and nodded at the shocked Sister Margarite and the Reverend Mother. "Yes-yes... I thought she may have twins when I last examined her." He positioned himself closer as the final push was exerted and the baby was delivered amidst cries of delight and utter shock. She faintly heard them say it was another healthy baby and more joyful cries.

She tried to open her eyes - engage in what she heard, but she was exhausted.

Once more she tried to speak and her eyes fluttered closed as she lost consciousness.

*****

Deagan and Loghan drove up to the curb on Powell Street and found the front of their hotel magnificent. He smiled at Loghan and shook his head with disbelief.

"This place is great, Loghan! Sir Francis Drake Hotel? I knew this is where we were going, but I didn't realize how...how..." He was at a loss for words. Loghan helped him out.

"Bougie?" She offered as she finished his sentence and laughed, reaching for her Kate Spade bag. "The wedding is here and Megan and Conner reserved a block of rooms for their guests." Loghan smiled at Deagan and tugged on his jacket sleeve. "Hey...thank you again for coming so last minute. I really do appreciate it." She smiled meekly at Deagan and felt a slight tinge in her cheeks.

"Aww... You're welcome. It's not a problem, really. Anything for a friend."

He felt a twinge in his gut when he used the phrase "friend," but he was glad to be here with Loghan, especially now, since all seemed to be well with her friend, Jodie.

Loghan reached for the door handle and she was greeted by a young man who hustled out and opened her car door. She stepped out and Deagan was already at her side.

"Valet, please? Deagan slipped a bill in the young man's hand discreetly.

"Yes, sir. I will take care of that for you. Please see the concierge or front desk if you wish to use your car anytime, sir. Here is your ticket." The young man took their luggage, bags and garment bags from the trunk and handed them to a porter. He placed them on the bell cart and wheeled away quickly.

The rain finally stopped, at least for the moment and the air had a crisp winter scent. Loghan pulled her jacket collar around her neck closer and felt a light touch on the small of her back. She turned to see it was Deagan and he smiled and nodded toward the hotel doors.

They were met by a man dressed as an old-world, Beefeater, in his best attire. Complete with ruffled white collar, cropped breeches and buckled shoes. He whisked them into the ornate lobby with high ceilings and opulence.

Deagan allowed his eyes to survey the expansive lobby and appreciate his findings. The gilded ceilings, marble walls and statues enhanced the feeling you had been swept away to another time. As they approached the counter, he noted that while much of the hotel had the air of days past, it was discreetly updated.

Loghan reached the desk first and gave her information to the attendant. she asked if the wedding party had arrived and was told many were. She didn't know if she could say hello to Megan and Conner before the wedding, but knew there would be opportunity at the wedding, along with seeing college friends.

The fog had lifted for her and she wasn't feeling as desperately sad as she once had when she learned Megan was getting married. She had always been happy for her, but the bittersweet feelings the two had once daydreamed of planning their weddings together were hard to shake.

Deagan offered his information to the second desk clerk, who appeared and Loghan leaned over to say something. "Would you please see that our rooms are next to one another or at least close by?" she asked the woman behind the counter. "Of course, I'm happy to assist."

Loghan gave her the room number and the desk clerk typed a few keystrokes and looked up. "There you go, Ms. Riley. You're next to each other." She held out the envelope with the card keys to Deagan. "Thank you," he smiled and nodded at the desk clerk, tucking his credit card and card keys in his wallet.

"I hope you don't mind that I took the liberty to have our rooms next to each other?" Loghan looked over at Deagan as they made their way to the elevators.

"Mind? No, not at all. I think that would be good so we don't spend time riding the elevator looking for each other's rooms." He chuckled and tried his best to be casual about it and was quietly pleased she asked for their rooms to be next to one another.

They rode up quietly in the elevator and exited on the 19th floor.

"I'm going to freshen up. Would you like to meet up in about an hour?" Loghan looked over hesitantly at Deagan.

"You know what? That sounds great. I'm a little tired and keyed up from the drive," he smiled gently at Loghan and added, "Waiting to hear about your friend Jodie and all. It will allow me a little time to check emails, check in on Jenny and see if that little weirdo, Dexter returned my email to meet up with him."

"Oh God, that's right." Loghan almost forgot that was one of the main reasons Deagan had come to San Francisco to see if he could meet up with Dexter and find out why he was sending him cryptic messages.

"I'm sorry, Deagan...I almost forgot about that." Loghan appeared to be contrite and Deagan waved her off.

"It's not a problem at all. Really." He smiled at Loghan and continued, "I almost forgot about him, too, in all the excitement." He ran his hands through his hair and rolled his head around to ease his muscles. "I'll text you in a little bit. Sound ok?"

"It sounds perfect. See you soon." She smiled at Deagan and they each entered their separate rooms.

Loghan closed the door behind her and reached into her jacket pocket. Her phone was buzzing and she glanced to be sure it wasn't a follow-up from Jodie.

It was from David. He messaged her three times in a row and each seemed more insistent.

'Hello darling. Have you a moment to talk now?' **2:24 PM.**

'I'm sure you're able to speak now and have time to talk to me. What can you tell me about your earlier problem?' **2:26 PM.**

'I'm not sure what to make of this, Loghan. I deserve a response from you, don't I?' **2:29 PM.**

Loghan creased her brow as she looked at David's messages. What the hell is going on here? She thought with slight agitation. He's being a bit obsessive - I don't have to answer his every whim!

Loghan dropped the phone to her side and walked into the room. They already delivered her bags in the room and she was trying to figure out how that happened without her seeing them go by.

Her phone buzzed again and her head jerked to look, "What now?!" She said aloud and saw it was Deagan texting.

'Hey. How did they get the bags in our rooms so quickly? LOL!'

Loghan felt her shoulders drop down and relax. Jesus, she was ready to pounce on David. She was relieved to find the text was Deagan and also thankful for his sense of humor and timing.

'I know, right? I was literally thinking the very same! LOL...!'

She smiled and walked over to the windows in the room. What a beautiful view, she thought.

The city below was glistening with the rain-slicked streets and buildings far below. She loved this city and was glad to be here, even more so knowing Jodie was safe. Her mind drifted for a few minutes while she moved about the room, unpacking and washing her face.

She had a twinge of guilt that she quickly concluded Barrett was the man in the photo this morning. Obviously, she was wrong. Jodie not only made sure she and Tina knew it was her texting, but Jodie also said they were having a wonderful time. Everything was good. Jodie was a brilliant woman and didn't make foolish mistakes. Loghan had to dismiss the thought about Barrett and she was confident she was just being overly paranoid.

She texted Tina and told her what she thought and Tina was already well ahead of her. She too, felt the same and even though the photo was super close, it couldn't have been Barrett, as he was with Jodie the entire time.

Tina and Loghan texted back and forth for a few minutes and Loghan said she would call the police department. She added she would let them know she was incorrect about Barrett. She needed to do that as soon as possible. She knew the police needed to have all the information about whoever the man was in the photo.

Tina agreed she would do the same and they signed off.

Loghan had a lot on her mind today. She was troubled by the way David's texts came across and it wasn't like him to be so...so...possessive. Insistent. She didn't like it and was just fine making him wait for her response. David needed to learn she wouldn't drop everything when he wanted her to. That was crazy. She shrugged off thoughts of David and rested a little bit, changed and reapplied minimal makeup; light foundation, blush, lip gloss and a touch of mascara.

She felt an unspoken ease in Deagan's presence, a rare comfort that allowed her to simply *be*. He witnessed her at her best - radiant with laughter, eyes alight with mischief, - and at her worst, when the world crashed down around her, at the loss of Ian. Through every storm and every sunrise, Deagan remained, never flinching, never wavering. She smiled at the recent memory of Deagan being so helpful and thoughtful toward her this morning and the drive to San Francisco.

She was slightly surprised Deagan seemed equally concerned about Jodie's well-being and supported going with Loghan today to find her. He was sure she would be alright, which meant the world to Loghan, when he told her that in the car. She needed his reassurance this morning when everything seemed to be falling apart.

She appreciated that Deagan didn't hesitate and was such a strong and kind man. She smiled slightly and shrugged off the thought to focus on the rest of her day.

She contacted the police department, asked to speak to Detective Kinder and received her voicemail. Loghan stated she could have been incorrect with the name she provided for the possible composite photo. She briefly said she had contact with Jodie and everything was fine. Sorry for the imposition and to please contact her if she had any other questions.

She hung up the phone and was happy that was out of the way. One more thing behind her as the short weekend of fun looked to be happening now that Jodie was ok.

Her phone buzzed again and she glanced down as she began to apply her mascara.

It was from David...again.

'Hello, my darling. I think it's time we meet in person. Don't you?'

Loghan screwed her face up at the message. What the heck is he talking about? she thought. All the drama earlier and now he wants to meet in person? He's in London, for Christ's sake.

She usually would be happy to hear from David. Excited to talk to him and most of the time, she found herself deep in the midst of steamy sexting with him.

Not at all like her, but it certainly was when it came to David. He brought out things she didn't know existed in her and she liked dabbling into what she thought was her "darker side."

This morning, the veil finally lifted and what once felt like an intoxicating connection now sat bitter on her tongue like stale wine. David's words - once thrilling in their precision, their ability to draw her in - suddenly revealed themselves as threads of control, disguised as care. The red flags she'd ignored fluttered boldly like banners in a stiff wind. It was unnerving, how quickly the shift had come, as though someone had flipped a switch in her mind. Lucid and sharp, she felt as if she were stepping out of a fog, seeing everything for what it truly was.

Yes, she had allowed herself to feel drawn to him, to explore edges of desire in the safety of distant words, but what had once seemed liberating now felt like chains tightening around her freedom. It wasn't him exactly - it was the hold he'd managed to cultivate without ever meeting her face-to-face. The grip had loosened. That spell was broken.

This morning was her reckoning, the quiet awakening she hadn't known she'd been waiting for.

She picked up her phone and tapped out a message quickly. She didn't want to be rude to David, but she felt their "time together" had reached the end. It was getting too weird for her, it no longer felt safe and time for her to move on. Time to be part of the real world and not lost in this world that lacked reality and security.

'Hello, David. I'm sorry I've been out of touch today. I've had some personal business to attend to and it was important. Everything turned out fine and now I'm out of town for my college roommate's wedding. No time to talk today, but I'll contact you in a few days.'

She paused and read the message over once more. She knew it was dismissive compared to their regular exchanges, but today really creeped her out. Maybe she was just tired, or, she may never ever reach out to David again, but he deserved an initial response. She justified her short message by telling herself she wasn't lying to him. She was satisfied with her answer, hit send and set her phone down on the bathroom counter.

Loghan put the last touches on her mascara and texted Deagan to see if he was ready to go and venture into the city.

*****

She woke and was acutely aware of the quiet surrounding her. She stirred and opened her eyes and was greeted by the serene smile of the Reverend Mother.

"My dear, you look much better after that long rest," Reverend Mother reached to the nightstand and picked up a steaming mug of clear broth.

She continued. "Here you are, my dear, have some bone broth. It's rich in minerals and nutrients. It will help get your strength back."

She sat up, reached around to prop her pillows up and gratefully accepted the hot mug. She cupped her hands around the warmth and nervously looked around. She remembered at that moment, there were two babies. Where were her babies?

Reverend Mother knew exactly what she was thinking and calmed her concern.

"The infants are sleeping and Sister Margarite will bring them to you shortly."

Mother Superior reached for some papers on the nightstand and held them close to her side. "There was a call from your father last night," Her smile faded somewhat and she continued, "He wanted to know how you were doing and if you delivered just yet."

Her hands nervously shook and to prevent spilling, she set the cup on the nightstand and adjusted herself higher in the bed.

"Did my father ask to speak to me?"

The Reverend Mother's kind face softened further, "My dear, your father is a complicated man...he loves you as best as any man of importance can. He loves you in his way and only wants the best for you." Her smile waned and she pulled a chair up the bed and sat down.

"I have a couple of documents for you to sign regarding the birth certificates. May we please complete this and continue our talk while we await your little angels?"

Reverend Mother handed her the papers and pulled a pen from some mysterious place inside the folds of her habit.

She took the papers and pen from Reverend Mother's soft yet firm hand and noticed her own hands were shaking slightly. She was still tired and overwhelmed by her experience. She wanted to see her infants and get her head around that she had two babies. What in the world would she do now? She had planned on one baby...but two? She stopped her mind from reeling out of control and looked for the place to sign her name.

"Right here, dear." Mother Superior pointed to the two blank lines on each page.

She took a breath and fought back the fear of her father's response to her birth of a child, let alone two. She knew there to be a fight waiting in the wings with that conversation once more. They had words so many times before, once he found she was expecting. He made his point very clear she would not ruin the family name with an illegitimate birth. He would cut her off from the family dynasty and earnings unless she did as he said.

Well, we'll just see about that, she thought. She took another deep breath and poised her pen on the line and with a shaky hand and signed;

Katherine Avery Stanton.

Chapter 29

Loghan and Deagan stepped out of the hotel into the rain-slicked streets of San Francisco. The city's damp air seemed to lighten Loghan's mood and atmosphere. The quick call to Jodie on Barrett's phone eased the weight on her and all was right with the world now. The time alone in her room made way for doubt to enter her mind if Jodie was really doing fine. She continued getting ready to meet Deagan to explore the city, but the need to settle those feelings pressed upon her. There was only one way to stop the thoughts, so she reached for her phone and called the number Jodie texted earlier. It would be nice to hear Jodie's voice to ensure she was safe and sound.

She was surprised when Barrett answered as she almost forgot he had a luscious Scottish accent. Loghan quickly recovered and reminded Barrett she was one of Jodie's overly protective friends. Barrett let out a great laugh and he was very kind and polite on the phone and reintroduced himself. He handed the phone over to Jodie and the two friends laughed again about Jodie losing her phone.

"Mmm...hmm...now that I'm reminded of his sexy accent, I can see why you lost your phone," Loghan's voice hinted at the naughty intention. She added, "I would have lost my phone as well to keep you ladies out of my hair for the weekend!"

Loghan laughed and the two spoke for a few more minutes, going over Loghan's plans for the weekend.

"Oh yes, I forgot about your friend's wedding this weekend in San Francisco!" Jodie exclaimed with remorse. "I'm a terrible friend! What are the odds I would be here with a man?! You're not going alone! I will work it out and I can go with you!" There was concern in Jodie's voice.

"No, no, don't be crazy! I asked Deagan to come with me when we left this morning to look for you," she paused briefly. "He's coming with me tomorrow as my plus one."

It was Jodie's turn to be surprised. "Really? That's great, Loghan. I'm glad you're not going alone," Jodie's voice took a conspiratorial tone, "Deagan, hmm...he certainly is easy on the eyes, my friend."

"Oh, my gosh... you're too much! "Loghan laughed and made a weak attempt at changing the subject. She was very good at shifting conversations away from those she didn't want to address. "Well, it's all worked out, that is for sure." Loghan smiled as she felt tension leave her body, knowing her friend was safe and well.

"Yeah, I wanted to ask you something," Jodie's voice turned serious momentarily.

"Why were you and Tina so worried about me bring with Barrett?" Her voice turned to more of a whisper. Loghan assumed Barrett must be nearby and Jodie didn't want him to overhear.

"Ummm...well, we hadn't heard from you for a while and it's out of character for you not to reach out." Loghan hesitated to continue, "And... umm...."

"What?" Jodie laughed slightly, but Loghan could tell that she wanted to hear what she had to say.

"We were worried...you haven't been watching the news, I assume...and..." Loghan opted not to worry her friend further and omitted the full details.

"It's a rough city in certain places and there was an attack on a young woman there and...well, ...we were concerned since we hadn't heard from you." Loghan would tell Jodie the full details once she had returned, as there was no need to worry her now. She wasn't in a hurry to tell her friend they thought the worst of Barrett. Clearly, they were incorrect assuming the man on the news was Barrett.

Jodie laughed softly and Loghan was relieved her friend didn't press further for details. She didn't look forward to sharing with Jodie that her boyfriend strongly resembled the man in the news. Jodie scoffed and her voice returned to a normal level. "You two need to stop watching Dateline!"

"Agreed!" Relieved, Loghan laughed.

The call wrapped with a brief back-and-forth exchange with Barrett joining on speakerphone. Jodie insisted Barrett tell Loghan they were happy and having the best time, which Barrett did gladly. Loghan heard his voice muffle a bit and Jodie laughed and squealed with delight. "Oh my gosh...! Stop, Barrett!" Loghan didn't think Jodie really wanted Barrett to stop whatever he was doing and she helped her by ending the call.

"Love you, friend! Text me when you get your new phone later on!" Loghan hit the end button, shaking her head and smiled as she set her phone down. Geesh, she is undoubtedly into him, she wistfully thought.

"There's our Lyft." Deagan's voice severed the call replaying in Loghan's mind. Her attention was pulled toward Deagan as he pointed to the curb across the street. He looked both ways, then took her hand with an easy confidence that made Loghan smile slightly. Together, they darted across the street, narrowly avoiding a bike messenger who zipped past with a muttered curse.

The car was a welcome escape, its warmth wrapping around them like a long - forgotten comfort. The driver greeted them with a friendly smile as they slid into the back seat. The air inside was immaculate, carrying a soothing mix of freshly cleaned upholstery, soft vanilla and the sharp tang of Amour All. For the first time that day, Loghan felt her shoulders relax. San Francisco could keep its damp; they had found their refuge, although briefly, for now.

They headed toward the San Francisco Ferry Building as the driver navigated around the busy streets. Earlier, Deagan texted Loghan to see what places she might like to see and she told him she was open to almost anything. She had a couple of places she might want to go to but was interested to hear what Deagan had in mind. She looked over at Deagan and smiled softly.

Today, Deagan was the picture of effortless style, donning a sharp, hunter green and deep black checked shirt layered under a vest, all topped off with a sleek winter jacket. His cuffed chinos added just the right touch of causal flair, with vibrant socks joyfully peeking out at the ankles. Loghan couldn't help but smile at how he managed to balance seriousness with a hint of playfulness in his attire. He never overdid it - his polished leather shoes grounding the look perfectly. Loghan found another moment where she looked at Deagan in a new light, realizing his understated sharpness had always been there, though she hadn't noticed until now.

"What?" Deagan was smiling back at her.

"Oh! Nothing...really," Loghan nervously sat up. "I was just thinking, I didn't realize you were such a... 'hip dresser'." She made a show of using air quotes and laughed.

"Oh really?" Deagan chuckled, while cocking his eyebrow for full effect. "Yes, I'm quite the hipster; you just didn't know it." He smiled and winked at her as he glanced out the window.

The time they shared was easy and the conversation never awkward or slow. Loghan appreciated the time with him in a new way and instead of overthinking everything, she decided to just have a great day.

Tomorrow was the wedding and now with the weight of worry regarding Jodie's safety off her shoulders, she could relax and enjoy a day of sightseeing and fun. There was still a nagging in the back of her mind regarding David. She never knew how deeply he got to her without ever meeting. Loghan knew she needed to reach out once more to him and end whatever it was they started, but that would have to wait just a short while.

The rain finally eased and there was a break in the clouds allowing slivers of sunlight to break through, casting long shadows on walkways and buildings. The driver expertly navigated his way toward the Embarcadero and pulled over when he found a break on the busy street. With grateful nods, they both thanked him and stood on the sidewalk as he drove away.

Making their way across the street into the busy crowd, it appeared everyone else had the same idea heading to the Ferry Building. There was an open Farmers Market and shops inside the old rustic structure. Their senses were immediately assaulted with the delectable aromas that came from the market. Coffee, chocolates and restaurants throughout the building, enticing the two with their goods.

They bypassed the open market and walked through the Ferry Building. With many small shops; sounds, people and music were coming from everywhere. They took their time and wandered through shops, looking at gifts and tasting multiple vendors' offerings.

Loghan loved the diversity San Francisco presented to its visitors and locals. There was never a dull moment or opportunity for new experiences, or to taste something you'd never heard of before. Loghan bought a few small gifts for her parents and Tina and Jodie. She felt a vibration on her wrist and looked down at her watch.

It was David - again. Asking what she was doing and when they could talk? His endless messages today were wearing on her, but she knew she'd have to deal with him eventually. She was enjoying the moment and atmosphere being with Deagan, who in contrast was refreshingly genuine and honest. No need to schedule conversations or tiptoe around topics. She wasn't ready to face the decisions she'd been making lately as they related to David, so she pushed the thoughts aside once more and let herself drift through the shops, browsing the displays. A cozy scarf caught her eye and she began trying on different colors. Just then, Deagan wandered over from the book section, a quiet presence in her thoughts.

"That looks nice on you, Loghan." He nodded and smiled as she pulled the scarf off and tried another color. "What about this one?" she smiled at him and batted her eyes playfully.

"I like that one too, but I really like the green one," he pointed to the scarf she had just put down. He didn't mention the scarf made her eyes look amazing.

Deagan was enjoying the time with Loghan and he felt their friendship growing and he reconsidered the idea of being in the "friend zone." He liked having a female friend even though he hoped they would connect one day. He accepted this wouldn't happen as she was so distant these days and knew she was interested in someone else. She clarified that to him a while ago, and he never asked about this mystery man again. He really didn't want to know about him. After all, he was the guy taking her time and possibly, her heart.

"I'm hungry" Loghan tugged on his sleeve "are you?" Deagan looked at her delicate hand as she pulled on his sleeve and grinned. She reached again for the green scarf and smiled at Deagan. "I'm getting this one," she held up the scarf he admired and smiled at him.

"Good choice," he returned her smile. "Yes, I'm starving." Deagan rubbed his stomach for effect. "Do you want to eat here or head up to the wharf for something?"

"Let's go to the wharf. I like it here but enjoy the vibe more at the wharf." Loghan handed the clerk her debit card and they quickly checked out.

Back in another Lyft, they headed to Pier 39 and Fog Harbor Fish House for lunch.

"I haven't been to Fog Harbor for a while," Loghan beamed and continued, "They have the most delicious clam chowder." She made a swooning motion and Deagan laughed. "I agree. They have great oysters, too, if you like that."

They navigated through yet another bustling crowd, climbing the steps toward the restaurant. By the time they reached the door, Loghan's hunger hit full force, her senses overtaken by the mouthwatering scent of fresh seafood drifting through the air, teasing her with the promises of fine food waiting for them.

Deagan gave their name to the front desk host and was told there would be a 15-minute wait. He took the pager from the host and looked around the restaurant.

"Let's get a drink." Deagan gestured with his thumb toward the bar and Loghan nodded in agreement. She glanced at the bar and saw it wasn't too busy, with plenty of seats open for the taking. As they approached, the bartender flashed a smile, his eyes lingering a little too long on Loghan as he looked her up and down with clear interest. Deagan did his best to remain composed, resisted the urge to raise a questioning eyebrow. It was obvious the bartender wasn't making any effort to hide his attraction and Deagan certainly took note.

"Hello, gorgeous," the bartender greeted, his smile oozing flirtation, as he blatantly ignored Deagan's presence beside Loghan. His teeth were blindingly white and even Deagan had to admit, the guy was annoyingly good-looking. "What can I get started for you?" Continuing to ignore Deagan, he leaned on the bar. Loghan remained completely unfazed and seemingly unaware, her expression cool as she causally turned her attention back to Deagan without missing a beat.

"I don't know about you, Deagan, but after the stress of this morning, I'm ready for something strong. You?" She felt her Apple Watch vibrate and casually looked down at the message. It was David... once again. He was becoming more insistent – '*I would suggest you let me know when we can spend time together.*' Together?... That was an interesting concept, wasn't it?

She flipped the message away with a swift upward motion of her man-icured fingertip and looked at Deagan. She hoped he had a good idea for a strong drink to recommend. She was usually a wine drinker, but today, she needed something that burned going down. She was concerned with David's attention today and how his tone increased to the point that made her uncomfortable. She winced slightly and pushed thoughts of him away. *Not now, damn it,* she thought.

The bartender looked away from Loghan, seemed annoyed and turned his smile down several notches. He approached Deagan almost reluctantly. "Well, what can I get you?" He thrust his chin upwards at Deagan and looked bored, realizing Loghan was not interested in his attempt to dazzle her.

Deagan smiled at Loghan. "I know what will do the trick," turning to the bartender, "two Long Islands, please." Deagan turned back to Loghan, smiling. "I like to cut out the middle-man and go right to the source." He laughed and Loghan couldn't help but join in. She liked how he thought and the Long Island would do the trick and take the edge off the bitter start of this day.

They took their drinks to a surprisingly open corner booth and Deagan stood while Loghan was getting settled. Loghan placed her shopping bags in the booth and started to remove her jacket.

"Here. Please, let me help with that." Deagan offered as she moved in closer to him and he gently pulled her jacket off her shoulders. A hint of her perfume reached his senses and he didn't know it was coming from her hair or skin. She smelled beautiful and he pushed the scent from his mind. *Focus,*

Deagan...Jesus, get a grip. He reminded himself.

They settled in once more and Deagan picked up his glass in an offer of a toast.

The clink of their glasses echoed softly, swallowed by the hum of the surrounding world. Deagan's smile lingered just a little longer than necessary, something thoughtful flickering in his eyes. Loghan felt the warmth of it, as if he'd wrapped the moment itself in a quiet intention she hadn't quiet anticipated.

"To Jodie being safe and sound," Deagan said, in a soft voice, as though he truly meant every word. She nodded," To Jodie, "her fingers curing around the glass firmly as she took a slow sip. And then, unspoken, but present and *to us–this day.*

Their gazes met again, the silence between them feeling less empty and more like a space they could share. She held onto his look longer this time - longer than polite, longer than casual–until it seemed that words weren't necessary at all. There was something steady about him, an ease that settled into the quiet. Loghan could see it now: the way his kindness softened the sharp lines of his face - the gentle confidence that made him seem somehow familiar and unknown all at once.

That flutter in her chest stirred again, fragile and fleeting, as though her heart wasn't quite sure whether to trust it. *Look away,* a voice inside her nudged, but her body didn't quite listen, it was only when Deagan's expression shifted - something knowing and patient, his head tilting ever so slightly - that she felt heat rush to her cheeks.

Clearing her throat, she broke the gaze and let her attention fall to her glass, fingers fidgeting as if the glass needed adjusting. The sip she took was more hurried than intended, as if the drink might distract her from the strange vulnerability that had washed over her.

When she dared look up again, Deagan was still watching her, calm as ever. But there was no smugness, no teasing in his smile. Just understanding. Hope.

"Drink ok?" he teased lightly, breaking the tension.

She closed her eyes and smiled, "Perfect," she took another sip as if she were evaluating her decision and nodded. "Oh yes... it's tasty, not too strong, but enough to where I feel a slight burn." She laughed and Deagan joined in appreciating the cocktail. Loghan was in the moment and turned to Deagan as she placed her drink down.

The edges of her nerves softened, a small grin pulling at her lips despite herself. Something between them had shifted in that moment, imperceptible yet undeniable. It was subtle, like the first few notes of a song you couldn't yet name but knew you wanted to hear it again.

Loghan pushed away the thoughts and nervously shifted in her seat.

"Tell me something about yourself that I may not know, Deagan."

Deagan's face became thoughtful, "Oh, wow...I wasn't expecting that," he smiled and leaned back, taking a moment before he responded. "Well, I want to take time off and write a book." He paused and she could see he was gathering his thoughts before continuing, "I've wanted to write a book for some time now, just haven't had the time or the exact story I want to write, you know?"

Loghan nodded, "Deagan...I didn't know that about you. Please go on!"

"My grandfather was a professor and an incredible writer and master storyteller, "he said, a touch of admiration in his voice. "He encouraged me to write, so I chose this path." He shrugged slightly and continued, "I love what I do, the exposés, the thrill of chasing stories - but I want to write something more," he paused to consider the words he was seeking, "more grounded and real, I guess. Something that speaks to me."

Loghan leaned forward, interested in this new revelation of Deagan. She knew he was an excellent writer but had no idea he wanted to write a book. She admired this and encouraged him to share more. "I love this, Deagan. It sounds like you should do it...make it happen." She smiled at him, her green eyes glistened in the muted lighting and she sipped her drink.

"Yeah, I'm going to one day. My grandfather gave me his old oak desk some years ago before he passed. He wrote many great stories there and told me the desk was mine with one caveat, to write from the heart," Loghan watched Deagan's eyes close as she could see him drift in this poignant memory briefly. He continued, "I loved him very much and to honor his memory and all he did for me, I will write that book one day. I promised him I would; I'm just not quite there yet." He took a healthy sip of his cocktail and smiled at Loghan.

"I love this... thank you for sharing your story with me, Deagan." Loghan tipped her glass to him again and they both smiled.

Their conversation drifted to work as it often did and they recapped what Deagan had been working on for some time now; the unsolved murders of the young women across the country. Deagan went over his work thus far and mentioned he hadn't heard from Dexter yet.

"That seems odd he hasn't responded to your emails, Deagan," Loghan's brow furrowed as she considered this news and continued. "Do you think it's weird he hasn't reached out to you again? I mean, he was emailing you tips about the women...the ones who were murdered in other parts of the country and now..." she drifted a moment, "now...this assault with Jenny... and it was right here." Loghan tapped her long fingertip on the table. Deagan agreed and checked his email once more as they were talking.

"Nothing. Well, I know where Dexter works. I guess I could go by and see if he's there and just play it off like I'm an old friend visiting if anyone asks anything, you know?" Deagan put his phone down and shrugged it off. "I think he would have contacted me if he found anything more compelling. He's a strange dude, for sure." Deagan looked down as the pager lit up and vibrated. "Table is ready," he smiled.

They followed the server through the busy restaurant, weaving between tables until they reached a cozy spot by a window in the back. From there, they were treated to a stunning view of the San Francisco Bay, where boats glided gently over the water and tourists wandered along the walkways below. As Loghan settled into her seat, the warmth of the drink began to take effect, a sense of ease washing over her. The tension of the day melted away and she felt a growing anticipation for what she knew would be a pleasant, unrushed lunch.

They looked over their menus and with no surprise, Loghan ordered the clam chowder in a bread bowl and a small salad with salmon. Deagan took a few minutes longer to decide, as his appetite and inability to select just one item on the menu, he opted for a small order of baked oysters, linguine and clams. They both ordered a glass of malbec for their meal and Deagan smiled as they shared a love of wine.

As the server left with their order, Deagan remembered the Blue Cheese French Bread was excellent here and ordered it to come before their meals. "Why not have more bread?" Loghan smiled. "I'm going to be in a carb coma by the end of tomorrow!" She laughed and they returned to their conversation.

Deagan returned to their earlier conversation and said he thought he would talk to Dexter once here, but without his response, he still wasn't quite sure how to approach it. He shrugged off the thought and stated he wasn't overly concerned he hadn't heard from Dexter, commenting that he was a flaky dude. The more Deagan thought about Dexter, his not responding to him yet didn't surprise him. As they wrapped up their conversation about the "creepy little man," it allowed Deagan a little more time to consider if he would pursue that lead or move on to another.

Deagan changed the topic as he was ready to move on to something more interesting: Loghan and her article. "Hey, tell me more about this network of people you've uncovered in your article." Deagan's eyes changed immediately and were filled with questions.

Loghan re-positioned herself anxiously. "Did you finish reading it?" Her expression couldn't hide her anticipation of Deagan's thoughts on this topic; she continued, "I mean, I did ask for your feedback... I'm really interested in what you have to say."

She was slightly anxious at his thoughts when she sent over her completed article for him to read. She wouldn't send it to her editor, John, without Deagan's weigh-in. Deagan offered to give his feedback a few days prior and she had forgotten, with everything leading up to Jodie. It all came flooding back to her now and she was curious what Deagan's take would be on her discovery of the people, sex and darkness that was hiding in plain sight on the internet. She nervously wondered about his thoughts on her article - her writing style. What would he think of her? Would he look at her differently?

Loghan spent hours messaging people online, asking questions she would never ask face to face. She found the anonymity of being online a safe space for her. There was an invisible wall of protection around her. She could sign off and close her computer if things were too much for her. It allowed her distance and the ability to control her involvement. It also allowed her to be brave, open and forward. She felt these last weeks, working on this article and spending time online with David, revealed a part of her that she was unaware of until now.

Loghan allowed the darkness that followed her since Ian's death to finally fall away from her. She felt her mind was open to areas she would never have explored otherwise. Case in point: her involvement with David.

David continued to message her throughout lunch and she knew he would call her if she didn't respond soon. That would be so embarrassing in front of Deagan. She didn't want Deagan to see her react to David. She was increasingly irritated with David today and was apprehensive to have a conversation with him tonight - she was going to tell him it was time they move on. This, whatever it was, she thought, was no longer working for her. It was now feeling unsafe and bordering on creepy with his constant messages and demands to talk.

Loghan thought about sharing with Deagan what was going on with her and David, but immediately felt her cheeks flush with embarrassment.

Embarrassed? She thought...why? She pondered for a moment longer.

She had to tell Deagan everything, it wouldn't make sense otherwise-not the fractured pieces of her actions, not the subtle changes of her demeanor that he'd probably already noticed. She couldn't hide the depth of her involvement anymore. To unravel the mess, she'd have to explain why she'd been so drawn to David, how he chipped away at her defenses, brick by careful brick, until there was nothing left of the cautious, guarded woman she used to be.

The shame burned hot as she replayed it all in her mind. David had made her feel alive at first, like he'd uncovered a part of her she didn't even know existed. His words were magnetic, laced with a kind of energy that bypassed her logic and went straight to her heart - and her desires. They were intimate in ways she hadn't thought possible without being in the same room. He made her feel seen. Wanted. Excited.

But that excitement came with string she hadn't noticed until it was too late. She'd given him access to part of herself she'd sworn no one would ever touch, all under the guise of exploration, research and curiosity. Slowly, subtly, David had pulled her into his orbit. He controlled everything - the timing of their conversations, the tone of their interactions, even what she wore. His suggestions weren't suggestions at all. They were directives, cloaked in flattery and sweet words.

Loghan's stomach twisted as she remembered the things she couldn't being herself to say aloud. How they interacted, how she'd let his words shape her responses, her thoughts, even her sense of self. She'd told herself it was harmless, just a game, but the truth was darker. It had felt real-too real.

And now, she felt hollow. Used. The intimacy they'd shared, though virtual, had left emotional scars she couldn't ignore, as she peeled away the layers of memories. He made her feel powerful, awakened and then he'd twisted it. It now felt, with his recent turn of mood and his insistence at her jumping when he texted, she felt like a pawn. The veil was lifting from all the magic he wove around her - she realized it was always on his terms. How she should act, what she should say. Even, what she should feel.

That was it.

As the realization swept over her, Loghan froze. This wasn't just a mistake or a lapse of judgment. This was control. Manipulation. She'd been blind to it, lulled by the thrill, but now it was painfully clear. She wasn't the woman she'd been before David.

Why hadn't she seen that before? Jesus. How in the hell...?

"Loghan?"

Loghan stopped herself and looked up at Deagan. He was looking at her with a genuine concern is his eyes.

"Loghan. Are you there? Are you alright?" Deagan's eyes showed worry and he reached across the table and placed his hand on Loghan's.

"Yes - yes... I'm sorry...I was," Loghan was clearly shaken but rapidly regrouped.

"I'm fine, Deagan." The server came to the table with their food and it was a welcomed interruption that allowed Loghan time to think of her response to Deagan. Once the server ensured nothing else was needed, he left them to their meal.

Deagan wasn't one to let anything go and he further pressed Loghan. "You looked really shook. What happened?" Deagan's expression was unchanged. Loghan knew she was caught in the moment. She knew her facial expression must have communicated a thousand words.

"Deagan," she began hesitantly, "I was thinking about many things. Things I haven't been very open about with my research. It made me feel uneasy and I...I felt...I feel you deserve **all** of the story and background on my research." She reached for her napkin and Deagan followed her lead. "Let's get started on this deliciousness in front of us and I will tell you everything over lunch." She gave Deagan a soft and reassuring smile and he relaxed.

They enjoyed their lunch and wine and Loghan launched into her explanation. She told Deagan about being on the sites, finding women who only wanted to hook up for sex and some of the other darker aspects. She wavered with how she would tell Deagan more details about David. How they met and where and how their "relationship" had turned into more than just chatting online.

She swallowed hard, her pulse racing as she carved out her words to explain it all to Deagan. He had to know - had to understand. Not just the sanitized version, but the whole truth. Because if she didn't, if she held back even a little, nothing else would make sense. And Deagan was the one person who deserved her honesty, no matter how much it hurt to give it.

Loghan started at the beginning and Deagan was attentive and asked a question occasionally, but overall, he seemed unfazed by her details. His reaction made Loghan more comfortable and she shared some of the details of their time spent online enough that Deagan fully understood. She watched his face closely when she danced around the subject of David and her sexting. It was embarrassing, but she felt better being honest with Deagan.

The table was cleared and they settled into their glass of wine. Deagan leaned back in his chair and looked directly at Loghan. "May I ask a personal question?" He looked at her kindly and Loghan couldn't help but laugh out of nervousness.

"Of course! I just shared with you the most embarrassing and intimate details in my life and you want to know if you can ask a personal question?" She sat back in her chair and lifted her glass to her lips. The sun graced itself through parted clouds at the end of the day and started to dip on the horizon and the last dregs of light filtered across Loghan's face. Deagan paused before he spoke and took in the way she looked for a moment. She was stunningly beautiful, with the light tracing over her auburn tresses. He dismissed that notion from his mind took a sip of his wine and returned his glass to the table.

"Are you in love with him? This, David?" He was direct and even though Loghan responded he could ask her a personal question, she wasn't expecting this question. His deep blue eyes were intent and he patiently waited for her response. Loghan fidgeted in her chair and gave up, leaning into the uncomfortable moment.

She cleared her throat and sat up straight. "Well...I thought so. At least, it felt like that. I...I wait for his calls. I clear my calendar for him. I make time for him...I..." her voice trailed off and her face flushed, "I find myself wanting to be...you know...be with him." Loghan felt her face flush even more and she couldn't believe she was sharing this with Deagan. "I know that sounds crazy and impossible. He's not physically here, but it feels like he is." She dropped her chin slightly in resolve.

"Well, I can see that he's affected you. He somehow got into your mind," he paused and considered his next statement, "your heart." He looked at her and gave a gentle smile. He felt the fate of his hopes sealed. Loghan was too far into this situation with David. He settled that knowledge in his mind and moved forward gently.

"Thank you for sharing that with me, Loghan. It must have been hard, but it's ok - really." He looked at her across the table and his eyes were filled with reassurance. She was so grateful for his friendship, but there was more to share with Deagan. She wanted to share that she just realized David was trying to control her. This was too much to share with him now. She was overwhelmingly embarrassed at her judgment for letting things get where they were with David and now this too? Allowing herself to be controlled?

She still didn't know why she didn't realize David's control earlier, but she knew it now. She needed to let David know-it was finished and while others may think it was "OK" to just ghost him, she knew that wasn't right. He was a person with feelings. He deserved a conversation and a reason.

She felt a vibration and looked at her watch. It was David again. She ignored it and felt a smirk teasing the corner of her lips at his impeccable timing.

"Do you need to get that?" Deagan asked with hesitation. He knew it was David. He could tell by the look on Loghan's face and he was uncertain why she looked so worried.

She looked up and flashed a smile at Deagan. "I do not," she said, smiling with deliberation. "I'm enjoying my time with you." She picked up her glass and Deagan did the same. They clinked glasses once more. He couldn't read Loghan and her meaning here, but he decided it didn't matter what her intentions may or may not be as long as they were in each other's space.

"Let's get the check and go do some sightseeing." She beamed a bright smile at Deagan and he warmly accepted it and politely flagged their server.

*****

Katherine Avery Stanton had only been home for two weeks. She was tired from her months abroad and her father's demands on how she could best, return home. The Reverend Mother was vital in helping young Katherine return home to her father. She communicated to Katherine's father the status of her health and well-being, along with the health of the infants. After she gave birth, there was a flurry of activity surrounding Katherine. She had a traumatic delivery and one of the infants was whisked away into another room. She was told one of the babies was not doing well and needed additional care. They didn't have the means at the convent to attend to the ill infant and the doctor in attendance wasn't certain of the infant's condition, or how to treat the frail newborn.

Katherine could see the infants after she woke and was overwhelmed with emotions. The sisters brought both babies into her room briefly. They were beautiful and she was told they were both boys. She was so happy and yet shocked she had twins. She wasn't aware that anyone else had twins in her family.

They were so small, seemingly fragile and both had tufts of dark hair peeking out from under their matching knit caps. Katherine didn't know what to say, nor did she have any idea how she would care for one, let alone - two infants. She was a young, unwed mother and her father would have nothing to do with this situation. He was bracing himself for one child, but now two? Rhonert Stanton was mortified once he learned she had two infants. He had made that very clear to the Reverend Mother and she gently conveyed this information to Katherine.

As the first few weeks passed, the ill infant was sent to the Children's Hospital in Basel, Switzerland. The doctors were able to diagnose the condition of the infant almost immediately. He was born with a heart condition and his lungs were not fully developed, which gave way to a difficult prognosis. They weren't confident the child would live. More testing would be needed and Katherine had no idea how this would be paid; it was the least of her concerns for now. The infant would be treated to the best of their ability, but the conversation of how this would be paid for would need to transpire at some time.

The hospital was almost four hours from the convent and Katherine was still in the care and hospitality of the sisters and Reverend Mother. She had no place to go at this time and her father was not at a place to welcome her home just yet. Katherine called her father several times to speak to him directly and he finally took her call.

He railed against her again for "getting herself into this situation," and now she had to live with the consequences. He demanded the father's name again and when he realized Katherine would not disclose the father's name, Rhonert Stanton finally gave up.

He remained furious with Katherine and believed she besmirched the family name with an illegitimate birth. For Christ's sake. No one cared about unwed mothers this day and age, did they? Katherine didn't know the answer to that question, but she knew it made all the difference to her future with her father - as well as the security she desperately sought. She wanted more than anything to continue to work with him in the family business. Couldn't he see the value in her being part of the business ? Not to mention, there were male heirs to consider now.

Time marched slowly and Katherine cared for her small, healthy son at the convent for those early months and learned how to be a mother. Caring for this tiny being was intrinsic in her nature, but the infant was fussy and didn't sleep well. Katherine quickly learned what it was to mother a child and had many restless nights, even though the sisters were there to help.

Once Katherine's strength returned, she could travel to the hospital to visit her ill infant. She peered at him through the nursery glass, her heart heavy. He was far smaller than his brother and his coloring wasn't vibrant and healthy. Monitors and wires were attached to the tiny infant that appeared to monitor his heart and breathing. Katherine was overwhelmed with sadness. Her beautiful baby, without his mother and cared for only by nurses at this time, broke her heart. She wanted to do nothing more than bond with this child. Her time with him was always short and hovering nurses made quality time impossible.

On this visit, the doctor in charge met with Katherine and Reverend Mother, he asked to meet him at his office, which was at the end of the hallway. Katherine sat in shock as the doctor reviewed the infant's diagnosis details. The infant had heart problems, they believed surgery may help, but more testing was needed to determine the path. In addition, his lungs were still not fully developed. They were treating him for his undeveloped lungs and he needed time to gain strength. All was still uncertain as he was too small and fragile to consider surgery at this time.

"What does this mean?" Katherine's eyes filled with tears. Dr. Mueller pushed a box of tissues across the desk to her. Katherine turned and looked to Reverend Mother for support. Dr. Mueller placed his arms on his desk and looked at Katherine compassionately. "It means until the child is stronger and able to withstand the possible surgery, which, I'm afraid, there is no guarantee he will...he must remain here." He leaned back and cleared his throat looking uneasy. "I must also speak to you about something most unpleasant," he began hesitantly. "Your father, Mr. Stanton, has been in contact with us. He has offered to pay for all the infant care," the doctor paused and continued, "he's also made certain arrangements." He glanced at the Reverend Mother, then nodded, signaling her to explain the rest.

"My dear child. I know this time is most difficult for you and we are truly sorry," her eyes were tender and filled with compassion. "Your father has agreed to allow you to return home and prosper alongside him in the business. You've made it apparent how much working with him and taking on the family business means to you and your father has acknowledged this." The Reverend Mother looked uneasy and looked to the doctor a moment. He nodded gently to encourage the Reverend Mother to continue.

"Your father will pay for the care of the infant...indefinitely and he's made arrangements..." her voice drifted slightly. "He will allow you to come home if you agree to leave the ill child here." Katherine blinked her eyes, fighting to get clear. "You've already said that. I understand the baby needs to stay here while he gains strength." Frantically, she looked back and forth between Dr. Mueller and the Reverend Mother.

"There is more, I'm afraid, dear," Reverend Mother pulled her chair closer to Katherine and took her hands in hers, "He says you may return home with one healthy child, but arrangements must be made for the other...he must be put up for adoption for you to return home and be a part of your family inheritance." Katherine sat frozen in her chair, unable to speak and knew her fate and her children's were sealed.

*****

Jodie sat down on the comfortable couch in the hotel room. Kicking off her heels and rubbing her feet, Barrett sat down next to her. "Here, lass," taking her feet in his large hands, he began to rub the aches away. "Let me help. We did enough walking today for anyone's feet to hurt... but in those lovely heels..." He smiled and wiggled his eyebrows. Jodie laughed and tossed her head back. He took this as an invitation and leaned in, nuzzling her fragrant neck. "Oh...my...whatever *do* you have on your mind, Mr. Rohan?" Jodie purred in his ear and rewarded him with a deep kiss.

They lingered momentarily and Barrett's hands ran down her slim waist. "Today was another glorious day." His deep burr rumbled in her ear and she could feel his evening whiskers brush against her soft cheek. "It was a wonderful day, Barrett." Jodie smiled at him. They spent the day sightseeing and ended the day on a ferry to Alcatraz. They walked all over the island and learned the backstory of the prison, the inmates and how the prison eventually closed once the notorious escape was announced.

Barrett returned to rubbing Jodie's feet and they recapped some of their favorite moments of their day. "We should have a nightcap and take this conversation to bed." He winked at Jodie and rubbed her feet firmly for emphasis. She laughed and groaned at the delightful feeling when his thumb found a particularly sore spot on her foot.

"I love that idea, but I can tell you, I don't want to talk." She smiled wickedly at him and Barrett was up in a shot. "Sounds perfect, lass... I'm going to get ice for our drinks."

He grabbed the card key and ice bucket on the table. "I'll be back in a couple of minutes. The ice machine is at the end of the hall." He turned and winked at her and walked out into the quiet hallway. He heard Jodie laughing at him as the door closed behind him and smiled.

Barrett whistled quietly as he walked the length of the hallway. No one was in sight and while it wasn't late, it seemed most were out enjoying the night in San Francisco or, what he hoped to be doing soon. He grinned sheepishly at this thought and turned the corner to the hallway he knew housed the ice machine.

The hallway was dim, the flickering overhead light casting long shadows across the carpet. Barrett barely gave the figure at the far end a second glance as he moved toward the ice machine. It was late and while he was tired, he was thinking of Jodie - waiting for him most likely, under the covers. He smiled and bent over the metal scoop scraping against the inside of the machine, when a deliberate clearing of a throat stopped him cold.

He straightened, his heart skipping and turned slowly. Standing just a few feet away was a man - a man who made Barrett's blood freeze in veins. His breath caught in his chest as he eyes roamed over the figure before him, His brain stumbled, desperate to place together what he was seeing.

The man, standing there was...him. Not someone who merely resembled him, not some distant lookalike - *him.* A perfect reflection of himself.

Dark wavy hair, piercing blue eyes, same height and jawline. Every detail seemed to be Barrett's mirror image. The same piercing blue eyes bore into him, unwavering. Yet, there was something...wrong. Those eyes weren't his. Not really. They carried a glint of something foreign, something cruel - amusement mixed with a hint of malice.

"Hello, my dear *brother.*" The man smiled at him and tipped his head to the side. "Confused, are we ?" The words dripped from the man's tongue with a crisp, proper English accent, each syllable laced with condescension.

"What the...what the fuck is this?" Barrett's deep voice rumbled. He stood rooted, dropping the ice bucket to the tile floor. The sound echoed in the small space and Barrett's attention diverted to the sound. The man was on him, pushing Barrett against the wall and pressing his arm against his throat. Barrett gasped and tried to cough, his fingers clawing at this throat to release the hold on him.

"Yes, that's right... you're seeing it correctly. I'm the brother you never knew...the twin who is the smarter of the two, stronger of the two...and will clearly, outlive you." The words were quiet, seething out of the perfect, gritted white teeth. Barrett sputtered and continued to try to push Aric away but was unable to gain his footing.

"Oh, what's wrong, dear brother?" The tone was dry and pointed. "Are you putting it together yet?" Aric pushed his arm into Barrett's throat further. "The paperwork that your *Aunt Katherine* signed over to you... it's our family business...**MY** family!" The man's eyes narrowed, his tone peppered with venom and sarcasm. "It's worth millions. I did the work...not **you!**" The words spat at Barrett and he blinked, fighting to keep conscience and understand what was happening.

"You've been set up, you ignorant fuck," Aric continued to seethe, "You will never get the money, or the business...I saw to that!"

Barrett gasped for air, "Katherine...she - she's...my..."

Aric leaned in harder on Barrett's neck and finished the sentence for Barrett, Katherine is your **mother**....you insipid fool...and she's dead." The words bore into Barrett's mind as he fought off blacking out. He found a moment of strength and pushed his body forward. "No...no...she's not...!"

Aric gained momentum from Barrett and pushed him back into the wall, "I made damn sure she is dead and you will be rotting in prison for her death...my dear brother."

The sound of quick footsteps came down the long hallway and Aric shoved Barrett hard to the wall and ducked out of the enclosure. Barrett fell to the ground hard and gasped for breath. Hands were upon him and dragging him up as he coughed and sputtered for breath.

"Mr. Barrett Rohan. I'm Detective Kinder and this is Detective Thornton. We need you to come with us, please. You're under arrest for assault and murder."

Chapter 30

She woke slowly as the fog cleared her consciousness. Confused, she fought to sit up amidst the coughing and indescribable aches. She didn't have the strength and allowed her head to fall back. She needed help but was powerless to do anything at this time.

What happened? She thought as the question pounded in her head like an echo she couldn't escape. She sucked in another shaky breath, forcing air deep into her lungs, her ribs protesting with every expansion. Her chest burned, a reminder that whatever happened had nearly stolen that breath for good.

She continued to pull air deep into her lungs. How long had she been unconscious? She couldn't tell. Minutes? Hours? The disorientation was suffocating, the kind of panic that clings to your skin like a cold sweat. Her fingers flexed weakly, brushing and touching what she found to be carpeting. She had ended up on the floor somehow. She blinked into the void of darkness, her eyes darting around a room she could not see. No light. No sound. The silence was so absolute it had weight to it, pressing down on her like a heavy shroud. Evening maybe? If it were true, the hours had slipped away without her consent, stolen by whatever dragged her here...whatever happened.

"*Jesus,*" she whispered through parched lips.

She winced at the pain and pulled a hand up to her face. Her eyes fluttered as she fought to keep them open, continuing to look around the room. Her eyes slowly adjusting to the darkness. Yes, it was night as she could detect silvers of moonlight coming in the windows. Memories flooded her mind in fractured pieces as she began to recall what happened.

She recalled the eyes. Eyes filled with rage and the strength he had when he lunged. He was too swift for her response. Her eyelids fluttered as the story line unfolded itself in her mind. It had been morning in the hotel, breakfast... no, brunch, she fought to recall. She pushed through the shattered memory, but it was coming quickly. There were words. Strong words, loud and...an argument. Yes, an argument. Over? She had enough strength to run her hands through her hair and her eyes flew open in shock.

The memory locked in place and her blood ran cold.

The sound of her voice was raspy and weak.

"Aric," Avery whispered in the void of darkness.

*****

Loghan and Deagan made their way through San Francisco on a whirlwind sightseeing afternoon. It was a fun-filled day and their shared atmosphere was easy and enjoyable. After lunch, they walked through Pier 39 and lingered in the shops and people-watching. They ducked into Loghan's favorite sweet spot, Chocolate Heaven and bought truffles to enjoy later that evening. Loghan laughed at Deagan when he made a pouty face when she placed the bag of truffles in her purse.

"I don't want to wait." He playfully jabbed a finger toward her purse with the decadent chocolate truffles, hiding safely. She swatted at the air and they laughed and returned to the cool air outside.

Deagan couldn't recall the last time he saw Loghan laugh so much. It made him happy to see her so light-hearted. They enjoyed walking in the brisk, damp air on the pier. They walked to the back of Pier 39 to watch the boats and ferries slice their way through the rough waters. The rain was holding off, but dark clouds loomed west. Deagan pulled his jacket around his neck and walked closer to the railing.

Loghan was playful and taking pictures of the bay and Alcatraz. A selfie here and there and she asked Deagan to come over and they took selfies of the two of them with Alcatraz in the background. Loghan inspected their selfies with a discerning eye. She mused at how they looked with one another

- comfortable and happy. She liked them looking comfortable and familiar and tucked the notion away, no doubt to think about later. Standing at the protective railing, Loghan felt the wind whip up and pulled her new scarf around her closer.

"Isn't this beautiful, Deagan?" She waved her arm across the span of the bay and settled in on Alcatraz. She sighed and Deagan stood closer, his arm pressing against hers. She looked over at him and gently smiled.

"Yes, it's gorgeous." He didn't know if he was referring to the expanse of the choppy bay, seagulls diving and dipping into the water or, if he was referring to Loghan's smile that captivated him. She leaned against his arm and he smiled. "It's getting colder for sure," Loghan looked out to the dusk-filled sky and her face became pensive. He wondered what she may be thinking but leaned into her to help break the chill.

Loghan was deep in thought. She was aware Deagan noticed her texting off and on throughout the day. He was kind and gave her privacy as he assumed she was texting with David.

She appreciated Deagan for not prying or asking questions. He was indeed, one of a kind. He had every reason to ask her if all was ok each time she disappeared up the store aisle or, ducked around a corner. He didn't, though. He allowed her the space she needed; she felt like this weekend broke whatever spell David had cast upon her over these last few months.

She allowed herself to lean into Deagan deeper and he also noticed. "Cold?" He leaned in, reaching over gently and tucked her scarf around her neck and into her coat.

"Mmm, hmm. A little bit. It's nice here, though. I'm not ready to go just yet." Loghan looked up at him and offered a grateful smile.

"Me either. It's nice." Deagan detected the change in her body language and willed himself to take a small gamble. Deagan returned her gentle smile and put his arm around her waist, pulling her closer. "Here. I hope that helps warm you up a bit." Each quietly and without hesitation, leaning into the other. A feeling of calm and comfort enveloped Loghan as she allowed a small sigh to escape her lips.

The two continued to watch the turbulent water swell and the edges of light begin to fall on the horizon. There was a subtle shift in their energy they exchanged and an easy quiet between them. Each comfortable in the silence, allowing their thoughts to ebb and flow as the water splashed against the piers below. After a few minutes of silence, Loghan softly cleared her throat.

"I'm... I'm sorry you've seen me dodging a few times today when I'm texting." She turned toward Deagan, her eyes filled with apology.

"It's alright – I know you must have something going on. I wanted to give you the time and space needed." He looked at her with genuine concern. "You ok, Loghan?" Deagan sensed there was something more and searched Loghan's eyes. Her emerald eyes were soft and questioning.

"Yes...I'm fine," she paused, "thank you, Deagan." She tilted her head and looked at him as if considering what she would say next. "I'm working through some feelings. Feelings I shouldn't have...or, had...or why I was allowing David to get into my head." She dropped her chin down briefly and reconnected with Deagan's eyes. "Thank you for always being here for me," she continued, "...for listening, not judging...just being you." She smiled softly, the last flecks of daylight catching her eyes.

The corners of Deagan's mouth turned upwards, gently returning her smile. The space between them changed, charged with an unspoken understanding. Around them, the world carried on – the bustling of the wharf, laughter, footsteps, the hum of life – but in this moment, none of it mattered. Their eyes locked, searching, questioning, daring, each seeking answers in the depths.

It was Loghan who answered first.

Hesitantly, she leaned forward, her eyes focused on Deagan, gauging his response. He watched her eyes intently and gently leaned in toward her. Loghan's eyelids fluttered and she tilted her head slightly to the side. Deagan responded, his hand moved gently to her face, fingers brushing her skin as his eyelids closed, savoring the closeness of the moment. Their lips hovered, just a breath apart. Deagan paused, savoring the moment – as he tried to quiet his thoughts. The feeling of Loghan's body pressing into his, the warmth of Loghan's soft breath on his lips. He inhaled deeply, as if drawing in her very essence, before finally closing the distance, their lips meeting in a tender, lingering kiss.

Loghan pressed her body into Deagan further and his arms dropped and circled her waist. They kissed slowly and gently, lingering a moment and finding their way. Loghan's hands ran up Deagan's back and their kiss deepened briefly. As they both moved apart, the kiss easily ended with Deagan adding a small kiss on Loghan's lips and they held one another in a quiet embrace. The dark clouds delivered their promise and rain began to gently fall.

"Ready?" Deagan smiled at Loghan and extended his hand.

Loghan looked at Deagan's hand and all the confusion and questioning she had for herself this day, fell easily away.

Her decision was clear.

"Yes...very much so." She reached for his hand and felt his warm fingers entwine with hers.

*****

"What the hell is going on!?" Jodie's voice tapped on the fringe of panic.

"Barrett?!" Jodie stood in the hallway, frozen as she watched Barrett roughly pulled to his feet by a man and woman. They weren't just helping him up; clearly, something was wrong.

Jodie ran down the hallway and the woman released Barrett and nodded to the large man in a suit and tie. He took Barrett, moved him against the wall and firmly placed his large hand between his shoulders. Barrett wasn't going anywhere.

The petite woman stepped forward, placing herself between Barrett and the large man, this stopped Jodie in her tracks. She reached inside her jacket pocket and flipped her badge for Jodie's view.

"Excuse me, ma'am. We're taking this man to the police station and we ask that you to stay back."

"This man is my boyfriend - my partner!" She felt the hysteria climbing up her throat again and fought it down. "What the hell is happening? Is he hurt? What is he being charged with?" She forced her demeanor to instantly calm as she demanded answers.

Barrett turned his head and breathlessly responded, "It's ok, lass. I'm alright." He was still recovering from almost blacking out, sucking air into his lungs as quickly as possible.

"I'm Detective Kinder and that's Detective Thornton," the slight woman nodded toward the large man as she placed her badge back inside her suit jacket. She shouted over her shoulder, "Detective - Mirandize him, please." The large man reached behind him, pulled out his handcuffs and pulled Barrett's wrists behind him. "You have the right to remain silent. Anything you say can and will be used against you..." Jodie heard the words coming out of the detective's mouth, shaking her head in disbelief. This couldn't be happening, she thought.

"Wait!" Jodie called out. "He's being arrested?! I want to know what is the charge?" She heard the handcuffs click and turned to see Barrett wince as Detective Thornton turned Barrett forward abruptly.

"Lass! Please...," Barrett coughed and sputtered, "Call my aunt. Call Katherine. She'll know what to do. Her numbers are in my phone!"

Several hotel guests had heard the disturbance and stood in the hallway. They stood silently in different variations of their evening activities; some in robes, some in their evening clothes, or just coming in from the night. Jodie noticed a young woman standing in her room doorway - a young man stood behind her, partly shielded by the door. The woman was wrapped in a sheet, her hair disheveled. Jodie considered the young woman must have been more interested in the sounds from the hallway than the time she was having in bed. The young man behind her, gently coaxed her back into the room.

Detective Kinder handed her a business card and Jodie's trembling hand reached out numbly to take it. "Here is the contact information for the police station. My desk number is on the bottom." Jodie looked blindly at the card and blinked away hot tears.

Detective Kinder continued to speak and stepped aside for Detective Thornton as he guided Barrett past her.

"You should be thrilled that you have friends who care about you so much," Detective Kinder paused in front of Jodie; her eyes were filled with concern and kindness. "They told us who you were with and where we could find you."

Detective Kinder turned and followed Detective Thornton, leading Barrett down the hallway; it was a moment before the comment registered with Jodie.

"Told you what? Who told you!?" Jodie called after the detective as her questions filled the cavernous hallway. There was no response. Jodie dropped her arms to her side, the business card drifted to the floor in silence and stood as tears streamed down her face.

Chapter 31

The hotel door clicked and Deagan tossed the key card on the table. He turned slowly and was met with Loghan's liquid green eyes. She smiled and her eyes never left Deagan as she slowly moved past him.

She dropped her bag on the chair and Deagan laced his fingers in hers, slowly pulling her close. He raised her hands to his lips and kissed them gently. Kissing her fingers, Loghan leaned in and kissed Deagan gently. He released her hand and she reached around his neck and began to remove his coat and scarf.

Deagan helped, shrugged off his coat and returned the favor by removing Loghan's. She pulled the emerald green scarf from her neck playfully and provocatively, smiling at Deagan.

He gently laughed, unbuttoned his vest and removed his shoes. Loghan was already ahead of him, barefoot and walked toward him as he sat on the bed.

"How about some wine?" she nodded and smiled. "I would love some." Deagan reached for the phone and called room service.

Loghan took this as an opportunity to freshen up and excused herself, grabbing her purse for a last-minute touch-up. She looked at herself in the mirror and chuckled. The rain wreaked a small amount of havoc on her hair, but it was quickly corrected.

Placing her hands on the sides of the sink, she took a shuttering breath and closed her eyes momentarily. She was filled with excitement, nervousness and anticipation at the turn of events with Deagan. How could she not have seen this coming? She gently chastised herself for being so blind to Deagan.

She brushed her long hair and tousled it by flipping it over. She looked back in the mirror and smiled at the antics that women go through to look more appealing. She shrugged it off, put on a little lip gloss and touched up her mascara.

Her Apple Watch vibrated and she looked down.

"I can't believe how you've dismissed me today, Loghan. You tell me something is wrong and then you disappear. You text me later in the day and tell me you aren't sure I'm the man you thought me to be? I won't stand for this!"

Right behind the text came three more:

"You have been beyond rude and thoughtless today! I deserve better than this! You're messages today indicate you've had a change of mind! Call me now, or you'll be very sorry you crossed me!"

"Shit," she whispered, her brows creased in concern; she reached down and with a delicate touch, turned off the notifications. Jesus, he's lost his damn mind! Loghan thought as she shook her head at the extreme change in David's responses.

She was grateful she came to her own conclusion today and would break it off with David. She thought letting him know she wasn't fond of how things were going - her responses to him would more than hint, she was going to end things. She was now, more than confident of this decision. She continued to turn the text exchanges over in her mind, again and again. She wasn't heartless - she knew David was a person who had feelings. She wasn't going to ghost him, but she needed time to get her thoughts in order and find the words to let him know she no longer wanted to interact with him. *Who in the hell talks like that with anyone? Thank goodness he knows nothing more about me or where I live.*

She removed her watch, tucked it in her bag with her phone and stepped out of the bathroom. She put a smile on her face, glided past Deagan and dropped her purse on the chair once more.

Deagan was opening the wine just delivered by room service and looked over his shoulder at her. "They are speedy and efficient here," he smiled as the cork popped and poured two glasses.

"I would welcome a glass of wine about now." Loghan reached for the wine, realizing it may have sounded off-putting to Deagan. She quickly recovered and added more thought.

"I've had a few *really* harsh messages from David this evening. That is where my need for a glass of wine comes in." She coyly smiled at Deagan and continued. "I left my watch and phone in my bag and will deal with him tomorrow with a conversation that needs to happen," she paused and looked solemnly at him, "I will let him know I no longer want to interact with him."

Deagan was relieved to hear the last part of her comment but wasn't going to let the first part go. He looked questioningly at Loghan, "Define, harsh?"

She thoughtfully sipped her wine and set the glass back down. "I'm sorry this is going on in the background, Deagan. David's been very pointed with me today and you should know why I was disappearing texting with him. She continued; I was explaining to him I didn't have time today. I told him I would contact him tomorrow and we would talk."

Deagan wasn't letting it go. "What did you mean by harsh, though?"

She reached for her wine and took a sip once more, hoping to find courage. "David wanted my time today and didn't appreciate that I didn't give it to him." Her eyes grew soft and serious. "I found someone I want to give my time to...my real-time...not virtual. My personal time." She reached out and touched Deagan's face.

Loghan searched Deagan's eyes and continued. "I thought if I let him know I wasn't appreciating his tone and responses with me today, that I would plant the seed I was breaking things off," She pulled away and her eyes dimmed. "He didn't seem to grasp my meaning just yet...that I'm breaking things off..." her voice drifted briefly, "I didn't want to get into a deep conversation with him today - I will tomorrow."

Deagan mulled over this information and reached for her hand" As long as you're ok, Loghan. That is all that's important. "He doesn't know where you are, or where you live, right?" He worried quietly as he waited for her response.

"Well, he doesn't know where I live - I mean, I never gave him any specifics. He knows I'm in San Francisco this weekend for a wedding, but I don't believe I told him where…I will have to check our messages…" her eyes clouded briefly as worry crept in. *What had I exactly shared with him?* She raced through her conversations and it was as if Deagan could tell and he squeezed her hand reassuringly.

"It's ok – it's ok, Loghan." Deagan leaned in and gently hugged Loghan. She immediately felt safe and secure. "I know – I'm fine, Deagan – really," she smiled a soft, yet bright smile. She was with Deagan and she knew she was safe and tomorrow was another day – she didn't want to be paranoid. She was fairly certain she hadn't shared her address, but she knew she did tell him she would be in San Francisco for a wedding. *She could be anywhere in the city – right?* She would do the right thing and have a proper conversation end things with David – but not tonight. Tonight was for beginnings and she was ready to move forward.

Loghan locked eyes with Deagan and the energy in the room shifted.

He pulled her down to him, their gazes locking in on a new understanding. They looked at one another through fresh eyes, the silence between them thick with curiosity and wonder. Staring softly at one another, searching and questioning. Deagan's thoughts swirled around his mind, pushing them away, he wanted to remain in moment and not overthink. Loghan's body was warm and instinctively responsive as Deagan drew her in for a long, deep kiss. He nuzzled her neck and became lost in her scent, dizzy with intoxication. He let himself surrender completely to the sensation, lost in her.

His fingertips danced down her arms and waist. Loghan reached back, pulled her long, auburn hair to the side and slowly pulled her shirt over her head. Deagan watched as her shirt fell to the floor. She lay back down and turned to Deagan. He pressed his lips to her neck and gently kissed and grazed her tender skin softly with his teeth. Dancing gently and teasingly around her neck and ear.

Loghan's breath at first quiet and rhythmic and as Deagan continued to gently kiss her neck, his lips followed along to her clavicle, Loghan's breathing became fractured as she focused to keep her breathing even.

Deagan was acutely aware of their contrast; his evening beard stubble and her silky skin. He allowed his hands to explore her body as he gently ran his fingertips over her sinewy body. They melded to one another effortlessly; Loghan felt as if she was floating. Every moment, every year, every experience Loghan held on to - the last three painful years fell away.

Loghan felt free and without guilt. She allowed herself to fold into Deagan's body without fear, or thoughts of what "others may think." She finally allowed herself permission to move on. She felt the weight of pain lift from her and at this moment, she knew this was her destiny. She and Deagan were meant to find one another.

Deagan shifted onto his side, guiding Loghan with him, their movements slow and deliberate as if time had paused, falling away. Her hair fanned out across the pillow, the strands catching the dim light like threads of auburn. His fingers combed through her locks, his touch gentle, exploratory and their eyes never wavered, lock in a silent conversation, a language of curiosity and wonder.

As Deagan pulled is shirt off, Loghan's gaze followed, tracing the contours of his lean frame. His body was unassuming, yet captivating - fit, lithe and real. She let her eyes wander, but never linger too long, as though savoring a secret meant only for her. Deagan, feeling the weight of her gaze, turned slightly his movements modest and careful as he shed the rest of his clothes. He slid into the bed beside her, the crisp coolness of the sheets meeting his warmth, a subtle contrast that made him shiver.

Loghan was already there, waiting. Her breath was steady but shallow, a quiet rhythm betraying the mix of anticipation and vulnerability she carried. The rain returning, steadily tapped against the windows, a soft, persistent reminder of the world beyond. Both paused at the sound, their stillness shared and when their eyes met again, they smiled faintly. It was the kind of smile that spoke of safety, of solace, of something rare being discovered.

Deagan leaned in, his lips brushing hers with gentle touches. There was no rush, no urgency - only exploration of a moment they had been unsure they would find.

Together, they let the night envelope them, the rain playing it's melody in the background as they quietly ventured into the unfamiliar terrain of each other, uncovering not just what was new, but what they had both feared may never be found.

*****

Avery coughed and tried again to pull herself up. This time she was successful and pulled her body into a half-sitting position, though she couldn't do much more. She was intensely aware her throat was parched. She needed water and a phone, but as soon as she pulled herself up, she felt dizzy and had to lay back on the floor... A tear snuck out of the corner of her eye, *"Damn it,"* she hoarsely whispered.

She lay back and allowed the memory of the days' encounters to unfold before her eyes.

Aric had been furious with her and made it well known. He knew of Avery's recent comings and goings and she still had no idea how he knew she met with her attorney, Roger Murphy. Aric ranted at Avery for what seemed like an eternity, looming over her and shouted he knew everything. *Everything?*

Avery dragged her hand across her forehead to move her hair out of her face; she felt tiny beads of sweat and something sticky. Blood? Her head was tender and her fingers lightly examined the area only to find a cut and more stickiness.

She continued to process their earlier discourse, the memory finally releasing from her fog and she replayed it in her mind. He screamed he knew of her business dealings - how she turned over Aric's percentage to his brother. The phrase, *brother*, he spat out as if profane. Aric tossed papers on the table and there it was in black and white. He somehow had got his hands on the draft documents that Roger drew up earlier in the week to bring Barrett into the family business and the birth certificates.

Avery shook her head, clearing her thoughts. How was this possible? How did he know about Barrett? She had done her absolute best over the years to keep her life separate and private from Aric. He had somehow found the birth certificates. She held the birth certificates; for the twins and the falsified one for Aric.

She kept the birth certificates closely guarded over the years, locked away in a safe. Where did Aric find them? Had she been sloppy at one time and allowed the documents out in the open on her desk? Avery had no idea and continued to process her memories and unfortunate mistakes. She maintained her privacy from everyone...the only two privy to her secret of the twins, were her Roger and her father.

Her father.

The uncharitable and self-serving bastard. Avery sneered at the memory of him and how he made her life so difficult after birth of the boys.

He was so caught up in his fucking appearances and ruled his empire with a tightly held fist. Avery felt she had no choice as a young woman but to do what her father demanded. He would cut her off from all money and means to her inheritance if she didn't consent to his threats. He obviously had the power to do just that, as he sent her away to Switzerland.

She could no longer hold the tears back. They flowed from the outer corners of her eyes and she did her best to wipe them away with a weak hand. Her thoughts washed over her in waves.

Why? Why didn't she make other choices in her life?

Maybe she could have cared for both children? Avery pushed away the thoughts as she recalled she had no money at the time to pay for the ill infants' care. Barrett was so sick when he was born. She remembered the doctors telling her the odds of him living through the surgeries were slim. Her father wielded the proper care for the ill infant if only Avery would leave him in Switzerland. She remembered making the difficult decision to leave him in Switzerland - this was the only way to offer her son a chance to live. She wanted her baby the opportunity to live a full life...if there was a chance, even the smallest amount.

Further insult and pain came when the ill infant was placed for adoption and another family was allowed to step in. Rhonert made sure everything was taken care of in advance. They were a good family and in Rhonert's mind, he cleared the path for his daughter to return home with no shame of an illegitimate pregnancy and a story to make others weep at her bitter loss.

She recalled how angry and filled with rage she had been with her father.

Leaving her sick child and returning home with only one baby was too much for the young Katherine to bear. She punished her father by keeping to herself in her small wing and cared for Aric with the help of a nanny. She let her father carry on with his fabricated story of Katherine losing her husband to an accident and she was carrying their child. Did people really believe this story? Katherine could have cared less. Her father worked at drawing her from her seclusion at home, but it would take several years for her to come to terms with her life and publicly show her face.

She recalled discovering that baby Barrett was more robust than doctors initially considered. He pulled through not one, but three separate surgeries and was beginning to thrive. Katherine was resourceful and with her own research found information regarding the family who adopted Barrett. They were Scottish and reasonably well-off. She didn't know how, but she would find a way to contact her son. She would find a way to care for him and be part of his life.

It took several years, but once she found the strength and planned to find her way back to her child, she inserted herself fully back into her privileged life. She was no longer the shy, hesitant young woman who came home after her "husband" died. She created her own story, her own path. She was more intelligent than her arrogant father and knew how she would find her way back into her son's life. She would grudgingly sit at her father's right arm and learn the business, but she would now be taken seriously, insisting on her new identity. She wanted to separate herself from her past, as much as she could.

She left the name Kathrine behind and Avery Stanton emerged from her years in the dark and into the bright light.

Now, feeling weakened and possibly defeated, Avery wiped the tears from her eyes again and lay back in the darkened room. She was weak and her mind raced how to get help before it was too late. She was in deep trouble and she knew it.

Her arm draped across her eyes.

Perhaps she could locate her phone if she allowed herself to sleep or rest longer. She could wait for the morning. The housekeepers would come by in the morning...or, what about her assistant, Gwyneth? She would be here at 7 AM sharp. Avery felt herself fading once more and knew if she didn't stay alert, something dreadful might happen. She knew she was in worse shape and needed medical attention and this realization startled her.

"Is this what my life has amounted to?" She whispered into the void of her room. "I need help...I...I..." her head swirled and the hazy thoughts entered once more.

She drifted and dreamed...dreamed of babies and her youth, dreamed of baby Barrett, his cries...long and languishing cries...

The ringtone shattered the silence in the room and jarred her from her foggy haze. The sound sharp and cutting through the darkness like a knife.

Avery stirred, her body heavy and uncooperative. For a moment, she wasn't sure if she was dreaming. The sound felt distant, muffled, like it was coming from underwater. It came again, louder this time and her pulse quickened.

The phone!

Her chest rose and fell in shallow, erratic breaths as she forced her head to turn toward the source of the noise. Across the room, on the end table, the faint glow of the phone lit the corner of the darkened room. It felt impossibly far away. Her lips parted as if to call for help, but no sound came. The weight of her weakness pressed down on her, anchoring her to the floor.

She closed her eyes, just for a moment, trying to gather the strength she didn't have. The ringtone persisted, relentless. With every chime, it felt like a countdown and she knew - this was her only chance. She had to get to the phone.

Her arm trembled as she reached out fingers curling weakly against the carpet. She pushed forward, dragging her body inch by inch. The effort was excruciating. Her muscles screamed in protest and the room tilted violently, the edges of her vision swimming. Her breath game in ragged gasps and sweat beaded on her brow mingled with the blood from her forehead.

The phone rang again and her head dropped to the floor in frustration. It felt so far away still - unattainable, but she refused to stop. Her nails scraped the carpet as she pulled herself forward again, her entire body shaking with the strain. One hand after the other, she crawled, her legs dragging, almost uselessly behind her.

The phone's glow seemed brighter now, closer. She reached the table and stretched her arm toward it, her fingers trembling as the grazed the edge of the phone. It wobbled, tipped over and fell to the floor with a dull thud.

Her breath hitched, tears welling in her eyes. She didn't have the strength for this. Her vision blurred, she forced herself to move again. Her fingers clawed forward, searching blindly until they brushed against the smooth surface of the phone. Avery curled her hand around it, the weight of the device almost too much to bear and pulled it to her chest.

Turning onto her back, she brought the phone to her face, blinking against the faint light. Her hands shook so badly that the phone slipped, but she caught it again, gripping it as tightly as her failing strength would allow. Squinting her eyes as she tried to focus on the name on the screen, she made out the blurry edges; Barrett.

Her fingers shaking, she tapped the button and, in a fractured voice, whispered:

"Hello? Barrett....? Help me...please."

Chapter 32

He escaped within moments of the detectives arriving as he rushed down the hallway, ducking into the elevator. He quietly pushed the button marked eighteen and smirked at his cleverness. He heard the faint footsteps before they were upon him. The sound brought him out of the darkness and the pure sensation of the rage that overcame him.

He fantasized of the moment he would encounter his brother face-to-face for the first time. He anticipated every word and the very moment of realization in Barrett's eyes when he understood he had a brother...his exact likeness.

"My brother." He whispered thickly with sarcasm through gritted teeth as he leaned against the hotel door to his suite.

He knew of Barrett's existence for years.

Long ago, he snuck into Avery's office at her estate. He was a young man then, still trying to figure out where he fit into the big picture of his family and RHS Communications. Why did his grandfather treat him so distantly and, more so, his mother? It was before he understood the voices that began whispering to him and slowly haunting him.

He instinctively knew something was wrong with his relationship with his mother. There were too many signs; his mother leaving for long trips that had nothing to do with business, the quiet tension over the dinner table between his grandfather Rhonert and Avery when she returned from her "excursions."

Through the years, hushed whispers meant solely for Avery and Rhonert found their way to young Aric's ears.

One of those occasions when Rhonert was ill, Avery and Rhonert exchanged harsh words. Aric was older now and planned to find out what secrets were being held from him. He lingered outside Avery's office door and overheard Rhonert saying something about "the young man" and "you need to stay out of *their* lives." Curiosity continued to build in Aric's mind, enough to rifle through papers in Avery's office when he was home during his college break.

He saw the envelope under papers and ballet invitations; it called to him: the perfect penmanship of Avery addressed to Roger Murphy, Avery's attorney.

He slipped the papers out of the envelope, listening for any footsteps that may warn him of someone coming - that someone being Avery.

He remembered his confusion as his cobalt blue eyes gulped down the words on paper: legal documents, shareholdings, birth certificates and adoption documents. None of this made sense to Aric. Certificates? Adoption?

He couldn't read through the documents fast enough. He saw his birth certificate - from Switzerland - Aric Rhonert Stanton - 5 lbs, 2 oz...nothing out of the ordinary here. Details he was aware of; father's name: Unknown. Try as he might over the years, when he asked Avery who his father was, she would never disclose, flipping her perfectly manicured nails in the air and saying it didn't matter.

He pushed the memories away and returned the paper to the envelope and looked at the other birth certificate. It was also stamped Switzerland at the top. Same date as Aric's, same doctor. His eyes scanned the certificate and he froze: a box was checked; Multiple live births.

His eyes followed the lines of the paper and he found Baby A and Baby B:

A: Aric Rhonert Stanton

B: Barrett Avery Stanton

He heard the familiar heel clicks rapidly descending the hallway and he knew it was Avery. He quickly looked at the papers and found current dated stock shares in the name of Aric Stanton and Barrett Rohan. He slid the documents into the envelope and tucked them inside his jacket. He would make his copies and return the documents - no one being aware.

Avery was none the wiser as she passed the office door and he heard her steps fade into the eastern side of the estate. It wasn't until later that night, when he was in the safety of his bedroom that he could read through the documents.

All the pieces of the puzzle came into place. Aric now understood why he was always an afterthought with his mother. Always left out of conversations. Always kept at a distance by his grandfather. Where she disappeared for several weeks at a time. Avery was living a dual life and it was right here in the documents he found.

He was not the chosen one. His mother didn't care about him...she cared about her other son. The son she gave up for adoption. Aric was devastated at this news. Yes, he knew he was a problematic child and lashed out at Avery often, but didn't she see it was her doing?!

Aric failed to recall his nasty attitude toward all things, especially when it came to Avery. Years before finding out about Barrett, he failed to remember that he was bitter and ill-willed. It was far easier to blame his behavior on someone else, more straightforward to blame the reason the voices surrounded him inside his head. He blamed much of his problems on learning about his brother's circumstances and Avery's not caring for him.

The early years, when Avery learned of his voices, were the worst. He went to therapy at Avery's insistence. Many specialists and doctor's appointments filled with testing. Why was Aric so mean-spirited? What were these voices he spoke of? Why did he find nothing wrong with hurting others as a child? Aric said it was the voices that told him what to do. It wasn't his fault.

As a young boy, he heard the doctors talking to Avery about every possible diagnosis, but Aric would not accept it. It was far easier to block out these memories and blame the voices on Avery. He didn't recall any of these memories as the years went on. The story he told himself left him faultless and able to carry on with his life. The many medications he was prescribed didn't seem to make him any better; they left him lethargic and numb and finally, he quit taking them. There came a time when no one discussed his illness any longer. He could hide it and when Avery asked him how he was feeling, he told her he was never better.

He struggled through his teenage years and into college, but he was determined to be part of the family business. It took years of research and looking for Barrett's adopted family, but he finally located them in Scotland. Avery was sloppy when she left the envelope out the day Aric discovered it. The names of Barrett's adoptive parents were on more documents inside the envelope. It was a huge clue left for Aric and he was determined to find his brother and take back what was his right...his destiny to the family inheritance.

He quietly kept tabs on Barrett throughout his life and knew of his success. Both brothers followed their paths and lives, but one was given everything: opportunity, wealth, success and family love. Aric fought for everything: attention from his family, learning the family business and his mother's love.

He fought his way to the table of RHS Communications and would be the last one standing. He would make damn sure of this, he would tell himself over and over.

He made particular work of that pesky matter when he killed Avery.

He smiled at this memory and scoffed. It would be the last time Avery thought she had the upper hand...

He had known he would kill Avery, it was just a matter of when the opportunity presented itself. The timing had come as a surprise to him when he lunged at her in the hotel penthouse. She wasn't going to sign everything over to Barrett and kick him to the curb...she had another thing coming if that is what she thought.

He reminisced happily over the feeling of overtaking her and pressing the pillow against her shocked face. She barely fought him off, he recalled. She was weaker than he thought and...she was dead.

Gloriously dead. Aric smiled again at the memory.

Crimson lipstick smeared against her face and cheek; he dropped the pillow and stood over her. He left as quickly as he could, undetected by the privacy of the penthouse floor. He would pack tonight and head back to

London on a red eye, but first, he had to finish his business and confront Barrett.

He shook off the memory of Avery and walked to the fully stocked liquor cabinet in the back of his suite and made a pitcher of martini's. It was all so perfect now. Everything.

That stupid fool of a brother had no idea what was happening. Aric had plotted out this ending for years. The timing couldn't have been better as he followed his dear brother to San Francisco. He didn't know Avery would meet with Barrett, but the odds were good.

He knew he had to make Barrett pay for stealing his family's fortune.

He paced back and forth, sipping his martini. The voices grew louder with each step, relentless as they jabbed at him like tiny needles piercing through the fabric of his frayed mind.

"Destiny! It was **MY** destiny!... NOT HIS! SHUT UP!" His voice cutting through the quiet of the room.

He drew in a shuddering breath and sat down on the corner couches. Trying to regain his composure. "Think - think..." He whispered into his glass while he sipped.

While Barrett traipsed around San Francisco with his whore, Aric set him up for the fall. Leaving a trail of bank receipts for the authorities to follow... but things got a little...complicated with Aric's new interest. Aric couldn't stop thinking about her. Sweet, beautiful Loghan. He usually could take women or leave them. His interest was never held long and he could shift from women to men...this time was different.

She got under his skin. Made him miss a few steps and he was sloppy with killing Dexter.

He was just a stupid fuck, the voices hissed at him.

"He was in the way," Aric responded to the loudest voice. They came at all different times and patterns, some louder than others.

She will be the demise of you.

"No, she won't! She loves me!... **ME.!**" He slapped his palm on his chest with a thud, creating a sting and he moved quickly, pouring another martini. He returned, sinking further into the couch, gazing out the window, drink in hand. He almost didn't remember their earlier text exchanges; so much going on around him.

Agitated, he pulled out his phone and tapped the screen, with a nervous intensity. Her messages popped up and his eyes darted across the words. She had dismissed him. Ignored him. The last text was hours ago, leaving him in a limbo that felt like eternity.

She doesn't care about you... a softer voice whispered, it's tone mocking and sweet. *She's playing you, Aric. Stringing you along.*

"She thinks she's smarter than me?" He muttered, his grip tightening on the phone. and looked for the app he needed on his phone. "Oh, but she's not."

*She **is** more intelligent than you...*the voices hissed in unison, louder now, a crescendo of cruel laughter ringing in his ears.

He shot to his feet, the martini sloshing over the edge of the glass onto the carpet. He didn't care. His head throbbed, his chest heaved. "She's **NOT** smarter than me!" he shouted, his voice cracking, "She doesn't know who I am. What I can do!"

The voices didn't relent. They twisted his thoughts, pulling at the loose threads of his sanity. He paced to the window, glaring out again at the rain slick streets below, his reflection distorted in the glass.

Gathering his wits he located the application he sought on his phone and tapped. It opened and a bright light illuminated his shadowed face.

A blinking dot appeared on the screen, indicating a location found.

"There you are, dear Loghan...Aric murmured, his lips curling into a twisted smile. He pressed his forehead against the cool glass of the window, his breath fogging the surface. "There you are. I see you...I see you..."

She'll outwit you ...she's done with you...she's already dismissed you... the voices warned, softer now, almost drowned out by the sound of his own breathing.

Aric's smile widened as he whispered into the night, "No. I say when we're done....I control the outcomes.... and, he tapped his finger against the window... "I'm done."

*****

"Hello?...Aunt Katherine?" Jodie was confused. This was the number in Barrett's phone, but this did not sound like his aunt. This person was weak and crying out for help.

"Yes...please...please...I need help...who - who is this? Where is Barrett?" Coughing and wheezing followed the soft voice.

"Aunt Katherine! This is Jodie, Barrett's girlfriend! Where are you?" Jodie ran to the desk to get a pen and paper.

"I'm at the hotel...Presidential suite. Mark Hopkins...my...my son tried to kill me...Please...call for an ambulance."

Jodie froze and blinked as the realization cascaded over her.

The Mark Hopkins?

They were staying in the same hotel.

Jodie quickly recovered and shouted into the phone, "Your son?... Aunt Katherine...! I'm calling right now! Barrett and I are here too...well... I'm here...Never mind! Hang on! Help is coming!"

Jodie ran across the room, found the hotel phone and pressed zero. Impatiently swaying back and forth - one ring - two rings. "Hello? Concierge." A confident masculine voice answered.

Jodie blurted out the details as quickly as she could and the gentleman on the line was calm when he responded.

"I'm happy to help you, miss. I'm confirming this is Mr. Rohan's room? I just need a little more information, please. You are?"

"Yes! I'm Jodie Rice; I'm here with Mr. Rohan. His aunt is staying here, in the Presidential Suite. She needs help immediately! I don't know what's wrong, but I just called her and she needs help! Please!" Jodie was exasperated and pushing back the concern of Barrett at the moment. First things first, Aunt Katherine needed help. She continued, "Her name is Katherine - Katherine... Rohan, I think! I'm sorry, but I just met her and I'm unsure if that is her last name."

"I'm calling 911 right now, miss. Please stay on the line with me a moment."

"Yes, of course! Thank you!" Jodie sighed a breath of relief and sat down on the edge of the bed. She could hear the concierge conveying information to 911, his voice muffled but audible.

"Yes, I'm not certain of the Emergency. We need someone here immediately," he paused and returned to Jodie. "Miss Rice," his voice was even and steady as he continued," I know you stated the woman in the Presidential suite is named Katherine, perhaps Katherine Rohan," he paused, "The ambulance is on its way and should be here within minutes. I'm afraid I don't have that name in our system."

Jodie shook her head, recalling the brief call with Katherine. She was confident she said the Presidential suite at the Mark Hopkins. She pressed on. "I'm sorry...I know that is what she said; the Presidential suite at the Mark Hopkins."

The concierge continued, "I have two members of the hotel and security on their way up to the room right now; the name I show, however, registered to that room is; Stanton. Avery K. Stanton."

Jodie didn't care at that moment what the name said on the register. Aunt Katherine needed help and she dropped the phone and headed for the door.

*****

The day started early and there was a remarkable break in the weather. A small beam of filtered sun made its way through the drapes. Loghan's eyes fluttered open and she stretched the length of her body and quietly yawned. She felt a warm arm around her waist, smiled and rolled over.

Deagan made a low rumbling sound in the back of his throat and mumbled something Loghan didn't understand. She chuckled and nestled into his arm. He pulled her close and wrapped both arms around her. He was warm and sleepy and she loved this new feeling of waking up beside him.

Last night had been a revelation. A blur of shy smiles and whispered confessions as they transitioned from friends to lovers, exploring a side of each other that was new and exciting. It had been sweet and slow, with moments of unrestrained passion that left both of them breathless. Loghan welcomed her feelings, so natural, at ease as she folded into Deagan's arms. Every touch, every kiss, every shared laugh seemed like it had been waiting for this moment.

The morning, the connection lingered, unbroken and was filled with more exploration of one another, each unable to pull themselves away to prepare for Megan and Conner's wedding.

"Good thing we woke early and the wedding is here." Deagan winked at Loghan as she reluctantly tossed back the rumpled sheets and climbed out of bed.

"Don't go," Deagan teased, smiling after her.

"I have to... all my things are in my room...we don't want to be late." She smiled and winked slyly at him. Deagan leaned back against the headboard, watching as Loghan searched for her room key on the cluttered dresser.

"Shower here. You can run next door and get ready *after* you shower." He smiled and stood from the bed. "Besides, we can save water if we shower together." He gave her a wicked grin, pulled her close and kissed her. Loghan didn't require any additional coaxing and responded to his warm kiss. She laced her fingers through his and followed Deagan to the shower, closing the bathroom door behind her.

The wedding was beautiful and the venue couldn't have been more perfect. Loghan had never attended a morning wedding and loved the idea as it was fresh and added to the new experiences of this weekend.

Arm in arm, Loghan and Deagan climbed the majestic, grand staircase. The walls leading up were a symphony of granite, their surface alive with intricate veins of silver, charcoal and soft rose hues that that caught the light from the chandeliers. Reaching the top of the stairs awaited the equally majestic mezzanine. They walked past the wait staff in white dress coats, black ties and gloves. Deagan stopped and looked around briefly; his eyebrows shot up in appreciation. The ceilings must have been at least twenty-five feet high. A grand piano was tucked in the corner with large windows overlooking the city; melodic strains drifted through the expansive room. A young man wearing a luxurious tuxedo with tails, sat at the piano, smiling as he played.

There were elegant chandeliers and overstuffed, red velvet chairs facing one another over large coffee tables. Deagan looked over and noticed a group of people. They appeared to patiently wait for others to join them as they watched people arriving for the wedding at the top of the grand staircase.

Deagan's eyes continued to scan the large room. He noted small tables with champagne and mimosas and a large fireplace against the back wall, fire crackling and popping.

"This is really nice," he admired as he continued to look around the expansive room.

Loghan appeared impressed as well as she surveyed the room and its attendees.

"It really is. I've stayed at this hotel a few times, but I've never been to a wedding here." She smiled, threaded her arm through Deagan's and turned toward him.

"Mr. McGrath, may I say you clean up nicely." She smiled and pecked him on the cheek. He wore his black tuxedo, with his signature color pop, and sported a deep purple bow tie.

"Well, thank you, Ms. Riley. You do *more* than clean up nicely," He smiled at Loghan and took all of her in. She was beautiful in a light grey, form-fitted dress that clung to her and showed off her curvy body. He had no idea about women's clothing and shoes, but he knew she looked stunning in this dress. Unbeknownst to Loghan and without planning, she matched his deep purple bow tie with her heels in a rich shade of lavender and the two made a striking couple. Loghan always looked beautiful to him but today was slightly different. She was radiant and he couldn't take his eyes off her. She seemed to sense this and her face flushed as she returned Deagan's smile.

They turned and walked toward the Franciscan Room and Loghan waved at several of her friends from college. Everyone was filing into the room and settling into their seats, the air filled with anticipation. Loghan quietly eased into her seat, arranged herself and was flooded with happiness. It had been so long since she felt joyful and today she was grateful as she leaned into the sensation.

She had finally allowed herself to finish grieving Ian's death.

Loghan knew she would never forget Ian and would cherish and honor his memory forever and all he brought her, but she knew she had moved on in her heart. She felt it the instant she and Deagan kissed by the waterside. It was at that moment time froze and she felt a shift in her heart as she looked into Deagan's eyes. It wasn't the first time this happened. She *looked* into his heart when their eyes met. It happened a few weeks earlier when she was at Deagan's house and they were going over her article. And again, when she was at his house for wine.

She felt her heart stir when Deagan looked at her a certain way, but she had pushed the thoughts away. She noticed her attitude and feelings about Deagan shifting when they messaged back and forth during the same time frame, but she shook it off. No, Deagan couldn't be considered, as she was wrapped up with David. David was safe and easy to talk to. The physical distance allowed Loghan to open up and share with David. He wasn't physically here, but she was connecting with him. She blushed and shifted in her seat; she had more than *connected* with David, she thought. Deagan noticed her blushing and tilted his head, looking to her eyes and gently smiled.

"All good, Loghan?" His blue eyes filled with slight concern.

She reached across her lap taking Deagan's hand in hers. "Yes, I'm fine. Just thinking about a few things," she said, offering him a soft smile. Deagan squeezed her hand gently and continued to hold her hand - her cool hand, quickly warmed as they sat together, watching the last guests take their seats. A hush of anticipation fell over the room as the small string quartet began to gracefully play.

The ceremony was every bit as elegant as the venue. It was a brief ceremony, but full of personal touches to the bride and groom. Loghan smiled and dabbed a few tears during the ceremony and Deagan continued to hold her hand. She smiled at him, tears threatening to spill over her brilliant green eyes should she blink. She reached into her bag for new tissue and saw her phone lighting up. She stole a quick look. It was David.

Damn, she thought, *I need to find time to talk with David today.* She thought as she reached past her phone to locate the tissue.

Loghan thought David should know she was at the wedding now. He must understand she was otherwise occupied and would get back to him as soon as she was free. She had told him for weeks the day the wedding was being held, so it couldn't have slipped his mind. She furrowed her brow, briefly dabbed her tears and smiled at Deagan. He looked at her quietly and quizzically, but she smiled reassuring all was well.

Conner and Megan kissed as the officiant announced, "Married and as one." There was a great thunder of applause and smiles as the newly married couple walked down the aisle and out to the mezzanine.

The guests quickly spilled out to the mezzanine area and enjoyed light hors d'oeuvres and champagne. Staff brushed past the guests as they turned the scene from wedding to brunch in the Franciscan room. This transition allowed time to mingle and meet some of Loghan's friends from college.

He sensed genuine happiness that Loghan had brought "someone" as he talked with a few of Loghan's friends. He felt their eyes fall on him and caught the look of slight surprise on a few faces when Loghan introduced Deagan as her "friend."

Deagan smiled each time he was introduced and knew this must be odd for Loghan - introducing a new 'beau' to those who knew Ian. Deagan, always a gentleman, stood quietly through many conversations and spoke when it seemed appropriate. He didn't want to make anyone uncomfortable to those seeing Loghan for the first time with a man other than Ian.

He met a few of her sorority sisters and laughed at the stories they shared about Loghan's antics in college. It was all innocent and good fun and only validated Deagan's infatuation with her.

As the morning wore on and moved to the early afternoon, the dancing started and the champagne continued to flow. Loghan, while she tried to be fully in the moment, she couldn't help but think of David's anger with his biting, harsh texts. Not at all like him, she thought, but then, did she really know him?

A bit of guilt entered Loghan's mind as she knew she needed to contact David as promised. He must be so concerned and not understand what was happening, thought Loghan. He deserved an explanation and Loghan should provide that to him now, not later. It didn't feel right that she had left him lingering while she was falling for Deagan.

"Deagan, do you mind if I excuse myself?" She looked at him and unexpectedly felt butterflies in her stomach. She couldn't help but smile at him as she tried to look in control of her feelings.

"Of course," he returned her smile. "Take your time. I'm enjoying my conversation with your friends." She leaned over and kissed him gently and lingered for just a moment. She reluctantly pulled away and touched his hand and walked away.

Deagan's eyes followed her and he felt a quiet sigh escape his lips.

"She is a striking woman, isn't she?" Deagan was jarred from his thoughts and looked over to who made the comment.

The bride and groom walked toward him and he smiled, knowing he was caught.

"Yes, she is wonderful," Deagan continued to smile, extending his hand to Conner in introduction, "I'm Deagan. Deagan McGrath."

"Nice to meet you, Deagan,"

"We hoped to catch you both, but I see we just missed Loghan." Megan smiled as she looked around the room.

"She'll be back shortly," Deagan extended his hand toward Megan. "Hello. It's so nice to meet you. It was a very nice ceremony," he smiled as Megan gently shook his hand. "I work with Loghan at Forefront Magazine."

"Oh, my goodness!" Megan looked surprised. "Yes, of course! Deagan McGrath. You're an incredible writer!" She looked over at Conner and continued, "Deagan is the head writer for Forefront. He writes in-depth exposés of the most fascinating topics."

"Wow...Thank you." Deagan modestly shrugged off the compliment just as a server arrived with a silver tray of champagne and offered politely. Deagan reached for two glassed, handing one to the bride and then the groom. Once he secured his glass they continued to talk and get acquainted. The conversation was easy and Megan and Conner seemed happy that Loghan was clearly interested in Deagan. They laughed and chatted for a few more minutes, promising to circle back as guests waited to greet the newly married couple.

Loghan found a chair in a quiet place and sat down, reaching into her bag and pulling out her phone to check her messages.

Her phone had a text from her mom; "Just checking in," she said. One from Tina, doing the same; "Checking in, friend! Hope all is going well. Text when you can." She smiled at Tina's message and moved on. As she scrolled down one more, she paused and saw she had multiple texts from David:

'Darling, please forgive me for my strong words last night. I don't know what came over me.'10:03 AM

'I suppose you feel I deserve no response after what I said to you. Can you please just let me know you're alright? I should at least know that, don't you agree, my dear Loghan?' 10:26 AM

'I had hoped it wouldn't come to this, but I fear your lack of response has triggered my mood. I'm not just something, or someone you can cast aside as if I've no feelings!' 11:02 AM

Well, that was short-lived, she thought of David's brief attempt to apologize for his shitty texts.

Loghan thought for a moment and started to tap out her message. She would keep it brief to let David know she was fine and the earlier "problem" was solved. She would make better contact with him when she returned to Sacramento.

'All is well and I'm fine – we can chat further when I return from SF;' she finished and hit send.

The response came quickly.

'Is that it, dear Loghan? I'm fine and you'll talk to me when you return? You are more to me than a text message. You gave yourself to me and I felt it. It was real.'

It had all started so innocently – a private message that spiraled into brief messages, contacts and then finally, long texting conversations. David's words had captivated her, his charm and fascinating way with words drawing her in like a moth to a flame. She could still remember the way her heart would skip when his messages appeared, how her pulse quickened as his carefully crafted sentences unraveled her inhibitions. His descriptions of their imagined moments together had burned into her memory, sparking feelings she hadn't dared explore before.

David's words would run across her computer screen and her imagination was rich as she could visualize his fingers dancing across her skin. His description of himself was masculine and his words captured her imagination. She recalled the times she had to find release from his words - the fire that consumed her - needed release...he created the need for her to touch herself in ways she would never admit.

But it wasn't real. Not truly.

She shook her head and cleared the memory, sitting up straighter. No! Whatever spell David had over her was over. She had to let him know it was done.

Loghan bit her lip, her stomach twisting as she typed, erased and retyped the first few words. She hated this. Hated the guilt that weighed heavily on her chest. David deserved honesty, didn't he? Or maybe he didn't. After all, they weren't real to each other - just names behind screens, trading pieces of themselves through the glow of their devices.

Her fingers moved again.

"David, I don't know where to begin..." she typed, her thoughts stumbling over themselves. *"This feels so strange because we've never met and yet, I feel like I'm breaking up with someone who's been a part of my life in a way I can't really explain. I'm sorry, but I can't keep doing this. It's not fair - to you or to me. Somewhere in all this - I got lost. Thinking it was just words on a screen, right? And yet, it became more for me. Maybe you too."*

She paused, her throat tightening.

"I don't regret knowing you, but this needs to end. I'm not the person I think you imagine me to be. And maybe, you're not the person I've built up in my head. Either way, I need to move on from this...from us. I hope you understand and I hope you find someone who can give you the things I just can't provide."

Loghan read the words over, her heart sinking deeper with each line. It felt clinical and detached.

Her finger hovered over the send button, shaking slightly.

She wanted to move on, leave this behind her, but yet, she knew she was hurting an actual person - one she never met in person, yet they'd helped her more than she could explain. Once she sent this, it was over. She would delete the messages and block him if she had to.

This tryst - if she could call it that - had been an escape, a brief plunge into fantasy, but fantasy wasn't sustainable. She had a real life to live, a real person she wanted to give her all to - Deagan - wonderful, loyal, loving Deagan.

Loghan paused a moment, gathered her thoughts and continued;

"Please forgive me if I've hurt you in any way. I'm sorry, but I've met someone and I care for him deeply.'

She hit the send button and followed with one more text.

'I wish you nothing but the best, David. Please take great care.'

She sat for a moment and waited. No response came and she waited a few minutes longer, but still nothing.

Such conflicting feelings she experienced today, she thought.

For a moment, she just stared at the screen, her chest tightening with an odd mix of relief and sadness. The message was out there, waiting for him to read it. Whatever came next, she'd deal with it. At least for now, she had started to gain her time and her life back.

She tipped her head back a moment and gathered herself. She sighed and stood, moving toward the door to get back to reality and to Deagan.

Chapter 33

The nurse entered the room quietly, her movements precise and practiced. Balancing a tray of medication and a glass of water. She was a young nurse with warm eyes and a calm demeanor. "Ms. Stanton?" She skillfully tiptoed across the sterile floor and placed the tray on a small counter next to her computer cart. "How are you feeling?," she asked softly, her voice kind but clinical. The nurse took her temperature and stared intently at her computer screen.

Avery cleared her throat and watched the nurse, "I'm far better than I was a few hours ago; thank you for asking, Nurse."

"Rebecca. Please call me Rebecca." The fair-complected young nurse smiled at Avery and returned to tapping away at her computer. Avery watched her with quiet curiosity, her eyes trailing the flurry of unfamiliar medical jargon filling the screen. "Your vitals are much better, Ms. Stanton, than when you first arrived." She moved about Avery astutely, changed her IV fluids and took her blood pressure. "The fluids have helped tremendously. You're recovering well."

Avery allowed herself a small sigh of relief, her shoulders relaxing as the weight of uncertainty began to lift. "I'm so glad to hear that, Rebecca." Avery closed her eyes briefly and relished in calm as she knew she was out of the woods. She turned as she heard someone at the door. It was Jodie holding a cardboard drink holder. She stopped instantly at the door as a huge smile crossed her lips.

"Aunt Katherine...I mean...Avery...," Jodie quickly corrected herself as she resumed walking into the room. "You look so much better! Look at the color in your cheeks!" She placed the drinks down and walked to the edge of the bed. "I haven't been gone that long and yet, you look like a different person!" Jodie reached for Avery's extended hand.

"Well, I do hope I still look like me," she winked at the nurse and continued, "only better."

Jodie patted her hand, pulled a chair over to the bedside and sat down. "I brought you juice and coffee for me," looking at the nurse, she asked, "Can she have some juice?'

"Of course, I can have some juice...although, I would prefer a drink, but...." her voice trailed off and she winked at Jodie. Avery pulled herself up to a better sitting position. She slyly looked over at her nurse, who nodded discreetly.

Avery gratefully accepted the juice as Jodie settled in a chair and sipped her coffee. "Is this your daughter, Ms. Stanton?" Avery beamed at Jodie and turned to her nurse, "Why, yes...she is just like a daughter to me." The two newly found friends turned to one another, acknowledging their connection and Avery leaned back and smiled.

The hours spent in the emergency room had felt endless. Jodie paced the floor, her nerves fraying with every tick of the clock. She had ridden in the ambulance with Avery, her hand clasping hers as questions swirled in her mind - questions she had no answers to. Even in her confusion, a deeper, more unsettling thought clawed at the edges of her mind. Who was Aunt Katherine?

Jodie replayed the events leading up to their arrival at the hospital. It was in the chaos in the hotel suite that she stumbled upon Avery's purse. Digging through it for something-anything - that might help the paramedics, she'd found the passport first: Avery Katherine Stanton. The names seemed straightforward enough. Then there was UK driver's license: Avery K. Stanton. Katherine. Jodie tried to rationalize it. Maybe "Katherine" was the name Avery preferred, her middle name, it appeared. People did that sometimes. But the last name, Rohan, didn't appear on any of the documents.

Sitting in the cold, fluorescent-lit waiting room, she couldn't shake the nagging suspicion there was more to it. After all, everything in the hotel suite - from monogrammed stationary, to a paperwork on the desk stated her name was Avery Stanton; but why did Barrett know her as Aunt Katherine? All the stories told over drinks that night were about Katherine. Katherine Rohan. How could someone live with two names so seamlessly? Two lives? And why didn't Barrett make any mention of this to her? Maybe, Barrett only knew her as Aunt Katherine - a mysterious, eccentric and rich aunt who floated in and out of his life over the years.

The ER nurse's words from earlier echoed in her ears. "We'll let you know as soon as we have news." Jodie had been ushered to the waiting room, left to piece together the fragments of her night like a puzzle with missing edges. Jodie immediately contacted the police station looking for news about Barrett. She couldn't leave Aunt Katherine now; she had to stay where she was needed. She was transferred to Detective Kinder. She reached into her purse, pulled out a card and read the name. Yes, this was the detective who pressed her card into her hand when Barrett was being led out of the hotel.

"Detective Kinder." The voice was even and light.

"Detective, this is Jodie Rice. I'm Barrett Rohan's girlfriend." Jodie fought to keep her voice from shaking. She was so focused on getting Aunt Katherine to the hospital she put her emotions and response to Barrett on hold. She continued and kept her voice from quivering. "I'm calling about Barrett. What is happening? What can you tell me?"

"Ms. Rice, Mr. Rohan is being questioned and fingerprinted currently. I'm sorry, but I have nothing more to share now." Jodie stood and paced the length of the small waiting room. "I want to speak to him. I can't - I can't get there right now. There is another emergency that I have to attend."

"I'm sorry to hear that, Ms. Rice," the detective's voice remained soft, yet targeted. "He is cooperating with us fully and we're waiting for his prints to return." There was a pause and the Detective continued, "Mr. Rohan has currently waived his right to an attorney right now."

"Fingerprints come back?" Jodie felt her anger rise, "Come back from what? What are you talking about?" Jodie froze in her path and demanded a response. "I need to get a call in to Barrett's lawyer and I don't have that information!”

“We have fingerprints from another scene that we are trying to rule him out.” Detective Kinder continued, “Ruling Mr. Rohan out is good, Ms. Rice. This is what we do.” Jodie sat down on the nearest chair and took a breath. “You have fingerprints? To a crime?”

“Ms. Rice...,” there was a pause, “I’m afraid I can’t tell you anymore. I can call you when I have more information.”

“I would appreciate that very much. Is Barrett being held? Are there charges?” Jodie pushed away a rogue tear with the back of her hand. “He is being questioned now and no charges have been filed.”

Jodie let out a deep sigh of relief. “Please tell him I’m at the hospital with his Aunt Katherine. She’s in rough shape and I’m waiting to hear her prognosis.”

“I’m sorry, Ms. Rice. I hope she is alright.” Jodie could detect genuine concern in the detective’s voice. “Thank you. I appreciate it. Please call me as soon as possible.”

An hour later, a doctor finally approached Jodie in the waiting room. He let her know that Ms. Stanton was stable and very fortunate. The assault created minor fractures on her right cheekbone. She also suffered a deep cut on her forehead, her nose was broken and she was severely dehydrated. They had sedated her, took x-rays and an MRI, she was otherwise healthy. She was still groggy from the sedation, but they expected she would be alert within the hour.

The doctor mentioned they contacted the police to inform them of the assault and were on their way.

“On their way?” Jodie looked at the doctor. “Yes, it’s just protocol. The police want to speak to your aunt. Get details while they are fresh.” The doctor took her gently by the elbow and led her back to the couch. “We’ll be out shortly and you can see your aunt then. Please sit; you look like you could use some rest yourself.”

Jodie tried to gather herself, but it was pointless. She paced back and forth, too anxious to sit down. Worried about Barrett, what was happening at the police station and, Aunt Katherine. There was much to mull over and it made time pass quickly, when she was called in to see Katherine. She was so relieved to see her alive and seemingly well. She was tired and still a little groggy, but the doctor said the sedative would wear off soon. He checked her vitals once more and left the room.

Jodie sat beside Katherine's bedside and they quietly became acquainted once more. "Let me properly introduce myself to you, dear," Her voice was stronger but wavering slightly. "You know me as Katherine, Katherine Rohan - Barrett's Aunt Katherine," she smiled softly and closed her eyes briefly. "My name is Avery Stanton. Avery *Katherine* Stanton." When she opened her eyes, they were bright and filled with emotion.

"I have a story to tell you, dear and I hope you will believe me and," she paused slightly, patting Jodie's hand, "...forgive me."

Jodie had her own story to share with Barrett's aunt, but she opted to hold back and hear what Katherine had to say.

Jodie sat riveted in her seat for the next hour as Avery shared her story.

"I was just a young woman," Avery began, her gaze distant as if she were looking through time. "I had dreams, ambitions...but when I found out I was pregnant, it was as if my world suddenly stopped. My father, Rhonert Stanton, made it clear that I marry the father, whose name I would never disclose, or, I would have to give the baby up for adoption. The Stanton name, the family business - everything came first. There was no place for a child born out of wedlock."

Her voice faltered for a moment, but she continued." I had no choice, Barrett was born prematurely and the doctors didn't think he'd make it. I was so torn and Barrett was so ill - he needed many surgeries and my father said, the only way he would pay for the surgeries, is if I would come home without the child." She winced as the memory and maintained her concentration. "I made the difficult decision to leave my baby behind to get the care he needed for a chance to live. I still remember the feeling of leaving my baby behind - like a part of my soul was ripped away."

"For years, I lived in one of the smaller wings of our estate, suffocated by grief and the iron grip of my father's control. To explain away my melancholy and depression to others and to maintain appearances, he fabricated a story about my "young husband" who had a tragic accident while we were away in Europe." Avery paused, her eyes glistening with tears brimming. "I had to find a way to be part of his life. Not for my own sake, but for his. It took some time, but I found my son and the couple who adopted him. I traveled to Scotland and spoke to the couple and told them I was Barrett's birth mother. It was a difficult meeting initially, but we found an unusual friendship over time. They allowed me to see Barrett and I felt as if my heart was finally - whole."

Jodie listening intently, leaned forward, captivated. "What did you do?"

Avery smiled faintly, "I did the only thing I could think of. I reinvented myself. I found the best way to unassumingly insert myself into Barrett's life, was to appear under an assumed identity. At home, I stopped responding to the name Katherine and stepped out as Avery Stanton."

"For the other life I needed to lead, I created Katherine - a well - traveled, eccentric 'aunt.' It was the only way I would be in Barrett's life without disrupting the stable, happy home the Rohan's had given him."

Jodie smiled at the idea, this strong, educated, brilliant and beautiful woman, had a plan and from the sounds of it, her father, Rhonert Stanton was none the wiser.

Jodie's heart ached as Avery continued. "Being 'Aunt Katherine' allowed me to watch him grow, to support him in ways I never thought possible. I helped pay for his education, contribute to his future. I was there for his birthdays, his milestones - always on the sidelines, but always present."

Avery's voice softened and she looked directly at Jodie. "It wasn't the life I'd envisioned, but it was enough. Barrett had the love of two wonderful parents and the subtle guidance of a mother who loved him from afar. That love gave me strength, even when the pain of what I'd lost felt unbearable."

The room fell silent, Jodie absorbing the weight of Avery's story. In that moment, she understood the depth of a mother's love - the sacrifices, the resilience and the quiet determination to be present, even if it meant doing so in disguise.

"Barrett doesn't know, does he?" Jodie finally asked.

Avery shook her head, her lips curving into a bittersweet smile.

"No, to him I am, Aunt Katherine. I always thought that was enough." She paused her smile fading." I have to tell him truth now and ...I'm afraid there is more to what I told you. Something I've not told you, or obviously, Barrett."

Jodie tilted her head slightly, not certain what Avery had to share.

"Excuse me, Ms. Stanton?" The doctor entered the room, interrupting Avery and moved efficiently around her, checking her vitals and taking her temperature.

"You're doing far better. How are you feeling?" The doctor smiled gently at Avery.

"Just sore and tired." Avery's hand touched her bandaged forehead as she winced slightly.

"You're very fortunate," the doctor stated matter of factly. "Another hour and the outcome could have been far different."

"I'm very fortunate." She smiled at Jodie.

The doctor continued, "The police are here to take your statement. Are you feeling well enough to speak to them?

Jodie began to stand, wanting to hear the end of Avery's story, but thought this was a good time to call the station again. Avery was under enough stress, so Jodie opted to hold off telling her, saying that Barrett would be here as soon as he could. Jodie decided she would wait until she spoke to the detective again and then would have something more to share.

"Yes, I was finishing up a story, but let's get this unpleasantness behind us." Avery smiled briefly at the doctor.

"That's fine. It will be a short visit. I'll be sure of that." The doctor walked to the doorway and nodded affirmatively to someone outside.

"Keep it short, Detective...Ms. Stanton needs rest. Go easy...please. "

Jodie began to excuse herself momentarily and turned to the sound of footsteps.

"Hello. Ms. Stanton. I'm Detective Kinder and this is my partner, Detective Thornton. We're here to get your statement."

Jodie's felt her mouth gape.

"Detective Kinder?"

Chapter 34

"Look, over there!" Loghan pointed and grabbed Deagan's hand as they walked over the rocky path. "Oh yes...there it is!" Deagan squinted his eyes slightly in the direction Loghan pointed. Deagan laughed at Loghan's exuberance; his eyes continued to follow the cliffs and remains of the Sutro Baths. "That looks like a great place to explore! Just like Conner and Megan recommended." Deagan followed alongside Loghan and held her hand tightly as they navigated over a narrow, rocky section of the path.

"I've been here many times to eat or have cocktails at the Cliff House but never have gone down to look at the remains of the baths." Loghan considered out loud as they continued to traverse the path.

As they moved along the pathway, Loghan recalled the prior hours. They had a wonderful time at the wedding and ended the event dancing in each other's arms. The morning and early afternoon were filled with laughter, talking with other guests and meeting more of Loghan's college friends. Deagan couldn't stop smiling and while Loghan seemed to be enjoying herself at the wedding, he couldn't help but notice a few times as she looked pensive.

During the celebration, Loghan remained in the moment with Deagan, but the knowledge she hurt David didn't sit well with her. She looked up and caught Deagan's eyes filled with concern and smiled at him.

"Hey, are you ok? Is there something wrong?" Deagan reached out his hand and took Loghan's.

"Deagan, I'm so sorry. I'm ok, really. I didn't want to ruin our day and, I was going to tell you later." She pulled him aside, squeezed his hand and continued, "My phone was filled with messages from David." She detected the slightest flicker in Deagan's eyes.

"Oh...well, you said you were going to text him or call?" His eyes left hers a moment as he tried to hide his thoughts. "Did it go alright? Do you need to call him?"

Loghan pulled Deagan's hands close to her chest and stopped him from continuing.

"Deagan, no, that's what I did when I excused myself a little while ago. I told him I would text him and I did. It's done and over. I'm here." She emphasized, "Here." and looked into his eyes, reassuring. She didn't know if she was reassuring herself or Deagan.

She knew she and Deagan were moving fast, but it felt like they'd been together for years. How could this be possible? She was just thinking a few days ago about David. It made her slightly uncomfortable, but she didn't want to try and figure it out; she just wanted to leave the experience with David behind her.

She knew the years of friendship with Deagan and working closely together fused their bond with one another. Deagan felt right and that reality is what Loghan held on to. For once, she wouldn't question or try to make sense of something. She would just 'be' and lean into her feelings for Deagan. "I'm here and I'm with you," she reached up and touched Deagan's cheek. "We can talk more about it later, but I feel terrible for hurting him. You caught me thinking about it and contemplating how I hurt him. I foolishly didn't think it would get so complicated." Her eyes narrowed, "It felt real...like I just broke up with him." She paused and dropped her hands to her side. "So much for not wanting to ruin our time today," she sighed, "I'm sorry, Deagan."

"I understand, Loghan, really. You've never done the whole 'connect' online with someone before" he used air quotes and gave a weak smile, "real people are behind the keyboard, just like you were. You talk and share things in a more intimate setting. We can be more open and free with our communication behind the screen."

"Damn, you do get it…" Loghan shrugged her shoulders. "I just didn't want you to think there was more going on with me and David, or that I'm a terrible person, to just ditch someone and, move on to another." She looked down at the floor and the music transitioned to a slower pace, subliminally announcing the end of the wedding celebration was near.

Deagan gently lifted her chin, his eyes meeting her usually bright green gaze, now muted with emotion. "I would never think you were a terrible person. Ever." His voice was level and sincere. "I would think it odd if you didn't feel something…I get it. Really."

She smiled softly at him. "Thank you, Deagan," she whispered. He lingered in her gaze for a heartbeat, aware that the melody had shifted with the mood. His smile deepened and with a grateful, almost theatrical flourish, he extended his hand. Straightening his posture, as if preparing for a grand occasion, he asked, "May I have this dance?" His blue eyes glinting in the flickering lights and with a subtle tilt of his head, his smile continued to fill her with Deagan's charm and sincerity. He tipped his head slightly and smiled. Loghan laughed, shook off the last of her insecurities and took Deagan's hand, offering a slight curtsy. "I would love to have this dance with you, good sir."

Loghan melted into Deagan's arms and they glided around the dance floor, surrounded by the last of the wedding party and the bride and groom. It was a perfect way to dissolve the lingering awkwardness and unspoken words. As the music swirled, so did her thoughts - reflecting on the journey that led her here. Venturing into the unfamiliar world of meeting someone online, had been a leap of faith, one that had pushed her to lower her guard and break through barriers she never imagined she could. With each step on the dance floor, the past slipped further behind her. Her experience with David, though unexpected, had taught her something invaluable about herself - a lesson she would carry with her into whatever came next.

Loghan was filled with life, a woman full of potential, her heart alive and full dreams and desires. Yet, she had caged herself in guilt, a heavy burden she carried since Ian's death. For so long, she had convinced herself that grief was the only proper way to honor him. It had been three long years.

The weight of that sorrow still clung to her, but now, finally, she realized – she would never forget Ian. But the guilt, that anchor holding her back, had to be cast off if she was ever to truly live and love again. It was time to allow herself to feel, to move forward and to let go.

She swayed to the music and pressed herself into Deagan's arms, giving in to the moment. She thought she had moved through her emotions the other night, but clearly, she hadn't cycled through them entirely. She let her emotions fall away and immediately felt lighter and looked up to a smiling Deagan. "This is what I like to see...you smiling and looking happy." He continued to smile and rocked her back and forth to the fading music. "I am happy, Deagan...so happy." She leaned into him and dissolved into his arms and a lingering kiss.

They left the wedding around 3:30 P.M. with time to explore the city before nightfall. A quick change into casual clothes at the hotel and they were off. They headed out to Highway 1 for a walk on Ocean Beach and to hike around the remains of the Sutro Baths. The weather held off with rain threatening from the west, with brief stints of sunshine fighting through the clouds from time to time. They found a place to park on Point Lobos and Highway 1, at the end of the steep incline leading to the Sutro Baths and the Cliff House. "I love that restaurant," Loghan nodded toward the Cliff House. "The next time we come here, let's go there for dinner or cocktails." She smiled brightly at him and Deagan reached for her hand. "That sounds great. I would love to go there with you." He smiled at her and laced his fingers through hers.

They walked along the beach and watched the waves crash against Seal Rock. The ocean appeared angry as the waves thundered over the rocks and sand. "The wind has picked up a bit," Deagan pulled Loghan closer to him. "Let's start walking back and then head up the hill to the baths."

Loghan loved the history of the Sutro Baths and her fascination and knowledge ran deep. The Sutro Baths were long part of San Francisco culture. Constructed in 1896 by Adolf Sutro, a German philanthropist. He came to the United States in 1850, built his real estate wealth and continued to increase his prosperity through the years. Sutro built the opulent and pretentious saltwater swimming pool establishment under his moniker, Sutro Baths. There was nothing like this anywhere in the world. It was once nestled into a small beach inlet and seascape on the west side of San Francisco; the glass, wood and steel-beamed structure gleamed in elegance. It was built next to the Cliff House and the surrounding buildings and landscape changed over many years.

Ahead of its time, the Sutro Baths offered healing saltwater baths and pools in varying temperatures of heated swimming areas. Six saltwater pools to choose from and ten to twenty-five cents for entry. A museum was filled with taxidermy, ancient artifacts and paintings from Sutro's travels worldwide. A significant observation area overlooking the pools and food concessions were available for those who wanted to stroll and take in the sights. A large glass roof allowed the inclement weather of San Francisco to remain outside while, the temperatures inside were balmy and warm. The atrium showed off exotic plants and foliage many had never seen.

Leading up to the baths was an elegant pedestrian entrance with archways and pillars calling to its patrons to enter. Walking through the significant Promenade, patrons were greeted by the warm, salty air and elegance. While the initial excitement and patronage from the public were evident, the baths took a lot of work to maintain and were quite costly. The saltwater was hard on the machinery, primarily the boilers required to keep the water heated. Sutro added events with entertainers, high divers and swimming events to help offset the costs. People came through the years and as the new century entered, so did more families, events and children learning to swim at the Sutro Baths. San Francisco embraced this family venue and held it near to their hearts.

As the years wore on and Sutro passed, his daughter, Emma Merritt, a physician, inherited the baths and tried to maintain the image for a time. Unfortunately, Emma wasn't invested in her ownership of her family heritage and The Sutro Baths shifted possession several times through the years. Face lifts and changes to the venue included a beach atmosphere with palm trees and sand and an ice skating rink.

As times changed through the late '50s and '60s, so did the appeal of the Sutro Baths. While many San Franciscans may not have patronized Sutro Baths, they were endeared to its history and familiar landmark. Sutro became synonymous with San Francisco. The last owner, George Whitney, owned through the years 1958 - 1966. They were charged with maintaining the venue and eventually abandoned the area with the now-empty swimming tanks. The lack of maintenance and wear and tear from the salty rain and surf deteriorated the structures. The family sold off part of the land to a developer, Robert Frasier, who, in turn, wanted to build high-rise apartments overlooking Ocean Beach.

While the attendance at Sutro's was down, it was still a beloved historical site and San Franciscans would not hear of tearing Sutro down. It was clear the developers had no intention of keeping the baths. A bitter debate would ensue between the properties, with the Whitney family continuing to try and maintain the skating rink while Robert Frasier offered to buy the family out. Dejected and out of money, the Whitney family accepted his offer and demolition began on the west side, including the swimming tanks and surrounding land.

What happened next remains to be proven, but two weeks after the Whitney family sold the final parts of Sutro property to George Whitney, the building was enveloped in flames. People stood back as billowing black smoke filled the northwest San Francisco sky. The beloved Sutro Baths were no more.

The remains of the Sutro Baths continue to be maintained by the National Park Service and thousands of people visit the ruins to explore and reminisce. Loghan was excited to roam around the decayed remains of the baths.

Deagan and Loghan walked up the twisted dirt path as they looked at what was left of the baths below. The outline of the large swimming tank was down below and pooled with salt water. The remains and shape of the powerhouse and filtration system jutted above the ground. "That's the settling pond right there." Loghan looked at the map she picked up at the gift shop and pointed to the structure. A large open area with concrete stood out as they detected the outline. They walked to what looked like a concrete walkway and moved across it, looking down at the settling pond. With the sound of the crashing waves behind them, they began to explore.

They walked along the concrete ridges and reviewed the map to understand what they were looking at and standing on.

Over to the right was a large concrete pad and ledge, dropping off into the angry surf. Deagan peered at the map and then back up again to the area.

"Look, that's called the main tunnel," his finger tapping on the map, indicating the location. "It's kind of creepy looking from here," Loghan considered the dark, cavernous opening. She spied a small sliver of light through the gap in the rock and waves, the last edges of daylight. The waves pounded relentlessly, the surf pulling in and out of the caves with a steady rhythm of breath, as if the ocean itself were inhaling and exhaling through the rocky lungs of the caves and shoreline below.

Loghan shivered and pulled her jacket around her.

"Damn... that's quite a drop from up there." Loghan pointed from the cave to the top of the cliff. "That tunnel pulls the water from that small pooling area and then goes through that tunnel. Looks like it goes right out to sea." Deagan followed Loghan's view and looked up the cliff and back to the tunnel some 30 - 40, feet below.

"What's up there? Let's go look." Deagan continued to eye the top of the cliff. He noticed a platform overlooking the ocean and baths from that location on the map. They teeter-tottered on the concrete edges of the pool outline and made their way back to the flat surface.

"Oh wow! Deagan, this was one of the diving tanks here." Loghan looked down at the water-filled section and handed the map to Deagan so he could also gain a visual site.

Loghan shared more of her knowledge of the baths. "They had diving exhibitions back in the 1890s." She peered down in the water and imagined what glory this incredible place must have been.

Deagan looked up at the sky and winced as the wind picked up and whirled around them. "Whoo...damn. It's kicking up, for sure. Dusk is coming soon. Let's get up there to see the sunset before we miss it." He pulled his scarf around his neck closer and did the same for Loghan. She smiled and laughed. "Taking care of me, are you?" She winked at him. "Always," he returned her smile and they headed up the rocky path to the remains of the Sky Tram platform. Their map stated the platform was installed when the Whitneys owned Sutro's in the later '50s. They walked along the path and passed a few people coming down.

"How's the view up there?" Deagan asked one couple as they walked down the uneven path. The scruffy-faced young man responded. "It's great. Those are good views, for sure. Heading back, though. Looks like rain again."

"Yeah, thanks." Deagan held Loghan's hand as they walked toward the platform. A significant concrete observation area overlooked Sutro's ruins and the wild, angry ocean below.

They walked across the platform. "This is amazing." Loghan pulled her phone out and started taking pictures, scanning the horizon and ocean. The impassioned waves were full of show and continued to angrily crash against the rocky landscape. Loghan wiped a few remnants of water that splashed on her cheek. She looked around at the waves below and then at the sky. Small and sporadic raindrops fell.

"Ahhh...I wondered where that water came from," she laughed and continued to take pictures.

Deagan came up behind her and snuggled into her neck. His strong arms wrapped around her waist. "It looks like the rain is thinking about it...not a soul to be found. We're all alone." He kissed her neck. "You want to wrap it up and get out of here?" Loghan turned to him and smiled, "Are you kidding? Let this moment pass? Not on your life." She tilted her head up toward him and his lips met hers. They kissed in the faint mist until Loghan felt she was out of breath. She pulled back a moment and looked at Deagan.

"What?" He smiled at her and the look of curiosity filled his eyes.

"Nothing...I just...I...you make me feel...like...I can't catch my breath. "

Deagan smiled his huge grin and pulled her close. "It's ok...me too."

They held one another and watched the sunset dipping on the horizon. Savoring the moment of watching the evening fade in each other's arms, they felt safe and serene. The quiet settled between them easily. The clouds rolled in along with the wind, but they were warm and comfortable in their space.

"This has been great, Loghan," Deagan smiled at her briefly and turned his sights back to the ocean. "I'm so glad everything has worked out. Jodie is fine, the wedding was nice and spending time with you...well, it's been more than I could imagine." He squeezed her gently and Loghan leaned against his shoulder.

"I couldn't agree more. Today has been a roller coaster of emotions for me." She turned to him once more. "I'm grateful everything turned out well. Jodie is safe and clearly, things between her and Barrett are more than good!" She laughed at the recollection of her call with Jodie the day before. "I'm happy for her... and the wedding," she paused and sighed, "it was perfect. The only thing we haven't been able to square up is getting in touch with Dexter."

"Oh, hell," Deagan chuckled, "I almost forgot about that, geesh!" He slapped his palm to his forehead, "I've checked my email several times and no response-so, I guess I'll call the coroner's office tomorrow and see if I can reach him at work."

"I know, so much has been happening these last few days." Loghan folded herself into Deagan's arms, "I've hardly been thinking about work and turning my article into John, but tonight when we get back to the hotel, I'm hitting the send button." She pulled back and smiled at Deagan.

"That's fantastic, Loghan! I'm excited for you and it will be great! You'll see! John's going to love it." He beamed his bright smile and Loghan could see the pride in his eyes. He was so helpful through the process of her writing this, what she felt was her break-away article. Deagan, encouraged her to stretch, proofed the article and offered input.

It had been somewhat embarrassing that Deagan knew Loghan had ventured deep into the realm of her story. He was aware she met someone and found intimacy in his words - let her guard down and, in doing so, allowed a man other than Ian to arouse her. She wasn't the first to find pleasure in the form of "sexting," but it was so out of the norm for her.

Loghan was ready to turn in her article and move forward. If John wasn't happy with the story, it was due to his perception of Loghan. John looked at her as a daughter and it would be hard for him to move past that, but it was time to crush this stereotype.

Loghan was finding love again, even if she initially allowed her emotions to get caught up with David. David led her to Deagan and she would be forever grateful for that.

"Let's capture this." Deagan's voice interrupted her thoughts and gladly, she shook off the thick cobwebs of memories. He reached for his phone and they took several pictures of them smiling with the darkness of night beginning to surround them like a cloak.

They talked for a few minutes and pointed at locations beyond the horizon. They could see the diners inside the Cliff House from afar and the silhouettes of people on the platform outside the restaurant enjoying the evening view.

"Let's go look where that cave outlet is." Loghan pointed over the roped-off, dilapidated stairs that led down the cliffs. "Ok. Do you mind if we take a couple of pictures from the other side over there?" He tugged at her hand as she was going in the opposite direction. "I'm going to be right here. You go ahead, Deagan."

Deagan smiled, "Alright. I'll just be a couple of minutes. I want to take a few pictures from that corner," his thumb jerking in the direction across the platform, "the waves make amazing shots." He beamed a smile and winked and she laughed. Deagan walked to the west corner of the platform and began taking pictures of the ocean and cliffs. Dusk had fallen, but he was finding some light from the moon shimmering on the water.

Loghan walked to the edge of the platform. She paused momentarily, looked at the rickety stairs below and wondered how long the stairs had been roped off. Clearly, people had still gone down there, as she could detect from the dimly lit sky that beer bottles and wrappers had been left behind. She rolled her eyes at the thoughtlessness of people.

She gently traced along the rock lined ledge with her fingertips to where she thought the cave was below. She looked over her right shoulder and saw Deagan still taking pictures. She chuckled and felt her phone buzz in her hand. She looked at the screen and it was Jodie. She felt something wet on her cheek and wiped another rogue raindrop, looking outward at the dark sky. Her phone buzzed again and her attention returned to Jodie's message.

'Hey – All is well. Call me when you have a moment. You're not going to believe what I have to tell you. I hope you're having fun with Deagan.'

Loghan furrowed her eyebrows, "Hmm...wonder what this is all about," she whispered.

"It's about me, I would imagine, dear, Loghan."

Chapter 35

L oghan whirled around and stood, mouth agape. That voice, the description...the hair, eyes, everything was spot on.

It was David.

"David...?" She didn't finish her sentence and he was on her in a flash. He twisted her around, her back against him and wrapped his arm around her neck, the other hand across her mouth. His hot breath whispered in her ear. He smelled of alcohol and leather.

"So nice to meet you face to face, dear Loghan. Thought you would get away from me that easily, did you?" His voice quietly surging in her ear. Loghan twisted, her eyes wide with fear, darting, looking for Deagan. He was still in the far corner and didn't see her.

"Not so fast, dear Loghan," his words whispered through gritted teeth - hot and angry. "You taunted and teased me - thinking you were smarter than me. You thought you could just cast me aside...toss me away as if I were nothing." His arm pulled tighter around her neck and he dragged her to the edge of the barrier.

"No, I don't think so, beautiful, Loghan." Her feet were kicking, twisting as she feverishly tried to escape to no avail - he pulled tighter against her neck. "I wanted you...you were different than the others," his voice seethed. She couldn't breathe and she fought off the darkness that quickly closed in around her. Fighting to stay conscious, she twisted and pulled once more.

"I didn't want to kill you like the others, but you're just as bad as they are... just like Dexter...he's dead now, as well...you are next." Loghan registered the name and continued to fight for conscience. She blinked, did she just hear the name, Dexter?? His grip tightened around her neck and she felt her air cut off. "*You* will be the one tossed aside...you are mine...not his...you belong to me," he whispered through clenched teeth.

He pulled at her neck again and she felt her back against the concrete barrier. His sweaty palm clasped over her mouth and she felt his leg sweep firmly against her ankles, pulling her off her feet. Loghan panicked as she felt her body being lifted up over the rock lined barrier.

She knew what was waiting below; the rocky cliff and the gaping black water tunnel.

"What the fuck!" Deagan's voice pierced the night. A shuddering thud resonated through Loghan's body.

Strong hands released her and Loghan crashed to the ground with a heavy thud, her head thumping hard against the earth. The impact reverberated through her skull momentarily stunning her and knocking the remaining breath from her lungs. Rain began to pelt her face, as the sky unleashed relentless sheets of water. She gasped for air, each icy drop, colder than the last, intensifying the pain in her head. She struggled against the encroaching darkness, her vision fading at the edges, but the world continued to slip away despite her fight. The weight of exhaustion pulled her under and her head sank to the earth as the shadows claimed her.

Moments before, Deagan turned around expecting to see Loghan taking more pictures; instead, he was horrified as he saw someone dragging her to the wall. His heart leapt in his throat and he took off in a sprint.

Whoever that son of a bitch was, he didn't see Deagan coming as he rushed him. He had to get there quickly as Loghan fought, but her assailant lifted her over the wall. He slammed his body into the man and tried to stay clear of Loghan as best as possible. The two men fell to the ground in a thud and scrambled on the platform, soaked in rain. The sounds of dirt, sand and pebbles grinding under the men as they grappled in the darkness.

Loghan began to slowly recover and pulled herself up, trying to get to her feet.

Still shaken, she found her voice. "David! Stop! She gathered all the air she could pull into her lungs, "Help! **HELP! SOMEONE!**"

Deagan pushed himself up as the assaulter slammed a fist in his stomach. He grunted, doubled over and stood upright once more. Deagan lunged at him and they wrestled and scuffled, fists and foul language flying. "I'll kill you, mother fucker!" The man grunted as another blow to the body connected. Deagan slammed his fists into his face. He felt the connection as his knuckles made hard contact - blood gushing from the man's nose.

Loghan was on her feet now, running toward the men, as the only barrier between them and the darkness below, was a flimsy, nylon rope. Deagan saw her from the corner of his eye and yelled, "Loghan! - No! - **Stay back!**"

Deagan was caught off guard. A sharp, searing pain exploded in his face as the assailant's fist slammed into his chin, sending him reeling backward. Desperately, Deagan clawed at the air, trying to grab hold of the dark-haired man looming over him. He remembered those eyes - unnaturally blue and filled with a malevolent gleam - the bloody, maniacal grin at Deagan was unnerving. Deagan pushed with every ounce of strength he had left, but it wasn't enough. Another blow landed squarely, driving him back further. Deagan's body collided with the ground, just shy of the jagged opening in the wall, but the back of his skull met the concrete with a sickening thud. His vision blurred, the remnants of light dissolving into a haze of rain and shadows. Through the haze, he heard muted sounds, rain, perhaps? Screaming? He wasn't certain, but he thought he saw the man's feet slipping over the edge of the cliff - gone and over as quickly as it started. Deagan blinked once, twice - and then everything faded into darkness.

"Deagan! Deagan...!" Loghan scrambled to Deagan and fell over him. He wasn't moving and she looked in all directions. Her heart and breath racing at a frantic pace.

Where was he? Where was David...? Did he...did that just happen?

The rain pelted on the ground and Loghan turned to Deagan. Sirens were in the distance. Someone must have heard her screaming for help. Her mind was fuzzy and tears mixed with rain streamed down her face.

Deagan wasn't moving and she touched his head where he lay. Her fingers came back and were covered in blood.

"Oh, my God! NO!" She tore off her scarf and held it to Deagan's wound.

Listening for his breath, she found none. She began to breathe for him. Pressing her lips to his and breathing out... in between the sobs, she kept breathing.

"Deagan, Deagan...please...don't die...please...I can't do this again..."

Loghan checked for a pulse and couldn't tell if she was missing it or if his pulse was nonexistent. She tore at his coat and shirt, locating his chest and listened... there was silence.

"No - no, no..." Loghan quietly whispered. She moved past her tears and knew what needed to be done, return to breath. It was a centering life force.

She repeated silently to herself: Breaths - one...two...three... compressions - one...two...three...four...five... breaths - one...two...three... compressions - one...two...three...four...five... Through the sound of her tears, wind and rain, she quietly whispered, "Please, Deagan...no...you can't be... I-I-I love you..."

She crumpled against his chest and held him, listening for any sign of life. She heard several footsteps thudding near and knew help was here. She kissed Deagan's cheeks repeatedly and his eyelids fluttered. He began to cough and sputter and his eyes closed.

"Oh my God! Deagan!" A rush of relief ran through Loghan's body and she lay limp against his chest.

"Miss... Miss...let us get to him, please." The EMTs circled around Deagan, their gear, fluids and other equipment placed next to him, along with the gurney. They started fluids, checking his heart and placing leads on him. The rain was relentless now and Loghan shivered, realizing they were both soaked to the skin.

One of the EMTs wrapped Deagan's head and continued to take his vitals; the others gently rolled him onto a spine board. They placed him on the stretcher and continued to work around him.

"Let us look at you, miss." She waved off the EMT momentarily and inserted herself next to Deagan, squatting down to his side. "Deagan..."

He opened his eyes in a slit and peered at her. "I know...I know, Loghan...I do, too."

*****

Epilogue

The spring breeze drifted through the open windows, carrying the scent of star jasmine and fresh blooms. In the kitchen, Loghan placed the last clean plate in the cupboard, then hesitated, pulling down two wine glasses instead.

"How's it going out there?" she called, already knowing the answer. "Ready for a break? Can I bring you some wine?"

A familiar voice responded from down the hall. "Yes, I would love some. Thank you, babe." Smiling, she reached for the bottle of malbec, she pulled earlier from their ever growing wine collection. The deep red catching the light as she set it on the counter to open.

Their new life together had just begun and it already felt like home.

Seven months had passed since the accident - seven months that changed everything.

Loghan poured a generous splash of wine into each glass, smiling as she glanced at the glass-front cupboards. Her grandmother's goblets and her mother's crystal now sat beside his everyday glasses and coffee mugs, a quiet testament to the life they were building together. The home bore traces of them both, their styles effortlessly intertwined, just like their lives.

As she walked down the hall, her bare feet brushed the smooth hardwood floors. This place was home now - *their* home. It had only been a month since she moved in and they made it official, but Deagan proposed two months ago. In truth, she's already been living here, never once leaving his side since the accident. Life was good and for the first time in a long time, it was exactly as it should be.

Deagan had suffered a fractured skull and a significant concussion that kept him in the hospital for several days. Along with bruised ribs and a cracked collarbone, but otherwise, he was in good health. Loghan was grateful that was all that happened. She was checked out and had a large bump on the back of her head and some scrapes and bruises and was discharged the same night. She cared for Deagan at his home and they had been inseparable ever since. She entered the large office and leaned against the oak door frame.

"Wine, my love?" She smiled at him and he rose to take it from her hand.

"Thank you, babe...I need a break. This came at the perfect time." He smiled at her and both slipped onto the burgundy leather couch. Loghan loved this quiet and creative part of their home.

Deagan sipped on his wine and smiled. "Still wish you would move in here and we can share this office space." He looked at Loghan again as if in question. Loghan smiled over her glass, "Absolutely not." She giggled slightly and continued, "You know how I feel about this, Deag. This is your space - your creative place for you to write and I don't want to encroach on that one bit," she smiled again, "Besides, I love my new office next door. It allows you to continue your work here and I can start my own vibe in my new office." She tipped her glass toward him and Deagan nodded in acquiescence.

As with everything they did, it was easy and made sense.

Swirling her wine, she studied Deagan. "So, how does it feel? Tomorrow's your first day on sabbatical."

Deagan exhaled, the weight of the moment settling in. "It feels - right."

He had finally done it - stepped away from the magazine, given himself the time he'd always promised. His grandfather's voice echoed in his mind, a reminder of the book he swore he'd write one day. Now, with everything that has happened-with Loghan, with Aric-there was no question about the story he needed to tell.

"Do you have everything you need?" Loghan asked, taking a sip of her wine, her expression shifting into one of quiet appreciation.

Deagan smirked. "It's good, isn't it?" She chuckled. "The wine? Yes, it is." He leaned back, his gaze thoughtful. "I think so. I've got the notes, the research, the timelines. And most importantly, I have your blessing."

"All of it," she assured him.

Their eyes met and Deagan knew this was more than just a story. It was the truth, wrapped in fiction. A tale of love, survival and the darkness that had nearly stolen everything from them. Loghan raised her glass in a silent toast. "And I'm glad I already know how it ends." She let the words settle, then added with quiet satisfaction, "The killer is dead. **D-E-A-D**."

She clinked her glass against his and Deagan responded with his own emphasis.

"Yes. D - E - A - D." He spelled it to mirror her emphatic words.

Deagan moved over to his desk, the last of his notes spread before him, the weight of the past several months settling into something almost manageable. The final pieces had fallen into place. The story that had nearly torn Loghan's life apart - and bound them together - was closing.

Detectives Kinder and Thornton had shared everything they could. The connections were staggering, a tangled web of names and fates: Loghan, Jodie, Barrett, himself. Even Dexter, the quirky assistant from the San Francisco Coroner's Office, had unwittingly played a role in the forensic puzzle that finally led to the truth.

Aric Stanton was dead.

The fall from the Sutro Bath ruins had been final - no body, just the unforgiving pull of the sea. The investigators had searched the cliffs, the tunnel and the canal. In the end, only a single shoe and the rain-washed remnants remained. Fingernail scrapings, barely-there skin cells - proof of what had happened that night.

And now, Deagan was writing it all. His first book. Their story.

It was still hard to believe Loghan somehow got twisted up in the article Deagan had been researching about the women mysteriously being murdered across the country, but she certainly did.

Aric Stanton, in all his stalking, had left behind a labyrinth of digital misdirection, his VPN marking his trail of terror. In the end, even his cunning wasn't enough. The detectives had pieced together the puzzle and with the incredible testimony of Avery, she was able to finally share her three decade long secret and the truth had come into sharp focus; she was mother to Aric and her beloved, Barrett. Avery shared her heartache of leaving Barrett behind, raising a troubled Aric through the years, ending with her terrifying encounter with Aric.

Barrett, once buried under suspicion, walked free as the evidence continued to unfold. Across states, law enforcement worked collaboratively, turning their findings over to the FBI. Loghan, still haunted by the weight of it all, had played her part willingly - turning over conversations with "David," the man she allowed to reach into the most sacred of places - the man who tore down her walls and her soul. Only now did she realize he had been one of the many faces Aric wore.

"Do you have it all mapped out where you will go with the story?" Loghan's green eyes filled with questions. "I do, babe. I have it all mapped out and the rest will organically find its way to my fingertips." He smiled and wiggled his fingers in the air, as he lowered himself to his desk. Loghan laughed and stood and walked toward Deagan.

"Well, I don't want to interrupt you any longer. Break time is over." She smiled and playfully gave him a peck. "Ok - ok...what will you do while I write?" Deagan tipped back in his chair and sipped his wine. "I have my own article to write. You know, I'm the co-head writer now." She batted her eyes at him and laughed. She turned on her heel, flipping her auburn tresses. "That - you are...," he laughed after her, "that you are. I'm proud of you!" He called out to her. "Thank you," came the muffled return.

Loghan took a seat at her desk and lifted her laptop. Setting her glass down and rolling her head around to loosen her tight muscles, she found her document.

Ding - Messenger announced. She glanced down and smiled; it was Jodie.

'Hi Loghan! Thanks again for brunch today. It was so great to catch up!'

Loghan poised her fingertips and responded.

'It was! I loved seeing you and Barrett! You look so happy, Jodie. I know you've been through a lot, but seems like Barrett is doing well given all that has happened... I just can't imagine what he must feel after learning about his

brother, Aric.'

'It was hard for him initially, but I think he's settling in well. He still catches himself calling Avery, Aunt Katherine but I suppose that will take time to unlearn.'

Loghan gently smiled. She couldn't imagine what it must feel like to learn your aunt is truly your mother - not to mention, learning you had a twin brother. Loghan felt a shiver run up her back. She shook the feeling and continued her text:

'I can't wait to come and visit you in Scotland!'

'Me too! Thank you...for both! I'm over the moon in love with Barrett! Speaking of happy, you're a fine one to talk...already engaged!'

'LOL! Well, we decided, why wait?! We know what we want and can't wait to get started on our lives together. I'm sure you and Barrett feel the same! What time is your flight tomorrow?'

'That is right! We do feel the same. Between you and me, I think he's going to ask me when we're back in Scotland. All my things shipped over last week, so I hope they arrive soon with us moving to our forever home.'

'OMG! That is so exciting, Jodie! I can't wait to hear the details. I wish we could attend the party in your honor. I'm sure Avery throws incredible parties! LOL!'

'I will let you know. I totally understand, though. Christmas will be here soon enough and you and Deagan will be here to celebrate the season with us...and hopefully more!'

'LOL! You're terrible! Don't ruin his surprise, Jode!'

'I won't....promise! Well, I have to run. We're heading out to meet Tina's new man before I leave. I'll let you know what I think...I know you already met him.'

'He's great - you'll approve - Promise! Love you! Text me when you land in Scotland!'

'I will!'

Loghan moved over to her document, opened her article file on her computer and leaned back in her chair to read where she left off.

Her eyes glanced over the last paragraph and she recalled precisely where she would pick things up.

Ding-messenger announced again.

She must have forgotten to mention something; Loghan returned to messenger, smiling and picked her wine up again.

"What else, my friend", Loghan whispered smiling as she clicked on the message; she stopped short - her blood ran cold and she froze, her eyes running over the message.

'Hello, my dear beautiful, Loghan...how are you tonight?'

He leaned back in his chair and stretched out his long legs. Smiling, he reached for his martini and took a long and thoughtful sip.

Yes, yes...she is perfect...still beautiful and utterly perfect.

He finished his martini and waited for her response.

~End~

About the Author

V. Carson Taylor makes her debut in the Psychological Thriller/ Romance/ Mystery Genre with this novel. An accomplished poet, her work has appeared in Emotions magazine and various news publications featuring poetry and short stories.

Originally from the Bay Area, V. Carson now resides in Sacramento, California with her wife, Kelley and their four beloved cats, Kahlua, Tiki, Finley and Cobie (affectionately known as Baby Girl).